W9-BUO-162

Heir to Destiny

Cumhal MacTredhorn, the proud chieftain of the Fianna warriors, had defied Conn the Hundred Fighter, Ireland's cruel High-King. Urged by the whispers of his evil Druid Tagd, Conn ordered the murder of Cumhal— and all his kin.

Warned by a vision, Cumhal's bride escaped with her newborn son. Raised in secret in the depths of the forest, this golden-haired youth learned the stealth of the fox, the speed of the stag, and the strength of the bear, and grew into the mighty hunter called Finn the Fair.

Pursued by the High-King's armies, and the dark powers of the Sidhe, Finn began a heroic odyssey to reclaim his heritage, aided by the mystic harper Cnu, the giant warrior Caolite MacRonan, and the hotblooded Fionulla, who taught him the ways of love. Then, at last, came the hour of his destiny, and he was determined that no sorcery or might of arms would stop his thirst for justice.

Bantam Books by Kenneth C. Flint
Ask your bookseller for the titles you have missed.

CHAMPIONS OF THE SIDHE
MASTER OF THE SIDHE
RIDERS OF THE SIDHE
A STORM UPON ULSTER

CHALLENGE OF THE CLANS

Kenneth C. Flint

BANTAM BOOKS
TORONTO · NEW YORK · LONDON · SYDNEY · AUCKLAND

CHALLENGE OF THE CLANS

A Bantam Spectra Book / March 1986

Illustrations by Maureen Monigal.

All rights reserved.
Copyright © 1986 by Kenneth C. Flint.
Cover art copyright © 1986 by Steve Assel.
This book may not be reproduced in whole or in part, by
mimeograph or any other means, without permission.
For information address: Bantam Books, Inc.

ISBN 0-553-25553-3

Published simultaneously in the United States and Canada

Bantam Books are published by Bantam Books, Inc. Its trade-
mark, consisting of the words ''Bantam Books'' and the por-
trayal of a rooster, is Registered in U.S. Patent and Trademark
Office and in other countries. Marca Registrada. Bantam
Books, Inc., 666 Fifth Avenue, New York, New York 10103.

PRINTED IN THE UNITED STATES OF AMERICA

H   0 9 8 7 6 5 4 3 2 1

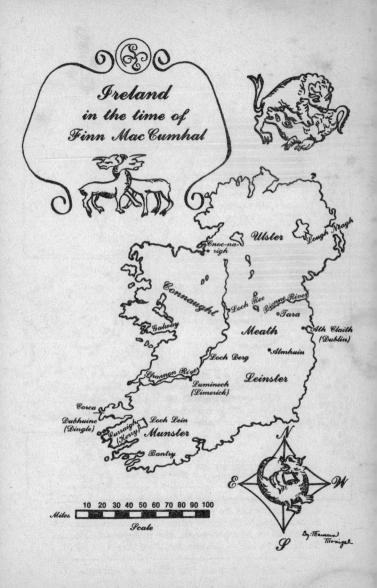

Ireland
in the time of
Finn MacCumhal

Cnoc-na-righ

Ulster

Lough Neagh

Connaught

Loch Ree

Boyne River

Galway

Tara

Meath

Ath Cliath
(Dublin)

Loch Derg

Almhuin

Shannon River

Luminech
(Limerick)

Leinster

Corca
Dubhuine
(Dingle)

Curraigh
(Kerry)

Loch Lein

Munster

Bantry

N

E

W

S

Miles   10 20 30 40 50 60 70 80 90 100

Scale

By Maureen
Monigal

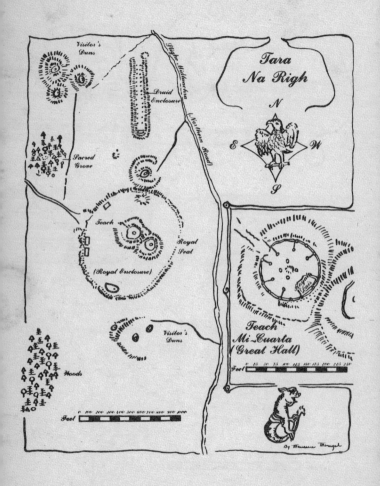

Book One

THE JOURNEY BEGINS

Chapter One

CONSPIRACY

"I will not allow you to leave Tara before the Samhain festival, Cumhal!" threatened Conn, high king of all Ireland.

"There's little you can do to stop my going!" came the heated reply from Cumhal MacTredhorn.

The angry voices echoed clearly, hollowly in the vast hall of Tara, rebounding from the circle of timber walls and the planks of the high peaked roof. Their violence drew the startled gazes of the servants working in the room to the two men arguing by the main doors.

Conn was of truly aristocratic bearing, lean and long-featured and fair, with ice-blue eyes and blond hair curling loosely about his shoulders. He glowed richly with the gold ornament of his station. His four-folded dark red cloak was golden fringed. The enameled brooch that fastened it was of red gold, as were the torc about his neck and the wide bands at his elbows. He was a wily and ruthless leader who had earned the title of Hundred Fighter in as many savage battles, but he had met his match in the man who faced him now.

Cumhal was both larger and darker than the king. His body was more massive and his features more broadly drawn. His eyes were the deep brown of Ireland's rich sod, and the long hair plaited loosely at his back was coarse and black. In dress he seemed only a common warrior, unornamented save for a simple iron pin to fasten his woolen cloak. In truth he was the captain of the *Fianna*, those bands of professional soldiers whose task it was to serve the ruling classes of Ireland.

"It is unknown for any *Fian* chieftain to refuse to attend me here," Conn pointed out with towering indignation.

"Then I will be the first," Cumhal told him, unmoved by his king's ire. "My wife will be giving birth to our first child very soon. No power—no power at all—will keep me from being with her."

With these words, he turned and strode through the open doorway, out of the hall.

Astonished by this insolence, Conn stood frozen a moment, staring after him. Then he noticed the servants' curious eyes upon him. He cast a chilling glare about at them, then started in pursuit of the departing warrior.

He followed Cumhal across an earthen causeway that bridged a defensive ditch and linked the hall to an encircling outer mound of earth, and down a steep slope to the level of the fortress yard. This was an area of several acres in extent, enclosed by a high palisade of thick logs. It was now bustling with the inhabitants of Tara, busily making preparations for the *Féis* of *Samhain*.

This yearly six-day festival to mark the end of the growing season brought chieftains, territorial kings, and learned men from all over Ireland to the great fortress. One party of mounted warriors was even then riding in through the outer wall's main gates. They were closely bundled against the chill air of the fall day, the brightly checked cloaks of their clan making a brilliant flash of color against the brown countryside and the iron sky behind them.

As Cumhal started away from the base of the hall's mound, Conn came up close behind him.

"How dare you defy me before my own people!" the high king said in outrage. "You have forgotten yourself, MacTredhorn!"

The leader of the Fianna stopped and swung toward Conn. His expression was hard and his voice chill.

"I've forgotten nothing, High King," he said, spitting out the title with contempt. "Every day I'm reminded that you are the Great Master of Ireland. But I know that it's the blood of my warriors that's soaked into the sod. For all these years we've fought to keep your power for you. And I never forget that, for all we've done, we're still treated with less kindness than you show your cattle and your hounds. Well, that time is ending!"

"Are you mad, speaking that way to me?" Conn asked in disbelief. "You are bound to me by the oaths of the Fianna. You must serve me!"

"I'll serve you, as I should. But I'll have everything that's owed the Fian bands, and I'll have respect for us as well. That, or you and your rich, pampered lords will find yourselves enforcing your laws and fighting your battles yourselves."

Conn choked off his angry reply. He knew well enough that no fighting force in Ireland, or possibly the world, could match the strength and courage of the Fianna warriors. And he knew that, for all their oaths of service to the king, their true loyalty lay with their own captain. He could not risk pushing Cumhal to open rebellion. By an effort of will, he remained silent.

"Now, I am leaving for Almhuin as soon as my warriors are ready," Cumhal went on, as if he were a teacher instructing a small child. "I mean to be there before my wife gives birth. And there I mean to stay for the winter. When Beltaine comes, I'll return here and be at your service, as is proper. I'll not return before. So, my high king, a fine Samhain to you."

Once more he turned away, crossing the yard to the stable buildings with a confident swagger. This time, Conn let him go, staring after him in hatred and frustration. Many more of his subjects about the yard had witnessed this second humiliation. He wanted no third confrontation with the Fian captain.

Casting a burning gaze about him at people who hastily averted their eyes, he started back toward the hall, shaking with barely suppressed rage that had no outlet. As he came through the gate onto the causeway, he saw with some surprise that someone awaited him at the hall's threshold.

5

It was Tadg, his court's highest-ranking member of the druidic class, that learned body of men who served as advisors to Ireland's rulers. Known for their great wisdom and their proficiency in the magic arts, they were very powerful figures in the Irish hierarchy, and very dangerous ones as well.

Like the high king, Tadg was a slender man, but his features were finer, almost to the point of frailty. He had a delicate beauty, like that of a winter's new frost, and he had its chill quality as well. His eyes were large, bright silver gray, his nose slender, his mouth small and finely shaped. His high-domed head was covered wispily with white-gold hair. His thin body was draped in the gleaming white robe that marked his status in the sacred order.

"Where did you come from, Tadg?" Conn asked, somewhat surprised by his unexpected appearance. "I didn't know you had arrived."

"I've been here for some time, High King," Tadg answered, his voice a soft, clear melodic sound. "I've watched your confrontation with Cumhal. Now do you agree with me?"

"Yes!" Conn tersely replied. "Cumhal has gone too far. He's become dangerous."

Tadg's lips parted in a sweet, engaging smile. "Yes, High King. And he must be destroyed."

The stark pronouncement caused Conn to glance about him quickly. But there was no one nearby to hear them. He moved closer to the druid.

"How can I act against him?" he asked in a hoarse whisper. "It would bring the chieftains of all the Fians against me!"

"Ah, but you've no need to worry," Tadg assured him in a soothing way. "The answer to your problem is arriving now. Look." He lifted a slim hand to point down into the yard. Conn turned to see another mounted band of warriors, in the green and yellow plaid of the Morna clan, riding in through the gates.

"It is others of the Fianna clans who will deal with Cumhal for you," said the druid. "All you must do is

see that tonight, after the festival is under way, young
Aed MacMorna is sent secretly to me."

Conn eyed the druid closely, seeing in that guile-
less, gently smiling face the real intent behind his words.
He nodded, and then he quickly walked away.

After that evening's feast, Aed MacMorna and his
brother Conan slipped from the fortress into the night
and moved down the hillside toward the sacred enclosure of the druids.

Both of them were dark, thick-bodied men, their
features similar enough to prove their blood relationship. But Aed MacMorna was the more pleasant looking of the two, his features coarsely handsome, his form
solid, powerful, and moving with an aggressive sure-
ness. His brother Conan was larger, inclining toward
stoutness, his movements more ponderous. His round,
soft face was marked by an enormous, spiky mustache
that seemed to be vainly trying to make up for his
balding head.

A chill, nagging wind tugged at their cloaks as it
worried the fall-browned grasses of the fields on either
side. Aed strode along briskly, looking neither right nor
left, intent only on his goal. Conan moved with an
obvious reluctance, casting nervous looks about at the
dark countryside and gazing back often and longingly at
the fortress fading away above them. He was yearning
for the comforts of the hall, with its blazing fire, and for
the companionship of his clansmen, now earnestly engaged in their late-night carousing. He had no wish at
all to be out in the chill and blackness of a Samhain
night, and especially on such a strange mission as this.

"Are you certain we have to go there, Aed?" he
asked in a growl.

His brother cast an exasperated glance at him.
"Conan, I'll not warn you again. If the high king commands us, there's nothing for us to do but obey!"

"I don't like this. Not at all, I don't!" Conan mum-
bled on. "Him pulling us away from the feasting like
that and sending us out here. As if he didn't want the
others to know of it. And this high druid of his. There's

a very unpleasant sort. Nasty sorts of powers I've heard he has. They even say he's of the sidhe blood himself! That he—"

"I know the rumors as well as you," Aed said sharply. "Now will you please close your mouth and keep up with me?"

They reached the bottom of the hillside and skirted a small copse of trees. The moon made a sudden appearance, the clasped hands of the clouds opening, pulling back, to release it momentarily. Its stark white light turned the sky gray, throwing the bare tree branches into sharp relief, revealing the wood as a grove of oaks, the sacred trees of the druids.

Their upper branches thrust like skeletal fingers toward the sky, the shifting breezes making them seem to clutch desperately for the sailing moon before it could drift into the sheltering banks of clouds again. And the wind made the trees wail mournfully like a discordant chorus of Ban-Sidhe keening for some hero's death, accompanied by the dry rustling of the few dead leaves still clinging stubbornly to their limbs.

Conan hurried by them in his brother's wake, careful not to look into the blackness lurking deep within the grove. Past the oak trees, the two men reached the druid's sacred enclosure. It was another stockade of upright logs. But, unlike the fortress above, this one formed a long, narrow rectangle.

The walls were solid save at one end, where a single, narrow opening allowed entrance. Conan stopped some distance from it, staring at it with uncertainty. Aed paused by the opening and looked back at his brother, his face taut with impatience.

"Are you coming, then? He'll be waiting for us."

"Yes. All right," the other said without enthusiasm. He moved on, following Aed into the enclosure, out of the wind's punishing blast.

The interior was one long open space. Along either side, just within the wall, was set a row of stakes, each topped by a human skull that gleamed in the moonlight. Down this macabre avenue they passed, toward a small roofed structure at the farthest end.

Before this hut there burned a fire in a circle of stones. The white smoke of it streamed upward until it reached above the sheltering walls where the harsh winds snatched it abruptly away. To one side of this fire yawned the black mouth of the druid's sacrificial pit. Behind the fire, just before the doorway of the hut, Tadg sat alone on a mound of piled furs.

His eyes remained closed until the two men stopped across the fire from him. Then they opened and the gray eyes fixed on them. A gust of wind flicked down into the enclosure, whipping the smoke into a sudden wreath, striking cold through the visitors. Conan shivered.

"So, you've come," Tadg said, the soft voice rustling like the night breeze through the dry leaves of the fall trees.

"Yes," Aed replied. "As the high king wished."

"And no one else knows of your coming here?"

"The way they were when we left them, they'll not even know where *they* are come morning," Conan said, essaying a smile in an attempt to counter his nervousness.

The gray eyes shot a glance at him, its intense chill striking the smile dead at its birth. They shifted back to Aed.

"Very well. Then I can speak openly to you, MacMorna." The druid's gaze met and held Aed's. "It's certain that you know what difficulty your high king has had with Cumhal MacTredhorn of late."

"Cumhal is leader of the Fianna," Aed replied. "It was the high king who gave him the captaincy, and we all agreed."

"Perhaps," the druid said in a meditative voice. "But the Fian bands were created to serve the will of the rulers of Ireland, not their own ends. Cumhal has taken too much power for himself!"

"He acts as he thinks he must to protect our rights," Aed responded defensively. "He's seen we gained the pay and shelter due us for our service."

"His arrogance is too great!" Tadg said, the gentle tone sharpening with irritation. "He has challenged the

9

authority of the high king. He has broken the Fian oath to serve."

"Then let the high king remove him," Aed suggested.

"You are no fool," Tadg retorted. "You know Conn does not dare to act. He is convinced Cumhal would defy him. It would spark open rebellion among the Fian clans. No. Cumhal must be removed another way."

"What do you mean?" Aed asked suspiciously.

"He must be killed." the druid said bluntly, his gray eyes flaring with the light of a polished blade.

"Why are you telling this to me? I am a Fian chieftain. My own loyalty is to Cumhal."

"And is this loyalty greater than the one you owe to your high king?" Tadg challenged.

"It's a hard place you're putting me into," the warrior protested. "Between the well-honed edges of two blades."

"Come now, Aed," Tadg cajoled, the fall chill of his voice warming like a spring breeze. "The Clan na Morna and the Clan na Baiscne have often been at odds for supremacy within the Fianna. You yourself are Cumhal's greatest rival. And you can't deny that you have long coveted the leadership for yourself."

"He's right in that, Aed," Conan spoke up in a helpful, eager way. "You have wanted to be captain."

"Oh, Conan, please be quiet!" Aed told him impatiently. "I can't think!"

"There is nothing to think about," the druid said with finality. "It is for the good of Ireland that this must be done. The Fianna must be brought to serve the high king again, as they are pledged to do. They must have a loyal captain who will use them properly, without questioning our leader's commands. You must challenge the Baiscne clan and win the leadership. Then the high king can proclaim you his captain rightfully."

"And just why is it that the high king isn't telling me this himself?" Aed wondered.

"Be sensible," Tadg answered loftily. "The high king cannot be openly involved in any way. Cumhal is much too popular. For Conn to act against the captain

10

of the Fianna would surely raise the wrath of many of its warriors against him. This must seem solely a battle between two rival clans for the leadership."

Of course, Aed realized. That was the reason for Conn sending them here secretly, and for his letting the druid strike this treacherous bargain.

He felt the forces tearing at him: his own ambitions, his loyalty to Cumhal, his bonds with the high king. He looked toward his brother but found no help there. Conan was only watching him expectantly. He looked back toward the druid.

"It . . . would not be easy," he said finally in a cautious way. "Cumhal is not our captain by chance. His clansmen are the finest warriors in Eire. No one has ever defeated him."

"Have no fears in that," Tadg said with great assurance, his mouth rising in a smile as he sensed victory. "I will use my own powers to help you destroy him."

Aed wondered if Tadg had a personal reason for being involved in this. After all, the druid's own daughter Muirne was married to Cumhal and was now pregnant with their first child. And there were rumors that her marriage to the Fian captain had enraged her father.

"Why are you so eager to see Cumhal dead?" he asked. "He is your son-in-law."

"My personal feelings have no place in this," the druid assured him coolly. "My only interest is to serve the high king and Ireland. It should be the same with you."

"I see," Aed said, not fully convinced. "And just what is it that you would do to help me?"

"Of course, as the high king's druid, I could do nothing openly against Cumhal," Tadg replied. "And there must seem to be no treachery involved. Still, there are ways I can insure that you and your warriors surprise and defeat the Baiscne clan with little danger to yourselves."

"No, Druid!" Aed protested. "I'll use none of your magic against Cumhal. If the high king means for me to challenge him for the leadership, then I am bound to

11

do it. But there'll be no treachery. It will be my clan against his, and if we fail, we fail. That way or none."

Tadg fixed the chieftain with a searching look, but there was no wavering in Aed's stubborn expression. The sense of honor of the Fian chieftain was famed in Ireland. He realized that it would not be shaken by any force.

"Very well. But you must promise that the clan will be completely wiped away."

"Is that necessary?" Aed said angrily. "Once Cumhal is dead and the leadership taken—"

Tadg interrupted sharply. "There is no other way! The high king must be assured that the Clan na Baiscne can never be restored. All of Cumhal's blood must die."

"But what about your own daughter? It's said she'll soon be bearing Cumhal's child."

"Once he is dead, I would have you return Muirne to me."

"And the child?"

"You know the answer to that question as well as I. If it carries Cumhal's blood, it is a threat. We must take no chances. Do you understand?"

"I understand," Aed said reluctantly. "The child will die too."

Chapter Two

THE TRAP

The woman hurried acoss the yard of the fortified house known as Almhuin. One bony hand clutched a bouquet of dried herbs. The other held a long coat tight about her lanky frame.

The chill wind swirled the dead leaves trapped within the encircling stockade in a forlorn, rattling dance about her. She glanced up at the lowering gray skies and then abruptly stopped, head cocked in a listening attitude, her gaunt face stiffening.

There was something, some unsettling sound rising in the mournful keening of the wind. A note, a wailing note there for an instant, faint and far away, then gone again.

A frown of worry deepened the creases about her eyes and mouth. She did not like that sound. But there were other things more pressing now. She hurried on, heading for the round thatched house in the center of the yard.

She pushed against the plank door, swinging it inward on its leather hinges as she passed through, kicking it closed behind her. Shutting off the blasting wind alone made the air much warmer, and it was further heated by a blazing fire in the central hearth. The wind roaring across the peak was sucking the trail of smoke out the roof hole in a straight stream, and making the fire burn all the hotter.

The room was large, but seemed cozy, with bright tapestries on the wattle and daub walls to reduce the drafts, and rushes spread thickly on the earthen floor. The reddish firelight glinted on the bronze, copper, and even golden appointments of a rich household.

A second woman was sitting by the fire, tending a large caldron. She was much younger, much smaller, and much plumper of figure than the one who had just entered, with a pleasant, round-cheeked face and large brown eyes. She gave the other woman a bright welcoming smile as she moved toward the fire.

"Ah, so you've got them!" she said cheerily as she saw the bundle of herbs. But then she noted the anxiety that tightened the older woman's face and her own sunny expression grew clouded.

"Bodhmall, what's wrong?" she asked.

The other shook her head. "I don't know," she said vaguely. "I felt . . . very strange. Very—" Here she saw the alarm in the younger woman's face and stopped

13

abruptly. She shrugged and forced her thin mouth into a smile. "It's nothing, Liath. Just the chill in my old bones. Never mind. Tell me about her."

Liath recovered her spirits and grinned. "Ah, well, she's doing just fine, that she is. A few of the early pains, but they're bothering her little. It's rest she's needing most."

"These will see to that," Bodhmall assured her, lifting the herbs. "Fetch me some broth."

Liath quickly scooped steaming liquid from the caldron into a small bowl. The older woman selected certain bits from her collection and crushed the dried leaves and petals, sprinkling them into the broth.

She carried it across the room to a wall woven of wicker that separated a small chamber from the larger, central room. Softly she pulled the light screen back and peered around it. The room beyond was softly lit by a pair of candles. They threw a gentle, wavering golden glow across the face of the woman who lay on a pallet there, apparently asleep.

She looked very young. Her features were fine and smooth and unlined, like those of a child. Her skin was so pale as to seem almost translucent in the candlelight, and her hair was like a stream of bright white gold flowing in a spreading wave across the dark covers of the bed.

Bodhmall moved quietly to the woman's side and knelt down by her. At her movement, the lids fluttered and then rose, revealing light, clear gray eyes. They lit with expectation as they focused on the other's face.

"Has he come?" she asked hopefully.

"No, Muirne," the older woman told her, laying a comforting hand on her arm. "Not yet."

Muirne's flush of excitement faded in disappointment. "Oh, Bodhmall, I'm so afraid he won't be here in time. I want to feel that he's near me when it is time."

She sounded so weak and she seemed so frail that Bodhmall, not a woman given to nonsense, grew a bit impatient.

"Now, look here, my girl," she said in a scolding way, "this is not the pampered life of some Sidhe palace

14

or of the high king's court you've chosen. You're the wife of a man of the Fianna now. A chieftain he may be, but a warrior first, and his life is a hard one. It was certain he had to go to Tara for the Samhain feast, as all chieftains must. So I want no more complaining from you. You're not the first to have a baby, nor will you have the greatest trouble with it, no matter how you feel. If Cumhal is meant to be here, he will be. But whether he comes in time or not, he'll be expecting to find a brave, strong wife here when he does arrive."

At first shocked by Bodhmall's harsh words, the girl now smiled and took the stern woman's hand. "Ah, what would I do without your help and your truths," she said earnestly. "You're right. And for my love of him, I'll complain no more."

A spasm of pain wiped away her smile. She stiffened, throwing her head back. Bodhmall tightened her grip and held on until the pain passed and Muirne relaxed.

"All right, girl, just you be easy now," she said. "It's coming surely, and very soon it may be. You need your strength for that."

She turned and signaled to Liath, who stood watching around the edge of the wicker screen. The younger woman moved forward obediently and Bodhmall handed her the broth.

"See that she drinks this," she ordered. "I'll prepare more."

Liath nodded. Taking the broth, she replaced the older woman at the bedside. She lifted Muirne gently and held the bowl while the girl sipped.

"Have all of it, now!" Bodhmall instructed sternly before leaving the room.

Returning to the fire, she began to crush more of the precious medicinal herbs in a stone mortar with a heavy pestle. But as she worked, she glanced up often to the roof hole where the winds howled angrily and the smoke was blown away into oblivion. She realized that she would be easier of mind herself if she knew that Cumhal was safe.

15

She lifted the pestle and poured the powdered contents into the liquid bubbling within the pot.

A brew surged, boiled angrily in the caldron of the high druid Tadg. He fed the sacred fire blazing beneath it with great care, lovingly laying bits of sacred ash and yew upon its flames.

The warriors of the Clan na Morna were gone now, set out in the darkness of the early dawn to pursue Cumhal's band. Tadg was alone in the druid enclosure, free to raise the spell that would insure the destruction of the Fian captain.

As the druid stood looking down upon the steaming liquid, he saw an image there. He was reliving the marriage of his daughter to Cumhal, recalling his rage and frustration as he watched, renewing his resolve to see the captain dead.

For he had lied to Aed MacMorna. It was his own need for revenge that lay behind his desire to destroy Cumhal. That savage, ill-born creature had taken his daughter against his will! He had despoiled that fair, pure, innocent girl! Worse, he had sullied the sacred blood of the high druid's ancient family, and brought unbearable shame upon Tadg himself! For such outrages, there must be revenge. The offender must be exterminated like the vermin that he was. All trace of Cumhal or any of his blood must be wiped away as if they never existed.

And so the high druid was about to disregard the refusal of the honorable Aed MacMorna to take his help. The odds for Cumhal's survival were too great. He meant to insure the defeat of the Baiscne clan.

Into the caldron he slipped the elements whose mystic properties were unknown even to the other high-ranking druids of Ireland. Over the steaming contents he made a strange incantation. He invoked the powers of ancient gods whose names the mortal races of Ireland dared not say aloud.

"Great Danu, Queen of the Blessed Isles, and Manannan MacLir, Ruler of the Sea, give your energy to the working of my spell! Let me have the magic that

I need to make my curse fall upon the Baiscne clan. Help the sons of Morna to bring Cumhal MacTredhorn's head back to me!"

As the high druid worked to raise his incantation, the object of his hatred was leading his clansmen away from Tara at a swift and steady pace.

On either side of the captain rode his two most valued comrades. To his left was Crimall, his brother, a square-faced warrior whose long black hair and mustache were neatly braided and whose manner was just as fastidious. To his right was Fiacha, a squat, smooth-faced, and rosy-cheeked young man with a carefree air.

"I think that this is madness, Cumhal," Crimall loudly complained. "To travel through the night without any rest, and so close to Samhain eve on top of it!"

The Fian chieftain laughed good-naturedly at his brother's concern. "Are you still going on about that? There's nothing to fear."

"Don't be laughing at me," the other retorted. "There is no sense in rousing the anger of the Others so near the time when their own full power is loosed upon the world. It's at the festival we should have stayed, giving our proper respects to them and to all the gods."

"Even those of the Sidhe wouldn't keep me from being at Muirne's side when my child is born," Cumhal told him stubbornly. "Not the Dagda nor the Morrigan herself would be taking such a thing from a man."

"I'm not so certain of that as you. Maybe you can defy the high king and get away with it, but the Others are something else. You've gotten entirely too full of yourself, my brother. It will make trouble for you one day. Don't you believe it's the truth I'm saying, Fiacha?"

The other warrior only shrugged and smiled at Crimall's dark foreboding.

"Ah, man, we're well enough on our way now, and there's little use in turning back," he said. "We may as well go ahead."

Crimall snorted. "I might have known you'd side with him. So I'll say no more to either of you!"

He fell into a hostile silence and they rode along

peacefully for some time. The day had dawned faintly, the sun heavily cloaked by thick, gray overcast like rippling folds of coarse wool. But the rain the dark clouds threatened held off, and the earth was dry and firm beneath the thick-furred hooves of their horses, so the powerfully muscled animals were easily able to keep up a rapid pace.

Then, so suddenly it seemed as if the overcast had plunged upon them, the party found themselves engulfed in fog. The large-bodied warriors wrapped in their bright cloaks became like phantoms in the eerie grayness. And the fog heightened this effect by swallowing all noise, muffling even the horses' clopping so that the company seemed to float along.

The warriors now peered about them constantly as they rode. They felt oppressed, uneasy with the gray shroud upon them. They disliked the look of the bare trees that loomed up ever thicker around them like a host of black skeletons interlacing the bony fingers of their branches in an uneven web that caught and held drifting patches of the fog.

And there was another sensation, too, that crept upon them with the increasing dampness. It was a peculiar feeling of weariness, of weakness, as if the effort to press ahead through the clinging stuff was somehow draining their strength.

Cumhal seemed the only one unconcerned with the strange conditions, so intent was he on reaching his wife's side. But Crimall was far from unconcerned. And when the twisted stump of a rotting tree trunk appeared suddenly, like something leaping toward him from the fog, he yelped in surprise and then spoke out angrily.

"That is enough! I say that it's time for us to stop and let this pass. Some harm will surely come to us if we continue traveling blindly this way."

"It's only a bit of fog," his brother replied. "It's not likely to cause us much harm unless you ride into a tree while you're so busy peering about."

"There's more in this than you think," Crimall insisted. "It's not natural, I tell you. I can smell it. And I can feel it too!"

18

"It's only the wear of riding through the night that's made you feel this way," Cumhal said. "Better to ride on through this. The sooner we reach home, the sooner we can rest."

Again, Crimall fell silent, but he continued to stare about him, trying to guess at the dim shapes that came and went and almost seemed to flitter around them in the fog.

Soon the impression came to him that he had seen before some of the trees they were passing. This was a foolish notion, he told himself. Still, the fancy came into his head that the trees were really shifting about, waiting for them to pass and then lifting their roots to scamper on and join their fellows ahead.

There was surely no question that the number of trees was increasing, the woods growing denser, the trunks closer together, as if the trees were gathering to hem them in.

And then there was a line of them ahead so thick that they nearly formed a stockade wall, the trunks so close that the horses would barely be able to squeeze between them. The party reined in, peering at them with curiosity.

"What's happened?" said Cumhal. "There's no forest like this on our way." He gazed about him in growing bewilderment. "They're as thick on both sides as well! Where are we?"

"We should be in the woods of Cnucha, near to Ath Cliath," said his brother.

"It can't be so!" Cumhal said. "I don't know this place at all. Can we have strayed?"

"Look there!" cried a warrior in a warning tone, pointing back the way they had come.

Behind them figures were visible, like shadows moving in the fog, growing as they came steadily nearer.

Several of the warriors pulled back their cloaks and put hand to sword or spears. They watched intently as the forms became darker, clearer, finally resolving into a band of horsemen.

The warriors of Cumhal knew them. They were the Clan of Morna. At their head rode Aed himself, flanked by his brother Conan and a giant champion of the Connacht Fian known as Luachra. This fierce, glowering bull of a man towered more than a head above the brothers Morna. The planes of his broad face had the hardness and sharpness of a cliff of stone, with thrusting chin and jutting brows.

The company of warriors drew up a spear's throw from Cumhal's clan. Aed moved on, crossing half the remaining distance before reining in. Cumhal turned his horse and rode back through his men to meet the other chieftain.

He meant to give a friendly greeting, but as he neared Aed he became aware of his grim expression. His warrior instincts told him that it was not comradeship that had brought the son of Morna to this strange place.

"What is it, Aed?" he demanded.

"I've come to challenge you for the leadership, Cumhal," the other answered tersely.

"Challenge me?" Cumhal echoed in surprise. "But why now? You've accepted my leadership before."

"You no longer serve the Fianna or Ireland," Aed told him in a flat, mechanical way.

"That's the high king speaking in you!" Cumhal accused. "Is obedience to him more important to you than your own warriors?"

"I am loyal to the bond we have made, as I must be," Aed told him gravely. "They are bonds of loyalty that we have all sworn to keep. I will do so."

"Those bonds were not meant to make us slaves to the selfish rulers of Ireland," Cumhal responded earnestly. "Listen to me, Aed: it is ourselves who are the real power now. We can use that power to bring ourselves and all the people of Ireland more freedom, more respect—"

"Enough talking!" the other said impatiently, sweeping Cumhal's logic savagely away. "Yield the leadership to me, or we must fight."

Cumhal sighed wearily. "Then we must fight," he said with great sorrow.

Both chieftains slid from their horses' backs. Their

warriors followed. There was a sharp clattering of arms as shields were adjusted, spears readied to the hand, gleaming swords drawn. Then the two forces faced one another, waiting, bodies tensed, eyes already searching among their opponents for a suitable adversary to challenge in single combat. But as they set themselves for battle, the men of the Baiscne clan became more acutely aware than ever of the peculiar weakness of their limbs and of the weight of fatigue upon them like a cloak of lead.

Aed began the fight, striking at Cumhal. As the two leaders engaged, their clansmen surged forward, the sides clashing together with the savagery of two sea waves colliding. The chill air was filled with the sharp clanging of iron on iron, the thud of weapons against thick leather shields, the battle cries of the Baiscne and Morna clans.

The battle grew quickly confused in the swirling fog. With the two sides tangled closely together, moving constantly, their clan colors almost indistinguishable in the grayness, it was hard to judge comrade from enemy until nearly within sword's length. At one point, Crimall—having hacked the sword arm from one opponent—sensed movement behind him and wheeled in time to fend off a savage cut. He found himself looking into the startled gaze of Fiacha!

Though the two groups were closely matched in numbers and in fighting skills, the strange weariness upon the Baiscne clan threw a great advantage to their foes. Inspired by the effort of their chieftain, the warriors fought on doggedly, managing to hold their own for some time. But as the battle dragged on, exhaustion came upon them more rapidly. Soon the Baiscne men were falling in far greater numbers than their opponents.

Luachra was causing the greatest devastation in the Baiscne ranks. The giant bashed his way through the melee with his broad shield, jabbing out at any vulnerable man with a heavy spear. His own clansmen scrambled to be safely out of the path of the lumbering champion.

After cutting a wide swath of destruction through

the embroiled warriors, he paused to tug his weapon from the body of his latest victim and scan the fight to pick the best direction for a new assault. It was then that he saw his chieftain in great peril.

The battle between Aed and Cumhal had been a hard-fought one. From the first the two men had been locked together like two bucks contending for mastery of the herd. The fight had been an equal one at first, but soon Cumhal had become aware of the effects of the growing fatigue. A glance around him had shown his clansmen in similar straits, with many warriors already down. He realized that unless he could defeat Aed, and quickly, they would be finished soon.

Mustering all his remaining energy, he dove upon MacMorna in a desperate move. He feinted with lightning speed, then managed to thrust Aed's shield aside with his own. Over its rim he swung a swordstroke at his opponent's unprotected head. Aed jerked back, managing to save his skull, but the tip of Cumhal's well-honed blade just touched him, slicing down through the skin of his forehead, piercing his eye, laying open his cheek.

Aed staggered back, dropping his shield. Cumhal, his energy nearly drained by this last, all-out effort, forced himself to move forward, determined to finish the Morna chieftain. But as he started toward the wounded man, a figure came in his way, looming over him.

He looked up into the stony face of Luachra.

Before Cumhal could lift a weary sword arm in defense, the giant struck, flinging one of his spears. It was a massive weapon, its pole the thickness of a man's forearm, its iron point as broad as a man's hand. The force behind the spear drove it through the leather of Cumhal's shield and on, slamming its point into the hollow just below the young chieftain's ribs.

Luachra yanked back on the leather strap of the weapon. His move tore the spearhead from Cumhal and the shield from his hands. Cumhal dropped to his knees, his sword arm falling to his side.

Now the giant stood above him, lifting his spear to

22

strike the final blow. But Aed appeared beside him, one hand clasped to his own streaming wound.

"No!" he commanded his champion, using the tremendous will of a trained Fian warrior to fight back the pain. "It is for me to finish this!"

Luachra stepped back. Aed moved forward to stand before Cumhal. The captain of the Fian, too weak to move his body, managed with an effort to raise his head. Knowing what was now to come, he still met his opponent's single, glittering eye unafraid.

"It was a good fight, Cumhal," Aed told him. "You've taken my eye; but in return I'll take your life."

With that he thrust out in a swift, skillfully aimed blow that struck through MacTredhorn's breastbone and impaled his heart. Soundlessly the stricken warrior toppled backward onto the bloody ground.

With the death of their chieftain, the spirit went from the men of his clan, while the Clan na Morna, intoxicated by this triumph, attacked with greater vigor. The battle went against the Baiscne warriors, and there began a great slaughter.

Crimall saw that there was no purpose in continuing this now hopeless fight. He shouted to his comrades to leave the battle. The warriors tried to break away and escape into the woods. But many were trapped against the dense wall of trees that hemmed them in and were cut down. Only Crimall and a handful of the clansmen managed to force their way through narrow openings into the woods beyond the trap and fade away into the fog.

"Get the men after them!" Aed ordered Conan. "Hunt them down. Kill all that can be found!"

While the warriors began their pursuit, he and Luachra went back to stand over Cumhal.

"Luachra, it was you who saved my life," Aed told the champion, looking down at the fallen warrior's body, "and your blow that defeated Cumhal. You have given me the leadership of the Fianna. What reward can I give to you?"

"Only one," the giant said. He stooped and yanked a bag of white skin covered with elaborate stitching from the shoulder of the dead man. He held it up with a triumphant air.

Aed knew what it was: the sacred treasure bag of the Baiscne clan. The collection of items within it were said to be the most prized possessions of Cumhal's people.

"Our taking this is our proof to all of the complete destruction of Cumhal's clan," Luachra told him. "I would become the carrier of the treasure bag for the Clan na Morna."

"Then that honor I will give you, and gladly," Aed told him.

Luachra slipped the pouch onto his own harness. "Then we have our prize," he said. "Now for a prize to show your high druid Tadg."

He leaned down again, grasped the plaited hair of the dead chieftain, and pulled his head up from the ground. His other hand pulled his sword from its sheath and swung it high.

As it swept down, a great raven lifted from the gray-shrouded branches overhead and flapped away, giving voice to a rasping cry that echoed mournfully in the foggy woods.

Chapter Three

ESCAPE

The battle raven soared above the house of Cumhal, voicing its rasping death cry. But within the dwelling, the sound was lost in the birth wail of an infant.

Bodhmall looked toward the wicker screen and allowed herself a small smile of satisfaction. Then she rose to fill a bowl with more of the medicinal broth, for Muirne would surely have need of it now. But as she stooped over the caldron, lowering the ladle toward the surface of the broth, she stiffened, staring down. For there, within the boiling liquid and the rising steam, strange, wavering shapes were beginning to appear.

Liath appeared from behind the wicker screen, beaming with exuberance.

"A boy!" she announced joyfully. "As pink and fat as I've ever seen, and as fair as his mother!"

She stopped then, noting the peculiar, frozen position of the older woman.

"Bodhmall?" she said in puzzlement. "What is it?"

"Hush, woman," the other commanded. She was trying to concentrate. This was not the first time in her life that she had experienced such a phenomenon as this. She knew she had to focus her mind and will the image clear.

Slowly it did become clearer, like the rippling waters of a pond calming to produce a mirror image. The vague forms grew sharper, taking on color and solidity and depth and, finally, movement. And suddenly she found herself looking upon a scene of savage battle. It was nearly ended. Many bodies littered the field, their steaming crimson blood bright upon the frosty sod. Other men were running, escaping away into fog-cloaked woods.

Then came a sight more dreadful: the head of Cumhal MacTredhorn, white-eyed and mouth gaping, dangling from a horse's bridle by its own long hair.

On this the vision faded, replaced again by the steam and swirling waters of the caldron.

Bodhmall straightened slowly, the ladle and bowl forgotten in her hands as she mused upon what she had seen. There was no sense of shock in her. To one who had tended warriors of the Fian as long as she, such grim sights were familiar ones. Her hard and practical mind was fully occupied with the implications of the event she had witnessed.

For she had no doubts of the truth of her vision.

25

Always before they had proven true. And this one meant that they would have to move very quickly.

She turned toward Liath, who still stood watching her with some concern.

"Is Muirne awake?" she snapped.

"Why, yes," Liath answered, surprised by the other's curtness.

Dropping the utensils, Bodhmall moved quickly past the nurse and around the screen. Beyond she found Muirne propped up against a mound of sleeping rugs, cradling the newborn in her arms. He was asleep, his tiny face nearly lost in a mass of linen.

Muirne was staring down raptly at the baby, but looked up as the gaunt woman entered and smiled brightly. This smile quickly faded, however, as she saw the chill expression on the other's face. Some premonition that something had happened filled her as she asked fearfully: "Bodhmall, what has happened?"

Bodhmall knelt by the bed. "There is no way to make this gentle news," she said bluntly. "Cumhal is dead. His company was attacked by the Clan na Morna. The rest of his warriors have been killed or scattered."

The girl's face was drained of its warm flush and she seemed to shrink back, wilting like a flower touched by winter's chill.

"Cumhal!" she said. "Oh, my Cumhal!"

Bodhmall leaned closer. "There is no time for sorrow now, Muirne," she said sharply. "It is the child you must be thinking of."

The harsh reality in these words recalled the girl's sense. She looked down at the sleeping infant, then back to Bodhmall, a new terror filling her eyes.

"Of course," she said. "The ones who killed Cumhal will not let any son of his survive to carry on a blood feud. What can we do?"

"We must leave here quickly," the gaunt woman said. "My brother has a large cart. He can carry us away safely."

"No!" Muirne said with a new firmness. She drew herself up and set her young face with a woman's determination. "It is I they will hunt for. I cannot have him with me!"

"What are you saying?" Bodhmall asked.

"That you and Liath must take my son to safety. You must hide him away and see that all I have of Cumhal lives!"

The families of the defeated Clan na Baiscne warriors streamed out from the ring fort and its surrounding cluster of huts. Some riding or in carts but most afoot, they fled into a surrounding countryside turned white by a sudden, rapidly thickening snowfall.

At the fortress gates sat a heavy four-wheeled wagon behind a team of aging draft horses. A scrawny and craggy-faced old man held its reins, gloomily watching as Liath and Bodhmall finished loading bundles of clothing and food into the back.

Muirne stood near them, the infant in her arms. When they had finished the loading and were ready to depart, she prepared her child for his journey. Carefully, tenderly she pulled the wrapping blanket tightly around him against the cold. Awake, wide-eyed but quiet, he watched her. His tiny, pale face was almost lost among the thick clothes that bundled him. A few stray whisps of his fine, blond hair showed about his head, the curling strands a glowing, almost silver-white, like his mother's.

She finished her arranging and just stood, holding him, looking down at that peaceful face, untouched by the sufferings of the hostile world he had been brought into. She cursed the violence that would part them. Anguish nearly overwhelmed her as the images of the life they would have had flashed through her mind. The experience of his first words and his first steps would be lost to her. There would be no playing together in the sun-warmed meadows, no watching his glowing wonder at a butterfly, a rainbow, a budding flower. It would not be her arms which hugged him close to calm his fears at the howling of a winter gale. All these images of a future she had looked to only yesterday were whirled away now like the snowflakes in the gusting wind. Now

27

she was looking upon the face of her only child for what might be the final time.

"Your father is lost to us both, my fair, my only son," she told him softly. "And without him, there's not another sorrow greater in the world to me than knowing I'll not feel your warmth against me or hear your voice or see your smile. But I will have a joy in knowing that you live, and that must be enough."

His glowing gray eyes stared up into hers fixedly, as if he listened and understood. She found herself unable to say more. Controlling her emotions with a great effort, she pulled the blankets tightly around him a last time, folded down a flap to shield his face, and put him into the arms of Liath.

"I've named him Demna," she told the nurse, whose round face streamed with tears. Then she turned to Bodhmall. "Take him into the fastness of Slieve Bladhma. Into the deepest glens. They are the lands of my own people. No one will find you there."

"And what will you do?" the gaunt woman asked.

"I will lead the hunters in another way," Muirne said with resolve. "They must never know of you or of Demna." She gazed searchingly into Bodhmall's eyes and her voice took on a pleading note. "Please, keep him safely. And see that he is happy. Don't let what killed his father destroy him too."

"I will do what must be done," Bodhmall said earnestly. "Good fortune go with you, Muirne."

With that, she and Liath climbed into the cart and settled in its back. Bodhmall signaled its driver and he urged the team forward, along the snow-blanketed roadway.

Muirne stood at the gateway and watched them move away until they had faded into the screen of white. Tears welled in her eyes, slid down her cheeks, and blended with the snowflakes melting there.

The door of the *liss* shattered as it was driven inward. The party of warriors, weapons ready, shouldered into the room, accompanied by a heavy swirl of snow.

Aed led them, a thick pad of linen soaked with red-black blood now tied across his wound. His pain made him impatient. His frustration enraged him. He kicked over the abandoned caldron upon the burnt-out fire and swung around, scanning the shadowy interior. His warriors moved about, poking into the corners with their blades and spears, tearing down tapestries and wicker walls.

"No one here," said Conan, peering under the pallet in Muirne's alcove.

"You noticed that, did you?" his brother shot back. "Where did they go?"

"They must have left here before us," Conan said.

Aed gave him a withering look. "Your brilliance astounds me! By the Bloody Raven, how did they know we were coming?"

He walked back toward the door. The night was fully on them now, the winds rising, sending the snow in scouring blasts across the yard, piling it in drifts against the inside of the walls.

"We have to find her," he said fiercely. "She can't escape." He looked back at the others. "Every man must go out. Scour every thicket and cave."

Conan moved up behind him, looking out into the storm. "What, go out in that?" he said complainingly. "We'll not find anyone's track in that. We'll only be frozen ourselves to try it!"

Aed wheeled on him, his voice low and savage. "I don't care. We will hunt her down no matter how long it takes. It's begun now, Conan. Don't you understand? It's begun and, like it or not, we have to finish it!"

The snow had ended but the wind was still sharp, wailing through the trees, tearing at those in the cart as it moved on into the heart of the forest called Slieve Bladhma.

The brother of Bodhmall struggled at the reins, using whip and curses to force the weary animals ahead

29

through the banks of snow. He was a skinny crow of a man, big-beaked and sharp-eyed. His voice, too, was that of a crow as he cawed his complaints to his sister.

"It's a carpenter I am, not a warrior. I must be mad to bring you out here in this night to this cursed place."

"We had to bring the child away," Bodhmall told him brusquely. "You were the only one I could trust to do it."

"There's another thing as well!" he went on. "We'll all be dead if we're caught with Cumhal's son. It's not for me to take a risk like that. I'm not of the Fian."

"You are of the Baiscne clan and your bonds should be enough to make you help," she pointed out. "No more talk, now. Keep your eyes on the way!"

He was forced to keep a closer watch on their path, for the woods became ever denser as they moved inward, with tree trunks, brush, and the furry boughs of evergreens brushing against the sides of the wagon. But this ended suddenly as they came into a small open valley along a narrow stream that cut a black sinuous line through the smooth field of white.

In the center of this glen, near to the stream, sat a round thatched house, unfortified.

"Thank Danu!" Bodhmall said wholeheartedly. "Brother, take us there!"

The wagon pulled up before the house. It was dark. No smoke rose from its smoke hole. She climbed down and peered in through its doorless entrance. It was a tiny dwelling, single-roomed, wattle-sided, and in poor repair, the clay dropping from its walls in chunks, its thatch festooned with cobwebs, its floor empty of furniture. Wind whistled in through the chinks and snow had filtered down through the smoke hole. Still, it was shelter.

"Take the child inside," she ordered Liath as she moved back to the cart. "I'll bring in some food and coverings. Use blankets to seal the door and cover the holes."

Liath obeyed as Bodhmall began to pull bundles and baskets from the wagon. But she paused as she

30

noted her brother still holding the reins and staring glumly at her activities.

"Don't be sitting there and watching," she told him curtly. She pulled a woodsman's ax from the back and tossed it to him. "Cut some wood! We'll need a fire, and quickly!"

He caught the ax and looked at it with distaste. His eyes rose to her. "I've never liked being at your command, you know, Sister," he said coldly. "Just because it was you who had the healin' and the seein' powers, it was you who served the chieftains." He threw the ax down into the snow. "Well, that's ended."

"What are you saying?" she demanded.

"I'm saying I've done all I mean to. You plan to stay here and hide from the Sons of Morna. Well, I don't. I'm leaving you."

"You can't!" she protested. "What if you're caught! You might tell them where we are."

"They'll not find me," he said. "They'll not even be looking for me."

"But you know how you are when you've had too much of the drink," she reminded him. "You might speak of us. Brother, it's too great a risk you're taking."

"There's little you can do about it," he said, smiling insolently over his new independence. "You can't leave here yourself. I'm free of you and your orderin'."

She saw that he meant to go and sighed. "All right," she told him in a resigned voice. "I can't stop you. But you might at least help me take out these other things from the wagon. It'll speed your going."

"I will do that," he said and climbed down from the seat.

As he began lifting the rest of the baskets and piles of clothing from the back, Bodhmall set down her own armful and stooped to lift the ax from the snow.

"You might leave us this as well," she said. "We'll be needing it to cut our own firewood now."

"Take it and welcome. It's a little enough price to be rid of you."

He leaned down to lift another basket from the cart. As he did, Bodhmall stepped up close behind him.

31

In a single, savage stroke, backed by all the strength in her sinewy body, she buried the broad ax deep in her brother's back.

His head snapped back. He gasped, then sagged forward, tumbling limply into the snow.

Bodhmall heard a terrified shriek behind her and turned to see Liath in the doorway of the hut, the baby in her arms, staring with wide eyes at the awful scene.

"What have you done?" she cried. "He is your brother!"

"He meant to leave us. He might have betrayed us," she answered simply, and then her voice assumed its brisk, commanding tones. "Never mind him, woman. Get that child inside. Do you want it to freeze? Keep it warm. I'll get a fire started soon!"

As Liath disappeared obediently into the hut again, Bodhmall jerked the ax free of the fallen man's body.

"Sorry, Brother," she told him grimly. "I could take no risks. The life of this boy is too precious. Someday he'll be ready to take Cumhal's place!"

Chapter Four

FINN'S CHILDHOOD

Through the long, bleak winters, through the wet springs and glowing summers and brilliant falls, the child lived hidden away in the glen of Slieve Bladhma with the two women as his only company. They became his parents, with Bodhmall his teacher and Liath his nurse and comforter.

From the time that he began to walk, Bodhmall was a harsh taskmistress. She spared the boy no pain or hardship that might make him stronger, faster, more clever or more skilled.

She would pursue the toddling child up rugged hills or through the trees, swinging a stinging switch behind to urge him along. Often she would test his speed and reflexes by placing him in a meadow with a brace of young rabbits and charging him to see that neither escaped. The earnest boy tried desperately to please his stern teacher. He would chase the bounding creatures about, throwing his entire body, will, and strength into the impossible task of heading off the departing animals. Always he failed, ending exhausted, red-faced, and humiliated. But as the years passed, as he grew in swiftness and cunning, he came ever closer to success.

The tender-hearted Liath, always the mother to him, lived in constant distress at Bodhmall's harsh treatment of the boy. Over the years of isolation there, he became her sole reason for life, and each hurt he suffered was one for her as well.

One day, when Demna was only three, Bodhmall had hauled the lad squealing and squirming to a nearby pond, lifted him, and, to Liath's horror, flung him out into the deepest part.

With a scream, Liath had sprung forward to rescue him. But Bodhmall had knocked her to the ground with a single blow and stood over the sobbing woman, her body rigid, her face drawn with anger, her voice threatening.

"Quiet, you foolish woman! What I am doing is to save his life. If he means to survive, someday he will need all his courage, all the toughness we can give him. Don't you ever think to interfere with that again!"

And Liath, remembering Bodhmall's ruthless killing of her own brother, had lain still, trembling with fear, watching as the boy had splashed and cried and spluttered and then managed to thrash his way safely to the shallows. From that time on, she had watched the older woman's training with alarm and disapproval, but also from afar.

But as the years passed by, even she was forced to

grudgingly admit that Bodhmall's methods seemed to be successful ones, for all their cruel look. The boy actually seemed to thrive on them, growing astoundingly strong and fast, moving in the woods with a fox's stealth, a stag's speed and grace, a bear's power. Liath also came to recognize that her hard companion's treatment of Demna was never unfair nor meant to cause real harm, but always carefully disciplined.

Still, when the training ended, it was to Liath that he turned for soothing, or binding of his hurts, or laughter and affection. So that kindly woman was able to touch him, too, instilling a sense of gentleness and consideration in him. While Bodhmall taught him the forest lore and how to track and hunt, Liath taught him its beauties and sang him songs of it. While the gaunt woman told him to be wily and hard and trust no one, Liath told him to love and understand all living things. While Bodhmall gave him the skills and courage of a savage beast, Liath saved him from having a savage heart as well.

Both of them tried also to teach the growing boy what they could of the life beyond the confines of their hidden glen. But this knowledge was very limited in two women who had lived their whole lives as servants within a chieftain's dun and never traveled more than a day's walk from their home. They could tell him of the dress and style of life and tribal customs they knew, but for knowledge of the wider world they could only pass on stories they had heard.

Some of the tales were vague, ill-remembered, or fanciful, and these were highly suspect to the cautious Bodhmall, who wanted the boy to learn only what she knew to be the truth. Often she admonished the romantically minded Liath when she caught her filling the rapt child's impressionable mind with legends of golden duns, magical heroes, and fabulous monsters. For Bodhmall understood that what he must learn about the outside world would have to come through hard experience. She could only hope that what she was teaching him would help him to survive the perilous journey of discovery he would someday have to make.

"I heard you telling him that old tale of the Boyhood Deeds of Cuchulain," she remarked to Liath one night as she watched the woman gently tucking in the sleeping boy. "I wish you'd not be always doing that."

"Ah, it was only for fun," Liath answered. "The lad is six years old today. He deserved a bit of fun."

She smoothed back the thick crest of glowing hair from the white forehead. "Good night, my Finn," she said softly. Finn—the Fair—had become her own pet name for him, and he now answered to it more readily than to his given name.

"Liath, you'll be ruining the boy with all these foolish tales and songs and motherings," Bodhmall said disapprovingly. "He'll become too soft."

"He must have love to survive," Liath responded, leaving his sleeping alcove to join Bodhmall by the fire. "All children need love."

"Love may destroy him," Bodhmall warned, as she had countless times before. "It will take a ruthless heart for him to succeed in the world he must enter."

"You are wrong, Bodhmall," the little woman said with some force. She had slowly learned to stand up to the other, and she could be stubborn now. "If he is truly to be the man you wish, all things must be equal in him. Warmth as well as hardness. So don't be taking that deadly tone with me. You can threaten me as you like, but you'll not stop me."

"And I thank you for that," said a voice.

Startled, both women whirled about. Muirne stood at the doorway of the hut.

She had aged very little in the years that had passed. She had become more mature in looks, but it had only added to her beauty.

"Muirne! You are alive!" exclaimed Liath.

"I managed to flee to Carraighe," she said absently, moving forward, her eyes fixed upon the figure in the bed. "I'm married to its king. He has hidden and protected me."

"Still, to come here is a great risk!" Bodhmall said gravely. "If you were seen and followed or if you were found here—"

"I know, Bodhmall," she answered, her pleading gaze going to the older woman. "I know it was a risk, but still I had to come. I had to see him and know that he was well. I've searched the glens of all Slieve Bladhma to find you. Please!"

Bodhmall eyed her coldly for a time without reply. Then she relented, shaking her head impatiently.

"Ah, well, you're here now, and the damage done," she said. "You may as well see him." But as Muirne started eagerly toward the bed, she added warningly, "But take care not to wake him. That I'll not allow. He mustn't know you came here."

Muirne looked back at her in shock. "What? I can't speak to him?"

"Bodhmall, no!" Liath protested, her own feelings for the boy making her know what distress must fill the young woman. "You must let her—"

"I will not!" Bodhmall said fiercely, cutting her off. "He can't know of his mother now. He thinks that she is dead."

Muirne stepped back toward her. "Why would you tell him that?" she asked in a stricken voice.

"There was no choice," Bodhmall told her bluntly. "You must understand that. As he grows older, keeping him hidden away here will become more difficult. Impossible, maybe, if he knows you're somewhere in the world outside. And he cannot leave here until he is ready."

"Ready?" Muirne repeated. "For what?"

"To claim the place of his father, as he should!" Bodhmall announced, pride ringing in her voice.

Muirne gripped the woman's arms. "You can't do that to him, Bodhmall!" she said in agony. "You'll be condemning him to his father's fate!"

Bodhmall looked down into Muirne's pale, frightened face. Her own was set stubbornly.

"It is already done, Muirne," she said with finality. "The boy knows who he is and what he must do one day. There is no other way."

"There must be!" Muirne said desperately. "There must be some way to save him!"

36

"And what would you do?" Bodhmall demanded harshly. "Would you have him stay hidden away here? Trapped here by fear all his life? No, Muirne. He is of the Clan of Baiscne. He is Cumhal's son. He must take the name and his place in the world as he should. And the only way he can succeed in that is to stay here until the time comes."

Muirne stared up at the tall, hard woman. "I hate what you have done," she said. "You have betrayed me."

"My loyalty is to Cumhal, not you," came the chill reply. "It is not for you to change this now, and I'll not let you. If you wish to see him, you may, but only as I say. Do you agree?"

The young woman's body sagged in defeat. Desolation filled her voice. "I've little choice, it seems. You've taken his life from me."

"No, Muirne," Bodhmall corrected. "You gave it to me when you put him in my keeping. Go to him now, but be careful."

Muirne nodded. Softly she crossed the hut to the small pallet at its far side. She stood for a moment, looking down at him. He lay on his side, his face relaxed in sleep. Lightly she stroked the white-gold hair, so like her own, and then gently sat down upon the pallet next to him. In a soft, almost inaudible voice, fine and high and sweet as a harp's tone, she hummed a lilting air to him. It was a mother's lullabye to her babe, the only act of love that she might show to him, though he would not know of it.

Tears filled the eyes of Liath. There was no jealousy in her at seeing Demna with his mother, but only sorrow for her loss. Even Bodhmall, who would have stopped the tune for fear of its waking the boy, could not interfere in Muirne's brief moment.

The tune ended. The young woman sat silently by his side, staring at his face, trying to memorize each feature, trying to drink in some sense of him. Then he stirred uneasily, as if her presence were reaching through his sleep.

"Quickly, he is beginning to wake," Bodhmall hissed. "You must come away! He cannot see you!"

Muirne leaned forward and, very lightly, kissed the smooth white forehead of her son. Reluctantly she rose from the bed and moved away, crossing the room again to the door. She paused there for a final look back.

"You will see him again, Muirne," Bodhmall promised. "One day you will see him captain of the Fianna of Ireland."

"Or laid on his funeral pyre," the young woman replied, fixing a hard stare upon the other. "It's my own heart you have in your hands, Bodhmall. If you destroy it, you will destroy me too. And may the curse of my people fall upon you then!"

She turned and passed out of the hut. The darkness swallowed her. As she disappeared, the boy sat suddenly upright in his bed, his eyes open, staring toward the door in a startled way.

"What is it!" he cried out. "Who was there?"

Liath moved quickly toward him, coming between him and the door. She pushed him gently back.

"Be easy, Finn," she told him soothingly. "It's all right."

He resisted her, craning his neck up to peer around her. His voice was insistent.

"But, Liath, someone was here! I know it!" Suddenly he stopped struggling and looked at her musingly, frowning as he sought to grasp a faint impression. "Someone was singing, weren't they?" he asked. "They sang, and"—he raised a hand to touch his forehead— "they kissed me . . . here!"

The little woman cast a pleading glance at Bodhmall, but the other's face was stone.

Liath threw her arms about the boy and pulled him toward her, hugging him tightly so he wouldn't see her tears.

"Hush, my son," she told him softly. "It was only a dream."

Chapter Five

DISCOVERY

The son of Cumhal slipped stealthily through the sun-dappled glade. His sinewy body, clad in a simple tunic of dressed hide, moved with the lithe grace of the deer he stalked.

Sixteen years had turned him into a man in size and form. Tall, broad, and sturdy of frame like his father, he had the leanness and suppleness of his mother as well. He had Muirne's hair too. The long, unbound flow that curled about his shoulders flared almost to silver when he passed through one of the scattered rays of intense spring sun.

His features were a blend of the best in each. The fragile, sculptured beauty of his mother had refined the coarseness of his father's traits while leaving their bold character in brows and nose and chin.

The years of Bodhmall's hard training had honed his forest skills well. His passage made no sound and left no mark on the bright, newly green foliage. Now he paused, standing totally motionless, listening intently. His eyes scanned the underbrush ahead for any movement. His slender, iron-tipped spear was held up, ready for the throw.

But there was no sign of his quarry ahead, no sound of its movement. This puzzled and irritated him. Game seldom managed to elude him now. And he was certain that this buck had come this way.

Of course, it was a new section of the forest, and much farther from home than he had ever ranged be-

39

fore. With age had come an occasional loosening of the reins by Bodhmall. Each time he had again stretched them taut in his exploring, impelled by a spirit for adventure and an insatiable curiosity.

He crept on, following the way he thought the deer had gone. He moved into a thicker section of trees, working his way carefully through clinging underbrush, and found himself suddenly on the edge of an open space.

This was no forest clearing. The view was unlimited by trees. The fields went on to the horizon in soft swells thickly furred with lush spring grass. Large herds of cattle grazed upon them. The many spring-born calves bawled and gamboled about their placid mothers or shakily tried to master their spindly new legs.

He realized with surprise and excitement that he had reached the forest edge and was seeing that world outside for the first time. It was a bit frightening, but it was fascinating too. And nothing held his attention more than a large knoll of earth not far away. For atop it was a manmade structure.

He stared at this with tremendous interest. Of course Bodhmall had told him of the homes of men that lay beyond the sanctuary of Slieve Bladhma, but he had never seen any building except for their tiny hut.

This was certainly something else. It seemed to him quite a grand sort of place. Immense in fact. From Bodhmall's descriptions of such things, he knew that it must be a rath. A wall of rough-hewn posts each thicker than his waist was set upright on a circular bank of earth. This ringed the *lios*, the central mound. The high-peaked roofs of several thatched buildings atop the mound were just visible above the stockade.

He examined all this carefully, absorbing these new wonders like a thirsty man at a cool spring. But he had to see it closer. All his life he had been warned of the danger of the deadly sons of Morna discovering him should he venture from the glens. And he knew very well the great anger that would be on Bodhmall should she learn that he had disobeyed. Still, he couldn't help it. His desire for knowledge was an easy defeater of his foster mother's rules. He would have just a bit of a closer look, he told himself. That was all.

With a fox's stealth he crept out of the woods and moved across the open countryside beyond. From ravine to bush to rock he cautiously made his way even closer to the ring fort, moving in a great curve that took him around its far side so he might take in every detail of it.

Finally he was just below it. He could see the wide notch that gave entrance through the outer ring. The large timber gates that secured it stood open. Beyond them a section of the enclosed lios was visible, a tantalizing thing, if only he could peep further into it. But his angle was not quite right.

He moved on, through a little grove of trees, and found that it edged a large field of beaten earth. Here he had his second surprise, for a score of young men were running about on it, shouting and cheering lustily, smacking a small object with large, curved sticks.

They looked to be of Demna's own age, and he stared raptly at them as if they were the fabulous creatures of some•legend. And so they were in a way. To him the existence of other boys was known only from Bodhmall's tales of the world. He had grown up without their company, without even seeing them until now. Not really knowing, he had not missed it. But now, watching them together, he felt the pang of something lost, of regret for the comradeship he had missed.

The sudden, intense need to be part of this tugged him forward. But he held himself back, again recalling Bodhmall's warnings to be always on guard, always suspicious.

His gaze assessed the youths. They were unarmed, save for the sticks. They seemed quite innocent, laughing in their play. There didn't seem to be anyone older about, certainly no warriors. As powerful and sinister as the grim woman's childhood tales had made the dark sons of Morna, he couldn't believe they could be everywhere. And he recalled the gentler words of Liath— usually given well out of Bodhmall's hearing—that all

41

men were not evil, that the great number of them could actually be trusted.

This was enough. Once more his need won out. A brief meeting with these boys was harmless enough.

He drew slowly out of the concealing foliage, moving forward onto the edge of the playing field to stand and watch. After a time one of the boys took note of his presence and began calling the attention of the rest to him. Gradually their play died, their shouts and laughing faded as they all turned to stare at this strange, wild figure who had suddenly appeared from the wood like some nature spirit.

A bit timidly, he smiled, hoping an open friendliness would be the proper start.

It seemed to work. They smiled back. Then one of them asked in a voice of amused wonder: "Well, by all the gods, what kind of a vagabond are you?"

The question was put rudely, but young Demna didn't note it, so anxious was he to establish a relationship. He started to reply, but decided that he must at least be a little cautious. He couldn't reveal anything of himself, even his name. Considering quickly, he recalled the pet name Liath had used for him as long as he could recall.

"I'm called Finn," he said, moving closer to them.

"The Fair One?" the other responded, laughing. "Well, that suits you well enough. And where is it you live? In the trees maybe?"

He laughed louder at his own jest and was joined by some of the others. Not understanding that this glee was at his expense, Demna laughed too.

"Please," he said, "could I join in your playing? I'd like to learn."

"Learn?" the same lad, clearly the leader of the group, echoed in surprise. "You mean you've not played at hurling before?"

"No," Demna said good-naturedly. "It looks to be great fun."

"You surely must live in a tree not to know of it," the other said. "But we'll let you play, and gladly, won't we, lads?" He turned to the others, winked broadly, and, in a voice Demna couldn't hear, muttered: "The game's dull enough. Thrashing this fool will give us a bit of sport!"

Excited by the prospect of joining in the game, Demna now tossed all caution aside. He grounded his spear in the sod beside the field and took the stick one of the young men handed to him. It was a carefully cut piece of hardwood, carved and smoothly finished. About the length of his arm, it curved at one end and flattened out into the shape of a disc. It was a well-balanced, heavy piece, and could be a quite deadly weapon as, unknown to Demna, it often was in this hard game.

"You hold the stick this way," another youth explained, demonstrating with his own. He gripped the haft firmly in both hands, holding the curved end close to the ground. Someone kicked a small, polished wooden ball toward him and he swung his stick, knocking it away. "You see? You use the stick to send the ball along." He pointed toward the far end of the field. "See that hole? Well, you hit the ball along until it goes into it."

Demna looked at the distant pit, then back at the stick he held. He gauged the smoothness of the hard-packed earth between and the distance to the goal.

"Is that all?" he asked.

The leader of the group grinned with a certain maliciousness. "Not quite." He looked around at the others, then back at Finn. "We're going to try to stop you."

Demna looked them over, then shrugged. "Still doesn't seem much of a sport."

At his self-assured tone, the smile of the other disappeared. "Oh, does it not?" he said sharply. "Well, that we will see!"

He signaled to his friends and they moved down the field, lining up before the goal. As they set themselves, sticks up, facing the stranger, he admonished tersely: "Give this oaf a fine thumping, lads. We'll beat some of that arrogance from him."

He dropped the ball before him and, with a well-aimed blow, sent it rolling down the field. As it ap-

43

proached, Demna charged forward, his first swing catching the wooden sphere squarely and sending it back toward them, much to their surprise.

So swiftly did he come against them that they were taken completely off their guard. No one was able to move fast enough to block him until he was nearly upon them. And even then their efforts were in vain. His speed and reactions were like those of no man they had ever met. He wiggled through their line, dodged about boys who seemed rooted to the ground and was past them, firing the ball on ahead with easy, accurate strokes. In what seemed an instant he was far down the field, leaving them to watch openmouthed as he gave the ball a final swipe that sent it rolling into the goal.

He retrieved the ball and strolled casually back to the group. "That was easy," he remarked. "Now what?"

"How could you move like that?" the leader asked him in awed tones.

He grinned. "I learned it from the rabbits!"

After that, the boys were clamoring to be on the team with this marvel. They divided fairly, and Demna led his new comrades in game after game, trouncing the team of the leader each time, piling more humiliation upon his head.

When the evening began to come upon them, Demna was forced to leave, against the protestations of many disappointed youths. He promised that he would return and faded back into the trees of Slieve Bladhma, aglow with his new experience and vowing to keep it a secret from Bodhmall.

". . . and he did Colm's team properly every time!" a youth proclaimed. "Left them all gaping after him, he did!"

His fellows and the company of warriors at the low tables of the ring fort's central hall were laughing heartily at the tale. But Colm, the leader of the band, listened in deepening desolation. He was son of the ring fort's chieftain, Cathal O'Ciaran, a beefy, red-faced man who drank heavily and glowered upon the speak-

44

ers from his table at the room's upper end. The other youths were in fosterage to Cathal, training to become warriors, and Colm tended to put on superior airs with them. As a result, they were using the evening meal to vividly recount the details of his defeat with great gusto. From their tables at the room's lower end they had taken command of the whole hall, drawing everyone's attention to their description of the games.

"He said he learned his speed from chasing hares," one lad said.

"He was like a hare himself, hopping through us," another put in.

"And the power in him!" announced a third. "He made Colm eat a nice bit of sod more than once."

The eyes of all the grinning company turned to the discomfited youth and he reddened further.

The chieftain had listened to this with displeasure, his own face growing more ruddy with anger and too much strong ale. At this last jab at his son, his temper finally flared.

"Enough of this!" he cried, slamming his heavy cup upon the table. "There'll be no more talk of this stranger. He made fools of the lot of you, not just my son. So have an end to praising him!"

But another man beside him spoke up quickly. "Wait, my chieftain. I think we should hear more of this."

It was the chieftain's druid. He had a sharp-featured, cunning face made forlorn by age, giving him the look of a rain-drenched fox. His once-brilliant druidic robe was dulled by wear. The torc of office about his neck was bent and hung askew. But he had listened to the boys' talk with increasing interest, and a spark of life had flared in the burned-out cinders of his eyes.

The chieftain gave him an irritated look. Respect for the old man's powers had largely vanished long before. Still, the druid's honored position required that he be heard.

"What is it you want to know?" the chieftain demanded.

45

The druid fixed a searching gaze upon Colm. "You say this lad called himself Finn. How fair was he?"

"His hair was bright as the straw bleached by the fall sun. I've never seen fairer," he replied.

"And he vanished into the woods of Slieve Bladhma?"

"From the look of him, he must live there," Colm said.

"But that land is said to be claimed by the Children of Danu, by the family of Nuada himself!" the old man said. "Few men would risk Their wrath by entering there. Could it be this boy was of the Other?"

"He had greater swiftness and strength than most, that's true," Colm admitted grudgingly. "Still, he was no magical being, as I'll prove if I get another chance."

"Will you?" the druid said with a certain skepticism in his tone. "Well, I would like to see you make that attempt. Do you think he will return?"

"He promised to come again tomorrow," said one of the other boys.

The old druid nodded, then turned to his chieftain. "I think that we should observe this meeting if it takes place," he suggested. "It would be entertaining, and it might be very important as well."

The chieftain was by now too far gone in drink to feel like arguing. "All right," he growled. "All right. But I'd best not be seeing my own son made a clown of again!"

His warning was unnecessary. Colm had already made a vow to himself that he would have his revenge on the one called Finn. If the youth came again to challenge them, he would not live to return to his Slieve Bladhma.

Chapter Six

THE CONTEST

It was the beginning of the afternoon when Finn came out of the trees onto the plain below the fortress.

He had said nothing to Bodhmall of the previous day's visit. After finishing his morning's work about the hut, he had announced his intention to go hunting again and marched boldly away. He felt a certain guilt at having to mislead her—she had taught him that honesty was a leader's greatest virtue—but in this he had no choice. And it would be just one more time, he promised himself.

The lads weren't on the playing field when he arrived. Puzzled, he made his way about the rath seeking them. Beyond the field he found a small lake whose dark waters indicated a fair depth. Here the band of young men were swimming.

It was another fair day for the normally rainy spring of Ireland. Sun was pouring like golden honey upon the fields and sparkling from the waters of the lake. The water was chill, but that meant nothing to young bodies hardened to the rigors of their life. And in an island country dotted with lakes and streams and pools, swimming was quite a natural thing for them.

They stopped their play when Finn appeared at the lake's edge. Some of the lads shouted for him to join them. This he did quickly enough, dropping his spear and stripping off his leather tunic. His hard, smooth body flashed whitely as he dove in and stroked out powerfully to where the others waited in the deeper water.

Up at the ring fort, the trainer of the young men was keeping a close eye upon his brood from the walkway inside the stockade wall. He saw the strange fair-haired lad appear at the lake and set off at once to tell his chieftain.

With the old druid joining them, they wasted no time in leaving the enclosure and moving down the hillside to the cover of a copse of trees near the water. They crept forward cautiously to a place where they could watch without being seen. The chieftain was irritated with this need for stealth, but the druid insisted. Sighing heavily, the chieftain agreed, peering out through the branches of a fir tree at the activity.

There was quite a bit of it in the lake. The company was engaged in a fracas whose verve and violence only boys could think of as play. One group had quickly seized upon Finn as their captain, and he was leading them in a spirited assault upon the others, led by Colm.

But the chieftain's son, still smarting from the drubbing of the day before, had plotted with some of his comrades to ignore the play of the game and concentrate their force upon Finn himself. He had a plan for taking certain care of this brash stranger.

But to trap Finn wasn't so easy. He was like an otter in the water, sleek and swift and slippery. And the others of his team stayed close about, protecting him. For his own part, Finn was reveling in the challenge of the sport, feeling a new kind of headiness in being able at last to test the muscles and skills he'd been developing for so long.

But Colm and his friends persisted. Finally, their chance came. Finn drove forward, separating from his team. Far away from their support, he suddenly found himself surrounded by grim-faced adversaries.

"Now!" Colm shouted triumphantly. "On him, lads! Together!"

The whole band of them converged upon him from all sides, bearing him down beneath the surface under their crushing, flailing mass.

"They'll drown him, they will!" cried the trainer, and he started forward out of the cover.

But the druid gripped his arm and pulled him back.

"No!" he hissed sharply, his own gaze fixed with great interest on the struggle. "Let them go!"

In the lake, some of Finn's team were fighting to reach him, but the solid wall of opponents held them back. Already he had been beneath the water too long.

"Let's let him up, Colm!" said one of his team. "He's been down long enough now to take some of the spirit from him."

"No!" protested the chieftain's son. "You keep him down until I say! Keep him down or you'll regret it!"

Suddenly realizing what he was meaning to do, the lads began to break up, pulling away from the mass angrily.

"We'll not be killing him for you, Colm," one told him. "Threaten all you want!"

He grinned cruelly. "Fools! It's too late to save him by now anyway! He must be drowned."

Several of the boys were peering down into the waters, thrashing about with their feet in the spot where they had forced Finn under. They looked puzzled.

"He doesn't seem to even be here, Colm," one said.

"What?" he cried, swimming forward, shouldering them aside. "He must be there. Let me look!"

Reaching the spot, he peered intently down into the dark waters, looking for a glimmer of Finn's body below. But there was nothing.

"He can't have gotten away," Colm said in rising concern. "Where could he—"

Abruptly he was jerked beneath the surface, disappearing with a gurgling shout. Only a spreading ripple remained.

The others splashed forward to rescue him, but he was gone. They searched the waters frantically but futilely.

"There he is!" one shouted suddenly, pointing. For

49

the young man had popped to the surface some distance away.

They started toward him, but he was only visible for an instant, long enough to take a desperate gasp of air, before he was jerked beneath the surface again.

Realizing what peril Colm was in, the chieftain shouted "My son!" and charged forward. Bursting from cover, he ran for the lake's edge, the trainer and the druid close behind.

They had just reached the water when Colm whooshed to the surface a second time, close to the opposite shore. This time a second figure surfaced beside him.

Once more Bodhmall's harsh training had served Finn well. His swimming skills had saved him and given him means to take his revenge. Now as those across the lake watched helplessly, he dragged a spluttering Colm up into the reeds at the water's verge. Dumping the bedraggled and much humbled youth there, he climbed onto the bank. It was then that he became aware of the three new figures watching him.

Two of them were warriors, and armed. Were there more? Were they the sons of Morna, meaning to capture him? He had to get away!

With a burst of speed that further amazed the watching men, Finn rushed to grab up his tunic and spear and then headed away from the lake, back toward the woods of Slieve Bladhma.

"Don't let him go!" the druid shouted. But his order was useless. Before anyone could act, the young man was far away, vanishing into the shelter of the trees.

"An amazing lad," the trainer said, staring after him with awe. "None I've ever known had such power."

"Maybe," the druid said thoughtfully. He looked at the chieftain. "Did you see his face?"

"I did," the man said irritably. He was more concerned about his son, who the other lads were now hurrying to help. "Why?"

"You didn't find it familiar?"

"Familiar?" he said, looking quizzically at the druid. "No. I didn't know him. Did you?"

"Not him. But years ago, when I was among the advisors to the king, I saw someone else much like him." His voice was excited and his dark eyes glowed. "That's why I had to see him, to be certain. Now I would swear by all the gods my people swear by that this boy carries the blood of the daughter of Tadg!"

"Alive!" cried Conn of the Hundred Battles, leaping up from his seat to stare down in shock at the two men.

Tadg stood before the high king's raised platform in Tara's central hall, the visiting druid beside him. On hearing his story, he had brought him at once to see Conn.

The sixteen years had made no impression upon the slender high druid. No gray touched his fine hair, no lines creased the smooth skin of the beautiful face. Conn, on the other hand, showed the wear of time. His hair had receded from his brows. His lean face and body were more gaunt. His energetic manner had become a slower and more careful one.

"Are you so certain that this is Cumhal's son?" he demanded.

"There is no way to be certain," Tadg explained. "But this druid vows that the resemblance to my daughter is remarkable, both in his features and in his hair. And he is of the right age to have been born around the time of Cumhal's death."

"But how could it be, Tadg?" Conn said accusingly. "You told me that Muirne and her child were dead."

"I told you that there were rumors of her death," Tadg reminded him. "All that we know is that she vanished and has not been heard of in all these years since. The child we know nothing about, except for the tales that a son was born. It is possible, my king. Muirne loved Cumhal. She was a woman of tender heart and great will. She would have done anything to save her child. And the glens of Slieve Bladhma would be a fine place to hide."

51

"Then it's clear that we can't take any risk," Conn said irritably, pacing the royal dais. "If Cumhal did have a son and he has survived, he could create a great danger. He might revive the Clan na Baiscne. He might carry out a blood feud, challenge MacMorna for the leadership, even renew the Fianna challenges of my rule!"

He shook his head as he walked, his mind filled with visions of a new Cumhal defying him, clamoring for ever greater power. It seemed all the more threatening to him now. The aches and weaknesses of age, the hints of his mortality had grown so insistent that he could no longer ignore them. And with the recognition of his frailty and vulnerability had come increased insecurity. The resentment of Cumhal that had led him to have the man destroyed had now deepened to fear of the challenge he symbolized.

He stopped pacing and fixed the high druid with a troubled gaze.

"Tadg, this cannot happen," he said emphatically. "I'll have no trouble again from that clan. If this MacCumhal were to appear—"

"I understand, my king," said Tadg, breaking in smoothly, his tones soothing. "Of course this boy must be found and destroyed without anyone knowing of it."

"But I mustn't be brought in," Conn quickly added, turning away as if to separate himself from the deed. "The Firbolg clans cannot think I had any part in it."

"Naturally, my king," Tadg assured him with a smile. "No one could think that the high king of Ireland would be involved in these petty feuds. This is a task that the sons of Morna must undertake. After all, the peace of the Fianna is at stake, not to mention their own leadership."

Conn glanced back at him, drawn against his better judgment by curiosity to ask: "What will they do?"

"My fellow druid," he said, nodding at the old man, "will tell us where the lad was seen. The Clan na Morna will simply search him out. He will die unknown in the lonely wood."

"Just be certain that he does die this time," Conn told him pointedly.

*   *   *

The main door of the ring fort's hall burst open and a group of warriors pushed through out of the darkness and the rain beyond. A stroke of lightning illuminated the yard behind them, throwing them for an instant into stark relief. They were an eerie sight, their drenched clothing clinging to their massive bodies, their long and dripping hair plastered about their grim faces.

At their head was Aed MacMorna himself. But he was called Goll—the One-Eyed—now. A leather patch was tied across the damaged eye. But the other gleamed with no lessening of energy, and the warrior's body still moved with a young man's vitality.

He glanced around him sharply, taking in the interior of the hall. All activity there had stopped. The ruddy-faced chieftain and his warriors, at their evening meal, sat with food and cups and knives suspended in their hands as they stared at this band who had appeared like storm demons from the treacherous night.

Goll started toward the chieftain's table. Beside him moved his brother Conan, made a bit balder, stouter, and more irascible by the years. They strode forward with the assurance of those who knew that they controlled.

"Who are you to be breakin' in?" angrily demanded the chieftain, who was as usual somewhat worse for the drink by this time of the evening. "Comin' in here as if you were the masters of this place! A sorry-looking lot of warriors as I ever saw. And dripping on my new rushes!"

"It is the captain of the Fianna of Ireland that I am," Goll shot back.

The chieftain blanched, sagging back in his seat. "Goll MacMorna!"

"Yes. And I've business here. Business that you will gladly help me with. Isn't that so?"

"Of course, Captain! Of course!" the other readily agreed. He knew well of the Fianna's power, and of the ruthless nature of the sons of Morna.

"Good," Goll went on brusquely. "We've come to find the lad—the one called Finn. Where would he be?"

53

"He disappeared into Slieve Bladhma, just to the southwest."

"You'll show us where," Goll ordered, then looked at his brother. "Conan, gather every man in this rath. See that they're ready to join us at once. We'll begin the search now!"

"Now?" repeated Conan incredulously. He looked past the band of warriors into the stormy night beyond the door, then around at the cozy hall. "But I was thinking of a bit of warmth, maybe some food and—"

"Tonight!" boomed Goll angrily. "We'll take no chances on this boy escaping. If this must be done, then it'll be done quickly, Brother, quickly! Gather the men!"

Chapter Seven

FLIGHT

The storm crashed about the tiny hut in the glen. Rain worked its way into the worn spots of the thatch and dripped through. The three inside huddled closer to their tiny fire and avoided the largest drops as best they could.

Young Finn honed a knife carefully. It was their only one, and it had grown thin from the years of use. Liath knitted a comforter meant to ward off the night's chill. Bodhmall was mending a cooking pot, worn through by its long service. But as her long, bony fingers worked the metal dam into the hole, she stiffened suddenly. A peculiar sensation, like the chill from a draft, was creeping over her. It was a sensation she had not felt in many years.

Her gaze lifted to the peat fire. There, in its glowing red heart, an image began to form. Soon she could recognize a dark image of woods swept by curtains of rain. Through the trees, dim but recognizable, moved a party of armed men. Their image grew larger, as if they moved toward her. Soon their faces became clear. She saw the man who led them, saw the patch upon his eye. She understood what her vision meant.

The vision faded back into the red glow. Her wits not slowed by age, Bodhmall was quick to react. She turned toward Finn. Noting her abrupt move, he looked up at her.

"Bodhmall, what is it?"

"You have left the woods," she said bluntly.

He was stricken. He should have known she would find out. He colored with shame as he blurted out the truth. "I wandered to the edge. I saw a rath. I—I met some boys." His voice was anguished. "Bodhmall, I only meant to play with them. I would have told you, but—"

She leaned forward and laid a hand upon his arm. Her voice was unusually soothing. "Demna, it is all right. I expected that this would happen."

His anguish turned to bewilderment. "Expected?" he repeated.

"Of course, lad. When I gave you the freedom to roam, I knew that one day your own courage and your need to know the outside world would draw you out in spite of my warnings. And I knew that on that day you would be ready."

"Ready for what?" he asked.

"To do what you were meant to do," she answered with force. "To enter the world. To ready yourself to take your father's place."

Entering the world outside Slieve Bladhma had been his dream since hearing his first tales of it. Since his brief adventure into it, it had filled his mind constantly. Now the time he had waited for had come.

"You must go out and learn what we could not teach you here," she went on. "You must gain the skills to become a warrior and a man of the Fianna. Only then can you hope to become the leader of the Baiscne clan, as is your right."

She rose and moved away, leaving him staring in a rather bewildered way as he tried to come to terms with this tremendous happening. She crossed the room to a large wicker basket and rummaged in its depths. She pulled forth some items and came back to him.

"It will be very dangerous," she told him. "The sons of Morna will hunt you. They cannot let you live. Here." She handed him a linen tunic and a heavy woolen cape. "These are the clothes of a common warrior. No one must know who you are until you are ready to act. Now, gather some food. You must leave here at once."

"Tonight?" he said in consternation, looking out into the rain-filled blackness.

"No, Bodhmall!" protested a stunned Liath. "You can't send him away like this!"

"There's little choice," the gaunt woman snapped. "I have seen the sons of Morna. Demna's journey outside the glens has led them to him. They are searching Slieve Bladhma now."

Liath knew there could be no argument with this. "My poor Finn!" she cried in anguish. Her head dropped forward and she began to sob brokenly.

Finn went quickly to her, kneeling beside her and hugging her close. Then her grief brought home to him the full meaning of what was occurring. He looked up at the sober-faced Bodhmall.

"But what about you?" he asked. "How can I leave you?"

"There is nothing else that you can do," Bodhmall told him firmly. "With you gone, we are just two harmless old women living alone. We will be safe."

Finn knew from long experience that when Bodhmall had made her decision, there was no shifting her.

"All right," he agreed reluctantly. "But leaving you will be the hardest thing I have ever done. I've been with you all my life. I don't know what I'll do without you."

"Yes, you do!" she answered fiercely. "Everything I have taught you was to this end. I've forged and hammered you into a sword of iron. Now you must hone its blade to a killing edge! Now make ready to go, and quickly. There's little time."

Swiftly he changed into the clothes Bodhmall had given him. He belted a sheath about his waist and slipped the old knife into it. Liath and Bodhmall gathered food and filled a leather bag. Finn slung this over his shoulder and took up his two hunting spears.

"I'm ready," he said.

"The hunt is coming from the north," Bodhmall told him. "Go toward the west. Go as far from here as you can. Hurry now! They must be nearly to the glen!"

He went to the doorway and paused there, looking back a last time at them. In the gesture both women were reminded of his mother making her last good-bye to her son so long before.

"I will miss you," he said in a voice hoarse with emotion.

Liath began to sob again.

"Be quiet, woman!" Bodhmall told her impatiently, then turned a stern face to Finn. "And you, son of Cumhal, just remember—it is your life you'll fight for now. To save it, you must earn your father's place and restore the honor of the Baiscne clan. Now run, before it is too late to escape!"

He hesitated no longer. Lifting the spears across his shoulder, he plunged out into the storm.

He started away from the hut at a trot, heading toward the west. Bodhmall and Liath stood in the doorway, watching until his figure was swallowed by the rain and darkness. They did not know that as soon as he entered the woods edging the glen, he turned and started north, moving through the trees with all the speed he could.

Once more he was going to disobey Bodhmall. He would not run away and leave the two who had raised him, the only people in the world he loved, to face the terrible Morna clan alone. The assurances of Bodhmall were not enough. Surely men as ruthless as the killers of his father would not leave the women unharmed. He had to lead them away from the lonely hut.

Once north of the glen, he slowed down, moving

cautiously through the underbrush, all his forest-trained senses alert for any sign of the warriors coming toward him. Then, in a flicker of lightning, he caught the sheen of light on the wet body of a horse. And, after the rumble of thunder had died, above the roar and rattle of the hard rain through the trees, he heard the sharp clatter of arms.

He stopped, standing motionless against a tree, knowing that in such conditions it was movement that was most visible. His eyes scanned the woods ahead as he waited for the next lightning stroke. When it came, it revealed a line of figures forcing their way toward him through the underbrush.

They were not far away now, and he waited patiently, not stirring, as they closed. Finally a trio of warriors, leading the straggling band, was right before him. He jumped out of the tree's shadow and landed a spear's length from their noses.

The sudden appearance of the figure startled the men. They recoiled, staring at him, forgetting even to move for their weapons. As they hesitated, he charged forward, pushing right into them, shouldering them aside and passing through, heading back the way they had come.

His movement brought the warriors to life. They seized their weapons and wheeled to follow, shouting out the alarm to their fellows: "He's here! It's the boy! Stop him!"

Finn had already darted into the scattered main body of warriors. He dodged around men who stopped in astonishment as this spectral shadow whisked by. More cries of warning were raised. Warriors turned back to pursue and collided with their fellows in the darkness. A tangle ensued, growing as more men, hearing the cries, sought their source.

Finn was soon through the main body of men. He glanced back to see if any were close behind, then looked ahead just as a massive form loomed up almost on top of him.

A warrior was pushing his mount forward at a risky pace toward the milling company. Finn had no time to dive from its path. Instead he raised his hands and gave a piercing hoot.

To the horse it was as if some monstrous being had erupted from the ground before it. It reared back in terror. The unprepared rider was thrown off, thudding to the soggy earth.

The horse plunged wildly. Finn ducked its flying hooves and then dodged around it. But the rider recovered with a speed that surprised the young man, leaping up directly in his path.

A long, ragged bolt of lightning crackled across the sky. For an instant its light sharply illuminated the scene. Finn found himself looking into a face whose left eye was covered by a great patch. Goll MacMorna stared back in surprise at the blond-haired youth as he realized who he faced.

The light flickered out as both men began to move. Goll's hand dove for his sword, but Finn was quicker. He swung his two spears around in a hard, sideways swipe that caught the Fian chieftain in the side of his neck. The force of the blow knocked him from his feet. He crashed to the earth again.

Other warriors, finally untangled from the mass, were coming toward them now. Finn left the downed man and sprinted away again. But he made no attempt to outdistance or lose his pursuers, either of which he could quite easily have done. Instead he now played the fox to their hunt, teasing them with brief glimpses of him to keep them following.

He led them far to the north, keeping them moving at a punishing pace. Finally, when he felt sure that the cottage was a safe distance behind, he left them, slipping easily away and turning toward the west. The warriors of MacMorna struggled on for some way before they realized that their quarry was no longer before them. They stumbled to a halt in the dripping woods, a bedraggled, angry, and exhausted company.

Book Two

A FIGHTING MAN
OF IRELAND

Chapter Eight

THE LITTLE NUT

Finn saw nothing more of the warriors of the Morna clan as he moved through the glens and woods of Slieve Bladhma. By dawn he was emerging safely from the last trees into the open countryside to the west.

The rain had ended, leaving the dawn sky striped with long banners of clouds. Before him the wide meadows of Ireland unfolded like spring leaves, bright and sparkling. He paused there to gaze out thoughtfully.

It was his future lying before him, he realized. He had not had time to consider it before, and he faced it now with a mixture of feelings. There was regret, certainly, over leaving Bodhmall and Liath and the glens of his childhood. Yet there'd been no choice in this. It was time for him to do what all his life he had been told he must do, and he was fiercely determined not to fail Bodhmall or his clan.

Without delaying further, he set out, striding boldly from the sheltering vastness of Slieve Bladhma into the strange lands. He did not look back.

At first he was a bit unsettled by the vast spaces. In the glens, he had always known a sense of being securely enclosed. Here, with nothing around but the smooth flow of hills, he felt exposed, like a hare out of cover. But this sensation faded quickly and he realized that, for all the unknowns and dangers that might lie ahead, he felt exuberant, reveling in his new sense of freedom. Very soon he was swinging energetically along, humming a light air Liath had taught him as he took in the new scene.

In a short while he came upon a faint dirt track. It ran to the west, so he began to follow it, staying on the grassy verge to avoid its rain-filled ruts. Bodhmall had told him to go west, far from Slieve Bladhma, and this was his first concern.

After half a day of traveling, any concern that the sons of Morna might be tracking him had gone. There had been no sign of anyone following on the road. In fact, there had been no sign of human life at all. This brought to mind a new concern for him. He must start to consider how he was to fulfill his quest for vengeance.

There was a fair amount of uncertainty in him about that. The first step in his quest, of course, was to learn a warrior's skills. Before he could hope to join the Fianna or even survive in the violent world Bodhmall had described to him he must know how to fight well. He had to find a place where he could acquire the proper training secure from discovery by the Morna clan.

This task might be a difficult one. Bodhmall's own advice in this area was sketchy at best, especially after sixteen years of isolation in the glens. And his own lack of experience with the world and its people would be against him. Still, he had been raised to be optimistic in outlook. Courage, strength, and wits could solve any problem, Bodhmall had always said.

The road was just passing by the tail of a tiny wood. The sky had cleared by now, and the sun through the rain-washed air gave a warm, hard light. The trees swayed gently in a light breeze, waving him into their cool shade. He decided to accept their invitation, eat a bit of his food, and think his problem over more carefully.

Beyond the outer fringe of trees, he came upon a small brook gurgling musically along its rocky channel. He dropped his spears, knelt down, and drank of the clean, chill waters from his cupped hands.

And then he froze, letting the water trickle through his fingers unheeded as he listened, all senses alert, body tensed to move.

A high, sweet musical sound was drifting, like the dust in the slanting beams of sunlight, in the air. It was not the brook or the birds or the leaves' faint rustling. It was a different sound, pleasant, but like none Finn had ever heard before. And he knew that anything unknown might be dangerous as well.

His hand crept to the spears. Once he had gripped them, he rose quickly, searching the foliage about him with his eyes. There was nothing close by.

He began to trace the sound, following it along the stream's bank, deeper into the wood. It was a melody, he decided, a definite tune with a repeated refrain, like the songs that Liath had taught him.

He came into a small clearing, stooping slightly to pass beneath a thick branch. It thrust out, like a giant's sinewy arm, from an enormous oak whose upper branches formed a canopy over the open space. Just beyond the tree he stopped to peer quizzically about. Suddenly he had lost the sound.

He stood motionless, not breathing, listening carefully. But it had stopped. He looked about him, trying to place its possible source. Then he jumped as a voice spoke from right above him.

"Hello there, lad!"

Finn wheeled about, raising a spear to strike. His gaze lifted to the branch he had just passed. Stretched out comfortably upon it, head propped upon a bag, legs crossed, lay a man.

From beneath a red cap pulled low upon his forehead, a pair of green eyes glinted merrily at Finn. He held a long, slender tube of wood in both hands, one end resting against the tip of a pointed chin. His manner was relaxed, showing no alarm at Finn's threatening posture.

"Where did you spring from?" Finn demanded. He was certain the man had not been on that limb when he passed beneath it.

"A father and mother, same as yourself, I would suppose," the man replied in a carefree tone, his small mouth stretching in a remarkably wide grin.

Though the smile and the voice were friendly, Finn remained on his guard. "Who are you?" he asked.

"It's Cnu Deireoil they call me—the Little Nut," he said, adding with a laugh, "though where I came to have such a name, I surely don't know."

With that statement he swung his legs about and dropped down from the tree in front of Finn. The young man realized that this Cnu was indeed little. His head came up only to the level of Finn's chest. In figure he was like a boy of ten, and with a boy's agility as well.

Finn lowered his spear. The pleasant aura of the man had convinced him that there was nothing to fear. He found himself smiling in return.

"That's much better," Cnu Deireoil told him. "Now tell me, who are you?"

"I'm Finn," he replied, reminding himself again that he must not reveal his identity to anyone.

"Finn, is it?" the little man said. He ran a scrutinizing eye over the lad, taking in his dress, his spears, and the bulging bag at his hip. "And doing a bit of traveling, I'd guess. Where are you bound?"

Though Finn felt he could trust the little man, he hesitated. The last time he had trusted, he had been betrayed. He had to be cautious.

"I'm heading to the west" was all he said.

"Ah, the west?" Cnu responded brightly. "That's the very way I was going myself! Would you be willing for me to keep company with you, lad? It's wild and lonely country we're heading into."

Finn's impulse was to say that he wanted no company. But the little man seemed harmless, amiable, and anxious for companionship. And, to be honest with himself, he was in need of comrades, too, right now.

"All right," he agreed. "But I was just going to rest for a bit and have some food. You wouldn't mind waiting?"

"Go right ahead, lad," he said. "You that are still growing need your nourishment."

Finn sat down against the trunk of the oak and opened his bag. Cnu dropped down nearby and sat, cross-legged, watching him as he pulled bread, dried meat, and apples out. When Finn glanced up at him, he noted a hungry light in the little man's eye. His own store of food was small, and he had no idea how long it would have to sustain him. But he recalled Bodhmall's teaching that, to a warrior of Ireland, generosity was one of the greatest virtues.

"Would you share some food with me?" he offered.

Cnu smiled in delight. "It's a very fine young man you are for asking me. I'll have one of your apples, if you've a mind to give it."

Finn tossed one to him. "Are you certain that's all?"

"More than enough for me," the little man assured him. "I've a linnet's stomach, so I have. Though he's always after me to give it back."

He laughed heartily at this, but Finn only stared blankly at him. Noting the reaction his bit of humor had received, Cnu sobered and shrugged.

"Ah well," he said resignedly, "I never claimed to be a clown."

"What are you?" Finn inquired politely.

"What am I?" he repeated, seemingly surprised by the question. "Why, I'm a musician, of course, traveling Ireland, trading a tune for a meal or a bit of gold. And couldn't you tell that when you heard my playing?"

To illustrate, he took up the wooden tube and blew through one end, while his slender fingers flew up and down its length. A sprightly melody issued from it and Finn listened, feeling the merry spirit of it catch him up. His body began to sway and his foot to tap, unbidden by him.

The Little Nut watched closely, then began playing with more energy. Finn was seized by an extraordinary need to move. The music tickled and teased at him, forcing him to rise. Soon he was capering about the clearing as if he had gone mad, throwing his legs high, waving his arms, whooping and whirling in time to the melody. He could not stop himself, but he had no desire to try, so fully possessed was he by the lively tune.

At last Cnu stopped playing and watched, grinning

widely, as an exhausted Finn, panting for breath, dropped down, staring in amazement at him.

"A very fine jig that was!" he congratulated.

"I don't even know what a jig is!" Finn answered in a bewildered way as he tried to understand what had happened.

"No matter!" Cnu told him airily. "The song knows how to do it for you. You've only to follow."

"You mean it's you doing that? But how?"

"It's a little gift I have," Cnu answered modestly. "I've music to make men laugh or weep, to love or hate, to make them sleep or make them dance their feet down to the stumps."

"It's a wondrous skill to have," Finn said, eyeing the little man with a certain wariness, "and a terrible one."

"It is, and it's done me good service many times. But don't fear, lad, I was only making a show of it to you. I'll not use it on you again unless you wish it."

Finn looked more closely at the instrument that Cnu had used to weave his spell. "And what is that thing you made the tune upon?" he asked.

"Why, it's my whistle, lad!" the man answered, amazed himself now. "Don't tell me that you've never seen one before?"

"Liath told me some about musicians," he said, "but I've never seen one, nor his instruments." He realized that Cnu was giving him a curious look now. "I . . . ah . . . come from a faraway land," he added quickly by way of explanation.

"A strange land, indeed, to have no musicians in it," Cnu said musingly. "And why is it you've come here? What are you seeking in the west?"

Again Finn hesitated. How much was it safe to tell this odd little man?

"Come on, lad. I'm safe enough!" Cnu urged, as if he had read Finn's mind.

Finn decided that he was right. There was no reason not to tell him anyway. He would have to reveal his intentions sometime if he meant to begin realizing them.

"I mean to become a skilled warrior," he announced, drawing himself up in what he hoped was a resolute pose.

"Well, well!" said Cnu, sounding properly impressed. He ran a critical eye over the young man's physique and nodded approvingly. "You do seem to have the size and muscle for it. Are you going into fosterage then?"

"Fosterage?" repeated Finn, not understanding the term.

"Yes, lad. You know. To be trained by some chieftain along with the sons of the other warriors of your clan."

"I have no clan," said Finn. "My parents are dead."

"Ah. I'm sorry for that," Cnu told him. "But where is it you'll go for your training?"

"I was told that there are chieftains who might take me into their service."

Cnu shook his head. "There are chieftains who hire warriors to strengthen their household companies. But they want only skilled fighters. They've no time to waste training young men from strange lands."

So, Finn thought, this first step in his quest was going to be even harder than he thought. He took a rather forlorn bite from his bread and wondered what he would do.

But once more the little man appeared to read his thoughts.

"Don't be despairing, lad," he said brightly, blowing a little warble on his pipe. "You've had good fortune meeting the Little Nut today. It happens that I know the king of Bantry. His fortress is some days west, near Lough Lein. He might help you. He's a good man, and a great friend of mine. I think I could convince him to take you in."

"You could?" said Finn with rising hopes. Then he grew wary again. "But why should you want to help me?"

"You are a suspicious one, you surely are," Cnu told him. "But don't worry, my young Finn. I'm a man who likes to help others, and I've a feeling you need a bit more help than you're letting on to me. Will you accept that?"

Finn shrugged and then smiled. "I will," he said. "I've little other choice."

"He couldn't find him!" Tadg said angrily. He threw a stick into his fire with a savage gesture. It flared, sending a red, wavering glow that gave false animation to the watching skulls. Conan looked about nervously.

"We lost his track in the storm," Goll said defensively. "We think he turned another way. But he's left the glens, I'm certain. He could be anywhere now."

"You must search for him. Hunt him down!" Tadg insisted. "He'll raise the blood feud against you one day if he is Cumhal's son."

"I've no doubt about that," Goll said. "I saw him clear enough. There's no mistaking he has his mother's looks"—he put a hand gingerly to his bruised neck—"and his father's strength."

"He's a dangerous lad," Conan put in, "running through us bold as you please and then leading us about in the woods! He left us so lost it took us all the next day to get out again. A long, cold, and soggy night that was! Why we—"

"Enough of your complaining, Brother," Goll said sharply, then turned to the druid. "But Conan is right, Tadg. This Finn has great courage and great skill."

"Your admiration is misplaced, MacMorna," Tadg said scornfully. "His skills could mean your own destruction. You cannot continue to fail me in this."

"Fail you?" Goll said in outrage. "And when do the sons of Morna act at your command?"

"To fail the high king I meant, of course," Tadg smoothly and hastily amended. "It's for Conn that I speak. He is very distressed."

"We haven't given up the search for him," Goll irritably replied. "I've sent a company of my best warriors to continue the hunt. They're led by Luachra, the finest champion and the finest tracker of all the Fians.

If MacCumhal is within the four corners of Ireland, Luachra will find him."

"I'm certain that we all hope so," the druid said pointedly.

Chapter Nine

CAOILTE MACRONAN

"You say that this boy you've come across is a fighter, do you, Cnu Deireoil?" the chieftan said, looking across the fortress's yard to where Finn stood by the gateway, gazing about him.

"And have I ever given bad counsel to you, Cian?" the little man answered easily.

The chieftain laughed. "Not when it suits your own ends." He examined the young man with a critical eye. "I suppose he does seem fit enough," he admitted, but added doubtfully, "still, he hasn't a warrior's look about him. He hasn't even got a sword."

"He's had no training in the warrior's arts before," Cnu Deireoil explained, putting sorrow into his voice. "Ah, poor lad! He's been an orphan since childhood, living on his own in the wilds, that he has. But he's very quick. I've seen few swifter or more agile in the moving. And if I'm any judge, he's a quick learner as well. A bit of training and you'll have yourself a marvelous warrior."

The chieftain listened to this cajoling speech with interest, watching the little man's face carefully. When it had ended, he asked, somewhat suspiciously, "What are you about, my friend? You sound as if you're trying to sell the lad to me. I've a feeling I should mistrust you."

"Me!" Cnu Deireoil said in an offended tone. "And when have I ever tried to take advantage of you?"

"Nearly always," Cian told him bluntly.

"Oh, well," the little man said, looking hurt, "if the poor Little Nut can't help a boy out of pity without being taken for a rogue—"

"All right, my friend," the chieftain said hastily, holding up a hand. He liked the musician and had no wish to anger him for fear of his not coming again. "If you are so concerned about this lad, we'll see if he's the sort that I can use. Just see, mind you!"

"I can't ask fairer than that," Cnu Deireoil agreed, and the two started across the yard toward Finn.

Throughout their talk, the young man had been quite rapt with his examination of the interior of the fortress. It was the first one he had ever been inside.

It was much as he had expected, though a bit less imposing than he had visualized. Like the other one he had seen, it was a rath—a lios surrounded by a bank of earth topped by a stockade. The whole ring fort sat on a high, smooth-shouldered hill that gave fine vantage over the broad meadows around. This view insured that no enemy could come upon the fortress by surprise and allowed herdsmen to watch over the grazing cattle that were the chief wealth of the tribal *tuath*.

Against the inner wall of the stockade there were some simple, rickety sheds that comprised the stables and storage sheds for the fortress. Near the center of the yard sat the meeting hall, a large, oval building that showed much wear. Its daub walls of mud and dung were cracked in spots. Sections had fallen away to reveal the basketlike wattle framework beneath. The thatched roof that rose steeply to a high peak was badly weathered, the straw torn away in spots, giving it the look of a hound balding with the mange. Around it were gathered other buildings, smaller and even sorrier versions of the central hall, like forlorn pups around their mother at feeding time.

The space between this cluster and the stockade wall was open, the ground bare and hard-packed by years of trampling feet. Here some two score men were hard at work practicing with weapons. From his examination of the fortress itself, Finn's attention went to them, and especially to one young warrior. He was working with a sword, holding two opponents at bay. This he did easily, almost playfully, parrying cuts and thrusts with casual gestures as he danced about the two befuddled men. Finn was quite fascinated with the warrior's skills and began to watch his moves carefully.

So absorbed was he that he didn't notice the chieftain and Cnu Deireoil approaching from the hall until his new comrade hailed him.

"Finn!" called the little man, and he turned toward them.

If he had expected his first sight of a chieftain to be an imposing one, he was much mistaken. Cian was an amiable-looking man, with a round-tipped nose and permanent laugh creases about his small, bright eyes. Fiery red hair was braided loosely at each shoulder and a thick mustache curled out and up on either side of a generous, smiling mouth. His dress was casual to the point of untidiness. A worn cloak hung carelessly around him and his tunic was gray with wear. He smiled warmly at Finn as he addressed him.

"Welcome, young man. I understand that you would like to join my household company."

"I would, sir," Finn said earnestly.

"It's not an easy life," the chieftain warned. "You must work hard and risk yourself for me, and get little for it but food and a roof to cover you."

"I'm used to hardships, and there's no risk I'll not gladly take," he assured Cian. "My chieftain, nothing in life is so important to me now as learning the warrior's skills."

Finn's determined attitude impressed the chieftain, but he still had some doubts. "I'd like to help you, lad, but all of my warriors have been trained since they were first able to walk. And the Little Nut says that you've done no fighting at all."

"True enough, sir," Finn admitted, "but I have learned the hunter's skills. I can track and stalk and use the spear better than most!"

The chieftain laughed at this boastful statement.

"Can you, indeed?" he said. "Well, let's just see." He glanced around the yard, then pointed toward a wooden tying post by a stable against the far wall. "See how close you can come to that."

At that distance, the post was a tiny target indeed. But to Cian's surprise, Finn seemed not at all concerned. He eyed the post for a moment to gauge the throw, lifted one of his spears, and with little apparent effort fired it toward its goal.

It flashed across the yard, arching slightly and then curving down to bury half its point in the hard wood of the thick post.

Warriors about the yard now began to quit their own practice and look about to see who had made such a throw. The chieftain stared in wonder at the quivering shaft. Then, not willing to accept Finn's skill so easily, he recovered himself and said in a careless way: "A fair throw. But it could have been chance. Try again."

Finn shrugged and repeated his throw with the second spear. It followed the path of the first, striking home less than a handbreadth below its fellow.

A cheer now rose from the assembled warriors.

"He's a master of the spear, that one is," one commented.

"Aye! Never seen such throwing," agreed another, and voices of praise were heard about the yard.

Finn beamed at their applause while Cnu Deireoil fixed a challenging look on the chieftain.

"Well, Cian, what do you think of the lad now?" he asked.

"He is as good as you told me, my friend," Cian replied, all his doubts gone. He grinned at Finn. "My lad, if you can learn the other fighting skills as well as that one, you could be a champion someday."

He turned toward the warriors in the yard. "Caoilte, come here," he ordered.

The young warrior Finn had noted before moved forward. As he came closer, Finn saw that he was perhaps five years older, a dark, lean, dour-faced man with sleek raven-black hair tightly plaited at his neck.

"This is Caoilte MacRonan," Cian told Finn as the warrior joined them. "He is the finest of all my warriors." He turned to the dark man. "Caoilte, this lad wishes to join our company. Would you be willing to train him?"

"Caoilte gave Finn a long, slow scrutinizing look. His expression was one of disinterest. He shook his head.

"No, my chieftain," he said flatly. "Throwing spears at a post is one thing. Throwing them at something alive is another. Trying to train this boy would be a waste of time."

"I'm not a boy!" Finn shot back, annoyed by this warrior's superior attitude.

"He could hunt for us in exchange," Cian suggested hopefully.

Caoilte was unmoved. "We've no need of more hunters," he countered. "Besides, this 'boy' is too old to begin warrior training. He'll never master the skills."

"I will!" Finn insisted hotly. "I'll work hard at it."

"I'd like you to agree to give the young man a chance," Cian put in. His cajoling tone surprised Finn. It seemed as if it were the warrior in charge here, not the chieftain.

"I'm sorry," Caoilte told him firmly. "We're helping neither him nor ourselves to accept him here."

"But there must be some way I can prove myself to you," Finn said desperately.

"If he's such a hunter, let him go against the Dovarchu," one of the other warriors called.

"Aye! Aye!" more of them shouted in agreement, many grinning. "Let him fight the Dovarchu. That'll prove his worth!"

Finn had never heard the name Dovarchu—Master Otter—before. But that made no difference. This might be his only chance.

"I'll go against this thing if you'll give me a place and train me in fighting skills," he said with determination.

The grins vanished. The men exchanged looks of wonder at this unexpected acceptance of a challenge made in jest. Caoilte fixed a disbelieving eye on Finn.

"You're not meaning what you say," he accused, "or else you've no idea what we're speaking of. It would be madness."

"Listen to the man, Finn," said the Little Nut earnestly. "He's making great sense."

"I've made an offer to you," Finn said stolidly, meeting Caoilte's eye with a bold stare. "Will you take it or not?"

"You must agree, if he defeats the Dovarchu, he's earned our acceptance here," Cian put in.

"He would that," the dark warrior said, shaking his head. "But what he'll gain from us will likely be a grave."

"All right, lad, just climb into the boat," Caoilte said as another warrior held the prow to steady it.

Finn handed his weapons to Caoilte and clambered over the side into the vessel. It was a curragh, a small leather-sided boat shaped like a round, concave shell. Of a size to fit no more than two passengers, and then uncomfortably, it wobbled as he dropped into it. Finn quickly sat down, and looked up at those grouped closely around.

All the Bantry warriors had trooped down from the fortress to the nearby lakeshore with him. They were watching his preparations now with expressions of interest, curiosity, and, in some cases, amusement. He didn't like the smiling ones at all.

"Just paddle out into the lake a way," Caoilte said, passing Finn's two spears and then some short wooden paddles to him. "Your disturbance of the surface will be enough to draw it. It'll rise as if you were a fly and it a trout come to strike."

"How do I know it'll come?" Finn asked.

"Oh, it'll come," a grinning, gap-toothed warrior said with confidence. "There's nothing crossed this lake in years without its being attacked."

The man's smile was nearly gloating. Finn wanted to know why, but he was reluctant to say anything that might make him seem uncertain or even afraid to these hard men. Still, it would be foolish to go against an enemy without knowing something of its nature. No one could begrudge him that.

"Could you tell me what this Dovarchu looks like?" he said, trying to sound casual.

"Well, there's no one too certain about that," the chieftain answered regretfully. "Some think it's like a great otter; of course, that's where the name comes from. Others say it's a giant serpent or an eel. But we've only had glimpses of it from the shore. No one's ever had a good look at it."

"What do you mean?" asked Finn.

Cian shrugged. "Those that've come close enough to tell have never made it back to speak of it."

"I'm sorry, làd," Cnu Deireoil said, greatly distressed. "I tried to warn you before. I'm sorry I brought you into this."

"You mustn't be," Finn told him stolidly. "It's my own choice." He looked at Caoilte. "I'm ready now."

The dark warrior looked down at the lad, seeing the determination in the young face. He sighed and shook his head.

"All right then. But you are a fool."

He and two other warriors shoved the little vessel off the shore. As Finn took up his paddle and began to push the curragh away, he told himself that there was nothing to fear. For all its strangeness, this Dovarchu was just a beast. Still, it gave him little extra confidence to see the Bantry warriors—once they had seen him well out into the lake—retreating quickly to a safe distance from the shore to watch.

Lough Lein was a large-sized lake to Finn, accustomed only to the pools of his glens. The shoreline he had left was low and marshy, softly fringed with reeds. The far shore was hemmed in by low hills covered with a forest so heavy it seemed like a thick, shaggy coat of dark green wool upon them.

It was late in the day now. The sun was sliding

toward a cozy haven in the soft cradle of the hills, sending its long, sharply slanting rays skittering across the wave tops. It created an effect dazzling and confusing to the eyes, with the points of light and the dark patches in the troughs shifting constantly.

He paddled out steadily until he was the length of two spear throws from the shore. The watching company of bright-cloaked warriors now looked like a flock of varied birds fluttering there. He stopped, putting down his oars, leaving the tiny boat to drift and rock slightly in the gentle swells. It was very quiet here at sunset, the breezes nearly stilled, the sounds of birds hushed in anticipation of the rising night.

He picked up his spears and sat motionless, squinting his eyes to see across the bright surface, all his hunter's senses sharp for the sound or sight or smell of anything unusual.

It seemed an eternity that he sat tensely waiting, but the sun crawled only a tiny span nearer to its final goal. He began to wonder if the thing would come.

Then his eye caught a movement on the surface. It was as if something were being dragged along, just below the waves. But in a moment, a smooth hump came into view, breaking the surface, rolling the water back on either side. He stared at it intently. It was like a cow's back, heaving up, or like the coil of an enormous serpent, black and shiny with water.

It changed shape as he watched, swelling up higher and then sinking back in a smooth, regular, fluid motion, as if the creature were undulating through the water. Behind it was visible for an instant a white line of spray as from a whipping tail or thrashing paws. Whatever the means of propulsion, it moved the thing along with great speed, drawing a foamy wake on either side as it shot across the lake's surface directly toward him.

He could get no clear idea of its shape or size, but his impression was that it was larger than his curragh. That was quite large enough for him. As it came steadily on, rose upright in the boat. His hand lifted the spear. When it was close enough, he would fire his weapon at the hump. It was almost close enough. He set himself. Just a bit closer . . . closer . . . closer . . .

It vanished.

The hump sank with a final surge of water and it was gone in an instant, leaving only a widening ripple to indicate where it had last been. He stood, spear still upraised, staring toward the spot. He could see no sign of it, no shadow beneath the waves. He scanned the surface to either side expecting it to reappear. There was nothing. Where had it gone?

There was a tremendous impact on the bottom of the curragh. It heaved upward from the lake, turning as it rose, slinging Finn violently out. The sudden shock knocked the spear from his hand. He fell back, crashing into the waves, sinking far beneath the surface before he could recover.

Quickly he stroked back to the surface and spewed out a great mouthful of water. He gasped for breath, shaking his head to clear his vision. He found himself looking up into the face of the Dovarchu.

Chapter Ten

DOVARCHU

The head of the creature was suspended above him on a long, curving neck that rose the height of two men from the water. It was flat and broad, rather doglike in appearance, with small, upright ears, dark eyes surrounded by patches of lighter coloring, and a short muzzle with bristling whiskers. The mouth was open in a sort of malevolent grin, revealing teeth that were doglike as well, quite adequate for tearing him apart.

He had only an instant to make this assessment, for, upon seeing him, the head darted down toward him on its flexible neck, the mouth opening wider to bite. He dove away and the head struck harmlessly against the water, but it lifted away instantly, water dripping from the jaws, and swept around to strike again.

Once more he dodged away, dismayed by the agility of a thing so large. The neck was like a serpent, powerful muscles rolling beneath the shiny, dark hide as it moved. It lifted, and the Dovarchu voiced an angry sound—part cow bellow, part deep bark—as if impatient with this prey who would not stay still and be eaten.

Finn used the brief respite to look around. He was weaponless, defenseless, and alone. He might be able to escape with his own swimming and diving skills, but he would not try. He had made a bond to fight the thing, and that he had to do. But how?

Behind the smooth mound of the creature's back he glimpsed the curragh, overturned and bobbing on the waves. If he could reach it, he would have some protection, and perhaps a way to strike back. He took a deep breath, slipped beneath the waves, and swam down, using all his power to dive right beneath the Master-Otter. If it could use that trick, why, so could he!

He glanced up at it as he passed under. It was like the rounded hull of a ship lying on the surface. At its front, short, broad flippers thrust out. At its back was a wide-bladed tail, notched like that of a fish. All were now beating the water as the creature, realizing he was gone, paddled its body in a circle. Their action made the water seem to boil.

Then he was past it, slanting upward to the surface and the curragh. He broke the waves beyond it and peered out past it cautiously. The creature was still looking the other way, the head swinging slowly back and forth as it scanned the lake for him. For the moment he was safe, but the Dovarchu would soon turn.

He needed some means to fight back, and the curragh offered none.

Then he noticed something bobbing on the surface not far away. Just a recurrent flash of something showing at the top of each passing swell. A stick? He looked more closely. No! The end of a spear pole! One of the thick wooden hafts had been buoyant enough to keep the weapon afloat, its point and forward three-quarters submerged.

He moved out from the shelter of the curragh, reaching for it. But his move attracted the attention of the beast. Its head swung around and struck down at him in a single, graceful move.

He ducked back. The head splashed harmlessly down upon the water again, the jaws grazing the side of the boat as he moved into its protection. The curving neck lifted and the head arched high above as the Dovarchu vented another and much angrier roar.

Finn started for the spear again. This time he stroked with one hand and pulled the curragh along with the other, keeping his body beneath it, making a great turtle of himself. This did not deter the beast. The head swooped down, jaws wide. They slammed upon it, the force of the blow driving curragh and warrior down. Then the jaws tightened, the sharp fangs puncturing the thick leather hide of the boat. The Dovarchu pulled its head up, easily lifting the frail craft from the water, pulling it from Finn.

The creature rose up to the full height of its neck, the curragh clamped firmly in its jaws. It shook the boat savagely, like a dog shaking a rodent, then let go, casting the smashed curragh far across the lake.

But while the beast vented its anger on the boat, Finn had a chance to act. He swam with all his speed for the floating spear.

He was nearly to it when the head descended upon him once more, with the force and speed of a great boulder plummeting from the sky. He glanced up to see the open jaws, the twin rows of jagged teeth dropping toward him. He made a desperate grab, his hand closing around the end of the spear pole, and then rolled sideways as the jaws crashed into the lake where he had been.

He was behind the massive head now, the neck a great curve above him. This might be his only chance to strike. He seized the weapon in both hands and, before the Dovarchu could lift its head again, drove forward, slamming the point against the underside of its jaw.

The spear penetrated the soft hide there, and Finn threw his whole weight against it to force it farther in, angling it up into the creature's head. His action drove the sharp point through the mouth and through the narrow head, into the base of the skull, into the brain.

Mortally struck, the Dovarchu jerked its head up. The neck began to shake as it bellowed its agony, blood pouring from the distended mouth. The body began to convulse, flippers and tail working in an uncontrolled, wild manner.

Seeing his danger, Finn began to swim rapidly away from it. The Dovarchu's death throes grew more frenzied, the long neck coiling, the barrellike body rolling, thrashing madly, churning the water to a white froth tinted red with its blood. He swam to a safe distance and turned to watch its struggles. They soon began to grow weaker. The body ceased to roll, the flippers to thrash. The graceful neck drooped downward to the surface of the lake in a gesture of immense weariness, of total defeat. A final spasm rippled through it, throwing the head up as if in a final act of supplication to the setting sun. Then all its final strength left it at once. The neck went limp, bringing the head splashing down for the last time into the waves.

For a long moment more Finn watched the still creature. Its massive form floated, stretched out across the surface. The low sun's rays, made crimson by a haze atop the hills, drew a blazing streak across the lake and across the creature, burnishing the smooth, shining skin to gold.

He always felt a pang of regret at destroying a proud, powerful beast, no matter how good the cause, and he felt regret now in the killing of this sleek, vital, and strangely beautiful creature, for all its savagery. Still, he had done what he needed to do. He had fulfilled his bond.

He turned away from the Dovarchu and began the swim back to shore.

The waiting men rushed to greet him as he emerged from the lake. They crowded about, their voices exclaiming a mixture of surprise, delight, and congratulation. Someone threw a cloak over his dripping body. Cnu Deireoil clutched his hand and beamed at Finn in relief.

"It's a happy man I am to see you win that fight," he said. "I thought you were a dead man, surely, and the fault for it my own."

"You have done it, and there's no arguing that," said Cian, clearly overjoyed at the young warrior's victory. He turned to Caoilte and said with a triumphant air: "Well, my champion, you can't refuse to take in this lad now!"

"You're right, my chieftain," Caoilte admitted grudgingly. He stepped up to Finn and put a hand upon his shoulder as he met his eye.

"You've won the challenge fairly, and there's no man who can say that Caoilte MacRonan doesn't see a bargain kept," he said with gravity. "If you mean to try to be a warrior, it looks as if I'll be having to see to your training myself."

"Thank you for that!" Finn told him earnestly, grinning at the man.

For the first time there came a return smile from the dark warrior. "All right, boy. But I still think you're a fool."

Finn's drink sat forgotten before him as he stared about the fortress's hall. Bodhmall and Liath had told him of the halls of Ireland's great chieftains and of their wondrous style of life. These stories had been precious fuel to fire the imagination of the isolated boy. But the grand and glowing images of such places he had created in his mind gave him no preparation for what he saw here.

The large room was oval, its center open, circled by a series of thick posts that supported a peaked roof frame covered with thatch. From the posts to the outer wall, wickerwork partitions radiated like spokes in a wheel, dividing the area surrounding the central space into wedge-shaped compartments.

The neat, symmetrical nature of the hall, however, was barely discernible beneath the overlying chaos, litter, and filth.

Objects were strewn everywhere, useful and broken, worthless and valuable jumbled together and treated with equal contempt. Carelessly hung tapestries covered the walls, sagging, ragged, their brilliant colors and elaborate designs discolored by wear. Weapons were everywhere, shields, swords, and spears stacked in great heaps or hung from every available protrusion. The floor was littered, too, ornate goblets of beaten gold rolling about with broken pottery and gnawed bones.

In the center of the room, several women labored around a large central fire in a round, stone-lined pit. Some turned whole carcasses of sheep and cow on massive spits of iron. Others stirred the contents of great cauldrons hung from iron chains. The steam and oily smoke wafted up in a thick cloud, some managing to squeeze out through the small roof hole, most filling the high canopy and turning the air hazy. The thatch above had long since been turned black by it, festoons of cobwebs dangling down in strands made thick by their coating of grease.

The space around the fire and the compartments were jammed with a raucous crowd of fortress inhabitants hard at the talking and drinking that preceded an evening meal. All sat on mats or furs on the earthen floor behind low tables of rough planks. The partitions allowed them to see into the center and the rooms across the hall, but gave them some privacy from those close on either side. Some rooms held whole families of

84

clansmen to the chieftain. Others were filled with single warriors grouped with their closest comrades.

Finn would normally have been relegated to a small compartment with the rest of the youngest warriors of Bantry. But his destruction of the Master-Otter, which had plagued them for so long, had given him a champion's status, at least for this one night. He dined with the best warriors of Cian's company.

Across from Finn's compartment was that of the chieftain. It was quite a bit larger than the rest, and with a higher table and benches for its occupants. At the place of honor beside Cian was now seated the Little Nut. He caught the eye of Finn and waved gayly at him.

Caoilte had stayed close to his new charge on Finn's first night here. He had noticed the young man's fascination with his surroundings and was watching the play of emotions in Finn's face with interest.

"It's a strange look you've got," he said at last. "What is it you think of our little rath?"

Finn started to reply, then stopped, not certain what to say. He could not insult those who had taken him in, but he also could not lie. He searched desperately for something to say while Caoilte stared at him, a slight smile revealing his amusement at the lad's obvious discomfort.

"It's . . . a most . . . ah . . . interesting place," Finn said at last.

Caoilte laughed. "Don't worry, lad. This place is a rubbish heap. We all know that, and it bothers none of us."

"True enough," a second warrior put in, wiping some globs of fat from his mustache with the back of his hand. "I nearly left Bantry the first time I came here. My own mother was a cleanly woman, praise her memory, and taught me to be the same." He burped loudly and tossed a well-cleaned pork rib over his shoulder. "But I've gotten used to it."

"Still, it's a good place," a third said emphatically, leaning toward Finn. "You mark me, lad: you'll find no place more a home to you, and no chieftain more generous, more friendly, or more kindhearted than Cian. And may the Morrigan take me if I'm telling a lie to you!"

"Of course, there's no denying that he's poor enough at running the tuath," the other said. "And he's no warrior at all."

"But I thought that a chieftain had to be a strong leader," Finn said, recalling more of the teachings Bodhmall had drilled into him through his childhood. She had talked often of the strong obedience and the great respect Cumhal had commanded from his clan, and that Finn would have to command if he meant to take his father's place.

"I've traveled much of Ireland and I've served in many companies," Caoilte said with the knowing air of one who has truly seen the world. "I've learned that there are things more important than a strong arm and a kingly manner. Cian treats us with fairness and respect. He doesn't make servants of us as many chieftains do. And in return for that, we see that things are run properly."

"Aye," one of the other warriors agreed. "Without our minding of him, he'd likely give away the whole tuath as a gift to the first who asked for it."

"He is a very openhanded man," said Caoilte, fixing a meaningful look on Finn as he added, "especially when it comes to taking in strays."

Finn understood and felt rightfully chastened. He owed much to Cian's generosity himself. It was not for him to judge.

"I'm sorry," he said. "I didn't mean—"

The dark warrior didn't let him finish. "No more now. The music's going to begin."

Finn looked around. Cnu Deireoil was now standing before the table of the chieftain. From the leather bag he carried with him he was carefully pulling a beautiful instrument. A *criusach* it was, he had told Finn. The musician's traditional harp. The graceful bow of yew was carved in a sinuous interlace design richly inlaid with silver and gold and colorful enamels. The fine strings running across it glinted as he lightly tested them, producing fine, high notes of a clarity like a bright, clear winter's day.

The sound of it carried across the talk and laughter in the hall. At once the sounds died as the attention of all turned toward the little harper.

He began to play. The sweet, sad, beautiful strains of the tune filled the room. In moments everyone was rapt, the power of Cnu Deireoil allowing him to enchant them with his music's spell. The warriors even stopped their drinking to listen, a certain sign of the greatness of his skill.

Finn listened with appreciation, too, though he was free of the control of the spell as the Little Nut had promised. He could understand why his friend was so well honored here. A tuath too small or poor to support its own resident bard was dependent on traveling performers for entertainment. And one with the talent of Cnu must be especially welcome.

He looked around the room at the people, his eager mind absorbing the new impressions. His eyes drifted across the compartments, around the circle to that of Cian. There he abruptly paused.

He realized that he was not the only one whose attention was not fixed on the musician. His gaze was met by another. Large, deep brown eyes were staring into his, and in their depths, even from so far away, he glimpsed an expression that he did not understand but found most intriguing.

Chapter Eleven

TRAINING

The eyes were still watching him.

Their owner was a woman who stood a safe distance from the training yard and the practicing warriors, gaze fixed solely on each movement of Finn's swordplay with Caoilte. There was something distracting in the dark, warm gaze. He could feel it on him even when his back was to it. As he spun about, his eyes again met hers and were held there for an instant. Caoilte used his hesitation to move in and slam his shield against Finn's side with great force, staggering him.

"Keep your mind on the fight, lad!" he scolded. "You have to watch every move I make, no matter how small."

Finn tried again to focus his full attention on his teacher, this time with better success. They began a long exchange of cuts, so frequent and so hard that soon Finn's sword blade began to twist and to bend.

"Hold on!" Finn said, stepping back and holding up a sword that more closely resembled a scythe. "I've got to do a bit of straightening."

He dropped the weapon onto the hard ground and began to hop upon it with both feet in an attempt to flatten the metal. Caoilte watched this activity with disapproval.

"You can't be doing that in a real fight, you know," he pointed out.

"In a real fight I'm not likely ever to meet a fighter so ferocious as yourself," Finn answered, grinning.

"That's a foolish thing to suppose," Caoilte replied tersely, appearing to ignore the compliment. But then he added in a grudging sort of way: "Of course, your own skills in defending yourself have improved a little since you came."

Finn knew that this was a great compliment, indeed, from the exacting warrior. Others of the company had told him they had never seen anyone develop the fighting skills so rapidly. Already he could defeat many of his new comrades.

He stopped pounding and lifted up the sword. His effort had been only partially successful. He examined the decidedly wavy blade doubtfully.

Caoilte moved up beside him and eyed the sword critically as well. "It might be you could use a better made weapon," he said. "I'll see to getting you one after your training's done."

"And how soon will that be?" Finn asked eagerly.

"Easy, lad," the warrior cautioned. "If you wish to be the great champion, it could take more than just a few days."

"Then let's be at it again!" the young man said, taking up a defensive stance.

"No, no. Enough!" Caoilte told him, as if curbing a leaping pup. "You've worked enough for one day."

"But I want to learn more!" Finn said earnestly. "I can't rest until I've become as fine a warrior as I can."

"Why?" Caoilte asked.

For a moment, Finn was nonplussed. All his need for caution returned. "What do you mean?" he asked.

"It's this need of yours. It seems to hold you too tightly. Other lads dream of the glory of battle, the riches to be had, the chance for fame. But it's something else with you. There's some other purpose."

Finn struggled within himself. He'd come to like Caoilte despite his individualistic and somewhat egotistical manner, but enough to tell the whole truth to him? Yet, to lie . . .

"I—I don't know what to tell you, Caoilte," he finally answered haltingly.

"Never mind, lad," he said quickly, seeing Finn's distress. "It's nothing to do with me, so I've no right to ask. If there's some strange ambition plaguing you, I don't want to know of it. I've no such terrible thing myself."

Finn eyed Caoilte quizzically at this speech. Having been raised with a single destiny himself, it was hard for him to conceive of someone else without his own.

"You mean, there's nothing that you care about?" he asked.

"Yes. Good wages, a chance to fight, and no man telling me what I have to do. Any more only sees a fighting man dead."

"Everyone must have something he's willing to fight for," Finn reasoned, "or there's little meaning to his life."

"I only fight to fight, the same as any other warrior of this company," Caoilte brusquely returned. "Now, why don't we go and wash the sweat of this day's practicing away? There's time yet for some hunting before evening."

Finn nodded and fell in beside Caoilte as he started toward their quarters. As they crossed the yard, he again took note of those brown eyes, still following his moves.

"Caoilte, who is that woman?" he asked.

The warrior glanced toward her and snorted. "Her? That's Cian's daughter. She likes hanging about the training yard, that she does."

"She's been watching me," Finn said, looking back again.

"I'm not surprised. She likes to watch the young ones especially. I've no doubt she's taken a fancy to you."

Finn looked at his companion in a puzzled way. "Why would she do that?"

Caoilte stopped abruptly and faced the young man, his cool, detached expression marred by a rare emotion: astonishment.

"Are you saying to me that you don't know? Come now, lad! You can't be so innocent as that!"

Finn stared blankly at the warrior, not understanding his reaction.

"I'm sorry, Caoilte, but I really don't know what you mean."

Caoilte looked narrowly at Finn, not certain whether to believe him or not.

"Maybe you don't," he said at last. "All I can say is, you'd best take care with that one, or you'll learn some things here that you likely weren't expecting."

Finn came out of the warriors' quarters with his two spears, ready for hunting with Caoilte. But outside the door he found someone awaiting him.

"Hello," said a voice as warm and soft as the brown eyes gazing into his. "My name is Fionnuala. I'm the daughter of Cian."

"I'm Finn," he answered, a little absently as he was absorbed in having his first close look at her.

He realized that she was very young, perhaps a year or two older than himself. He had little to compare her with in terms of judging her beauty, but he found her face quite pleasing, with even features and the whitest skin he had ever seen. But her most striking feature was the wealth of copper hair that billowed about her shoulders. This she was clearly aware of, for she tossed her head slightly as she smiled at him, making her hair dance with light.

"I must go out of the fortress," she told him. "It is a lovely day and I wish to pick some flowers in the meadow below. My father insists that I must have someone to guard me. I want you to go with me."

"But Caoilte and I are just leaving to hunt," he said.

Her smile vanished and her voice took on a spoiled child's petulant tone. "I've chosen you to go with me, and it must be you. You must obey me. My father is the chieftain."

Finn had to agree. As much as he would rather

have gone hunting, he was bound to serve his chieftain first.

"All right then," he said, sighing inwardly. "I'll take you if I must."

"Don't worry, I don't think you will be bored," she promised, smiling again.

He found the smile to be of quite a different nature from any he had encountered before. But without experience, the effect of it and the smoldering gaze and the low, slow, sensuous voice meant nothing to him.

Caoilte came out of the warriors' house then and saw the two. He moved to them, giving Fionnuala a hard look.

"Caoilte, I can't go hunting now," Finn told him, trying to disguise his disappointment. "She says I'm to escort her while she picks flowers."

"Yes, she likes to do that," the warrior said dryly, "along with other things."

"We are going now, Finn," she ordered curtly, her eyes casting a fiery dart at Caoilte for his last remark before she turned and flounced away.

"I must go with her," Finn said apologetically. "Sorry, Caoilte."

"It's all right, lad. Good luck to you," he said.

Finn turned away to follow Fionnuala across the yard, puzzling over his comrade's cryptic remarks. Caoilte watched the two go out through the gateway, then shook his head and shrugged.

"Ah well," he said resignedly to himself, "he's got to find out about everything in time, I suppose."

Finn sat on a soft, grass-covered mound at one side of the meadow watching her move about.

At first, he had only pined for the lost pleasures of the hunt. But soon he had decided that this activity had its own fascinating aspects.

Fionnuala had taken off her wool cloak and now wore only a long tunic of linen. It clung about her figure as she moved, revealing her form, and at certain times the sun glowed through the thin white material, throwing the body beneath into clear relief. It was then that his keen hunter's eyesight was at its most alert.

She was certainly different from Liath or Bodhmall. Her body was slender but not thin or bony, full and round without plumpness, stretching and turning and bending with an easy sensuality. Not self-consciously, though she had to know he was watching her, but self-aware.

After collecting an armload of bright flowers, she came over to him. She dropped down into the soft grass beside him, laying aside the bundle of flowers. Then she fixed that dark, penetrating stare on him again. The gaze flicked down his body then back up to his face, meeting his eyes boldly.

"You are a very handsome man," she said finally.

"Am I?" he said. It wasn't something he had ever thought about before.

She edged closer to him. Her hand lifted, stroked along the muscles of his upper arm. "Fine, strong body" —the hand moved up to his head, the slim fingers slipping through the silver waves—"wonderful hair"—the fingers slid down, softly tracing the firm line of his jaw—"a bold, warrior's face." The hand dropped down to rest against his chest. "Yes," she said with satisfaction, "you are indeed handsome."

"I . . . ah . . . thank you," he said uncertainly. He was very puzzled by her odd behavior. Her closeness and her touch had made him uncomfortable.

"Do you think I'm beautiful?" she asked him in a gently teasing way, shaking her flow of blazing hair and dropping her lashes to coyly veil the lustrous brown eyes.

He was at a loss again. He didn't know how to answer her honestly. He fell back on one truth that couldn't be denied.

"I think that you've very nice hair too."

She dove upon him suddenly, shoving him back with both hands against his chest. Taken by surprise, he was pushed down onto the grass with her now lying fully atop him.

She swung her head, shaking her hair down upon his face in a silken, fragrant cascade.

"Let's waste no time with these games," she said with intensity. "We both know why we've come here."

Finn tried to protest, but his mouth filled with hair when he opened it. He blew the strands out from between his lips and cried out desperately: "Fionnuala, what are you doing? I've no idea what you want from me."

"Ah, you're playing with me now," she said, laughing. "Can't you feel the warmth of me against you?"

He was beginning to be aware of that, and of the feel of her body pressed to his, and of the warm, sweet, musky scent of her. It was causing some peculiar sensations within him, a shortness of breath as if he had run, a tingling beginning in his stomach and spreading downward.

He rolled to one side to move her from atop him, carrying her down to lie beside him.

"Fionnuala, don't you think we should be getting back?" he suggested in a very strained tone of voice.

"We're only beginning," she said.

She leaned forward, pressing her lips against his. His shock at this was quickly overwhelmed by another when he felt her hand burning upon the bare flesh of his thigh. It rested there and then slowly, caressingly slid upward, beneath the hem of his tunic.

His first impulse to pull away at her rather personal actions quickly died, however. He soon found himself enjoying the sensations, relaxing and giving way to them. And very quickly thereafter, he was responding with an enthusiasm that matched her own. His arms slipped around her, pulling her more tightly against him as he returned the kiss. Then his hands began to move, roving down across the soft curves of her body with the adventurous zeal of a hunter in a new territory.

"Oh!" she exclaimed with pleasure. She pulled back and looked at him, smiling knowingly. "And you wanted me to think you had no idea what I wanted."

His return smile now was a bold one. "I've been told that I learn very fast," he said.

The sun slipped rapidly toward the western horizon in its final, steep plunge into night. Finn rolled to his side and looked toward it, suddenly conscious of how much time had passed.

"We'll have to be starting back soon," he said. "It'll be getting dark soon. We'll be missed."

"I don't care if we are," she said, stretching herself luxuriously in the soft cushion of lush grass.

He smiled, plucking a stray blade from her copper fan of hair. Then a distant sound reached him. His head turned away from her and the smile vanished, replaced by a frown of concentration.

"What is it?" she asked.

"Shhh," he told her, fixing on the sound. It was the drumbeat of many hooves.

He stood up. From their vantage point, the road to the hilltop rath was visible. He saw the dark figures of several mounted men heading toward the fortress gates at a rapid pace.

"Horsemen," he said. He picked up his sword and harness and began to buckle it on.

Fionnuala showed no interest. "My father has visitors often enough," she said. "No need to be hurrying back just because of it."

He picked up her cloak and tossed it to her. "Put it on," he said firmly. "I'm your escort, remember? I'll not risk your father's anger by keeping you out any longer. Besides," he added, looking back toward the rath, "I'm curious to see who's come, even if you're not."

He pulled her to her feet and she fastened the cloak about her. Taking up her bundle of flowers, now largely wilted, they started across the meadow toward the gates.

The horsemen had vanished inside the stockade long before they reached it. As they entered, Finn expected to see the arrivals being welcomed by Cian in the yard.

Instead, the yard was deserted. Only the row of lathered horses gave evidence that the riders were there.

Thinking everyone must be within the main hall, Finn and the girl started across the yard toward it. But as they were halfway to it, a figure appeared in the doorway, moving out from the shadows within into the light. On seeing him, Finn stopped, his hunter's sense for danger fully aroused. The warrior who faced him was a stranger, a massively built man who towered a full head above him.

"Welcome," he rumbled, a slow smile of pleasure spreading his wide mouth. "We have been waiting for you, Finn."

Behind him the timber gates crashed closed. He wheeled about to see a dozen men, their weapons in their hands, move out from their hiding places to surround him.

He was trapped.

Chapter Twelve

HUNTED AGAIN

Two warriors moved up closely on either side of Finn. They held their spears ready to strike if he showed signs of resistance. The others formed a rough semicircle between him and the gates. Only the giant stood before him.

"Make no move," he told Finn, "or you and the girl will die."

Finn believed him. A glance to right and left revealed the glinting spear points close to his throat. It might be he could move fast enough to draw his sword, but his fighting skills might not be honed enough yet to let him parry both weapons before they struck. And he could do nothing to risk Fionnuala.

"Are you the sons of Morna?" he asked.

"We are of the Morna clan. I am Luachra, its champion."

"Then you mean to kill me anyway," Finn said with certainty.

"What's happening?" said Fionnuala with rising fear. "Where is my father?"

"He and his warriors have chosen to stay within their hall," Luachra explained. "This has nothing to do with them."

"But you can't come into our fortress and do as you wish!" she protested.

"No one would dare to interfere with the will of the Fianna," he growled in return.

"One would," said another voice.

Luachra turned his head in surprise as a warrior emerged from the doorway of the hall. It was Caoilte. He strode boldly past the giant, stopping midway between him and the encircled young pair.

"Fionnuala," he snapped, "go in to your father now."

She looked at Finn in anguish. "I don't want to leave you."

"You can't help me," he told her earnestly. "Please, Fionnuala, I don't want you harmed. Get out of this."

Reluctantly she obeyed, moving away, cautiously skirting the watching giant to reach the doorway of the hall, vanishing inside. As she reached safety, Caoilte turned to confront the giant.

"Who are you?" Luachra demanded.

"I am Caoilte," he answered, "a champion of this fortress. I say that this boy is of my company. You'll not be harming him."

Luachra's smile vanished. His voice grew ominous.

"If you're mad enough to try helping him, he'll die on your first move, and your own life will end very soon after."

"Don't risk yourself, Caoilte," Finn called to the warrior. "This is my trouble."

"Quiet, boy," Caoilte shot back. "I would do the same for any of my men." He laid his hand on his sword hilt and fixed the giant with a chill glare. "I'll not be leaving this."

Luachra stepped forward, his voice an angry rumble now, his massive spear rising in his hand.

"Stand away, or I'll kill you myself! Stand away! You'll get no other warning from me!"

Caoilte stood his ground defiantly. The giant stalked toward him. The men near Finn edged further in, their spears ready. Finn braced himself for a desperate move. He would not die easily.

"Now, Finn!" Caoilte shouted suddenly. He whirled about and charged toward the young man, his sword sweeping out.

Finn spun, too, jumping away from the man on his left. He drew in a lightning move Caoilte had taught him and thrust out at the man on his left. He drove the blade past the edge of the shield, under the upraised spear arm, exactly as he had been shown. The point of the sword struck home, thudding into the warrior's belly.

An expression of pained surprise filled the man's face. His agonized gaze met Finn's, then he sagged back, falling to the ground. Finn stared, for a long, long instant frozen by the grim reality of an act he had so often visualized. He had taken his first human life. The memory of the man's face and the bright gush of his blood would stay with the young man forever.

The warrior behind Finn was ready to strike. But his thrust was blocked by the sword of Caoilte, and he was knocked back by a swing of the warrior's shield.

"Back-to-back with me, lad," Caoilte ordered. "Quickly!"

The rest of the warriors were closing in about them. There was no further time for thoughts of remorse. Finn's will went now to keeping him alive. He moved to Caoilte and the two stood back-to-back in the classic warrior's defense he had practiced often these past days. Their attackers came in more warily then, angling for positions, feinting in an attempt to get at either of the two from the side. But they shifted rapidly, guarding one another's vulnerable points, driving back every assault.

They soon earned the respect of the attacking warriors. The Fian men, for all their own great skill, realized that they had met their match here. Caoilte was a master of the sword while Finn fought with nearly the skill and with greater speed than his comrade, his sword a blur as it swung out. In moments another man had fallen and two more were staggering away with disabling wounds. The others were hesitating, each waiting for his comrades to make the next attempt.

It was then that Luachra, angered by the inability of his men to finish the pair, entered the fray. He lumbered toward Finn and Caoilte, towering above them like an upright bear.

Caoilte saw the giant coming first. He swallowed hard and raised his weapons in defense. But Luachra was not concerned with him. His massive shield swung out like a gateway, struck the dark warrior, and slammed him aside. Caoilte stumbled to one knee as the giant closed on Finn.

Finn had heard the sound of impact behind him and realized his companion had been swept away. He turned his head to see the colossal form looming above, the great spear lifted to strike.

Suddenly a high, clear music arose, filling the yard with its melody. It was a golden mist of sound, like a fine spring rain caught in a stray shaft of sunlight. It fell upon Luachra and the giant paused, his expression turning from rage to puzzlement. And then, as Finn watched in wonder, a look of contentment overspread his face. The young warrior realized that Luachra had been entranced.

Finn looked toward the source of this enchanting music and saw Cnu Deireoil perched atop the stockade by the gates. He was playing with great fervor at his harp, his fingers flying across the strings as he wove his spell. It had ensnared all the MacMorna warriors, bringing them to a sort of stunned immobility, their heads cocked to one side in listening poses, a foolish vacancy in their eyes, their weapons hanging forgotten in their hands.

"What happened?" Caoilte asked, getting to his feet. Only he and Finn had been excluded from the spell.

"Get away from there quickly, lads!" Cnu Deireoil shouted down to them. "My tune won't hold the likes of them for very long!"

The pair needed no further urging. They ran from the ring of frozen men to the gates, hauled them open far enough to allow passage, and slipped out of the yard. The harpist, giving over his tune, swung around and dropped lightly from the wall to join them outside.

Let's not delay a moment in being off," he urged. "Soon they'll be coming to life again."

"Should we stay and fight them?" Finn asked, thinking that running might be a bit less noble than a warrior's behavior should be.

"Go against that monster?" Caoilte said. "There's bravery and there's madness, lad. For now, we simply escape."

They headed away from the fortress at a run. Caoilte was nearly as swift as Finn, and the Little Nut, for all the shortness of his limbs, kept up quite easily. Behind them, in the fortress, Luachra was shaking his head like an angry bull. He looked around him, realizing what had happened.

"After them!" he bellowed to the rest, pounded to the gates, grasped them, and flung them wide.

Already far away, three figures were visible against the glowing crescent of the setting sun, just disappearing behind a low hill.

"Run all you wish, son of Cumhal," the giant growled. "You'll not escape me any more than your father did. If I have to hunt you to the rim of the world and beyond it, you will not escape me."

* * *

"He escaped again?" cried Conn of the Hundred Battles angrily. He reined his horse hard around so he might fix his gaze on Goll MacMorna. "And how did that happen?"

The rest of the hunt had moved on, a hundred warriors afoot moving through the woods in line to start the game while a score of noblemen rode behind with ready slings to bring down the flying birds. Conn had dropped behind to talk privately with his Fianna captain. An interested Tadg was beside him, as usual, to listen to the discomfited Goll's tale.

"The boy has friends now," Goll answered in defense, "They helped him to escape. Magic was used. Several of my men were killed or wounded. But Luachra is continuing the hunt."

"And if he does find our Finn again, why believe he'll have any more success destroying him?" the druid inquired.

"And just what's your meaning in that?" Goll demanded in rising heat.

"Only that we clearly cannot depend upon you to see this properly done," Tadg said. "Your famed Clan na Morna cannot deal with this single child yourself!"

Goll pushed his horse close to the druid's, leaning toward him, face flushed with his anger, his voice low and ominous: "You are risking a great deal to say that to me! This is the son of Cumhal we are facing. He has all his father's courage, skills, and wiles."

Tadg saw that he had gone too far with the touchy chieftain. With the adroitness of a skilled manipulator of men, he swiftly revised his approach.

"Calm yourself, my captain," he said soothingly. "I had no idea of suggesting that you were to be blamed in this. I only meant that if this boy is truly as dangerous as you say, you will need help in dealing with him."

"What do you mean?" Conn demanded quickly. "You know that neither I nor any of my court can seem to be involved."

"Not in an attack against one of the Fianna," Tadg said in a sly manner, smiling. "But this MacCumhal is keeping the secret of who he is. He seems only a

101

common warrior, with no identity. And he has, with no provocation, attacked and killed a number of Fian warriors. By Brehon Law you may ask your chief judge to have him declared outlaw. Then the hand of every honest man of Ireland will be set against him."

This notion seemed to appeal to the high king. He nodded and smiled too. "A fine notion, Tadg. I'll see it done at once!"

"I can do even more, my king," he said. "I can also use my own modest powers to seek the boy. I might even be able to bring about his end myself."

"None of your sorcerer's tricks, Tadg," Goll warned darkly. "I've told you before, there'll be no treachery used in this. It's still the son of a Fian chieftain we're speaking of, and he'll be treated fairly."

"But you said yourself that he has help now—supernatural help, from your report," the druid pointed out.

"It changes nothing," Goll shot back stubbornly. "MacCumhal will be dealt with honestly, or you'll not have the help of the sons of Morna in dealing with him."

"I think that Goll is right, Tadg," Conn quickly added. He wanted no rebellions in the Fian leadership created by this. "Nothing should be done that will violate our captain's sense of honor."

"As you wish, my king," Tadg acknowledged with apparent willingness. But neither Goll nor Conn noticed the flame of defiance burning deeply within the gray ice of his eyes.

The black eye sockets swallowed the flickering red glow that lit the rest of the skull to lurid brightness. Many similar death's-head stares, starkly revealed against the dark background of leaves, were directed down from the surrounding tangled branches of the oaks into the tiny clearing. For scores of weathered skulls, the grotesque ornaments of druidic ritual, festooned the limbs of the sacred grove.

Prodding the fire higher with the iron-shod tip of

his sacred staff, Tadg watched the sparks from the flaming yew wood fly upward, vanishing into the darkness above. It was deep in the heart of the night that he had come here. Alone he had prepared his ritual fire and said his charms. Now all was ready. He stood upright, eyes closed, head back. The crimson light beat upward against his face, drawing sharp, arching shadows above his eyes and mouth, replacing his fragile, innocent expression with one that seemed to expose his true sinister nature.

"I summon to me the messengers of the Sidhe," he intoned, lifting his staff toward the dark canopy of night. "Gather here, I command you. Gather now."

At first there was nothing in response. He stood, unmoving, arms lifted, for many moments. Then, faintly, came the sound of rustling.

It grew quickly louder, moving in from all directions at once. Soon the treetops began to shake, disturbed by something dropping through them from above. Objects like tattered shadows, like windblown spirits of the night began to flutter down through the branches, settling slowly and furling great wings as they came to rest.

They formed a ring on the lower limbs of the oaks, a flock of enormous blackbirds, sleek blue-black bodies shining in the light, watching Tadg with the glittering star points of their eyes.

As soon as all had found perches, a single, gray-necked bird, much larger than the rest, sailed forward to land neatly atop the skull that sat on a pole beside the fire. It gave a loud caw that held a distinct note of inquiry, then cocked its head to await the druid's reply.

"I cannot trust the mortals of Ireland to carry out my revenge," he said to it. "As the father of Muirne, it is my right to see it done. No threat of Goll MacMorna will stop me. I ask the help of my own race in wiping out this disgrace to all of us, this foul product of the violation of my daughter."

The bird gave a single, rasping cry, as if it understood.

"Good," he said with satisfaction. "Then I call upon

103

you, children of the Battle Raven. Fly from here and carry my message to every Sidhe, to every warrior of the Tuatha de Danaan. The son of Cumhal must be found and destroyed!"

Chapter Thirteen

FINN'S REVELATION

The raven skimmed low across the hills, its sharp gaze sweeping constantly over the countryside below.

A movement attracted its attention and it banked into a lazy curve over the spot. Three figures had appeared from a screen of thick woods and were moving onto a wide roadway. The bird spiraled down lower, sweeping in close above the trio. Then it lifted sharply away, voicing a triumphant caw.

Only Finn noted the peculiar action of the bird, but he quickly forgot it as they topped a rise and a large structure came into view ahead.

"Ah, I knew there was one close by," Cnu Deireoil declared with glee.

It was a large building of planks, six-sided and high-roofed. It sat at a junction of six wide roads that radiated away to the horizons in various directions. It was the scene of a great deal of activity, a number of men and horses and carts moving about it, coming and going on the roads.

"What is this place?" Finn asked.

"Why, it's a *bruidhean*, lad," Cnu answered, at first surprised, then nodding in understanding. "Oh, yes. I had forgotten you know little of our ways here. Well, it's a public house. A place where travelers can always find food and a place to rest, however poor." He grinned. "And never were there travelers poorer or more in need than ourselves."

That was true enough. They had been two days in constant flight through wild country to escape the tenacious hunters of the Morna clan. A chance to clean themselves and eat was tempting indeed. Still, though Finn felt certain that they had lost their pursuers, at least for now, he had misgivings.

"Is it safe for us here?"

"It should be," put in Caoilte knowingly. "And even if we were discovered here, we couldn't be attacked. No man may fight and no criminal may be taken within its sanctuary, or so says the Brehon Law."

"All right then," Finn agreed. "I'm willing to be led by you."

As they neared the public house, Finn noted that each of the three sides facing them had a large, open doorway. At the one they approached, as at the others, an unarmed man stood in the plain tunic and trousers of a servant. He greeted them in a friendly way and led them inside.

The interior was a single, large room with small sleeping alcoves along the outer wall. Most of the floor was given over to long tables where some two score men now sat. They were widely scattered, some in large groups, some in twos and threes, a few alone. Most were eating, though one group seemed more interested in drink and boisterous talk.

A dozen other servants bustled about the tables constantly. They served pitchers of drink and carried platters of hot food from the cooking pots and spits of the central fire. They also cleared away the tables after departing men to make way for new arrivals. This was done often, as the crowd was changing constantly. The room, Finn now realized, had a similar doorway in each of its six walls, and men were coming and going through all of them.

Their own servant guided them to an empty table and asked them to sit down.

"You'll be served very soon," he said politely, and then headed back to his door to await other arrivals.

As he moved away, a man left a group across the room and rushed toward them. He was a thickset, robust-looking man whose bald head was fringed by a bushy hedge of golden hair. His manner was enthusiastic as he greeted the harper.

"Welcome, my friend," he said heartily. "Welcome! Have you come to play for us?"

"Ah, no, sorry to say," Cnu Deireoil replied. "We'll not be staying that long today, Fearghal. But I promise you that I'll come back soon to play for you all you wish."

"Fair enough!" the man said. "And for now, you're welcome as you always are. Your friends as well."

He moved away and shouted orders to one of the servants to see to the Little Nut at once. Finn looked after him with curiosity. Though his manner was commanding, he wore no weapons.

"Was that the chieftain of this place?" he asked his companions.

Cnu Deireoil laughed. "This is no fortress, lad. There are no fighting men here and no nobility. Fearghal is the *bruighaid*. He sees that the place is run as it should be and that no man goes from here without a full belly, day or night."

"Why?" Finn wondered. "What makes this man and all these others laboring here choose to be so generous?"

"The law of Ireland does it, lad," the little man explained. "It decrees that no one be denied the hospitality of a bruidhean wherever he travels. And so each is required to keep sheep and cattle and hogs—a hundred of each—grazing on its lands and have the flesh of all three always ready to be served. They're to have a hundred servants and beds for a hundred guests. Always they're to offer the three cheers: the cheer of good ale, the cheer of warm food, and the cheer of the gaming board."

"Are there many of these places?" Finn asked, looking about with greater fascination now.

"Hundreds, lad. Through all the provinces. Not all so grand as this, of course. But it's for the province kings to see to their being properly endowed, and it's a great disgrace upon them not to do it well. So, war or peace, feast or famine time, the bruidheans are always supplied."

"It's a fine thing to be done," Finn said, marveling at such openhandedness.

"It is that," the harper agreed. "I've made use of more than a few of them in my own wanderings, and I've always found a blazing fire of welcome and a full kettle on the boil."

Their food was brought to them then. There were platters of all three meats, broiled and steaming. There were fresh vegetables and fruits and rough round loaves of hot bread. There was a thick white cottage cheese and a great bowl of soup of milk and oatmeal and leeks. The wonderful, fragrant bounty filling the table before him quite awed the young Finn.

"There's enough for a dozen men here!" he said, and turned to the Little Nut. "You surely have some helpful friends."

"It's the harp that makes them for me," Cnu Deireoil replied modestly, giving the leather bag containing the instrument a loving pat. Then he took up a mutton leg that seemed almost too big for him to lift, bit off a great mouthful of the juicy meat, chewed, swallowed, and sighed in satisfaction. "Ah, but good cooking—there's the finest bit of magic!"

The other two began to eat as well, for they'd had little chance for food since leaving Bantry. For some while they concentrated only on consuming, and the only sound from them was chewing and occasional slurps. But with the first, sharp pangs of hunger eased, they took up their conversation once again.

It was Caoilte who began it. Taking a swig of ale to wash down a mouthful of pork, he fixed his young companion with a searching eye.

"All right now, boy. Now that we've left behind your large friend and his warriors, I think it's time for you to tell us just why men of the Fianna are after you."

There it was, Finn thought. He had been expecting this since their escape. And once more the training of Bodhmall caused him to hesitate, reminding him that he must always protect himself.

"You said once that you'd not ask me for more than I wished to say," he told the dark warrior.

"It had nothing to do with me then. Now it does. The little man and I are in this with you now, like it or not. From here on those Fian men will be seeking us along with you, and there are no men I'd less want hunting me. So, if we're to become the stag to their hounds, I want to know why."

Finn knew that he was right. These men had earned his trust in the finest way; they had risked themselves to save him for no other reason than that he needed help. They deserved the truth.

"I will tell you then," he said. He looked around to see if anyone was nearby, and then leaned toward them. The two sat forward expectantly as Finn spoke in a hushed tone charged with great drama: "I am the son of Cumhal MacTredhorn."

The great revelation had less effect than he had pictured. To the Little Nut the name appeared to mean nothing at all. Caoilte's reaction was a raising of the eyebrows in mild surprise.

"Cumhal's son?" he said in a skeptical tone. "Try another, boy. There are none of Cumhal's family alive."

"There is one," Finn said. "I was saved. Just after my birth I was taken away to the forests of Slieve Bladhma by two women of my clan. I was kept hidden there until I was old enough to go into the world on my own."

"Hidden away, were you?" said the Little Nut with dawning understanding. "Well, it's no wonder you know so little of the way of things."

"And it does explain the warriors of the Morna clan wanting to see you dead," Caoilte grudgingly admitted. "Maybe your story's true, lad."

"I don't know anything of that," Cnu Deireoil said. "It happened before—" Here he stopped abruptly.

"Before what?" Caoilte asked, giving him a curious glance.

"Before I . . . began traveling about Ireland," the harper finished in a casual way. "So, could you tell me of it?"

"I don't know how you'd not have heard of it," Caoilte said. "I was only a small child myself when it happened, but I remember. The MacMorna clan challenged the Baiscne for the leadership of the Fians. Cumhal, their chieftain, died in the fight. The rest of his warriors were killed or scattered, the clan's power broken. Aed MacMorna earned the name of Goll in that battle, along with the captaincy of the Fianna."

"Goll MacMorna and the Fianna I do know of," said the Little Nut. "But what you're telling me must have happened years ago. What threat can this one lad be to them now?"

Caoilte shrugged. "I don't know, unless they believe he could still challenge their control."

"That is exactly what I mean to do," said Finn with grim determination.

The two men looked at him in astonishment.

"You're going to challenge the MacMorna clan for leadership of the Fianna of Ireland?" Caoilte asked as if he could not believe what he had heard.

"I am," Finn answered. "It's what I'm meant to do; what I was raised to do. All those years in the glens, all I've known was that one day I would go out and regain the place of my father."

"How did you know that?" the harper asked.

"It was Bodhmall, one of the women who raised me, who told me who I was and what I would have to do."

"And did she tell you how you were to do it?" the dark warrior wanted to know.

"She was a servant in my father's house," Finn explained. "She knew little of the ways of fighting men or of the Fians or of the world beyond the dwellings of our clan."

"Especially after being cut off from it for years," the Little Nut said dryly.

"She taught me all she could," Finn replied hotly in defense of Bodhmall. "She meant to see our clan's pride restored."

"Well, she set no easy task for you," Caoilte told him. "It's clear you've no idea of what you'll be facing."

"I know it will be difficult—" Finn began.

Caoilte broke in: "Difficult? Impossible is what I call it. You listen to me, boy, since you're so ignorant of the realities. To begin, Goll MacMorna will not just stand aside while some pup walks in and claims the captaincy."

"I mean to be ready," Finn shot back. "It's why I need to learn the best fighting skills I can."

"Being the greatest warrior in all Ireland won't be much help to you against his clan."

"I won't be alone. The others of the Clan na Baiscne will join me once they know Cumhal's son is alive."

Caoilte gave a short, derisive laugh. "You really don't see, do you? You have no clan. It ceased to exist years ago. If any of its members have survived, no one knows where they are."

"Then I will find them," Finn said stubbornly. "I will gather them and I will restore their power."

Frustrated by the young man's unshakable faith in his apparently ridiculous dream, Caoilte grew irritated.

"Why are you doing this?" he demanded. "To replace someone you never knew because this Bodhmall told you that you must? There's no logic to that."

"You don't understand, Caoilte," Finn said. "It's the honor of my family and myself that I'm fighting for. Without it, I'm nothing."

"You are alive!" Caoilte retorted. "That's what matters. Honor is an empty word that's done nothing but kill many good men fool enough to think it valuable."

"I didn't ask for your help," Finn told him. "I'm sorry you've become involved in this. But it is something that I have to do, and nothing will turn me from it."

Caoilte sighed in resignation. "Aye, lad. I see that. I knew you were a fool. Still, if you're bound to go ahead with this madness, then I'm bound to make you the finest warrior that I can."

"You owe nothing more to me, Caoilte," Finn protested.

"Of course I do. I said that I would train you, and that I will do."

Finn smiled. "Why? For your honor?"

"For my code as a warrior," he swiftly corrected. "If the word of Caoilte MacRonan couldn't be trusted, I'd have little worth to anyone as a fighter, now would I? So, you'll come with me. I know a place where I think we'll be safely hidden from your Clan na Morna, at least for a time. And you can gain some fighting experience there as well, if things are as they used to be."

"What about me?" the Little Nut asked with some anxiety. "You'll take me there as well, won't you? I'll go nowhere alone with that great monster seeking me."

"You can come if you wish," Caoilte said carelessly. "Though you'll be of little use to us, we might at least get some pleasure from your music."

"Little use?" he repeated indignantly. "And I suppose I was of little use at Bantry? It was I who saved you there, if you'd care to recall, not your sword."

"I would have gotten us out without your harp," the warrior told him with great confidence. "I need no help from anyone to see to myself."

"Is that right!" Cnu Deireoil said, getting to his feet, his face red with his anger. "Well, if you don't mind, I'll just leave you to yourself then for a time. I've lost my taste for the food and the company."

With that he grabbed up the bag containing his harp and stalked away.

"I don't think you should be making light of the man," Finn told Caoilte disapprovingly. "He has been a good friend."

"I won't have any harper putting on airs of his grandness with me," the warrior replied. "Never mind about him now. Just be finishing your own food. We'll have to push on soon. It's three good, hard days of walking to the place I was speaking of."

As they were cleaning up the last scraps of their

meal, the Little Nut returned to them. He was beaming in a smug and triumphant way.

"Well, my fine warrior, there'll be no more walking for us," he announced. "I've talked with our most hospitable bruighaid"—here he touched the encased harp lightly and gave a wink—"and he's so in love with my playing that he's offered us the use of horses for as long as we've need of them." He gave Caoilte a supercilious look. "How is that for being of little use?"

From Caoilte, the only response this drew was a cold return gaze. But Finn laughed heartily over the little harper's well-deserved victory.

So when the three were ready to depart, Fearghal took them to his stables and supplied them with stocky, strong-limbed ponies from his extensive herd. He had the smallest he could find given to Cnu Deireoil, but the little man looked absurd perched atop the barrellike back of the animal, his legs sticking out on either side.

Thanking the bruighaid for his generosity, they rode away from the house, taking the road that led to the north and west. None of them took note of the huge blackbird that swooped down from the sky and took up its vigil upon the trio once more.

"We'd best be looking for a place where we can sleep," Finn MacCumhal suggested. They had come a great distance since leaving the bruidhean that afternoon, but soon the night would be coming upon them.

"There's no shelter for us hereabouts," said Cnu Deireoil. "It'll be a night under the stars for us."

"Will it?" said Caoilte, pointing ahead. "Then what's that?"

Some way ahead, in a rocky hillside half shadowed with the night's rising darkness, they saw a house. The red-yellow fire from within it was shining from the door, throwing a wedge of light out over the valley below it.

The Little Nut frowned in puzzlement. "I never knew of a house in this valley."

"Ah, there are likely many things you've no knowledge of," the dark warrior replied in a superior tone. "It's best for us to go and see it. We've nothing to fear."

They moved toward the door. But as they came near to it, the form of a man appeared suddenly, black and huge against the light.

"My welcome to you," came the man's voice, a low and harsh sound, like a growl deep in a hound's throat. "It's a long time you were in coming here."

Finn shot a puzzled look at Caoilte. What had the man meant by that? His instinct for danger was aroused, tingling up his spine, lifting the small hairs at his neck.

But Caoilte seemed not to have noticed the remark. "We thank you for your welcome," he said politely.

The man moved aside to let them pass. He was broad and rugged in looks, roughly clothed, with a wild mass of gray hair and beard and a strange, intense light shining in his eyes. As they passed, he rudely jerked the bridles of the horses from their hands and drew the mounts into the room as well. Once all were inside, he slammed shut a thick wooden door behind them and shot home two heavy iron bolts with a final-sounding clank.

"I do not like this," murmured the Little Nut, looking uneasily at the locked door.

The closing of the door seemed to have extinguished the flames of the fire. The light that had attracted them had sunk to a few glowing coals. The room was very dark, everything beyond the small firepit concealed in thick, clinging shadows. To Finn, it was like a heavy covering had been thrown upon them. And the sensation of being smothered was made greater by an atmosphere both hot and nearly stifling.

The man pulled the horses further into the room. They balked and snorted nervously, but he had no trouble hauling them along. He tied them to a roof pole by the fire.

"Caoilte, are you certain we should stay here?" Finn said softly while he was doing this.

"Of course I'm certain," the warrior assured him. "The man's a bit strange, that's true, but we've been given welcome to this house and we've accepted it, so we're safe enough."

The man, overhearing this, stomped toward them, scowling.

"Are you thinking of leaving here?" he demanded angrily.

"We are not!" Caoilte answered with great earnestness. He shot Finn a meaningful look as he added: "No man of any worth at all would refuse another's hospitality."

This mollified the gray man. A smile of jagged teeth rent the beard. "All right then, sit!" he commanded, pointing to a bed of rough planks. "I'll serve you!"

The three moved back and dropped down side by side on the bed. Finn felt the sharp splinters of the unfinished planks striking up painfully into his flesh. He shifted, but that only made it worse.

"I do not like this. I do not like this," Cnu Deireoil was mumbling over and over to himself. He clutched the bag with his precious harp before him on his lap in a protective way.

The man, meanwhile, had gone to the low fire and was stroking it with tremendous energy. He shoved stick after stick of wood into the embers, burying all the glow. Soon a heavy smoke began to rise from the pile and mushroom out into the room. Still he threw on more wood. More smoke blossomed outward. A thick white cloud filled the room, making the air acrid with its scent.

Finn felt as if he were being suffocated. He took a breath, drew the smoke into his lungs, and nearly choked.

"It seems"—he coughed out—"a very strange way to treat guests!"

"Quiet, lad!" Caoilte muttered to him in a warning tone. "Whatever happens here, do nothing rude. Accept every hospitality that's shown us with good grace!"

"Why?" Finn asked.

The smoldering fire had reached its flash point. The mound of wood ignited in a great burst, throwing a bright red glare about the room, revealing suddenly what the shadows had masked before.

"Because if we don't," the warrior said tightly, "then I've a feeling that we may just be in a bit of trouble."

Across the fire from them they could now see another figure. It was an ancient hag, her bony limbs poking from her ragged gown. And growing from the long and scrawny neck, like hideous blossoms from some grotesque flower, were three heads.

Chapter Fourteen

THE PHANTOMS

Each of her heads was similar in its cadaverous thinness, its sickly whiteness of skin, and its greasy, straggling hair. Finn's first sight of the bizarre creature startled him, but he remembered Caoilte's warning and struggled to suppress any sign of it.

A third figure now moved forward into the light. This one, in contrast to the hag, had no head at all. But a single, large eye peered unblinkingly at them from the center of its wide, flat chest.

The lipless mouths of the hag's three heads opened and, in three voices screeching in unison, she spoke: "You have accepted the hospitality of our house. We are pleased to have you here, one called Finn. We also give greetings to Caoilte MacRonan and special greetings to our Little Nut."

Cnu Deireoil had lifted the bag before his face when she appeared, as if to hide himself. But now he lowered it, his expression fearful.

"Rise up, you that are in the house!" the three voices squawked. "Make music for our guests!"

And from the shadows to the right of the three, figures rose suddenly. They were clad as warriors, holding shields and swords in their hands. But though they moved like living men, they had no heads.

From the other side of the bed, heads rose into the air. They lifted as if held by unseen hands. Nine heads to match the nine headless warriors. Their bulging eyes rolled wildly and their throatless mouths moved as they all began to wail together.

As they raised their song, the hag's three heads joined their chorus. A wolflike howl rose from the gray man, and a high-pitched humming came from the body of the one-eyed man. All joined in a dreadful, discordant sound that Finn felt like a knife driving through his skull, rattling his teeth, breaking the bones of his head.

He wanted to lift his hands to stop his ears against it, but Caoilte, seeing him start to move, snapped another warning.

"Don't make a move! Don't do anything that could give them insult or it could be our end. Act as if it's the finest song you ever heard!"

So Finn gritted his teeth, clenched his hands tightly together, and smiled as warmly as he could. So did his comrades.

This seemed to work. When the singers realized their awful noise was having no effect on their guests, their voices died away. The warriors retired. The heads sank down. For a moment a blessed silence fell.

"The entertainment's done," the gray man said then. He lifted a great ax from its pegs upon the wall and grinned broadly at the three, an insane light glowing in his eyes. "Now it's time for eating!"

For a moment Finn wondered if he meant to eat them, but he turned away from the three toward the tethered horses, lifting the ax.

Realizing his intent, Finn started to rise, his hand moving to the hilt of his sword.

"You ca—" he began to protest.

116

The hand of Coailte jerked him roughly back and his sharp hiss cut Finn off.

"No! I said do nothing!"

Finn sat helpless, watching in anguish as the man approached their horses. They crowded back in terror, tugging at the reins. The gray man reached them. The ax flashed out. Quick, well-aimed, powerful blows severed each beast's head cleanly. They thudded to the floor amid streams of their pulsing blood.

The ax slashed out swiftly, rhythmically, hacking into the bodies even as they fell. Finn stared in shock at the violent butchering as the gray man, in what seemed only moments, flayed the carcasses, stripping great, ragged chunks of flesh from the bones.

The one-eyed man then brought him a bundle of long wooden spits. On each the gray man speared a chunk of meat and then laid the spits across the hearthstones. The fresh meat hung almost in the searing flames. The smell of blood and scorched flesh filled the room, mingling with the stench of smoke.

The man had just time to finish setting all the spits when the hag's three heads began to cry out: "Time enough for it to be done! Feed our guests! Feed our guests! Feed our guests!"

The gray man took spits from the fire and handed one to each of the three. Finn gazed down at his in disgust, for the meat upon it was raw, the red blood still dripping from it.

"Take your food away!" he told the gray man, handing back the spit.

"Don't do that, Finn!" Caoilte warned.

"I will!" the young man retorted in heat. "I'll not be made to eat raw meat for any reason. It's gone too far! This hospitality is madness if it means we can be treated so."

The gray man threw down the spit and lifted his ax to grasp it in both hands.

"If you have come into our house and refuse our food," he barked out angrily, "then you will surely go against ourselves, Finn!"

"Oh, no!" cried Cnu Deireoil. For at the man's

117

words, the nine heads rose up again, giving voice to a chilling battle cry. The warriors' bodies charged forward with the gray man, weapons rising in attack. At the same moment, the fire was extinguished.

"You've done it now!" Caoilte shouted. "Get behind the bed!"

In the blinding darkness, the three dove backward, barely escaping the weapons that swung out at them, wooshing harmlessly past. Caoilte seized the trestle of the bed and jerked it up. The heavy planks slammed into the bodies of the attackers, knocking them back.

"Get behind us, harper!" he ordered as he and Finn drew swords. "Finn, swing all about you! Keep them back!"

Finn began to swing out into the blackness, striking out at the invisible foes. Often his sword clanged against another blade or made a hollow thump as it struck a shield. But he couldn't tell if he was doing any harm.

As his eyes grew more accustomed to the dark, he could faintly discern figures shifting before him as thicker patches of blackness in the the black. These he would strike at, but still without any sign of effect.

He and his companions could not move. The logs of the outer wall were at their backs. So they fought doggedly on, Caoilte constantly urging Finn to keep swinging.

The young man's arm became weary, then wearier. It ached, it throbbed, it grew leaden. Moving the stiffening joints took a greater effort as the time crawled by, and he became certain that his sword's weight was increasing rapidly.

Still he continued to fight, holding back the shadowy horrors. Beside him Caoilte fought with like determination, while the Little Nut huddled on the floor behind.

It was at the point when the weary Finn was wondering if this ordeal would never end that the worst came. In a sudden move, the shadowy forms seemed to draw together and then rush forward in a single mass.

He felt a force, like a wind, come hard against him.

It pushed at him, swirled around him. He felt it tugging, grasping at him, trying to roll upon him like a sea wave, trying to force him down. With a new strength born of final desperation, he fought back, hacking about him with his sword, the blade raising a sharp wind of its own as he swung it back and forth. Still the forces were closing in, the pressure of them increasing. It occurred to him that this onslaught might be the finish.

It was. But not of him.

As abruptly as the attack had come, it was over. The force faded, and he realized that the shadows about him had vanished. Bewildered by this sudden end to the fight, he peered around him. He realized that the things around him were becoming more distinct. It was becoming lighter.

The air above was beginning to glow with a faint, rosy hue. He looked up toward it, at first further confused by the new phenomenon. Then he understood what he was looking at. It was the sky, growing brighter with the coming dawn.

As the light increased, he could see that the room had vanished, along with the forms of its strange occupants. He and his companions were now on a bare hillside.

With relief he found Caoilte still beside him, Cnu Deireoil crouched behind, both looking about them warily.

"Where did they go?" Finn asked.

"They were phantoms, lad," the warrior told him. "Things that haunt the darkness. The dawn wiped them away. That must be why they made that last fierce attack on us. Look there!"

Finn turned to see what he now pointed at. Their three horses, whole and alive as ever, stood tethered to a nearby bush, grazing peacefully.

"Was it real then," he said, "or some kind of dream?"

"It was real enough," the Little Nut said, climbing to his feet, "and its power would have destroyed you if your spirit had failed you." He opened his bag to assure himself his harp had gone undamaged. "We were lucky to have made it through the night."

"Well, it's certain that the enchantment was raised against ourselves," Caoilte put in, "for they knew our names."

"It was those of the Sidhe that did it," said Cnu Deireoil.

The Sidhe! For Finn this was another name from the tales of the outside world that both Liath and Bodhmall had told him. Their descriptions of the mystical race that had left the upper lands of Ireland to dwell in hidden palaces beneath it had been both fascinating and terrifying.

Caoilte fixed a scrutinizing eye upon the harper. "And how do you know it was the Others in this?"

The question seemed to discomfort Cnu Deireoil. He hesitated, then said vaguely, "I—I've had my meetings with them before."

"Ah, yes," Caoilte said thoughtfully. "They did show a certain special interest in you."

"They're jealous of my playing," he said, then added quickly, "but it wasn't myself they wanted. It was our young friend."

Caoilte looked toward Finn. "He's right, lad. It was you they were welcoming. Are those of the Sidhe really after you?"

Finn shrugged. "I don't know, Caoilte. That is the truth."

"Oh, that's fine, that is!" the warrior said irritably. "First the Fianna after you, and now the Others! It's a grand lot of enemies you have, lad. Are there any more that we should know about?"

"I'm sorry, Caoilte," Finn told him earnestly. "I told you before that you didn't have to help. I don't know why these 'Others' would be after me. I don't know who else might be."

Caoilte saw his distress and his own anger faded. "All right then," he said, sighing. "We've one more thing to be looking out for from here on. But," he added more sternly, "you be a bit less rash next time! If you had held your temper, we might have beaten them without a fight. Once they had welcomed us, they were bound not to harm us until we gave them insult.

That sword's not the answer to everything, you know. You've got to use your wits as well!"

"You're a fine one to be talking about using your wits," the Little Nut fired at him. "And you walking into that house without the least care when anyone with the wits of a nursing lamb would have seen there was something wrong."

"I knew there might be a danger!" Caoilte blustered in return. "I meant for the boy here to have a bit of experience with such things."

"How? By getting him killed?" cried Cnu Deireoil. "If you'd listened to me, we would never have gone in."

"Listened to you?" said Caoilte, laughing derisively. "And what help were you, cowering behind us like a frightened pup."

The harper drew his small frame up stiffly in indignation.

"I'm afraid of no mortal man of Ireland, MacRonan, including you," he replied fiercely. "And there's no shame in respecting the great powers of the Sidhe folk."

"Peace, friends," Finn said, holding up his hands between them. "You're neither of you fools nor cowards. We've survived, and that's all that matters now. Next time I'll be less rash and have proper respect. So, please leave off this quarreling, and let's be going on. We've still got our place of safety to find."

Grudgingly, the two antagonists agreed. With a last exchange of hostile looks, they and Finn mounted their horses and set out again. The animals seemed well rested and full of energy. The men were somewhat less eager after the long night's ordeal. But the Little Nut drew out his whistle and began a merry air. The music refreshed them like a chill bath, and soon they were riding with more vigor toward the west.

"This surely is a much wilder land," young Finn remarked.

The countryside had, in fact, been slowly growing

121

harsher for some time. The rolling meadowlands had given way to starker landscapes of rugged hills and fields of rock, and sharp, bonelike spurs of stone now often thrust jaggedly from the soft flesh of the green hills.

The pathway had grown narrower and less traveled, its surface often nearly vanishing across wind-scoured, barren plains.

Finn found the changed scenery as beautiful in its way as the wild glens of Slieve Bladhma or the wide, lush vales they had just left. But here there was a sense that the land was challenging him, like a wild beast, proud of its savage freedom, not ready to meekly serve man. And this sense made the country all the more intriguing to him.

"It's a very hard land for those who live in it," said Caoilte in a musing way. "You know, much as I was in a rush to leave it as a boy, I've never found another place in all my traveling that had as much hold on me. I always come back."

"I've never come here, myself," said the Little Nut. "It's not the best of places for the likes of me to make my living. And it's too cold." He shivered and wrapped his cloak tighter about him against the sharp breeze that whistled across the rocky fields.

Caoilte laughed. "Well, you'll never grow soft or rich living here, that's true enough. But it will be harder for our young friend's hunters to find him, or us."

On the morning of their third day of riding, they crossed a wide plateau and descended into a broad valley. Here they entered a forest of tall, slender pines. Caoilte led them through the confusing maze of trees whose high branches formed a lacy green canopy above. The wide hooves of their horses were nearly soundless as they plopped into the soft cushion of needles covering the forest floor.

Soon they came out onto the shores of a small lake. Before them was what seemed to Finn a most marvelous place. An entire ring fort seemed to float upon the water's surface. The circling stockade of logs rose like a ship's sides from the water, holding the waves back from the buildings within.

"What is this place?" he asked. "How does it float?"

"It's a crannog," Caoilte told him, grinning. "And it's not floating. There's an island built of stones beneath it. It's protection. Come along."

He led them along the edge of the lake to where a narrow bridge of earth led from the shore to a gateway in the wall. It was the only way to reach the fortress without swimming.

"Here's where we cross," he said to them.

"We're going there?" Cnu Deireoil. "But it's savages living there. They'll likely kill us!"

"That they will not," Caoilte told him in an angry tone. "Still, you two might be better to wait here while I go out to speak to them first. They are a bit suspicious of strangers."

A faint sound behind him alerted Finn then, and he turned to look.

"You won't be needing to ride out there to meet them, Caoilte," he said, his hand dropping to his sword.

A dozen men, all with heavy spears poised to strike, had moved from the trees and now formed a half-circle, trapping them against the water's edge. They were a fierce-looking band, all thick of build and well muscled, very dark, many heavily bearded, and all with a like grimness of expression.

"Savages! I told you!" cried the Little Nut. "They're going to kill us!"

Finn braced himself for another battle, his muscles still aching from the last one. But Caoilte rode close and put a restraining hand on his sword arm.

"No need for that," he said. Then he lifted his other hand in a gesture of greeting to the men. "My friends, it's Caoilte MacRonan!"

The weapons were lowered at once. Broad smiles appeared and there were shouts of welcome as the warriors moved forward.

"You know them?" Cnu Deireoil asked in surprise.

"Well enough," Caoilte answered. "This was my home!"

Chapter Fifteen

FIRST TROPHIES

The warriors had greeted Caoilte, their returning tribal member, as a hero, parading him into the crannog's gathering hall and bringing out enormous vats of ale to toast him with drink after drink.

The hall was much like that of Cian, but smaller and very simply decorated. Only weapons hung upon its roughly stuccoed walls. To its favor, however, it did lack the awful litter and decay of that careless chieftain's hall. The men themselves were of a different type than he had seen before. Their bodies were thicker generally, their complexions quite swarthy and large of feature. Their clothing was plain, with little of the fine linens and silks and rich brocades he had seen Cian's warriors wear, and the Firbolg men were largely free of adornment. Their hair seemed their one point of vanity, for it was long, elaborately plaited or waved, often hung with colored beads or metal balls. Mustaches were long, carefully tended and curled, sometimes neatly plaited as well.

Caoilte and his people, Finn had quickly learned, were of the race known as the Firbolgs. Finn knew someting about them from the stories Bodhmall and Liath had told him. They were said to be the oldest race of Ireland. Long before the coming of the Milesians they had ruled here. Then invader after invader had come against them, breaking their power and taking away their duns and herds. Some had retreated into the wild places of Ireland, living a primitive existence, but proudly keeping their tribes whole and their culture intact. Others had mixed with the newcomers, and their blood was now strong in the people of Ireland, save for the Milesian aristocracy. Even Finn's own roots, Bodhmall had told him, could be traced to proud champions of the ancient Firbolg clans.

They were a quite friendly lot, for all their coarse look and rough manner. Cnu Deireoil had soon gotten over his initial fear and begun to entertain the warriors with his harp. Finn himself had been readily accepted as a friend to Caoilte and supplied with endless quantities of ale. At first he had only sipped at his huge mug, grimacing at the taste of the strong, dark liquid. He'd had almost none of such drink before this, disliking the taste. But here he couldn't refuse, for hospitality's sake. After the first mug or two, he had noticed the taste improving a great deal.

As the pungent ale had become easier to down, he had drunk ever more deeply. He had felt a sense of pride that he could hold his own with these hard-drinking warriors. After a time he had also become aware of a curious exuberance he had never experienced before.

His talk and laughter with the Firbolg men became more boisterous. He discovered them to be a truly grand lot of fellows, growing grander by the moment. He danced in line with them to Cnu Deireoil's jigs. He cried with them to the harp's soulful tunes. He listened with proper respect and awe to their tales of savage fights and dangerous hunts. He felt more and more a part of their close company, and the impact of this new sense of fellowship was great.

While Finn was thus getting to know his new comrades, Caoilte had been engaged in a long and intense conversation with the tribe's chieftain. Now the two approached the young warrior. The chieftain, a brawny man whose broad nose had been flattened more than once, clapped a heavy arm across Finn's shoulders.

Finn, who was just taking another drink of ale, swallowed a large mouthful and nearly choked.

"So, lad," the chieftain said heartily, "Coailte tells

me that he's taken on your training as a warrior. Well, you couldn't find a better man to do it, so you couldn't. He's one of the finest fighters in all Ireland. Why, he could have been a champion of the Fianna if he'd wished it!"

This remark seemed to disconcert Caoilte, for he spoke up hastily. "Now, Uncle, don't you be bragging on me to the lad. I'm a simple fighting man, making my living the best way I can."

"Are you?" the chieftain said. "Then why don't you come back? It's yourself should be the chieftain in your father's place, not me."

"No, Uncle!" Caoilte protested. "You're leader now. You've children who will follow you. I've no wish to be married and less to be settled. That's as it should be."

Finn listened to all this with great interest. He was suddenly learning a great deal about this new comrade of his.

"Well, it's good to have you back anyway, Nephew," the chieftain said. "You know you can stay as long as you wish with us." He turned back to Finn, giving him another friendly whack across the shoulders. "And you're welcome here too, boy!" He grabbed up a pitcher of ale and refilled the mug of his young guest past the rim. "There you are! Drink up now! This is a celebration!"

"I was hoping that while we were staying here, the lad might have a chance to be in some real fighting," Caoilte said.

"Well, if it's a fight you're seeking, you've come here at the right time," the chieftain said. "We've been having great troubles with the O'Domhnall tribe up on the valley rim."

"Aye," another warrior added emphatically. "They've attacked our herdsmen and our hunting parties by surprise. Three of our best fighters they've killed since spring."

"We've lost half our herds as well," added another. "By the winter there'll be nothing left to us."

Their tempers raised by ale and their combative natures, other warriors now began to recount recent offenses against them with a rage that escalated quickly with the tallying of each additional wrong. Finn listened to them with a growing indignation of his own. Just who were these evil people to be treating his comrade's tribesmen, his fine hosts, his new friends, in this terrible way?

"We've not been able to go against them sword-for-sword," the chieftain explained to Caoilte. "There were too many."

"Not now!" one of the warriors cried. "We've got Caoilte back with us. He's match for a score of them!"

This was greeted by shouts of agreement from the company. Caoilte leaned toward Finn to call over the tumult.

"What about it, lad? Will you join us? It'll be your first chance for a real fight."

"Of course I'll join you," Finn answered fiercely. He was fully aroused now by the power of the drink, his new feelings of comradeship, and the contagious battle fervor of those around him. "I'm ready for a fight! Let's be after those treacherous raiders now!"

"There's surely a bold lad," the chieftain announced. "After my own heart he is." He looked around at his warriors. "What do you say? Shall we strike now?"

The response was wild cheers and shrill battle cries. Swords were brandished high.

"Then let's do a bit of raiding ourselves," he announced. "The day is young. We'll feast on their cattle this very night!"

"Just give me my chance at them," Finn declared in a combative voice, drawing his own blade. "Just give me my chance!"

"Easy, lad," Caoilte cautioned him, a little surprised by the young man's unexpected savageness. "This is new to you, so I think you'd better just stay close to me."

With a gathering of weapons and a final, hearty drink, the raiding party was off. Propelled by the energy of their fired anger, they sped through the woods and up the open valley beyond. Most of this journey was only a blur to Finn, but it seemed very soon that he stood looking across a wide meadow lit by the afternoon sun.

The cattle were there, a fat herd, its numbers swelled by those stolen from Caoilte's people. And just above, a ring fort perched on the upper rim of the valley, its timber walls glowing in the slanting light like a golden crown.

The warriors of Caoilte's tribe made no delay in attacking. They used no strategy at all, but charged directly in at their chieftain's command. Their high, trilling war cries echoed across the valley in the still, warm afternoon.

"Remember to stay close!" Caoilte reminded Finn.

But the young man was not listening. Still in the throes of his own battle rage, aglow with the heat of ale in his veins, he charged right ahead with them, voicing— and quite well, he thought—a war cry of his own.

The few herdsmen with the cattle turned with a start to see this screaming horde rushing upon them. They leaped from their resting spots and pelted for the fortress, crying for help. The attacking warriors were soon about the cattle. Some of them began driving the animals away. But this process was barely under way when a clanging sound rose within the fortress.

"The alarm's being raised," the chieftain shouted with satisfaction. "They'll be coming now!"

To draw the enemy warriors out to fight was as important a part of the raid as securing the cattle, for only blood could make revenge complete. Caoilte's tribe was not to be disappointed, for in moments the gates flew open and a stream of warriors was pouring from the fortress.

It spread as it came down the slope toward them. The warriors about the herd scattered to meet it. The style of fighting was strictly a matter of single combats, and both sides began to choose out opponents as they closed.

Finn was in the forefront as the battle joined. With a great yell of triumph, he leaped before a pair of advancing enemies and struck a challenging pose. The two hardened, burly warriors eyed the youth quizzically.

"Come on! Come at me!" Finn exhorted. "I'll take both of you!"

The two looked at one another in surprise at his audacity. Who was this beardless madman? Then they shrugged and moved in upon him.

He handled them with what seemed to him marvelous skill, sweeping about them with a dazzling display of swordsmanship. Caoilte, he thought, would be quite proud of his skills. He swept here and there, parrying their rather clumsy attack, lunging and cutting and thrusting, his sword a whirl of light as he danced about, throwing them both on the defensive. It seemed the most exciting thing he had ever done.

He managed to wound one of the warriors, swinging a hard cut across his chest that caused the man to stumble and then go down, his life's blood welling from the deep slash.

It was on seeing this that Finn found things starting to go badly. The rush of exhilaration that had taken him this far was suddenly gone and he began to feel just a bit queasy. The landscape about him seemed to be pulsing and heaving. His head felt as if it were starting to whirl. He tried to fight on, but this second fellow was being quite stubborn, no longer intimidated by his artistry with the sword. In fact, the man was becoming quite a nuisance.

Finn was forced to the defensive, backing up, trying to hold his determined foe away, shaking his head to clear it and only finding that it made the spinning sensation worse. Oh, he was not well at all, he thought. He began to wish that this stubborn lout would go away and let him lie down, or possibly just kill him and put him out of his misery. He looked about and found that Caoilte and the other warriors were fully engaged themselves. He could get no help from them.

So groggy had he become that he wasn't even aware of the rock behind him until the backs of his legs came in contact with it and he was toppling. But his fall saved him, for he dropped beneath a massive stroke that would have cleaved his head to the chin.

Finn crashed heavily to the earth. The pain cleared

his head a bit and he looked up as the warrior drew back his arm to make another cut. Realizing his peril, Finn sat forward, driving desperately upward with his blade. It sank into the man's belly and he doubled up. His own sword swung past Finn and he crashed forward like a felled oak trunk, across the young man's legs.

Finn was still struggling to pull himself from beneath the pinning weight when Caoilte came up to him.

"Are you all right?" he asked, rolling the body away.

"Yes, yes!" Finn said irritably, wanting to hide his unaccountable weakness. But as he tried clumsily to pull himself to his feet, his gaze fell on a scene not very far away.

A warrior of Caoilte's tribe had tangled one hand in the long hair of a downed adversary. As Finn watched, he pulled the head up by the hair, stretching out the neck, and then with three hard whacks of his sword severed it from the body.

That was too much for the young warrior. His stomach seemed to turn itself inside out. He turned away and was very, very ill.

Alarmed by his condition, Caoilte moved to him, throwing a supporting arm about his shoulders.

"Finn, what's wrong with you?"

"I—I don't know," Finn said shakily. "What about the battle?"

"It's ended," the dark warrior said. "We've won!"

Finn managed to lift his head and look about. The field was littered with corpses, drenched in blood. The few enemy wounded were being dispatched with ruthless efficiency. The survivors were retreating to their fortress, leaving their herd to its new owners.

The enemy dead were being systematically deprived of their heads by their victors, the grotesque objects piled neatly in a great cairn, their open eyes staring out in various directions, their jaws hanging open.

Finn felt his gorge rising again, but after some shuddering and gagging, managed to control it.

"The—the heads!" he managed to choke out. And

then a darkness he couldn't overcome swept through him, flooding over his mind. He struggled to stay above its surface, but its waves poured over him and he sank into the depths.

He was aware of being carried and being dumped down upon a soft surface. His eyes were open, squinting against the light. He was looking up at the thatched framework of a ceiling. Then two heads came into view close above him, peering down. Not severed heads, but those of two living beings he knew well: Caoilte and Cnu Deireoil.

The little harper, who had wisely decided not to accompany the raiders, looked distressed at the condition of his young friend.

"By Danu!" he exclaimed. "Is the lad badly hurt?"

"He's not hurt at all," the dark warrior assured him. "Just had a bit too much to drink is all. Fell down in the middle of a fight and nearly got himself killed."

"Drunk?" said Cnu Deireoil. "But how—" He stopped, then laughed in realization. "It couldn't be that in this strange land you come from you never did any drinking before, could it now?" he asked Finn.

Finn managed a shake of the head, though it caused a hard pounding in his brain, as if his heart were beating within his skull.

"It's my own fault," said Caoilte. "I should have seen the way he was. But I didn't think of it. Lad, why did you do it?"

"The others were doing it," Finn managed to get out, though his tongue felt as if it had sprouted fur. "So I thought . . . well, it seemed so easy. Like drinking water for them. Caoilte, how can they do it?"

"They have been drinking since they were old enough to hold a cup. Don't feel too badly. You'll learn to do it, too, with practice."

At that moment, Finn was sure that it was something he would never do again. He moaned softly, then realized that there were other moans coming from around him, and there was the sound of crying as well. With an effort he turned his head. Around him, on pallets of straw like his own, lay a dozen other men. But their agony was the result of wounds.

He had not considered the aftermath of a fight before. Now he saw clearly the effect of weapons whose purpose was to puncture, tear, or cut, weapons that maimed an enemy more often than they killed outright. The women and the healer of the tribe now worked feverishly to bind gashes, tie off bleeding stumps, plug gaping holes. Other women sat on their heels by dead or dying men, rocking and keening softly, sorrowfully.

"Caoilte, it's terrible!" Finn said, aghast. "All these men! Just for a few cows!"

"It's the honor of the tribe they were fighting for," the warrior told him. "Without that, they would have no life at all."

Finn recalled how eagerly they, and himself as well, had gone off on their raid, seeking revenge. Could he ever become accustomed to battle, with such images of the carnage it created?

The chieftain of the tribe approached them, beaming at his victory, so jolly and high-spirited that Finn felt a resentment for him.

"A good fight that was!" the man announced heartily. "They'll not be seeking to raid us again." He beamed at Finn. "And you were a help in it, lad, so you were! You took two of their best warriors alone, and it was a good bit of sword work for a whelp. I've got your trophies for you!"

He raised his hands. From each a dripping, leering head hung by its long hair.

Finn looked away and gulped. "No . . . no! I don't want them!"

The chieftain looked hurt. "But they're yours, lad, fair and proper!"

"It's the custom, Finn," Caoilte told him, puzzled by his reaction. "Your first trophies. Don't you want them?"

"I . . ." Finn began weakly. Then he pulled himself together. He couldn't insult his hosts no matter what his feelings. "I'm honored to have them," he said, "but I'm not one of your tribe. I think that these . . . trophies belong with the rest."

The chief was mollified. "A good idea, lad," he agreed. "Maybe they should go with the lot. But if you change your mind, you just let me know."

He moved off to place the two heads in the gruesome collection.

"What do they do that for?" Finn asked Caoilte.

"A very old belief," the warrior explained. "The head is the seat of man's power. Taking a head proves a victor's greater skill. Some collect the heads of rival chieftains and champions. Some keep the brains, too, mixing them with mud to make a hard stone ball."

"Enough," Finn groaned, his stomach near rebellion again.

A girl pushed Caoilte aside then and came up to the bed. Her expression was stern and her voice scolding.

"What are you doing keeping this poor lad in talk when he must be tended to? Now move aside and let me see to him."

She knelt down by the pallet to examine him. But as she saw his face closely for the first time, her expression changed. The sternness melted away and a light of interest filled her eyes.

"Oh!" she said with pleased surprise. "You're very . . . young!"

"He's not really hurt, you know," Caoilte pointed out.

"I'll be the one to tell that," she snapped back at him. "Just you two get away!" She looked back at Finn, her tone softening again. "I'll see to him myself."

Caoilte looked at Cnu Deireoil. The little man gave a broad wink and they exchanged a knowing grin.

"Well, then, I suppose it's safe to leave him in your hands," Caoilte said dryly. He patted Finn's shoulder. "Good luck on your recovery, lad. Enjoy it."

As his comrades moved away, Finn looked up into the girl's face, so close to his. Even in his state, he was aware of her pleasant look. She was quite as young and as comely of feature as Fionnuala, but in a much different way. She was darker, with large hazel eyes, a wide, sensuous mouth, and curling waves of unbound raven hair. And there was a look in those eyes that he found familiar.

She laid a hand lightly upon his breast. She placed the other upon his brow and began to stroke it gently.

"Now," she said gently, "you try to relax. We'll see what we can do to make you feel better."

He wasn't sure just how much he was going to be able to relax, but he was certain that he was already feeling much better.

Chapter Sixteen

INTO CARRAIGHE

"Finn!"

The small leather-sided boat drifted across the placid surface of the lake, apparently empty. But at the shout, the fair-haired head of the young man appeared, popping up above the side.

He peered about him, finally noting Caoilte Mac-Ronan on the edge of the crannog, waving to him.

"Caoilte!" he called back, sounding a little disconcerted. "What is it you want?"

"I've got to speak to you, Finn," he answered. Then with some curiosity, he added, "Just what is it you're doing out there?"

A second head now popped up by the first, this one distinguished by a billowing mass of shining black hair.

"I—ah—" Finn stammered, his pale face growing flushed.

"Never mind explaining," Caoilte said heavily. "Just get yourself in here, and quickly!"

Finn obeyed with great alacrity. He sat up—almost throwing the girl out of the boat—and took up the paddle. With powerful strokes he propelled the little craft toward the fort while his companion busily readjusted her clothes.

As the curragh grounded beside the fort's wall, Finn leaped out and then lifted the girl onto the shore. She looked flushed, too, Caoilte noted, though not from embarrassment. And both appeared to be out of breath.

"I think it's time you were getting back to your home," he told the girl in a lightly scolding way. "Likely you're needed there, and I've got to talk to Finn. So get along with you."

"All right," she said. She flashed the young man a brilliant smile. "But I'll see you again later!"

With that promise, she scampered away across the rocky shore, Finn watching her appreciatively until she disappeared around the crannog wall.

"There's a fine girl," he said sincerely.

"She is that. She is also my cousin," Caoilte said soberly.

"I don't understand you, Caoilte," Finn said in puzzlement. Then he noted an unusual grimness in his friend's expression. "What is it? What's wrong?"

"Finn, we have to leave here," the dark warrior told him bluntly.

"Leave here?" Finn said, not believing he had heard rightly. "Why?"

"One of my uncle's sons has just returned. He was at a fair in Luminech only a few days ago. He heard there that Conn, the high king himself, has declared you, me, and our little harper as outlaws. Every man of Ireland has been charged to look for us."

"Outlaws!" exclaimed Finn. "How could he do that?"

"By Brehon Law. We've killed men of the Fianna. Now our own lives are forfeit in exchange. We can't stay here any longer. My people would protect us, but we would be bringing great danger upon them. If we were discovered here—"

135

"I know, Caoilte," Finn said unhappily. "And it's because of me that all this has happened. Of course we'll leave here."

He regretted leaving the crannog. He had come to know a wonderful sense of home here, of belonging to a family, of having friends. They had taught him much in the past score or so days. He looked at the walls of the secure little island fortress and felt a pain like that when he had parted from Liath and Bodhmall.

"It will be hard to leave here, Caoilte," he said. "I have become very close to your people."

"I noticed that just now," the warrior said in a teasing way. "Very close indeed."

"What do you mean by that?" Finn asked innocently.

"I mean that it's a good thing that we'll be leaving here, or you'd likely have been in several duels before long."

"Duels?" Finn repeated, still not comprehending. "Why?"

"That young maiden—I hope—that you've shown such interest in lately is the object of a frenzied courting dance by several young bucks of my tribe. They've not taken well to your so easily cutting them out. Much more of it, and they would have been making challenges to you. Didn't you notice?"

Finn shrugged, completely at a loss. "I may have noticed some lads being short with me," he answered honestly, "but, Caoilte, I've had nothing like this happen before! I didn't know!"

"Your great, galloping ignorance is a constant amazement to me," Caoilte said, shaking his head. "I hope you come to understand women soon, or they'll likely bring your end someday."

"But what can we do now?" Finn asked, ignoring the sarcasm. "If every man in Ireland might now be seeking us, there's nowhere we can be safe."

"There may be one place," the warrior said. "One place where even the power of the mighty Fianna doesn't reach."

* * *

"There it is, lad," Caoilte announced, pointing ahead. "Corca Dhuibhne it's called. And in all of Ireland you'll find no place more wild of spirit or so free of will as here."

It looked to Finn as if the mountain they now stood upon had melted, flowing outward from its base, the waves of it hardening when they had reached the sea. From beneath his feet the land swept down in smooth, grass-covered slopes. To the north it rolled up again in a pair of rounded hills. Between them could be seen a wide area of lowland that spread out like a fan into a large bay. The bay's far side was bounded by a line of peaked hills, made blue-gray by distance. At its end, two of the more independent of the hills seemed to have detached themselves and crept out further into the sea, forming tiny islands. To the west of Finn, a long spur—a serpent's head of land with a protruding backbone of rock—thrust sharply out into the water, creating a sharp contrast with the soft lands to the west.

It had been a rugged journey here, far into the west of the territory that Caoilte had said was called Carraighe. But the journey had been an enthralling one for Finn. They had climbed through hills where lakes were set like glistening jewels in a great crown and slopes were vibrant with brightly colored flowers. They had skirted the long mountain range of Slieve Mish and followed the narrow way that led along the coast of the peninsula, then mounted abruptly to the Conair Pass across high Croaghskearda.

It was there, at the top of the pass, that the three travelers stood now, looking upon the scene spread below.

The sea itself was what had fascinated Finn most of all he had seen in his traveling. He was stimulated by the changing nature of its surface, by its clean, sharp scent, and by the tremendous power of its crashing waves. But the seemingly limitless expanse of it was a bit terrifying too. It made him feel uncomfortably small and weak.

"What else is there, beyond?" he asked his companions, staring toward the curve of the western horizon.

"Nothing else, lad," Caoilte said. "It's the last of Ireland and the rim of the world you're seeing now, and nothing beyond."

"Except for the Blessed Isles," the little Nut corrected.

Caoilte gave a short, scornful laugh. "Oh, aye. Far Tir-na-nog, if you've a mind to believe in such. But there's no sanctuary for the likes of us there. Here's the only land of safety we can believe in now. Come along. No reason to be wasting more time."

They urged their mounts ahead, along the road that wove its way down the mountain flank onto the plains below. It took them toward the south, between the two hills, onto the broad shorelands beyond. Ahead of them a harbor came into view. Its triangle of water was enclosed by fingers of land, the access to it from the bay a narrow opening between their tips. At the innermost point of the harbor was a village, its several dozen structures spread along the water's edge.

The harbor, Caoilte explained to Finn, was a fine place for ships to shelter, and there was clear proof of this in the score of craft pulled in to shore. Most were large, often with more than one mast. The shapes of them were widely varied, some with exotic decoration and elaborately painted hulls. One was long and sleek and seemed formed of polished iron. It reminded Finn of a spear point.

The town, Finn realized as they approached, was of an impressive size, and quite different in nature from those he had seen before. It was undefended, having no rath or walls. Its buildings were clustered tightly together along several avenues paralleling or running to the water. The buildings were largely made of stone, not wood. Square, rough-hewn gray blocks stacked neatly together formed the outer shells and flat slabs of green-gray slate roofed many instead of thatch. The shapes were various, some larger structures being square. A number of smaller buildings—individual dwellings, Caoilte said—were simply cones of piled rock.

The trio rode in, passing along a central street between the rows of buildings. Most of the inhabitants they passed were men in simple trousers and bulky sweaters of yellow wool. They were lean and sinewy of figure, their faces long and large-featured and weathered. They only glanced up incuriously as the newcomers rode by.

"Fishermen mostly," Caoilte explained. "They and the traders are the only ones who really live in the town. The rest we'll find here have no real homes."

"What do you mean?" Finn asked.

"Corca Dhuibhne is one of the busiest landing places in Ireland!" he answered. "Ships visit here from Alban, Espan, and even farther, come to trade or sell off contraband or even bring raiders here. You'll see some of the worst thieves and pirates of the world, lad. And outlaws, too, like ourselves. Oh, it's a most fitting place for us now!"

"Why do they all come here?" Finn wanted to know.

"Because the bay is a safe landing spot, and because they know they're protected by Mogh Nuadat, the chieftain of this territory. He's a ruthless man, it's said, and even great Conn of the Hundred Battles hasn't shown the stomach to come to this rough little end of land and challenge him."

They were just passing a large structure, square and featureless. But a number of men were hanging about its wide door and a sound of loud talk and laughter came from within. Caoilte reined in and the others stopped beside him.

"We've got to find ourselves some kind of place here," he told them. "This public house will be a good spot to start the searching. I can talk to the men and pick up word of anyone who might take us into service."

He climbed from his horse and tied it to a post. The other two followed, though with less eagerness, for the men about the door were of very rough aspect and scrutinized the newcomers with suspicious eyes.

Caoilte led the way through them, casually shoving one out of the doorway, and the three entered the house. It was crowded with men who sat at plank tables or stood about. They were a varied lot in looks and costume. Many were of types Finn had not seen before in Ireland. Some were very fair, with golden hair that rivaled even his own. Others were dark, with skin more swarthy than the Firbolgs, and smooth ebony hair. The dress of some was strange to Finn as well, usually colorful, sometimes gaudy. There were rich furs and fine skins, cloth of many textures and colors trimmed with gold and silver. Lavish jewelry winked everywhere, bracelets at wrists and elbows, torcs and necklaces about throats, brooches fastening cloak and vest, and all manner of baubles woven into the elaborate hairstyles. Intricately worked scabbards often set with jewels encased the blades of swords and daggers with ornamented hilts, and precious metals studded belts and boots and harnesses.

The impression created by all this on the still rather unsophisticated Finn was so wonderfully textured, so exotic, so complex that he had great difficulty even absorbing it. He was content simply to let Caoilte lead for now. The Little Nut followed as well, but with great apprehension, peering about him at the peculiar crowd.

They worked their way into the room, edging between tables and around knots of men as MacRonan sought a place for them to sit. But Finn stumbled over a stray foot and staggered into a group at one table. As he was opening his mouth to apologize, one of those he had landed heavily against leaped up and turned upon him with a snarl.

The young man recoiled from the face that was thrust toward his own. It was not human, save in its general features. Its eyes popped froglike from its squat head. Its nose was two pulsing nostrils and its mouth a wide, drooping slit.

"Are you looking for a fight, boy?" it asked in a guttural voice, revealing small, sharply pointed teeth.

"Just a drink," Coailte said quickly, coming up beside Finn and speaking in a calming tone. "We want no trouble here."

The being snorted and then turned away, sitting back down at its table. Finn watched it, realizing with revulsion that the others seated with it were as gro-

tesque, some even worse. The features of all were
horribly deformed in different ways. Many looked
reptilian, but the most awful were nightmare distor-
tions of a normal human face, with eyes, mouths, noses
missing or askew, heads flattened or bloated or deeply
grooved across the skull. A few wore scarves about their
features, masking everything but their eyes. What they
masked, Finn didn't want to contemplate.

"That was a near one, lad," Caoilte said with relief
as he pulled the stunned Finn away. "They are a touchy
lot."

"What are they?" Finn asked, still looking back.

"Fomor," the warrior told him. "Pirates mostly.
They raid the coasts or other ships and sell their goods
here."

"Why do they look like that? Are they men?"

Caoilte shrugged. "No one knows. They're always
roving. They seem to have no home. There are some
ancient tales that they once ruled Ireland, but I've little
belief in them."

He found them a place at a table and they took
seats. The primary occupation here seemed to be drinking, and Caoilte ordered ale for them from a harried
serving man.

"I know about the Formor," Cnu Deireoil put in.
"They did control Ireland once. It was the Tuatha de
Danaan who destroyed them."

"So you say," the dark warrior replied in a disbelieving tone. "Who knows how much of those old tales
are true? The only truth I know is one I can see before
me and jab with my sword."

"Is that so?" the harper shot back, sounding annoyed. "Well, I'm saying that those old tales are true,
and I know there are a good many other things that
might surprise you. You don't know everything, Caoilte
MacRonan!"

"Maybe," the warrior admitted, eyeing the little
man thoughtfully.

The mugs of ale were plumped down before them
then by the rushed serving man.

"No free drinks here," Caoilte said, tossing the

man a coin. He lifted the mug, sipped the ale, and grimaced. "Whoo! But they should be paying us to drink this muck."

Finn sipped at his own cautiously. He'd become more accustomed to consuming ale during his sojourn with the Firbolgs, but that wasn't enough to prepare him for this thick, acrid, muddy liquid. He set it down.

A gangly, hawk-beaked man pushed up through the crowd behind Caoilte and slapped a hand onto the warrior's shoulder.

"MacRonan!" he exclaimed, grinning. "Is it you? Still alive?"

Caoilte looked up at the man and broke into a smile of delight himself. "Seainin O'Conchúir! How long has it been?"

"Since we served that Ithian chieftain, MacNiad. What a time that was, fighting those bloody Ernaan! But what is it you're doing here?"

"Looking for a place, as always. Do you know of anything about here?"

"It's your good fortune, meeting me," the other said. "I'm in Nuadat's household companies now. He's always looking for good men."

"How about this lad?" Caoilte asked, nodding at Finn. "He's a good fighter, I'll give my word on that."

"If he's a comrade of yours, that's enough for me. We'll find him a place as well." He cast a doubtful eye on the Little Nut. "I'm not certain we can do anything for your other companion, though."

"Don't be worrying about me," Cnu Deireoil assured the man. "I'm a harper. Just you get me into Nuadat's hall and I'll have a place for myself," he said, grinning, "I'm certain of that."

O'Conchúir shrugged. "If you say it's so, you can come along. I'll take you up to the dun. The captain of the chieftain's companies will see to you."

The four left the public house, took their horses, and rode out of the village, along a path that led out along one of the harbor's sheltering points of land. The ground rose steadily to the tip of the point, which was several hundred feet above the bay. Finn examined the fortress as they approached. It perched precariously on the very edge of a sheer drop, looking very tiny in comparison to the immense cliff face below. It seemed to be almost a part of the cliff itself with its walls of the same gray stone.

A three-storied keep dominated the great dun, and was surrounded by several smaller structures. These were defended on the landward side by three curving walls of stone a spear's throw apart. The only way to reach the fortress was through a series of staggered gates.

O'Conchúir led them through the three gates under the watchful eyes of some two score heavily armed guards. Once inside the yard, he directed them to a large stable against the inner wall where grooms took their horses.

They had dismounted and started across the yard to the keep when another group of horsemen came through the inner gate. It comprised a man and a woman surrounded by a tight ring of warriors. Finn looked at the pair with great curiosity.

The man was quite short and very squat of build, his body hard and compact. His head was broad, with a low brow and almost no chin. Small eyes were set far to either side of a short, thick nose, and the mouth was wide and thin, like a scar across the lower face. The woman riding close beside him was, in contrast, tall and slim and elegant. Her beauty was striking, her skin white, her neatly plaited hair a shimmer.

She seemed to sense the young man's gaze and looked toward him. Their eyes met, and then they locked together. He felt a strange shock. She started as if struck, her own eyes widening.

The man beside her noted her reaction and turned to follow her gaze. He saw the rapt young Finn, and his eyes narrowed in annoyance. He slapped the woman's horse across the rump, urging it ahead at a trot. The action caused her to turn back, breaking the contact with Finn. He watched the company ride into the stable, out of sight.

"Who was that?" Finn asked, still feeling the odd sensation.

"That's our chieftain himself, Mogh Nuadat, and his wife!" O'Conchúir supplied. "You're blessed to be seeing her, so you are. It's seldom she leaves the keep."

"What is her name?"

"Well, you saw her. You can almost guess it from that. She's the smooth-skinned one for certain, that she is. Muirne is her name."

Chapter Seventeen

REUNION

"I've got to learn more about her," Finn said to his friends.

The three were perched atop the fortress cliff on the seaward side, watching a crimson sun fire a bank of clouds in its final, glorious act before sinking behind the ocean's rim. It had become a daily ritual for them to gather together here once their own duties were completed. They could be alone and talk freely.

"That's one woman you shouldn't be thinking about at all," Caoilte told him in a scolding tone. "She is the wife of Nuadat, and he is far too dangerous for you to be playing about with."

Finn had no doubts about the toughness or ruthlessness of Nuadat's nature. In the days he had been in the chieftain's company he had learned much about the man. Nuadat had gathered to him a massive force of hardened warriors, many of them outlaws, criminals, mercenaries—desperate men with nothing to lose and willing to sacrifice for the man who had given them a place.

With this power, he kept an iron grip upon his territories, held challengers from the rest of Ireland at bay, and exacted heavy tribute from the brigands who used his harbors for their landings. But though harsh and uncompromising, he was known to be a fair and honest man as well. His sword was always ready to protect his people, and he was a champion of their right to freedom. It was rumored that he one day planned to control all Munster province, breaking the power of the dreaded Ernaan tribe, who had, with the support of the high-king of Ireland, long oppressed the Ithian and Eberian races there.

"I know this seems madness to you," Finn said in an urgent way, trying to make them understand. "Maybe it is. I only know I can't do anything about it. Something is driving me to know more. There's a part of my mind that's gnawing at the rest. I see her face in dreams. I hear her voice—"

"Her voice?" Caoilte said, breaking in. "And when have you heard that before?"

"I—I haven't," Finn admitted, clearly bewildered by this himself. "But I know it's her voice. I hear it singing faintly, as if she's far away. The sound of it wakes me. I've got to know why." He turned to Cnu Deireoil. "Please help me. Have you learned anything about her?"

The Little Nut had, as expected, easily obtained a position as entertainer at the dun. And as the common warriors were not included in the chieftain's nightly feasts, he was the only one who had seen much of Nuadat or his wife.

"I've kept close watch on her, as I promised," he told Finn, "but there's little to find out, I'm afraid. She's well guarded, and she stays in her own apartments high in the keep most of the time. When she does appear, he's beside her and as protective as a hungry wolf on its kill."

"Is he cruel to her?" Finn demanded with concern.

145

"No, no!" the harper assured him. "He's very gentle toward her always! Very loving."

"But couldn't anyone in his court tell you about her?" Finn asked more desperately.

Cnu Deireoil shook his head. "That's all a mystery, lad. I even used my harp's charms to 'persuade' the folk to talk, but they knew nothing of her past or her family." He paused, then added in a thoughtful way, "Though I've had a strange feeling about her myself. There is something more to her. An aura about her, almost. As if—" He stopped abruptly and shook his head, saying quickly, "No, no! Never mind. I just can't tell you anything, lad. I'm sorry."

"So am I," Finn said. "It means there's only one way left to me. I have to speak to her."

"Speak to her?" Caoilte repeated, aghast. "Have you seen the warriors he has guarding her? Why, they won't even let you get close to that upper level of the keep."

Finn gazed up speculatively toward the structure. Its seaward side rose directly at the cliff's edge, the outer wall seeming to grow directly upward from the sheer rock face beneath. In its upper level, two small windows faced the ocean. He could picture her up there, standing at one of them right now, watching the blazing sunset as they were.

Caoilte followed the young man's meditative gaze and guessed at what he was thinking. He took Finn's shoulder and pulled him around to catch his eye with a threatening look.

"See here, my lad," he said sharply, "you forget about that woman. If you make one of your rash moves here, there'll be no one to save you. Do you understand? No one!"

"I understand," Finn told him. But the strange impulse that had claimed him immediately drew his longing gaze back toward the grim stone tower.

The loose stone gave way under the pressure of his foot, crashing down the cliff face in its long fall to the sea. Finn dropped abruptly, his weight nearly jerking him from his precarious handhold upon two other projecting bits of wall.

He tried not to panic, hanging still, then cautiously feeling about first with his left foot and then his right until he found another toehold that seemed firm.

The great trick, he reminded himself again, was not to look down. He had tried that once, and the sight of those waves crashing against the cliff base so far below had caused an unpleasant vertigo. Now he looked only at the wall before his eyes, with an occasional glance upward to gauge the distance to his goal: a small window in the top level of the keep.

This was, in any event, the only way he could get to Nuadat's wife. The cliff-side wall of the keep was considered inaccessible and went unguarded. It was also invisible to anyone within the dun. Finn had considered and planned his move for days, while the terrible impulse in him had grown steadily stronger, tightening upon his insides like a fist. Finally, when the chieftain had ridden out with a party of men on some errand of state, leaving his wife alone in her high sanctuary, the young man had decided to act.

The sea wind hauled at him as he went higher, the chill, damp sting of it driving through him. He felt very exposed here, stripped to just his linen tunic for the climb, his cloak, his weapons, and his sandals hidden in the rocks at the keep's base. But as his toes, scraped raw by the rough stone, worked their way into another small gap in the blocks, he felt very glad he'd brought no encumbrances.

The window was finally in reach. His hands gripped its stone still and he pulled himself slowly up to peep over it's edge into the room beyond.

He lowered himself quickly back. Not far away, the very woman he had come to see paced the floor with a restless stride.

He considered quickly. The rest of the room had been empty. She was alone. There was no reason to hesitate. He took a deep breath to overcome the violent pounding of his heart, pulled himself up again, and climbed through the window.

Her back was to him, and his entrance made no sound, but something warned her, for she spun suddenly around, her expression startled as she saw him.

"It's all right, my lady," he said soothingly, raising a hand in a gesture of friendship. "I mean no harm to you. I only want to talk."

He had rather expected that this feeble explanation would be ignored by her and that she would run screaming for the guards. But instead, her look of alarm faded, replaced by an expression of growing wonder as she stared at him fixedly.

"What do you want?" she asked in bewilderment.

The voice was one that he knew well, one that he had known would be hers. It was the voice that had haunted his dreams.

"I know you," he said earnestly. "At least, I feel I must know you. I've heard your voice before. I've seen your face. But that is impossible! Please listen. Some force that I don't understand has drawn me to you. If I don't discover why, I'll not have peace."

"This cannot be," she said with distress, shaking her head. "No! This is some awful dream. You cannot be . . . Demna!"

Hearing the name he had not used since leaving Slieve Bladhma was a shock to Finn.

"How did you know?" he blurted out.

A sigh welled up from deep within her and seemed to draw away her strength. Her eyes closed and she swayed forward in a faint. He swooped forward and caught her, scooping up the slender form in his arms easily. She was so frail to him! He carried her to a couch and laid her gently down, sitting beside her, watching her apprehensively. In a few moments she sighed again and the eyes fluttered open. The pale, bright eyes fixed searchingly on his.

"Oh, Demna," she said, "I have hoped so long for this. I thought it would never come. I thought that I would never see you again."

"What do you mean?" he asked beseechingly. "Please tell me who you are."

For answer she first drew down the long plait of his hair, laying it against her own unbound flow. The fair, fine strands mingled, were lost amongst one another, became a single stream of white-gold.

"This is the symbol of our link," she said. "This is the proof of the blood of my body that flows in you. The name Demna is the one that I gave you, son of Cumhal. I am your mother."

Mogh Nuadat galloped into the yard of his fortress at the head of his company. Caoilte, crossing the yard toward the quarters of the household troops, paused as they went by then continued on. But he stopped again as he saw the Little Nut hurrying toward him from the keep.

"What's wrong?" he asked, noting an anxious expression on the harper's face.

"The chieftain is back early," Cnu Deireoil replied. "It made me start to thinking. Finn was asking me about his going away only this morning. I've seen nothing of him since. Have you?"

"No," the other told him. "I was looking for him myself. It's very strange the way he disappeared. I wondered—"

And then the realization struck him. His gaze flew to the upper windows of the keep.

"My very own thoughts," the little man said. "What shall we do?"

"There's very little we can do now," Caoilte answered regretfully. For the chieftain and his guard were already moving toward the keep. "But I did warn him that there'd be no help this time!"

"You did that!" Cnu Deireoil agreed. "And very right you were too." Then, after a pause, he added, "So, how shall we go about it?"

"You see if you can delay Nuadat," Caoilte said, sighing. "I'll find some way to warn Finn."

Up in the keep, meantime, Finn was in deep conversation with his mother, unaware of his danger.

"Do you understand that there seemed to be no choice for me if you were to survive?" Muirne was asking in an imploring way. "It has been my greatest fear that you would hate me for leaving you. You must believe that I would never have done so if there had been a way to act freely."

"Yes, Mother," he said soothingly, laying a hand upon hers. "As strange as this is to me, I think that I always knew somehow that you were here, that something of you was in me. I know who it was who came to me and sang to me those years ago. Your love came to me in that song, and I've no question of it now."

Tears of relief and joy filled her eyes. "My son!" she said, sitting up to throw her arms about him and hug him close. "My Demna! I've waited so long to hold you, to talk to you, to hear your voice."

"I want to know everything that's happened, Mother. All those years—"

"I know," she said. "And I want to know about your life, and how you've come to be here. There is so much to speak of."

A loud sound startled them both. Finn jerked about to see a fist-sized stone rebound from the inner wall of the apartment and drop onto the floor.

He looked around for the source of the missile and saw a second sail in through a window, strike the wall, and drop down beside the first.

"What's happening?" he asked, running to the window. He was looking down from one side of the keep onto the storage sheds within the wall. Atop one now stood Caoilte, fitting a stone into the pouch of a thong sling.

With it ready for firing again, he swung his arm back for the throw, glanced up toward the window to set his aim, then stopped, seeing Finn. Then he began pointing in a rather emphatic way toward the front of the keep.

Finn wasted no time in shifting to a window on that side. He peered down and then quickly pulled back out of sight. Directly below him, Nuadat himself stood with his guard, listening to a tune from Cnu Deireoil.

"It is Mogh Nuadat," he told his mother. "He's come back earlier than I'd supposed."

"My husband?" she said in alarm. "But he mustn't discover you. I've kept your secret all these years. No one must find out now. You have to leave!"

"I can't just leave," he protested. "We have to talk again!"

"Yes, yes!" she urgently agreed. "I'll find some way that no one will suspect. But for now, please go, for your own sake!"

He obeyed her, leaving the way he had come in.

"Will you be safe?" she asked in concern as he slipped over the sill.

"Don't worry," he assured her. "I made it up, didn't I?" Then he was gone.

He made his way back down and across the wall, Muirne watching anxiously from above until he had safely reached the cliff edge. There he found Caoilte MacRonan waiting, frowning in disapproval.

"Don't scold me, Caoilte," Finn said as the other opened his mouth. "It's not what you're thinking. It's my own mother up there."

"Your mother?" the warrior echoed in surprise. "But how?"

"I'll explain it to you later," Finn answered, retrieving his clothes and weapons from a hollow in the rocks and quickly donning them. "We'd best be away from here now!"

They went back around the keep, reaching the front in time to see Mogh Nuadat wave the Little Nut away and stride into the building.

Cnu Deireoil looked after him in dismay, but when Caoilte called to him and he turned to see the two, his expression turned to one of great relief.

"Thank Danu!" he exclaimed. "I could only hold him for so long. He's a very strong-willed man, he is!"

"You've done well enough," Caoilte told him. "We've managed to save our lad again." He looked at

151

Finn. "And you come right along with us. You've got some explaining to do!"

The three went off seeking a private spot to talk. They were unaware of a searching gaze upon them. None realized that Caoilte's peculiar antics to warn Finn had attracted the notice of the captain of the household companies. That efficient and suspicious personage had followed the dark warrior, and from a vantage point along the cliff he had observed the young man's rapid descent from the high window of the keep.

He knew well enough whose apartments lay behind that opening, and he knew—like it or not—that it was his duty to carry his discovery to his chieftain.

He was certainly glad that he would not be wearing the cloak of Finn or his two friends after Nuadat knew of this. No man before who had even dared to smile upon the beautiful Muirne had ever survived.

Chapter Eighteen

REVELATION

A ship cut smoothly across the harbor under the powerful urgings of two-score long oars. It was a slender, graceful craft with a gilded figurehead of a serpent sweeping up at its prow and rows of bright shields hung along its sides.

"Lochlanders," Muirne commented. "Off on another raid, or heading back to their frozen home."

From the end of the inner battlements she and Finn watched the ship approaching the harbor mouth. The rest of her escorting guards—always with her when she left the keep, were waiting at a discreet distance, at her command.

"I've seen many ships sail away from here in these past years," she said wistfully. "Often I've imagined myself sailing away with them, seeing far lands, free to go anywhere I wished."

"I hate to think of your being a prisoner here all of this time," he said.

"There was little choice," she said, "and it was my own. I knew the sons of Morna would scour Ireland for me. This seemed the safest place to come, as it was for you. I lived always with the fear that they might yet find me and somehow discover that you were still alive!"

"It's for me you had to make that sacrifice, Mother," he said regretfully. "I'm sorry."

"Don't be!" she told him, putting her hand upon his arm. "It was something I did for my love of you and of Cumhal. There's nothing to be regretted in that. And it's not a bad life I've had here."

"Are you happy then with Mogh Nuadat?" he asked, feeling a special need for assurance in this.

"Oh yes," she said emphatically. "He may seem a hard man, but he has been loving to me and he has kept me safe. He's asked no questions of me, knowing only that I wanted to be hidden. In return I have been a faithful wife to him, and I have learned to feel very deeply for him. So we are content."

He nodded, not certain what else he should say. It was as if this story of her life—her hardships escaping alone across Ireland so long before, her meeting with the chieftain Mogh Nuadat—was a tale told of legendary folk. He felt a strong sense of attachment for his mother, but as strong a sense of detachment from her life.

The Lochlander ship was through the narrow gap now, onto the high sea. It raised a great square sail of red and white stripes and glided away, like a swan, across the waves. Finn and his mother turned away and started walking along the wall, back toward the waiting guards.

"I'm glad to find that you were raised well," she

told him. "I've often wondered if, when I saw you again, you would be like Bodhmall: lean and hard and grim."

He smiled. "She did try to make me so. But Liath managed to save me from her a bit."

"Ah, dear Liath," she said, smiling, too, but with some sadness, as she thought of the woman. "But, if it could only have been my own hands guiding you."

"I think your spirit was there with me, too," he said in a comforting way.

"There's much of your father about you," she said, a mother's pride ringing in her voice. "It's a fine, strong, handsome man that you've become." She turned suddenly away then, dropping down on the edge of the stone wall. "But there is a great sadness in me to see you in a warrior's trappings. I had hoped—I had prayed to Danu herself—that Bodhmall's plan would fail."

He moved to her, put a hand upon the slender shoulder. "There was no other way," he said. "I am the son of Cumhal. It must be that I take his place and see his vengeance done."

"You might be destroyed!" she said in anguish, looking up at him. "The ones against you are too strong! The clan of Morna does not dare to let you return, not when they control all the Fians of Ireland now. Think of that, my only son. Stay here. Stay safe with me!"

"No, Mother," he said earnestly. "I've the training of a warrior now. Soon I'll be ready to seek out my father's clansmen, to learn the ways of the Fianna."

"I see," she said with resignation, realizing she could not sway him. "You have your father's stubbornness as well, my son. If you have decided on that fate, it's clear that I must help you if I'll see you survive. Bodhmall has won."

"Help me?" asked Finn. "What do you mean?"

"Over the years I have used what means I could to find the remnants of the Clan na Baiscne," she told him. "I know where they and your uncle Crimall are. He is the one who must teach you of the Fianna and help you challenge the sons of Morna for your father's place. When you are ready, I will tell you where to seek him out."

Finn understood the sacrifice his mother was making to give this aid to him. He took up both her hands and held them tightly in his.

From the window of his apartment in the keep, Mogh Nuadat watched the pair with a baleful glare. Then, unable to watch any longer, he jerked about, slamming a heavy fist onto the table.

His blow made the gold playing pieces on the *fidchell* board jump. Doncha Kavanagh, his gray-haired advisor, had been contemplating a move. At the angry gesture he jumped himself, looking up at his chieftain.

"Mogh, what is plaguing you?"

"Help me, Doncha," Nuadat said in an imploring way. "Tell me what I can do about my wife and this young warrior."

This sudden appeal for help was no real surprise to the canny old advisor. He was well aware of the attention Muirne was paying to the handsome lad, and of his chieftain's increasingly gloomy mood. His answer to the request was direct and ruthless.

"Have him killed."

Nuadat shook his broad head emphatically. "I can't do that."

"Why not? You've dealt with others that way."

"None of them ever reached her or roused any signs of desire in her. This one has reached her—somehow—and it's clear enough she does desire him. She's placed him in her personal guard. He's with her everywhere. They walk together on the battlements and he visits her room late in the night. She smiles at me and acts the same as ever she did, but I know what's going on. Oh, Doncha, well I know!"

He began to pace the room with impatient strides. The advisor watched him, puzzled by his attitude.

"I still don't understand you, Mogh," he said. "She is your wife! She is sworn to you! It is your right to deal with this . . . threat!"

Nuadat stopped and turned to fix a look of disappointment on his advisor. "You really don't see, do you, my old friend? I love my wife. All these years I've sheltered her, cared for her because of that. And she has always returned my love with gentleness and warmth and even affection for me. Do you think I could do anything to hurt her or to cause her to hate me? If anything should happen to this whelp, she would have to know who was the cause of it!"

"The confront her with the truth," Doncha suggested. "Tell her that you know. Ask her to give him up!"

"And risk forcing her into making a choice? What chance would I have then? Just look at me, Doncha." He lifted his short arms away from his squat body. "Compare me with that bold young man. Which of us would you say might attract a woman more?"

"You are a strong and a . . . a striking man, my chief," the advisor answered diplomatically.

"I am a toad," Nuadat responded bluntly. "I've no illusions about that. It's only by the blessing of the gods that I've been given this woman, this sunlight, this spring! And I'll do anything that's needed to keep her with me."

"Even to tolerating this young man?" the advisor asked.

"Yes!" Nuadat retorted. "If it's the only way." He looked back out through his window. Muirne was very close to the young man now, a hand upon his arm, smiling up at him.

"But just how long can I stand to watch this before I go mad, Doncha?" he asked the advisor in a dismal tone. "How long?"

". . . and she's with the lad more often than she's with Nuadat himself!" the drunken warrior said loudly. "We've all made bets on what day the fight will come."

The gathering in the public house in the harbor town was listening attentively. No man before had dared the wrath of the harsh chieftain by approaching his jealously guarded wife. At least, no man living had.

Nuadat's failure to react violently had drawn the attention of an avid audience.

"That Finn," he went on. "He is a clever one. I've never—"

A heavy hand fell on his shoulder, dragging him around. He found himself looking up into a glowering face high above him.

"You say you've seen a boy named Finn?" came the growl of the MacMorna champion Luachra.

"Take your hand from me!" the warrior said, too drunk to be prudent. He pushed the giant's paw from him.

Luachra's other hand drove up, the palm slamming against the man's chest, forcing him back against the wall.

"I'll ask you only once again," he promised savagely. "What do you know of this Finn? Is he silver-haired? Has he two friends?"

The man was gasping for breath with the pressure of the hand against him, crushing his lungs. He managed to give an emphatic nod.

"Much better," Luachra said with a malicious grin. He lessened the force of his palm slightly to let the man breathe. "Now tell me where this fair one can be found."

"He's . . . at the fortress!" the warrior managed to get out. "In the . . . household companies!"

Satisfied, the giant released the hapless man, who dropped like a sack of grain onto the floor and lay panting for air. He signaled to the seven warriors with him.

"Come with me. We'll be going up to this fortress at once!"

He turned about to see a number of other warriors of the dun, as far gone in drink as their fellow and eager for a fight, close in around him.

"You've no right to be dealing so roughly with our comrade, you bloody great cow!" one said. "You're wanting manners, so you are, and it's just the likes of us who can teach a few to you!"

"Out of my way, drunken fools," Luachra said impatiently. He was in no mood to be delayed with his long-sought quarry finally so close by. He lifted a massive hand and shoved against the chest of the one who had spoken.

The force of it sent the man reeling backward until he crashed into a table filled with Fomor. The reaction of the deformed beings was spontaneous, instant, and violent. Snarling with rage, they leapt up from their table, drew weapons, and charged upon the MacMorna warriors.

Luachra seized the first attacker, effortlessly swung him high, and slammed him down into his fellows, driving several to the floor in a tangle. This gave the Fian warriors a chance to draw their swords to defend themselves. Then the Fomor were upon them, quickly joined by the rest of the pugnacious mob.

The room became the scene of a wild melee. A maelstrom whirled about Luachra's band, intent on destroying it. The score of Fomor warriors were the most savage. The fury of their attack and their numbers alone were almost too much for the Fian men. Though they fought back with skill and courage, inflicting great damage, their numbers dwindled fast. With two men dead and two more sorely hurt they would have soon been overwhelmed but for Luachra.

The giant stood in their midst like a great boulder in angry sea, unmoved by the crashing waves of attackers. With his bare hands he fought back. The thick tree limbs of his arms swung out, his huge fists smashing adversaries away. When warriors dove upon him he shook them off, tossing them away to crash down into the tables. Soon even the vicious Fomor lost their blood lust and began to retreat before him.

In a short time it was over. Luachra stood triumphant, out of challengers, glaring around him at the carnage.

A strange calm had fallen upon the room, the quiet broken only by some moans of pain. Of the giant's foes, only the fallen remained, their bodies covering the floor or draped across the splintered furniture, their blood mingling with spilled ale. The battered remnant of the mob had hastily departed.

Luachra snorted in contempt. "It's poor excuses for fighting men they are. They'll know better than to challenge Fianna warriors again." He looked at his men. "Come along then," he snapped irritably. "We must get to the fortress."

"But, the wounded—" one began, bending over a fallen comrade.

"Leave them," the giant commanded. "It's their own lack of skills that brought their harm. I'll not have them slowing us. Now, come along!"

He lumbered from the room without a backward glance. The three remaining men exchanged a look of resignation, sheathed their swords, and followed him. They were unhindered as they left the town and headed out the point toward Nuadat's dun.

The chieftain was still playing fidhcell with his advisor when the MacMorna warriors arrived. A timid servant came to the door of his quarters, inquiring nervously, "My chieftain? Can you be disturbed?"

"What are you talking about?" he shot back impatiently.

"There are visitors," the servant answered. "One of them was very . . . ah . . . insistent. We couldn't . . . we didn't think it advisable to keep him out. He—"

The man suddenly disappeared as the vast form of Luachra pushed past him into the room, followed by his last three warriors.

"By all the Powers!" the chieftain said angrily, leaping to his feet. "Who are you? What do you mean disturbing me here without my leave?"

"I am of the Fianna," Luachra told him. "I've come hunting an outlaw of Ireland."

"We've many outlaws—or those called that—in this place," Nuadat told him, eyeing the giant warrior suspiciously. "But none of your Fians has ever come here seeking one of them before."

"This one is . . . special," Lauchra said tightly. "I've been told he is here, in your household companies. You would know of him if he is. He is a young man with white-blond hair. The name he goes by is Finn."

"Finn, you say?" the chieftain said with surprise. He cast a meaningful look at his advisor, then moved toward the MacMorna champion. "And just who is this boy? What has he done to make him an outlaw?"

"He killed several warriors of the Fianna," the giant replied. "My own comrades among them."

"Did he, now?" Nuadat said with great interest. "And what would the punishment be, were you to find him?"

"Death," Luachra said bluntly. "In accord with Brehon Law, the chief justice of Conn has decreed Finn's life forfeit in exchange for those he has taken."

The chieftain turned to his advisor, his face alight with eagerness. "Do you hear that, Doncha? This lad they're seeking must be put to death. And it has nothing to do with me at all. I can't be blamed!"

Doncha understood what his chieftain was thinking, but he wanted to be cautious.

"Just a moment, Nuadat," he said, getting to his feet and moving closer. "Let me speak to you."

Nuadat stepped back to meet his advisor, his expression one of puzzlement.

"What is it, Doncha?" he asked impatiently.

The other man leaned close to speak in confidence: "Don't be so quick in condemning this Finn, Mogh."

"And why not?" the chieftain gruffly whispered back. "This is the perfect way to be rid of the whelp!"

"Not so rash!" Doncha suggested. "You don't want to be making any mistakes. I think that you should learn all that you can about him. There's something very strange here."

Nuadat shrugged resignedly. "Maybe you're right." He turned back to Luachra and said, "I'd like to know more. Why is this Finn so important to you? Who is he?"

"That's nothing to do with you," Luachra told him gruffly, glaring down at the smaller man. "It's enough that he's wanted by the high king of all Ireland and by Goll MacMorna, captain of the Fianna."

The combative little chieftain was not intimidated by his visitor's bulk. He walked up close to Luachra, strutting slowly, fearlessly, head high, body tensed, eyes meeting those far above him boldly.

"It's not enough for me!" he retorted with heat. "If you want my help, you'll have to answer my questions first!"

"It'll go hard with you if you defy the Fianna!" Luachra said darkly.

Nuadat lifted up on his toes, thrusting a finger into the giant's face to punctuate his words. "Don't be threatening me, man! We're not afraid of your bloody Fianna here, and they know it well enough. They'll not come here to war against us over this single boy. Now, you tell me what I want to know or by Great Danu, I'll throw you out of this dun right now myself!"

He stepped back, setting himself in a fighting stance, like a bulldog challenging a raging bull. It might have seemed ludicrous, the little man against the mountainous Luachra, had not both been so deadly serious in their intent.

The giant considered his situation here. He realized that he was beyond the reach of Fian power. He could not hope to take on Nuadat's entire garrison. Reluctantly, he decided to cooperate.

"All right then," he said, lifting his empty hands, palms out in a gesture of peace. "I want no fight with you. The boy we're seeking is the son of Cumhal MacTredhorn, he that was chieftain of the Clan na Baiscne."

"And the captain of all the Fians before your Goll," Nuadat added with a dawning understanding. "Now I see why this Finn's end is so ardently sought by you. But I had never heard of Cumhal's having a son."

"Only one," the giant said. "No one knew that he lived until a short time ago. He was hidden away in the glens of Slieve Bladhma by his mother, Muirne."

"Muirne?" repeated the chieftain.

The name struck him like a lightning bolt. In one bright flash the truth was clear to him. Relief and joy surged up in him and found its release in an outpouring of laughter.

He laughed long and loudly and with great gusto,

Luachra watching him as if certain the chieftain had suddenly gone mad. Finally, with an effort, Nuadat controlled himself. He set himself stolidly before the champion of the MacMornas, his expression gravely set.

"I find your tale . . . interesting," he said very seriously, "but it means little to me. There's no lad such as you describe now in my dun."

"What?" cried Luachra in astonishment. "But you said that you would help me!"

"If I could," Nuadat amended. "But I have no way of doing so. If this Finn was here, he's passed on."

"That can't be true," the giant protested. "In the village I met a warrior who—"

The chieftain cut him off sharply. "The villagers are drunken fools. There's nothing here for you. Our talk is ended."

"You'll not be rid of me!" the champion roared. "Not until I've looked about this dun myself!"

Nuadat drew himself up stiffly. "Are you saying that I lie?" he asked in indignation. "I'll tolerate no more of your arrogance. I've answered your question. Now get out of my fortress or I will have my warriors remove you. Take my word back to your Goll MacMorna and your Conn. If they don't like it, let them come to Carraighe and ask me themselves!"

Luachra ached to tear apart this little chieftain and his dun, but he was no fool. He swallowed his anger, promising that he would slake his thirst for blood in a more sensible way.

"Someday, Mogh Nuadat, I hope to meet you again," he snarled, and retreated from the room.

"See that our large friend leaves Corca Dhuibhne," the chieftain told Doncha. "And have the warrior Finn brought here to me!"

Chapter Nineteen

LEAVETAKING

The golden piece moved forward. Finn eyed it, yawned, then moved one of his own pieces across the board to counter it. He looked up at Nuadat, who was bent forward, frowning as he concentrated on the game.

"My chieftain, it is very late," said Finn. It was, in fact, well past the middle of the night. All others in the keep had long since gone to bed, leaving the pair alone in the main hall.

"Quiet!" Nuadat commanded brusquely. "I'm considering a move."

Finn watched him, wondering again why he had been brought here. There had been no explanations, only that he had been requested to appear before the chieftain. And here he had stayed through the evening, playing game after game of fidhcell. It was a disquieting thing. And he had the feeling that, eventually, something was going to happen.

Nuadat lifted a piece, moved it forward, hesitated, moved it back, then flicked it over in a concession of defeat.

"You are good!" he said, shaking his head. "That's seven games you've won. I've never known an opponent more clever."

Finn remembered all those nights when Bodhmall had drummed strategies for the game into him.

"I had a good teacher," he said.

"Was it your father?" Nuadat casually inquired.

"No," Finn said carefully. "My father . . . died."

"My husband?" came the voice of Muirne. She now stood at the doorway of the hall. Her expression was anxious, her eyes flicking from Finn to the chieftain. "What is it? Why is this warrior here, and so late?"

"Come in, my wife!" Nuadat said heartily. "I was about to fetch you anyway." He rose and lifted an arm in welcome. "Come here and join us."

She crossed the room to his table. He pointed to the bench beside Finn.

"Sit here!" he told her.

She exchanged a worried, puzzled look with Finn, then sat down next to him. Nuadat stayed on his feet, beaming down at the pair.

"I kept Finn here so late because I wanted to talk to him, and to you, alone."

That had an ominous ring to it, but a broad grin continued to split his wide face. "Muirne, I've become most interested in the young man, that I have. I wanted to see him more closely. I was noticing his hair especially. Most amazing. Its color rivals even your own, and I've never seen another that could come close."

He leaned forward suddenly, fixing a hard gaze on Finn. His voice took on a demanding tone. "Just who are you at all, lad?"

At first flustered by this direct question, Finn desperately fell back on the identity Caoilte had told him to use in such a circumstance.

"I—I am a son of the countryman of the Luigne of Meath, my chieftan," he said.

He cast a sidelong glance at his mother. She was trying to look calm, but the apprehension was clear in her drawn, pale face.

Nuadat noted it. He stood upright again and laughed. "Ah, please forgive me," he told them, all the brusqueness gone. "I didn't mean to be worrying you. My little game was cruel, maybe, but I had to repay you for the game you've played on me." He looked at Finn. "You see, I know that you are the son my wife bore to Cumhal."

"My husband!" Muirne said in surprise. "You know, and it makes no difference to you?"

He moved around the table to stand beside her. He placed a wide, short hand upon her own slender one. His smile was tender as he looked at her, and it gave his squat, homely face its own attractiveness.

"My wife," he said gently, "I took you in not caring about your past. I've sheltered you only because of my love for you. Nothing can change my feelings."

She lifted his hand and pressed her cheek to it. "Your understanding means very much to me," she told him with great relief.

"If I'm hurt in anything," he said, "it's in your not telling the truth of this to me before."

"My only thought was for my son," she told him. "I could risk no one knowing of him. Do you understand?"

"I do," he said. "Although your secret almost cost him his life this time. But for my advisor, I would have given young Finn over to a warrior of the Fianna."

"The Fianna!" Finn echoed. "Was it a warrior of the Morna clan?"

"Their champion," Nuadat said. "A huge and bearlike fellow. Very determined to find you."

"I know him," Finn said darkly. "He has hunted me here from Bantry. The Clan na Morna will not rest until they have my head."

"You could stay here," his mother suggested in a hopeful way. "You would be protected in Corca Dhuibhne."

"No, Mother," Finn said with determination. "I'll not ask Mogh Nuadat to protect me, and I'll not bring any danger upon you. It's time for me to go on anyway. I've learned the warrior's skills. Now I've got to find my father's clan."

"You're a courageous lad," the chieftain told him with respect. "It's a dangerous way you've chosen, but one of great honor. I know of your father. He used the Fianna for the good of all Ireland, not just that of the bloody Conn. If you succeed, I'd wish to see you make it that way again!"

"I will try, my chieftain," Finn told him.

"Good. When you are ready to leave here, ask me for anything you'll need. And be careful. That giant is no fool. He's likely doubting the truth of my tale that you were gone from here. He could be waiting somewhere out there for you now."

At these warning words, Muirne's gaze grew fearful. "Are you certain that you have to go, my son?"

"I am," he said firmly. Then he smiled regretfully at her. "Though it will be hard to leave you so soon after finding you. It seems as if always leaving what I love is what I'm fated to do."

She leaned forward and hugged him close. "Ah, I wish I might have done this when you were small," she said. "But at least I have you now. Please, don't be lost to me."

"Mother, when I regain my father's place, you'll be free of hiding forever," he told her fiercely. "We'll be together again, I promise that!"

"You could have stayed there," Finn told his two comrades as they urged their horses up the steep incline.

"What, be left behind in that place?" said the Little Nut. "Why, I'll be safer with you, even with all of Ireland after you."

"And what about you, Caoilte?" Finn asked the dark warrior. "I've the fighting skills now. Your task is finished."

"So you say," the other replied brusquely. "You're a sapling still, not the great tree you think. I'm staying with you to see that you remain alive to reach your people. Then I'll be done with you. So no more talk of it."

"Well, you'll neither of you have an argument from me," he said, grinning. "I'd miss you both."

They reached the top of the Conair Pass and he looked back onto the peninsula for the last time. The fortress was only a tiny bit of gray marking a small point. Its grim keep and stolid walls had dwindled to almost nothing against the glittering vastness of the sea beyond. Yet he could feel the eyes that must be looking up to him now, and he could feel the warm spirit wafting up to him like a caressing summer breeze.

"Good-bye, Mother," he murmured. Then he stoically turned and set his gaze ahead to the open, sweeping lands beyond the pass.

The road now slanted down along one side of a wide, smooth valley. Far below they could see the blue sheen of the sea on the north coast of the long peninsula. The horses could move with greater ease now, and the three riders urged them ahead faster, anxious to be away from Corca Dhuibhne soon.

From the rim of the valley's far side, watching eyes had noted their appearance in the pass. They had carefully scrutinized the trio, brightening with satisfaction as they noted the head of blond hair glowing like a silver flame in the sunlight.

"It is them!" said Luachra, turning to his companions. "I was right to wait. The boy was there, and now he's fool enough to come out again. One of you take word to Goll that he's been found again. The rest of us will follow these outlaws."

He looked back toward the three horsemen, grinning savagely with the anticipation of his victory. "When the time is right, when we are certain he cannot escape, Finn MacCumhal will die."

Chapter Twenty

THE GIANT

"It's a land with its own magic, so it is," said Cnu Deireoil. "Stay in it too long, and they say you may never be able to leave."

Finn could understand why such a tale might be true. The lands of Connacht that they had entered were indeed enchanting ones.

The countryside seemed to him composed of marvelous vistas, landscapes of rolling hills thickly fringed with trees or silken smooth with coverings of lush grass. The shades of green were so many that he could not count them all, and shifted often, the bright sun gilding them, the soft mists shrouding them in a mysterious gray, the blanketing overcasts giving them a darker, brooding look. It was like some enormous, billowing quilt sewn from cloths of varied and sensuous textures, so rich it could almost be felt enfolding him. Unlike the rugged seacoast, where the beauties stimulated, challenged, and awed, these lands comforted, like well-worn, familiar clothing or a friend's warm fire.

They had headed into the province of Connacht at the direction of Muirne. Though this large territory took up the west and central portion of Ireland just north of Corca Dhuibhne, their journey there had required a long ride back toward the east. This was necessary, Finn's well-traveled companions explained to him, to skirt the wide section of a river called the Sionnan that thrust far inland like a barbed spearhead of the sea.

They carefully avoided forts and villages, living off

the land, much to the dismay of the Little Nut. After three days of riding they were able to turn north, making a wide circuit of the large town called Luminech. Above it, the river narrowed abruptly, becoming a deep blue shining band that curled in serpentine loops through the countryside, and they were able to cross quite easily.

As they rode on north and west into the province, Finn noted that dwelling places seemed more numerous, and that the herds that grazed the meadowlands were larger, fatter, and more plentiful.

"Aye, it's some of the best grazing lands in Ireland we're in now," Cnu Deireoil agreed. "Some say Connacht is the finest province, and those who live here are certain of that. But there are a few in Ulster who might dispute such a claim, and with a sword at that!"

"Some of the most famous of the Firbolg warriors came from Connacht," Caoilte mentioned with a touch of pride. "Fardia MacDamann was said to be one of the greatest champions Ireland has ever seen."

"I know of him," said Finn, recalling one of Liath's tales. "To keep a bond with his queen he was forced to fight his closest friend, the Hound of Cuailnge, and was killed. It was a tragic story."

"He was just another fool to die that way," Caoilte replied derisively. "The only things a sensible warrior should be fighting for are to earn good wages and to keep himself alive."

"I don't agree," Finn told him with intensity. "Even being a great warrior can't give your life any worth. That's got to come from your having something you're willing to fight for—not for payment, but only because it's important to you."

The Little Nut gave an elaborate yawn. "That's all very exciting," he said, "but I'll not be living much longer myself if we don't get a chance for some rest and food, beneath a roof. How much farther is this place?"

"From what Finn's mother told him, I'd say about two days more," Caoilte estimated.

"If you can find it," the harper added.

"I can get us close enough," Caoilte shot back. "Would you care to try it yourself?"

"No arguing now," Finn said soothingly. "We're all tired of this travel."

"I'm tired of his constant complaining, is what I am!" the dark warrior exclaimed. "Every time he wants something, he toots his bloody whistle and expects us to hop about for him. I'd like to take that whistle and—"

"I'd like to see you try that!" Cnu Deireoil retorted, drawing his little body up to strike a challenging pose. "The music's all that protects me from your insufferable arrogance!"

"Arrogance!" cried Caoilte. "Arrogance! You're a fine one to speak of that, you little—"

"Wait!" said Finn sharply, pointing ahead. "Look there!"

They had just topped a rise and ahead the road entered an area of woods. By the roadside at the woods' edge sat an elderly woman, bent forward, her face in her bony hands. She was weeping loudly, her thin body shaking with the sobs.

Finn rode up before her and reined in, sliding from his mount.

"Good woman," he asked gently, "what sorrow is it that's troubling you so?"

She started and looked up, her old, care-worn face wet with tears, her expression hopeless.

"It's my only child," she managed brokenly to say. "All that I had left in the world to me. We were traveling on foot to my clan's home, for we'd only lost my husband these three days past. But brigands attacked us on the road. They took my son off. Carried him into the woods there. Oh me, if I'm ever to see him again!"

Her grief overtook her again at that. Her face dropped back into her hands and she wailed on.

Finn turned at once to his horse and began to unstrap the shield from its saddle.

"What are you doing?" Caoilte asked.

170

"I'm going to try to save this poor woman's son," he said simply.

"Finn, you can't be just rushing after them," Caoilte said in a reasoning way, trying to head off another of the young warrior's rash acts. "You don't know how many of them there are or where they went!"

"And I'm getting a scent of something very evil here," Cnu Deireoil added. "Remember, lad, that the hand of everyone is against us now. There could be great danger."

Finn fitted his arm through the straps of his shield. He pulled his two spears from their lashings and put them across his shoulder. Then he looked up at his comrades, his face set in determined lines.

"I'm going to help," he stated with finality. "Isn't seeing to others part of what makes a warrior, too, Caoilte?"

Caoilte sighed deeply. He cast a glance of resignation at the Little Nut, then climbed down from his horse and began to unstrap his own shield.

Finn grinned. "I knew you'd come."

"What about me?" Cnu Deireoil asked with some apprehension.

"Don't worry," Finn told him. "You can stay here and help this woman. Give her some food. She looks nearly starved."

"Ah! A very fine idea!" the harper agreed with renewed cheer. "I'm quite good at comforting, that I am!" He jumped down and moved toward her eagerly.

"Play her a tune," Caoilte said sarcastically as he slipped on his shield. "Maybe that will cheer her."

Finn went to her and laid a comforting hand gently on her bony shoulder. "My woman, if there is a way, we'll bring your son back to you. I give my word to you on that!"

This had some effect on her. She stopped her sobbing and looked up at Finn with hope in her tear-filled eyes. "Oh, it's a fine warrior you are to be helping me. If you could save my son, there's nothing I'll not do to repay you."

"You'll owe nothing to us," he told her. "It's only

what we should be doing. Now, where did these men go that took your son?"

She pointed to a faint path into the woods. Finn nodded and marched off boldly, Caoilte close behind. It was clear from the marks on the soft earth and the foliage that someone had passed quite recently.

"Looks as if a large party has gone through here," Caoilte said.

"I count the tracks of only four," Finn said. "One must be the boy, being dragged along."

"Why would they take him, though?" the dark man wondered. "This gives me a strange feeling I don't like."

They moved along the pathway cautiously, weapons ready, peering around and behind them as they moved. Soon they came upon a small clearing. In its center a thin young boy sat alone and trembling upon a fallen tree trunk.

"Boy!" Finn called to him from the clearing's edge.

The child looked toward them. His face was pale. He didn't move or speak. Finn thought of a trapped baby hare, paralyzed with fear.

He started into the clearing.

"Wait!" Caoilte said. "This is more and more wrong."

"I've got to get the boy," Finn insisted and went on.

Caoilte took a few steps into the clearing and then stopped. His suspicious gaze swept the surrounding trees. His sword and shield were up.

Finn was nearly to the boy when something odd caught his keen eye. The edge of a rope was visible above the collar of the boy's tunic. And another piece showed behind his elbow, running down behind the log.

"Caoilte, he's tethered there," Finn said, coming to a halt.

"Like a lamb to bring the wolf in," the other replied. "It is a trap!"

Even as he spoke, there came a crashing from the woods behind. Two warriors leapt into the clearing and charged upon him.

He whirled, raising sword and shield in defense. Finn turned, too, ready to help him, but swung back when more crashing sounded from the woods beyond the tethered boy.

A giant warrior Finn remembered well came into view, moving upon him swiftly, like a roaring avalanche. Finn had barely time to drop the two weapons and raise his shield in both hands as the huge champion's war ax descended upon him.

The thick iron boss of the leather shield turned the ax, but the shock of the blow shuddered through Finn's arms and sent him staggering back. The ax lifted and came down again. Once more Finn's reflexes saved his life. He ducked away and the ax swooshed past, burying its head deeply in the ground.

Luachra yanked the weapon free, ripping up a great chunk of sod as the gleaming head lifted and swung toward Finn once more. The brief delay, however, had given the young warrior a chance to draw his sword.

The ax came up. Finn's shield lifted to deflect the blow. It did so, but the heavy weapon dented the iron rim deeply this time, and the downward force drove Finn to his knees.

Still, the wiry young man managed to swing a cut up below Luachra's shield. The agile giant pulled back, saving his belly. The blade only touched it, slipping across the surface, drawing a line of blood across the flesh as it sliced his tunic.

This wound only seemed to infuriate Luachra more. He bellowed loudly, jerking up the ax for another blow.

Finn came off his knees, bringing his sword up to parry it. His blade did manage to turn the descending head, but this was the last service it did for Finn. The power of the strike snapped it off above the hilt as if it had been a twig, knocking it from Finn's hand with a force that nearly broke his fingers.

Finn gripped his shield in both hands once again and held it up as the ax once more swept up and down. This time the blade of it struck the leather covering within the iron boss. The sharpened edge slashed through the many stiffened layers and wedged tightly in the shield. The giant yanked back, hoping to pull it away from Finn. He threw the young warrior sideways. Finn's arm slipped from the thongs and he rolled away, coming to rest halfway across the clearing, head spinning, breath knocked from him, nearly stunned.

Having just dealt a death blow to his second man, Caoilte now pulled his blade from the falling body and turned to see the giant warrior descending upon the downed Finn. With a shrill battle shout to call Luachra's attention from his intended victim, the Firbolg charged in.

He had had experience with this bearlike man before. He told himself he'd not be beaten this time.

He was wrong. As he feinted for an opening, Luachra merely swang his massive shield out again to slam Caoilte's aside, then swept his ax around in a hard, sideways blow meant to take off the dark warrior's head. Caoilte threw himself desperately forward. The blade of the ax missed him, but the heavy handle didn't, slamming hard against his skull, knocking him from his feet. He crumpled to the ground and lay unmoving.

As Finn saw his friend receive this massive blow, a great anger surged through him, giving him new strength. His sword and shield were gone, but his two spears lay on the ground behind the giant. Before Luachra's attention was turned back to him, he was on his feet and running for the weapons. The giant swung at him, but his great speed carried him safely out of the ax's reach. He reached the spears and snatched them up, setting himself to face the huge warrior as he advanced, a moving mountain behind his enormous shield.

Luachra laughed. It was a low, grunting, savage sound.

"You've no chance against me with those puny spears," he said gloatingly. "You were a dead man when you left your magic little friend behind. I hoped you would do that. I hoped you would give me the chance to finish you. The chase has gone on long enough, Finn MacCumhal. It will end here."

He came on, seemingly unstoppable. Finn scanned him desperately with his hunter's eye, seeking a vulnerable point. He knew he had no chance of penetrating the fist's thickness of leather shield. It had to be like iron. And it left little uncovered save for the top of the head, the arm with the raised ax, and the immense feet.

It seemed far from sporting to Finn, but there wasn't any choice if he meant to survive. He brought a spear up, cocked his arm, and fired.

His aim, as always, was highly accurate. The spear flew to its target, slamming the broad iron head through Luachra's boot and deep into his foot just above the toes.

The giant roared in pain, drawing up the foot and hopping sideways, then crashing down on one knee. The shield dropped down, exposing the head, the tearing eyes, the wide mouth open to howl.

Finn lifted the other spear, took two leaps forward, and hurled the weapon with all his power. The deadly point flew into the gaping mouth, the force of its momentum driving it on through, to crack out the back of the MacMorna champion's broad skull.

Luachra's head jerked back and he shuddered. His eyes flicked up to Finn's with an astonished look before going blank. He toppled like a great tree severed at the base, slowly falling backward, landing with a thud that seemed to shake the woods.

Finn stepped toward him, watching the felled giant carefully. He made no move. His relaxing hand released the handle of his war ax, letting it slide away. He was dead.

The young warrior's attention now went to his friend. He rushed across the clearing to Caoilte, knelt down, and examined him. He was unconscious, but breathing. There was a swelling bruise on his forehead, but Finn could not tell what damage had been done. Gently he lifted his friend.

"Caoilte," he said. "Caoilte, wake up!"

The warrior moaned. His eyes opened and he looked up, eyes focusing on Finn. Then, to Finn's relief, he smiled ruefully.

"It's my fault, lad," he said. "I knew I should have gotten a new sword for you!"

He sat up, putting fingertips gingerly to his wound, grimacing at the pain.

"What's happened?" came the shocked voice of Cnu Deireoil.

The two men looked about to see the harper moving slowly into the clearing, looking about him at the carnage.

"We survived," Caoilte said dryly. "But only just. What are you doing here?"

"I . . . I was fearing for you," he said with some hesitation, looking embarrassed. "I thought I should just come along and see if you needed saving again."

"A bit late," Caoilte told him.

"But very brave of you," Finn quickly added. "It was very close." He climbed to his feet and offered to help Caoilte up.

"I'm all right," the warrior said irritably, getting up by himself. "See to the boy."

Finn crossed the clearing to the tethered youth, who had watched the fight in terror.

"Easy, lad," Finn told him. "You're safe now." He untied the rope and pulled the boy to his feet. "Can you find your way back to your mother from here?"

The boy nodded, still speechless with his fear.

"Then go to her. Run as quickly as you can. We'll be close behind."

He sprinted away at once, up the faint pathway out of the woods.

Caoilte picked up his fallen sword and shield. Finn examined his own ruined weapons, then selected the best replacements from those of the two men Caoilte had killed.

While the Little Nut waited, his gaze wandered about the clearing, but it came abruptly to rest when it reached the body of Luachra. He stared, and then he moved closer, his eyes fixed upon a pouch slung across the giant's shoulder on a strap.

With great reluctance, he moved to the enormous

corpse and, after some tugging, pulled the object free. His peculiar actions drew the attention of his companions.

"What are you about?" Finn asked him.

"I've got a sacred bag," he announced, holding it up.

"A sacred bag?" Finn echoed with curiosity, moving closer. "What's that?"

It was certainly a fascinating-looking thing, he thought. It was made of a fine-grained white skin, too soft to be leather. The surface was thickly covered with intricate decorations of gold and silver thread and brightly colored beads forming curling interlace designs.

"You see those signs?" Cnu Deireoil asked him, pointing to a grouping of spiral shapes. "Those are meant to protect the contents. It's one of the most wonderfully crafted bags I've ever seen."

"They're common to the clans," Caoilte supplied, joining them. "Each has a bag to store its clan charms and treasures."

The little man began to untie the thongs that bound it closed.

"What are you doing?" Finn asked.

"I mean to see what's in it," the harper answered, pulling it open. He upended it, pouring out its contents.

All three were astonished at the result of this action. For the mass of objects that tumbled from the bag were several times greater in bulk than it could possibly accommodate.

"There's magic surely in this," Cnu Deireoil said, peering into the bag and then down at the pile.

The items were peculiar ones indeed. There was a cone-shaped helmet ornamented with precious stones and golden filigree. There were skillfully crafted silver shears, an ironsmith's hook, a belt of curiously shining hide, an embroidered linen shirt, and a slender dagger. Mixed in with these things was a thick scattering of small bone pieces and brightly glinting jewels.

"Now, there's a rich treasure bag," Caoilte said, a covetous light appearing in his eyes as he moved in.

Finn shrugged. "It's of no value to me," he said indifferently. "Shouldn't we leave it with its owner?"

Dark warrior and harper exchanged a look of dismay and then moved upon their young friend together.

"Oh, no!" Cnu Deireoil said. "It's much too valuable to be left behind. There's no way of telling what good may be gotten from it."

"He's right, Finn," Caoilte put in supportively. "And if this is a Morna treasure bag, it's yours by right now. It's your trophy for the defeat of this champion."

"All right," Finn agreed, "if you both feel it's so important. Bring it along, Cnu Deireoil." He looked back at the fallen giant, his young face set in grim satisfaction. "But it's enough for me to know that I've begun to avenge my father on his enemies."

Book Three

THE WAYS OF
THE FIANNA

Chapter Twenty-one

CLAN NA BAISCNE

The eyes of Tadg, high druid of Tara, gazed upon the body of Luachra, alive now with a flock of hopping, pecking crows.

Tadg was not in the clearing where the fight had been. Instead, he viewed this scene in the glittering black eyes of a raven. The shining blue-black bird was larger than a hawk. It stood motionless upon a skull before the man, its gaze fixed steadily, unblinkingly on his.

Now, as Tadg watched, the image shifted. It rose from the body, lifting above the treetops of that distant wood, rising to provide a panorama of the countryside below. It swept along a narrow roadway that cut through the trees. Some way along it, three moving objects, tiny from that height, were visible.

Abruptly the ground seemed to leap upward. So vivid was the impression that Tadg felt his stomach heave with the sense of dropping. The three figures grew rapidly, almost filling up the image for an instant before they flashed from view. But that instant was long enough for the high druid. He knew that these were the ones he sought.

The bird cawed loudly, giving its wings a restless flap. Contact was broken. The image faded from its eyes.

"Very well," Tadg said to it. "I thank you for what you have given me. Inform me when you discover where they are going."

The bird cawed again and flapped away, rising from the clearing and out of sight.

Tadg lost no time in leaving the sacred wood and going up to the dun. He found the high king engaged in his usual midmorning pursuit, watching the youths in training at Tara play a fast-paced hurling match.

"My king, I have information that is vital," he said.

"What now, Tadg?" Conn asked impatiently, trying to keep his eye on a particularly skillful play of the ball. "The game is very close."

The druid leaned closer, murmuring, "It concerns the boy named Finn, my king."

Conn's gaze swiveled up to him at once. "I see! Well, come over here."

They moved away from the other spectators. The sound of their cheering and the shouting of the boys covered their talk effectively.

"Tell me what it is, then," Conn demanded. "Has Goll found him?"

"The men of Morna have failed completely," Tadg said. "I've just learned that their champion Luachra has been killed by MacCumhal. No one pursues him now. And he is heading into Connacht!"

Though this last piece of information seemed significant to the druid, Conn was puzzled by it.

"Into Connacht?" he said. "But that's still far from here. He's not likely to be any danger to us from so far away."

"You've forgotten, High King," Tadg said. "The last word we had of the survivors of the Baiscne clan was that they had fled into the forests of Connacht."

"Of course!" Conn said with new concern. "If he should join them—"

"The danger will be all the greater," Tadg finished. "Yes, High King."

"Goll must go to Connacht at once and begin the search again," Conn said with force.

"He tried long ago to hunt down the survivors of Cumhal's clan," Tadg pointed out. "He failed. In those forests it would take a thousand men to find warriors with the training of the Fianna."

"We can't send a thousand men!" Conn protested. "It would be known what we were doing. There would be a great outcry!"

"Of course, my king," Tadg said in his soothing way. "That is why I think Goll should be left out of this. Let me see to Finn MacCumhal this time, and the rest of the Clan na Baiscne as well."

"You?" the king asked suspiciously. "But Goll warned you that he would not tolerate your using druidic powers against the boy."

"Yes, my high king. But you and I understand that the destruction of Cumhal's son is more important than his feelings of honor. Why, your very power over Ireland might be at stake."

"Yes . . ." Conn admitted slowly, reluctantly. "Perhaps you are right."

"Of course I'm right, High King," Tadg said with smooth assurance, his small mouth bowing in a clever smile. "Goll need never know that I have done his task for him."

"Tell me no more of it," said Conn brusquely, turning away from the druid to head back toward the game. Then he paused, turning back to add an afterthought: "I do wonder just how great a threat this really is. After so many years, what can be left of the Baiscne clan?"

"Are you certain this is the place?" Finn asked in a disbelieving way.

"I followed the directions your mother gave us," Caoilte told him. "They were very exact. This must be it."

Finn looked around him again. How could this be the camp of his father's clan? It was only a few tiny huts of woven branches scattered through the trees, nearly invisible amidst the foliage. Without his forest skills, they might never have been found.

From the low door holes of the huts men began to emerge. They were gaunt and bearded, clad in animal skins and the worn remnants of warrior's dress. They seemed to Finn more like a winter-starved pack of wolves than men as they slunk warily forward, weapons raised in defense.

One of them cautiously moved forward a bit from the rest, a spear lifted threateningly. Shaggy hair and unkempt beard nearly masked his features, but his eyes revealed his hostility.

"Who are you then?" he demanded. "What are you doing here?"

"I've come seeking the Clan na Baiscne," Finn said.

The man's eyes flicked round the circle of his fellows, then back to the young warrior. "There's none of that clan left in Ireland," he snapped. "Now be away from here or we'll make an end of you."

"I have to find the Clan na Baiscne," Finn told him in an entreating way. "I mean to join them. My father was their chieftain, Cumhal MacTredhorn."

That name clearly surprised the man. He started, then shook his head angrily. "That's a lie! It's a trick of the Morna clan. Cumhal's child didn't survive."

"Please listen to me," Finn said. "My mother hid me away. I stayed hidden until I was able to survive on my own in the world."

"He's speaking the truth," Caoilte put in. "The warriors of the Morna clan have pursued him across half of Ireland. He killed one of their champions only two days ago."

"More lies," the man growled, pulling back the spear. "You'll die now."

"No! No!" Cnu Deireoil protested. "It's the truth! Look here! I took this from the body of the one Finn killed." He held up the pouch he carried.

As the man saw it, a look of amazement wiped away his expression of hostility. Exclamations of surprise came from among his fellows. All lowered their weapons and moved in closer.

"The treasure bag!" the bearded one said, walking up to Cnu Deireoil. He put out a hand and, in a gentle, reverential manner, touched the pouch. Then he looked up at Finn. "And you killed the man who had this? What was he like?"

"He was a giant," Finn said, a little bewildered by this odd reaction. "He called himself Luachra."

"Climb down," the man asked.

Finn exchanged a doubtful glance with Caoilte, but then complied, dismounting and facing the other courageously. The bearded man moved in, peering searchingly into his face. Then he nodded.

"Yes, I can see him in you now," he said. "You are my brother's son."

"Your brother?" Finn said.

"I am your uncle, Crimall," the other told him. "Welcome to the poor remnant of your father's clan." He gave Finn a great hug, then turned to the others. "This is the son of Cumhal," he announced. "And he has returned the treasure bag of our clan to us."

"What do you mean, Uncle?" Finn asked. "How can this treasure bag be yours?"

Crimall gave him a strange look. "You mean you don't know? This was the treasure bag of the Clan na Baiscne until the Morna clan defeated us and took it from your father's body. The man that you killed was the one who gave your father his mortal wound!"

The fire sent a stream of sparks up in a glittering column to wink out against the sky. It threw a ruddy light over the objects from the bag, now laid out carefully on a cloth before it.

Finn and his two comrades sat in a circle about the fire with the others of the clan. They chewed on roasted venison and listened—Finn quite raptly—as Crimall told them about each piece in proud tones as he pointed them out.

"The smith's hook was that of Goibniu, chief smith of the Tuatha de Danaan. These are the shears of the king of Alban, and that helmet belonged to Lochlann's king. The belt is made of the skin of a monstrous fish killed years ago, and the bones are of Asal's pigs brought to Ireland by the sons of Tuireann in the time of Lugh.

And this shirt and dagger are said to be those of the sea god, Manannan MacLir himself!"

One by one he carefully began to pick up the sacred objects and place them back into the pouch.

"The tales have it that the treasure pouch is made of a crane skin that was once the skin of the beautiful woman Aoife," he went on. "She was put into the crane's shape through jealousy."

"I've heard the tale," Cnu Deireoil said. "And a very tragic one it is."

"Your thanks should go to the Little Nut and to Caoilte as well as myself for bringing that here," Finn told his uncle.

"Then it's a great debt we owe them. For it was the honor of the clan that was lost with our treasure bag."

"We're happy to have helped," the harper said, but he watched the last jewels poured back into the pouch with a wistful eye.

As before, the objects were all accommodated easily by the miraculous treasure bag. Crimall tied its thongs carefully and set it aside.

"Tell me what it's been like for you out here, Uncle," said Finn, eager to learn more of his clan.

"It's not been so bad," Crimall told him. "The Mornas gave up hunting us long ago. Likely they think we're harmless now. We live off the land easily enough when the summer's here. It's only the winters that are hard, when the game is scarce, and we can't find a shelter with some obliging chieftain as we used to do." He sighed. "Ah, there are times when I do miss those days. It's a great sorrow to me to see what our clan's become."

"Those days will come again, Uncle," Finn promised. "I've come to join my clansmen and learn the ways of the Fianna. I mean to take my father's place and to challenge the Clan na Morna for the leadership that should be ours."

Crimall looked into the earnest young face and smiled sadly. "Ah, lad, it's a fine dream, but there's no means to make the truth of it. Look around you. We're all of the clan left."

Finn's gaze slid around the circle of men. He was forced to admit to himself that they were far from what he had imagined. He had expected a force of proud, stalwart warriors. Instead he saw men who seemed old and worn and without spirit, reduced to living like animals in the wilds.

"Understand, Nephew," Crimall went on. "We've lived all these years without any hope of recovering our power. There was only surviving left to us. Most of the younger men have scattered, joined other clans or gone into service, hiding from the Mornas. Those of us here have little time left to us. And when we're gone, there'll be an end to the Clan na Baiscne."

"And you mean to just sit here and wait for this end?" Finn said, outraged by these words.

He climbed to his feet and stood, a towering, powerful figure against the background of night, his muscular form and strongly featured face lit by the fire's crimson glow. He swept his clansmen with eyes that seemed to blaze. His voice took on an impelling force that Caoilte and the Little Nut had never heard before. It held them as it held the other men.

"I do not know you," he told them, "but I have heard the tales of the Fianna all my life. I have come to believe that those of the Fianna are the greatest warriors in all of Ireland. No real warrior would give up a fight, that I have learned. No man at all would let his honor be stolen away without sacrificing his own life to take it back. I am the son of Cumhal. I have come to take his place. I mean to restore the honor of my clan, even if I must do it alone. If you are of the Fianna, if you are warriors, if you are men at all, you must join me."

The speech roused a new fire in the hearts of the men. Crimall jumped to his feet.

"You are right!" he said, and turned toward his comrades. "We've nothing more to lose," he said to them. "Better to die fighting to regain our pride than to waste away here." He drew his sword and held its blade high. "Who will join me?"

As a man the others of the clan stood, their spare frames drawing erect with a vigor they had not felt in many years. Their weapons leapt up, sword and spear points flashing with red firelight.

"For Baiscne!" came the cry from Crimall.

"For Baiscne and Cumhal!" came the reply from the throat of every man.

Chapter Twenty-two

THE RED WOMAN

A baying pack of hounds bounded through the trees. Each of the lean and wiry animals strove to outdistance its fellows, to be the first to reach their quarry.

It was not far ahead now. The great stag was tiring after the long pursuit by the persistent hounds. It was reaching the end of its strength, and the pack was closing in.

Not far behind the pack ran Finn MacCumhal, Caoilte, and others of the Baiscne clan, moving at their greatest speed to stay close, to keep the stag in sight.

Suddenly the animal turned at bay. It dropped its magnificent head and plunged back into the hounds, who scattered before it. One dog was caught on the antlers, lifted and flung away by a shake of the stag's muscular neck. It landed with a yelp, bleeding from the stab wounds of the antler points, but these did not deter it. It darted back in at the stag at once.

The pack closed in around the stag then, the circle

of them barking and snapping at the animal to keep it trapped until the men arrived. It was Finn and Caoilte who leapt through their circle first to dive in upon the stag. Caoilte went bravely in over the antlers, plunging downward with his hunting spear in an attempt to strike the spine. But the animal twisted sideways, and the weapon missed its target, sinking into the tough muscle beside the bone.

The animal reared back, pulling free. Caoilte ducked away to avoid its hooves. Finn, moving in beside him, thrust upward with his spear, driving it through the soft belly of the stag, spearing its heart. It shuddered, and then sagged, crashing over sideways to the ground.

"Well done. Well done!" Crimall congratulated as he moved up beside the two and looked down in admiration at the enormous stag. "He was a good one. Gave us quite a hunt, he did." He shooed a few curious hounds back from the body and beamed at Finn. "You're doing very well on the chase now, Nephew."

That didn't surprise Finn. He had done very little else since coming here. It appeared that, next to war, hunting was the most important activity to a man of the Fianna. The summer was fully upon them now, and through days of warm sun or steaming heat or fine mist or driving rain the hunts had always gone on.

Partly this obsession with the hunt was practical, as a quantity of fresh meat was required every day. But the greater reason was the sheer enjoyment of the sport. If a warrior of the Fianna couldn't be fighting, Crimall had said, then it was only in the chase and the kill that he could really test his strength and skill.

Finn and Caoilte now moved back to watch as Crimall and another warrior swiftly slit the stag, cleaned out its viscera, and hung it on the carrying poles. Another pair of men lifted it, and the party started back toward their encampment.

The pack of hounds moved along beside them, seemingly untired from their long pursuit, bodies strained taut with suppressed energy, ready to run again. As Finn looked at them, he realized that learning to hunt with them was one of the most exciting things he had experienced these past days. For the slender, sinewy, small-headed hounds were one of the greatest treasures of the Fian men. They were most carefully bred and most lovingly trained to rouse and pursue and bring to bay any kind of game, from cunning fox or badger to savage boar or bear or even wolf. Around the fires at night there were almost as many tales of their courageous feats as of the deeds of heroes. And each man bragged proudly of his own hounds, giving them great praise and arguing hotly over whose were best.

When the men went out to hunt, it was always afoot, spears in their hands as they chased through the forests after the hounds. The pack would dash far ahead, in full cry, the wild, piercing shouts of the men adding to the din, stirring up every bird and beast for far around. Then some worthy game would be spied, and the hunt was on. And the harder the pursuit, the more rugged the ground, the more cunning and fast and dangerous the quarry, the more the Fian warriors relished it.

It was late in the afternoon when their hunting party came back into the encampment. It had been set up on an open, pleasant hillside surrounded by the thick woods. Each day now they camped in a different spot. Concerned that the Mornas might have begun searching for them again because of Finn, they had abandoned the wattle huts. They had taken up the nomadic life that was the custom for men of the Fianna during the warm half of the year, moving constantly and sleeping beneath the stars.

When Finn's group arrived, it was to find preparations for the evening meal well under way. As on every hunt day, some of the band had dug the cooking holes—wide, shallow pits—and lined them with the plentiful stones of rocky Ireland, heated in a nearby fire. As the hunting parties brought in their game throughout the day, it was dressed out, wrapped in green rushes, placed within the holes, and covered with more heated stones. There it was left to broil.

As the warriors finished their hunting and returned to camp for the night, they made ready for the meal.

First the dogs were seen to. Any wounds were tended, the coats were brushed free of burrs and twigs and mud, water and some of the choicest bits of the game they had helped to take were given them. Then the men went to a nearby stream to thoroughly wash themselves in the chill flow—an almost ritual observance for them—and comb and plait their hair before gathering about the dinner fire.

While the cooking pits were uncovered and the meat was passed out to the company, Cnu Deireoil, who had remained at the camp, brought his own skills into use. He entertained the men with tunes on his harp, the lilting strains drifting away into the clear night sky.

The men of the Clan na Baiscne had changed in these past days, Finn noted as they ate. The men around him now were far different from the defeated lot he had first met. Since they had chosen to support him, their vigor had grown rapidly. It was as if his own vitality had infused them. The ragged beards had been shorn away. Flamboyant mustaches and elaborately plaited hair had appeared. The warriors had begun to look and act like much younger men, which, indeed, many were. Finn had been both surprised and pleased to discover that most were still very much of active years. His own uncle was not far past thirty years of age.

With the meal finished, the talking began. It was in these evening discussions with the men that Finn had learned the Fian lore: its rules, its beliefs, its history. This night Crimall was telling him of the code of honor which a Fian warrior had to accept.

"So you see, Finn, you'll have to put away this thinking of yours that you must have some sort of revenge for your father's death," he was explaining. "When you join the Fianna, you give over any right to seek revenge or satisfaction for the deaths of your own kindred, as they must not seek satisfaction for any harm to you."

"But the Morna clan killed my father!" Finn pro-

191

tested. "They tried to destroy our clan!" He was having difficulty in understanding this philosophy.

"Aye, Nephew," Crimall agreed, "and it would be for his sworn comrades to get the proper revenge for a wrong. But only if it violated Fian codes or the laws of Ireland. The Morna clan's fight with us was a fair one."

"Fair!" exclaimed Finn. "And was it fair for the Morna clan to be hunting me across the land?"

Crimall shook his head. "No," he admitted. "That makes little sense to me. But then, neither did their coming against us, nor their ruthlessness in trying to wipe our clan away. We'd been rivals before, but not enemies. Still, their clan made a rightful challenge and won the leadership. Aed MacMorna—the one you say they call Goll now—was properly proclaimed the new captain by the high king."

"Then how is it I'm to regain my father's place?" Finn wanted to know.

"Ah, well, you have a right to claim the clan chieftainship your father held," Crimall explained. "After that, you can challenge the Morna clan for the leadership." He shook his head doubtfully. "Though whether we'll ever have the force to take it from them, I don't know. We're surely not strong enough to battle for it now."

"We'll find a way," Finn said determinedly. "First, Uncle, you have to see me ready."

"That I will do, Finn," the other promised. "That we will all do."

The talk and the storytelling and the playing of the Little Nut went on then until the warriors grew tired. The fire was banked for the night and the men moved into the woods. There, under the shelter of the sweet-smelling branches of the pine trees, Finn made his bed as the others did, in the way his uncle had taught him. Over a layer of freshly cut fir boughs that provided a soft and springy mattress, he laid a thick layer of moss and then a layer of rushes.

He lay down upon this comfortable, fragrant bed, putting his sword close beside him, and settled his head back upon his arms. He looked up toward the clear night sky, blazing with its now familiar embroidery of stars, and thought of the long and dangerous path still ahead of him.

Then something drew his attention. A shape flashed across the field of stars, blocking them out for an instant as it swept low above Finn. Then it was gone.

An owl, thought Finn, beginning its own nightly hunt.

But it was no owl that had flown over the sleeping men. It was an enormous raven with a glittering black eye.

Finn noted the black form of a raven drifting high above them, circling with apparent idleness in the air currents. It must be curious about them, he decided. It had been staying overhead for quite some time.

He had noticed it because there was little else to draw his attention. The hunt had been nearly fruitless through the day. They had wandered far to the north in search of game. The dogs had wearied of barking and the men had grown hoarse in shouting with no result. Now, with the afternoon well upon them, they were all growing irritable with their frustration.

"This is getting to be just a bit too much," Cnu Deireoil said in a complaining voice as they trudged along. "I've certainly picked a fine hunt to come on."

"Just recall that you did choose to come," Caoilte answered testily. "We certainly would never have asked you."

"I was becoming bored sitting about a camp all day," the harper said. "But now I've discovered what true boredom is." He appealed to Finn. "Couldn't we give it over?"

Before the young warrior could answer, Crimall spoke up in a stubborn tone: "No! We'll give up no hunt empty-handed. We go on!"

Finn shrugged and gave the weary little man a regretful smile. "Sorry, my friend. It's Crimall's hunt you're on."

"Forever, it appears," Cnu Deireoil said, sighing heavily.

Doggedly they pushed on, into territory new to them, hoping to find game more plentiful there. Then, as they were crossing a meadow toward another area of forest, a strange beast appeared suddenly from behind them.

It had narrow legs like a deer, but its head was that of a boar, and it had long horns. On its wide flanks were round spots that shone like moons. It swept by them with a speed like that of a passing wind, vanishing into the woods ahead.

"By all the gods," cried Caoilte. "What was that?"

All of Finn's curiosity and instinct for the hunt were aroused by the bizarre creature. He turned to the others.

"Have you ever seen a beast like that one before now?" he asked them.

"We never have," Crimall said, looking after it with a covetous eye. "And it would be right to set the hounds after it."

The hounds were already barking madly to be in pursuit. The men released them, then started after the flying pack at a full run.

Only Cnu Deireoil hesitated, feeling an intense foreboding.

"Wait!" he called after them. "There's something wrong in this!"

But they were already well away, caught up in the fever of the hunt. So, not wishing to be left alone in this unknown area of the forest, he sprinted after them.

As fast as the hounds and the men of the Fianna were, they were just able to keep the animal in sight. It drew them deep into the wood, which grew ever denser about them. They ran on and on, ignoring their weariness in their single-minded desire to win this chase. They ran on as the sun descended toward the horizon, as its light dwindled, and as a damp and clinging mist rose up around them.

The mist grew thicker, filling up the space between the trees as if it were a white liquid poured into

the wood. Soon it had swallowed up the fleeing creature. The pursuers were forced to slow down, the dogs
now sniffing their way ahead on its trail, the men moving along behind, peering about with increasing uneasiness.

"I recall a night like this," Crimall said in a gloomy
tone. "It was when your father died, Finn. The mist
was meant as a trap for us, I think."

"I told you there's something wrong," Cnu Deireoil
said. "Let's be out of this."

"I'm not giving that creature up," Finn said stubbornly. "Not when we've come so far."

"Look!" said one of the men, pointing ahead.

Something was visible in the fog ahead. A dark
shape, barely discernible, stood atop a low, treeless
hill. The creature had stopped and was awaiting them.

The party crept toward it, the dogs very subdued
now, almost reluctant to approach. Finn and the others
were all aware of a disturbing aura here, but they had
to go on, impelled by their need to know what they
faced. They reached the low hill and mounted the
slope, spears up and poised to throw.

The dim shape grew clearer, its outlines darker,
sharper, until it finally reached a recognizable form.
The men pulled sharply up, staring in confusion. It was
no beast that they faced, but a woman.

She was tall and slender and stood proudly erect,
her figure wrapped closely in a long robe of softly
glowing red. Her eyes were large and silver-blue and
lustrous, her hair a flood of golden radiance about her
shoulders.

Lowering his spear, Finn moved closer to her.

"Red Woman, we greet you," he said politely.
"We're seeking a beast with moons upon its sides. Have
you seen it?"

She regarded him for a long moment with her
brilliant eyes. Then she spoke, her voice soft and clear
at once.

"How far have you pursued this beast?"

"We have been on its track since we left the forests

of Lough Dearg," he told her, "and we are bound to follow it until it falls."

She smiled. "Many men have chased that beast across all of Ireland," she said. "None has ever caught it. None is swift enough."

"We are," Finn said with pride. "And I will not let it go until I know what sort of beast it is."

Her soft voice took on a threatening edge: "If you yourself or your men go after it, I will stop you."

"Stop us?" Finn said, smiling himself now. "It is a score of fighting men of the Fianna of Ireland I have with me here."

"It is little heed I give to yourself or your men," she said coldly. "And if you try to pass me, it will be your end."

"It will be a bad day when a threat from the likes of you will put fear in myself," Finn told her, angry now. He turned to the others. "Let's all follow, men and hounds, after that beast."

He took a step forward, and the woman before him began to change. In amazement he watched as her body grew fluid, swelling and shifting in an instant to the shape of a monstrous worm. Its shape was thick, slightly flattened, headless, its only feature a drooling, sucking mouth. The surface of it was smooth, soft, and covered with a shining mucous.

Before Finn could recover from his surprise and defend himself, it was upon him, throwing itself forward and wrapping him with its wet, sticky coils. He fell backward, the thing upon him, winding itself tighter about him. He felt it constricting, closing about him like a giant fist as it began to crush the life from him.

Chapter Twenty-three

THE KING OF THE HILL

Finn was battling, feeling his life being squeezed out. He struggled to keep his consciousness, squirmed violently to pull his arm clear of the coils and stab at the thing with his spear. But he couldn't move, and the grip on him was tightening, tightening. He could feel his consciousness slipping away with his last breath.

But Caoilte leapt forward, directly upon the sluglike creature, throwing his arms about its coils and wrenching at it to loosen it from Finn. Soon others of the band joined him, gripping the thing at several points to wrench at it.

They succeeded in forcing it to ease its hold on the trapped warrior, but they also brought its wrath upon themselves. It uncoiled suddenly, whipping about at them, sweeping several of them down in a heap. Then it was upon them, its pliable body spreading, oozing down over them in a sticky blanket that could smother them.

Finn, gasping for breath, fought his way back to full consciousness. Seeing the struggle before him, he climbed to his feet. He ignored a swimming head and charged to the attack. Locating what he thought must be the head of the thing, he leapt upon it, shoving the broad head of his spear against it.

The creature stiffened then, and from it came a voice.

"Keep back your hand," it said, "and you will not have the curse of a lonely woman upon you."

"Release my friends," he told it, "and take the woman's shape again."

It slid back from the men it had fallen upon, its form pulling together, rising, solidifying into the outlines of the Red Woman.

"Why do you leave me alive?" she asked him. "I would not have left you your life if I could have taken it from you."

"You are beaten," he told her. "I've no more need to harm you. Now, be out of our sight, and let us continue our hunt in peace."

"I'll bother you no more," she promised. "But you'll not catch the beast you seek."

With that she turned and, in two steps, faded into the mist.

"Now that was surely an unpleasant little fight," said Caoilte, trying to wipe some of the sticky substance from his arms in disgust. "For such a beautiful woman to change into such a horrible worm!"

"Look there!" shouted Crimall.

They all looked around in time to see the horned beast whisk by them once again and race away.

"Quickly, after it!" Finn cried.

"You are mad!" Cnu Deireoil. "There's certainly magic at work in this. The magic of the Others, too, I'd say. Don't challenge it, Finn. The last time it nearly destroyed us."

"We can't turn away from fear of anything," Finn told him. "I've said that I will not stop until that beast is caught, and I'm bound to that now. I'm going on. Will you others come as well?"

The challenge roused the other warriors too. To a man they started off again with Finn after the beast. The hapless Little Nut, drawn against his will, followed in their wake.

It was fully dark by this time, and between it and the mist they would surely have lost their quarry, but the moons upon its sides glowed brightly, giving out streams of light that showed clearly through the shrouding gray. So on they chased, keeping the beast always in their sight.

Through all the night they followed, until at last the sun rose, striking through the mists, burning them away with golden light, revealing the countryside around. The hunters found themselves in a strange and eerie land. Ahead of them, an enormous hill thrust suddenly, starkly from the gently rolling lands below it. Its sides were steep and rocky, but its top was softly rounded, green with grass and thickly covered with trees. Across the rolling meadows at its foot were scattered scores of the smooth earth mounds that marked ancient burial places, the great numbers clustered there indicating that some tremendous sacred aura existed about this place.

But this aura meant nothing to the band now. Their whole attention was directed on the beast ahead. For it was making straight for the hill, and they shouted in triumph, thinking it trapped at last.

They were wrong. Without slowing its pace, the beast rushed right against the steep, rocky cliff side at the hill's base and vanished there.

The men and hounds pulled to a stop, staring ahead in angry disbelief.

"How can it have gotten away?" said Crimall. "We had it there. We had it!"

"I know how it could escape," said Cnu Deireoil unhappily. He was not staring at the place where the beast had vanished, but up at the looming hill itself. "I know this place. It is Cnoc-na-Righ. It's truly the realm of the Others we're in now!" He looked pleadingly at Finn. "Please, let's be away while there's still time!"

"So, you did not take the beast," said a woman's voice.

Startled, they all wheeled about to see the Red Woman regarding them from a nearby mound.

"Maybe we didn't yet take it," Finn admitted, "but we know where it is."

"It is brave men you are to follow the beast here," she said. She lifted a hand from the folds of her long cloak. In it she held a long, polished stick of blackthorn, knobbed at one end, tipped with silver at the other.

"Come with me now if you are truly brave, and you will see this wondrous beast you've sought so long."

She moved gracefully down from the mound and past them, going to the foot of the cliff.

"That's a druid rod," Cnu Deireoil whispered to his comrades. "Careful. She might mean to try some enchantment."

But all that she did was to lift the rod and strike a blow against the solid rock. There began a shifting and a groaning deep within it. This grew rapidly louder, until the whole cliff face before them seemed to shake. A crack appeared in it, widening to a crevice. The rock pulled apart like a curtain being parted, revealing a wide, smooth-sided cave that ran deep into the mountain.

Far down that corridor the Fian men saw the wavering gold of firelight. And from the cave depths the sounds of music and the aromas of food drifted out to them.

The Red Woman turned and beamed upon them, the expression on her face now warm and welcoming.

"Come in now," she said, "till you see the wonderful beast."

Finn had never seen anything like this marvel. He was overawed by the power it represented. How could any magic rend a cliff? Then her welcoming words brought him back to practical reality. He looked down at himself and around at his mates. Their clothes were torn from the chasing, muddied from the fight.

"Our clothing is not clean," he told her, "and we would not like to go in among a company the way we are."

She nodded. Stepping into the cave mouth, she picked a golden hunting horn from a hook there, lifted it to her lips, and blew a single high note.

In a moment ten young men appeared from within the hill. They were tall, slim, fine-featured, nearly boys in looks. All were fair-haired, and all clad in similar tunics of green glowing silk fringed with red-gold.

"Bring water for washing," she told them, "and bring clean suits of clothing, and a rich cloak and tunic for Finn, son of Cumhal!"

"She knows your name, Finn," Caoilte murmured. "That's not good."

"We've no choice but to go on now," said Finn.

The young men left them, but returned soon after carrying silver basins for washing and fine new clothes for all the band. The men cleaned themselves and dressed. Finn's own clothing was finer than any he had ever seen. The tunic was of a soft, cool linen, hemmed with fine gold thread and patterned in elaborate spiral designs. Over it he draped a four-folded cloak of deep forest green, fastening it at his throat with a round brooch of gold set with precious stones. When he strapped back on his well-worn harness and sword sheath, they seemed to him very shabby in comparison.

When the men were ready, the Red Woman directed her ten serving boys to take charge of the pack of hunting dogs. Then she directed the Fianna men into the cave. Courageously, Finn led them forward, determined to show courtesy, whatever the danger.

Again, the Little Nut hung back, looking fearfully into that yawning cavern and up at the smiling face of the tall woman.

"Come along, harper," she coaxed in a friendly way. "You won't be harmed here, that I promise you. And if you try to run, you'll not escape"—her rod lifted and her eyes flickered with a dangerous light—"that I promise as well."

Cnu Deireoil gave a deep, despairing sigh. "I knew it would come to this one day," he said, and fell in behind the rest.

They moved along the long corridor in the rock, going down and into the heart of Cnoc-na-Righ.

The light increased as they moved forward, becoming suddenly intense as they came out into an enormous space. Their dazzled eyes slowly became used to the bright glow, clear, white, and warm as the sun, soft and gently pervasive as the moon. They were looking into a single room, so broad and high that Finn realized the whole inside of the hill must be hollow.

The roof of the chamber was a great vault, carved from the living rock, the strata of it showing in the smooth surfaces arching above. Far across the space, and from high above, a stream of water spouted from the stones, cascading down in a fanning waterfall to crash in shimmering explosions of spray against the floor. There the water pooled and formed a stream that flowed away to be lost in the distance.

In the center of this area was a ring of widely spaced stones, roughly man-height and of a crude pillar shape.

Within the ring of stones was a second ring, formed of tables set around a great bonfire. At these tables were many scores of people, all tall and slender, fair and handsome of looks. They were at a meal, the tables laden with quantities of food—meats and breads and fruits—filling elaborately crafted, gleaming dishes of gold. Musicians were playing a merry air on harp, pipes, and *tiompan* while others of the bright company performed a lively dance on the open ground about the fire. The clothes of these folk were a dazzling swirl of colors, shifting so swiftly Finn could not identify them all.

"What is this place?" Finn asked, gazing about in open awe.

"A Sidhe it is, my lad," answered Cnu Deireoil. "A hidden palace of the Others. To be brought into it means nothing good for us. Those that are taken Away by the Men of Dea are never seen again by mortal men."

As the Red Woman led them across the vast space toward the central ring, the little harper moved closer to Finn.

"There he is," he muttered darkly to the warrior. "There's the King-of-the-Hill himself. A dangerous one he is!"

Finn had no difficulty in knowing which one it was the little man was referring to. Across the circle from them was an enormous chair. It was of oak, its high back and wide arms carved deeply with designs of strange creatures—birds and serpents and beasts, stretched out in sinuous curves and intertwined. On this impressive throne sat a lean, lank-bodied man, long

202

of jaw and nose and high of forehead. His wide, elastic mouth was now stretched by a grin, and his large hands were clapping with the music as he watched the dance. His cloak was an almost painfully bright checkered pattern of reds and blues, and on his narrow head sat a golden crown that seemed a bit too large, for it had slipped down on one side in a rakish tilt.

"He seems a cheerful enough man to me," Finn commented to his friend.

"Oh, he is that," agreed the Little Nut. "But he'll also have your guts to feed the ravens if he has a mind. As changeable as Ireland's weather is our King-of-the-Hill."

They reached the stone circle, and the Red Woman signaled the Fian band to halt. She moved between the stones and approached the king. Drawing his attention from the dance, she spoke to him at some length while he listened intently, his broad grin slowly fading, the wide mouth drooping in a frown. When she had finished, he turned his attention toward the visitors. The gaze of his company had already been drawn to them, and now the music died away, the dancers coming to a stop. There fell a silence more deafening than the noise. Finn felt suddenly uncomfortable as the focus of so many curious stares.

"Come forward!" the king demanded in a sharp, supercilious way.

"Here it comes!" Cnu Deireoil said fearfully. "We're in for it now!"

But Finn pushed him forward, and the band moved past the stones, up toward the ring of tables and through an opening into the central area. They stopped again across the fire from the king.

He ran a cold, scrutinizing eye over the Fian men, then dropped his gaze down to fix upon the Little Nut.

"So, Cnu Deireoil, you've chosen to fall in with the likes of these mortals, have you? And just how low do you think we can let one of the Tuatha de Danaan sink?"

One of the Tuatha de Danaan? The words astonished Finn. He and Caoilte glanced at their little friend.

203

Cnu was white-faced, clearly terrified in this man's presence. Still he spoke up courageously: "I'm doing as I wish, as any man should be free to do. And these 'mortals' you're so scornful of are as fine as any man of the Sidhes of Ireland, as you'd know yourself if you'd ever leave this great rock tomb of yours."

"Your wishes don't carry to wandering about the surface of Ireland without the permission of your own people, harper. And as to your feeling about this race that has stolen away our lands and driven us into the hidden places, I can only call it madness."

Finn was not really paying the close attention to this exchange that he might have. His eye had been caught by that of a young woman seated beside the king. She was, he decided, quite the most beautiful woman he had yet encountered in Ireland. She had the fragile, finely sculpted looks of his own mother and a billowing mass of golden hair that glowed as if the sun were beaming upon it. She also had a most intriguing light shining in her large gray eyes, and because of his recent experiences, he now understood what that light implied. He smiled.

Then his attention was yanked harshly back to the conversation as the Red Woman said: "But, my king, do you really think that Finn MacCumhal must be destroyed?"

"Wait now!" he said quickly, stepping forward. "What do you mean, destroyed?"

The king cast a disdainful look upon him. "Stay out of this talk," he said curtly. "You've no part in it."

"But it's my own life you're speaking of!" Finn hotly replied. He put his hand to his sword hilt. "And I've no fear of your powers, no matter how great. If you wish to harm me or my friends, the Little Nut as well, you'll have a fight of it."

"Is that so?" said the king.

Behind them there arose a great rumbling and grinding sound. Finn's party turned to see the tunnel they had followed into the hill closing together, the sides of the rocky passage sliding in until they touched, wed perfectly together, fused tight as if never parted.

"You're sealed forever now within this hill, unless I choose to free you," said the king.

"Maybe," Finn said, showing no fear, "but if you come against us, you may find that you don't want us trapped with you in here."

"Still arrogant, are you?" the king said with some surprise. "Well, young warrior, and why should you not be killed by us? There are those among our people who want it done."

"Why?" Finn demanded. "I've done nothing to you."

"He's right, my king," the Red Woman said in support. "He's done nothing to earn our dislike, and he's proven to me that he is a warrior to be admired. He and his men pursued the beast without failing in their strength or courage. No others have ever been able to do as much. And he showed great honor in letting me go when he might have killed me."

"Perhaps," the king said thoughtfully, "but he has the blood of a mortal in him."

"There is as much reason to take his part as to be against him," she said in a reasoning tone. "He has the blood of the de Danaans as well."

"What do you mean?" asked Finn, bewildered by this cryptic exchange.

"Your mother, Muirne, is one of us, Finn," the woman told him. "She is a granddaughter of Nuada Silver Hand, who was once high king of all the Children of Danu."

"Can that be true?" Finn said, astounded by this revelation. "She said nothing of it to me."

"Of course it's true, Finn!" Cnu Deireoil said with sudden understanding. "I knew I sensed something in her when I first saw her. It was a kindred spirit."

"To accept your father's love, to live with him, she had to choose to become a part of his world," the Red Woman told Finn. "She could let no mortal know the truth."

"Enough, woman!" thundered the king. "You have told him more than it is his right to know. His father corrupted one of us. His mother turned her back on her people. That must be avenged."

"No! It must not!" cried the Little Nut. The king's words had made him angry, and the anger banished his fear. "You're meaning to punish this lad for our losing of Ireland, not his own wrong. Muirne's only crime was to wish to live amongst the mortals, as was mine. If the kings of the Sidhe of Ireland can condemn us for that, then there's no freedom left to us."

There were mutterings of agreement and support from the gathering of Sidhe people at his words. Some even spoke their sympathy aloud. Surprised by this response, the king looked around at them.

"Are you saying that this Finn shouldn't be harmed?" he asked.

"It's for those who think themselves wronged by him to take what revenge they can," a noble white-haired man of the company answered forcefully, "not for ourselves. We've no right to be interfering in this fine young warrior's life."

The golden-haired young woman beside the king then spoke to him, her gentle voice reasoning, coaxing, and caressing all at once: "If part of him is ours, then all of him is ours. That has been our way. To hurt one of our own would be a greater wrong than any done to us through love. My king, you would not seem just in it. You would seem evil."

These last words of hers were enough. He nodded, and then turned to the Fian men.

"Finn MacCumhal," he said sternly, "I'll accept these arguments for leniency toward you. You have won your life from us. You and your warriors will be allowed to leave here safely."

"And what about Cnu Deireoil?" Finn asked, putting a hand upon the little man's shoulder. "I'll not leave him."

"You are a lad of strong honor," said the king. He looked at the harper. "Well, I think his own courage in defending you has won his freedom as well. I'll give my own leave for him to go into the upper world again, so long as he vows to stay with you."

"That's fair enough!" the Little Nut said with glee.

"But listen to me, Finn MacCumhal," the king added. "Expect no more kindness from us or so fair a treatment from the next people of the Sidhe that you meet. Do you understand?"

"I do, my king," Finn answered earnestly. "You are a gracious man."

At such politeness, the king beamed with pleasure. "You have manners too, I see. Well then, before you go, you must accept our hospitality in return for the harsh treatment we've given to you. Join in our feasting."

Such an invitation could not be refused. Finn and his companions sat down in places opened for them among the bright company. They were given all manner of foods, rich beyond comparing with the simple warrior's fare. They drank of deep red and golden liquors that Finn found filling and warming, wiping away all his fatigue. They watched the dancers and they listened to the bards singing of the faraway islands of Tir-na-nog, where palaces were golden and there was only peace.

Finally the King-of-the-Hill rose on his throne and lifted a gleaming chalice toward his guests.

"It's time for your leaving now," he said. "A final drink with me before you go."

Pitchers were brought, and the cups of Finn's band filled again.

"May you do well in battle, Finn MacCumhal," the king said, "and may you die well when your time is come to you. Peace to you now."

They drank deeply. Finn felt the drink as a peculiar surge of heat that went through him like a wave. Suddenly he felt very heavy, his limbs going numb, his mind confused. Was he drunk again, he wondered?

"Wait!" he said, forcing the slurred words through lips that seemed to have grown very thick. "The beast. The beast we followed here. The Red Woman said that we would see it."

"And so you shall," that woman said, coming into the middle of the tables and stopping beside the fire.

Finn watched her, his vision blurring quickly. He

realized that her form was shifting again. Through a rapidly growing haze, like a sun-drenched mist, he saw that the beast stood before him. Its twin moons shone out like beacons.

But he could focus no longer. The glowing white was filling up his head, overwhelming him. This was wrong! This was not drunkenness. It was something else. Something else in the liquor. Was it poison? Did the King-of-the-Hill mean to destroy them after all?

With this last, awful thought, the swelling whiteness swallowed him and he was lost.

Chapter Twenty-four

A PARTING

When Finn awoke, it was to a familiar scene: the slowly lightening dawn sky.

He stretched and shook his head to clear it of the muzziness, then looked around. He saw trees, but no sign of Cnoc-na-Righ. The forms of his companions lay about him on the ground. He checked them all quickly. They seemed to be only peacefully asleep, although he couldn't wake them.

He sighed and looked around again. Once more the powers of the Sidhe had tricked him. He wondered if perhaps the whole thing had been some dream, some illusion, like the phantoms.

A hand touched his shoulder and he whirled around. He found himself looking down into the small, beautiful face of the young woman from the hall of the Sidhe. It had been no dream.

Her eyes still held that familiar, tantalizing look.

Her smile was warm. She moved close, touching his arm with a small, slender hand.

"You are all right?" she asked him.

"I'm not certain," he said truthfully, feeling still a little dazed. "What about my friends?"

"They are only sleeping," she assured him. "They will awaken when the sun is fully risen. From here you will be able to find your way easily."

"Why were we put to sleep?" he wondered.

"It was meant to keep you from discovering our Sidhe again. Now the power of Manannan that protects all the Sidhes of Ireland will lead you Astray should you go near it again. You are not even to know if your visit there was real."

"I wasn't certain, until I saw you," he said.

"I am not supposed to be here," she told him. "I wished to speak to you, alone."

"I am glad," he told her, lifting a hand to touch the fine hair.

She took the hand in her two small ones, holding it tightly.

"There is no time," she said earnestly. "Please listen. The king told you that you could expect no other kindness from my people. He was wrong. There are those among us who would help you, and I am one of them. You must know that the enemies you face are much more powerful than you think. You've a right to know who they really are."

"Really are?" he asked in puzzlement. "What do you mean?"

"It is Tadg, the father of Muirne, who wishes you destroyed by us. Though he is the druid to Ireland's high king he is of the Tuatha de Danaan."

"Why does he hate me?"

"Because his daughter Muirne was taken from him against his will by Cumhal. It was a great insult to him that he had to avenge, though even his daughter never knew of it. He schemed with Conn of the Hundred Battles himself to destroy your father, and to see you dead as well."

"The high king is part of this too?" Finn said in surprise.

She nodded. "Yes. He fears your leading the Fianna to defy him, as your father did. He cannot be trusted, Finn, nor can any of his court."

"All my life I was told that it was the Clan na Morna I must beware," he said. "I never realized."

"None of the mortal world did, save those involved. It was meant to be that way. You may find that Goll MacMorna is less the enemy than you thought."

"But, how—" he began.

She lifted a hand, touching her fingers to his lips.

"No more," she said. "The sun is almost fully up. I've risked too much already coming here. If the king discovers . . ." She left the punishment unspoken, but Finn understood.

"I don't know how I can thank you for what you've done," he said. "Why are you helping me?"

She lifted suddenly up on her toes, leaned toward him, and pressed her lips to his. It was a kiss more filled with warmth and energy than the magical drink of the Sidhe. He tingled from it still after she pulled away.

"I must go now," she told him. "Good fortune go with you."

As she moved away, Finn recovered from the kiss and called after her: "Wait! Tell me who you are!"

"I am called the Shadowy One," she said, and proved her words by fading away into the woods. But as she disappeared, her final words drifted back: "I will see you again, Finn MacCumhal."

He certainly hoped so, Finn thought, raising a hand to his still tingling lips.

A loud snort drew his attention to Caoilte. The man was stirring, coming awake. His eyes opened and he was instantly alert, leaping to his feet, hand on sword hilt, body set for defense. Then he saw Finn grinning at him and realized where they were.

"By all the gods my family swears by!" he exclaimed.

The Little Nut awoke then, sitting up and staring around him with great intent.

"Ah!" he said in a much relieved way. "So they did leave us alive!"

"Did you doubt they would?" Caoilte asked. "They're your own people."

"How do you think I know they can't be trusted?"

"Knowing you're one of the Others explains a great deal to me," the dark warrior said. "I thought there was something peculiar about you."

"At least I have an excuse for it," the harper shot back. Then he looked up at Finn. "It's our young friend's being of our blood that's wondrous to me. It must be what drew me to helping him that first time we met."

The other Fian men were awakening now. With varying degrees of alacrity they stretched and shook and climbed to their feet.

"Look there!" said Crimall, pointing westward toward a patch of sparkling light amongst the trees. "That's Lough Dearg! We're almost back at our own camp!"

He led the way through the woods, paralleling the lake. Soon they were coming out into a meadow. The camp and the figures of the older men who had remained behind were visible. So was a wave of furious activity that rushed toward them with a confused sound of frenzied barking. In moments a swarm of animals was about their feet, leaping excitedly.

"It's the hounds!" Finn cried happily. "The Others have sent them back as well."

The men of the camp explained that the animals had returned during the night, raising some concern as to the fate of the hunting party. Crimall recounted their adventures, and Finn added to the tale what he had learned from the Shadowy One. The news disturbed his companions greatly.

"I've not met this Tadg," Cnu Deireoil said, "but it's certain his powers are great. We'd best be watching always."

"It's hard to think the high king himself is in this," said Crimall, "but it does explain the Morna clan challenging us."

"What do you mean?" asked Finn.

"Well, you know that the Fianna are meant to serve the high king. But it's true your father had become a bit . . . well . . . arrogant. I'd warned him about it myself. I feared he'd push the king too far one day."

This was a most peculiar notion to Finn. In Bodhmall's teachings, there was no suggestion that Cumhal might not have been blameless in his own downfall.

"Your father wanted more power for the Fians," his uncle went on. "But to Goll the bond to the king was always before any other. If Conn wished him to take the leadership from us, he would have obeyed."

"If the high king is part of this," said Caoilte, "it'll make your task all the more difficult, Finn."

"He's right in that," Crimall agreed. "You'll not be able to simply walk into the hall of Tara and proclaim yourself openly. Conn will likely have you killed as an outlaw when you step through the gateway."

"But I've got to make myself known, or I've no way of claiming the chieftainship," Finn said.

"There may be a way," Crimall said thoughtfully. "At Samhain time, the chieftains of Ireland gather at Tara for the celebrations. During that time, no one is allowed to take up a quarrel with another. All men are protected by a peace. If you could make your way into the fortress then, you could make your claim without the Morna clan or the king being able to act against you."

"And with all the other Fian chieftains there, Conn could do nothing else but acknowledge you," Caoilte added with a grin. "It's a brilliant notion, Crimall."

"It will be, if Finn is ready to prove himself worthy to be a Fian warrior and a chieftain by Samhain."

"What do you mean, Crimall?" Finn asked him in surprise. "You said that I had learned the Fian knowledge well. I'm ready now!"

"No you're not, Finn," his uncle replied gravely. "It's true that you have the strength and courage needed. And you know the Fian skills and lore as well as any of us. But there's one other part of the training that you're lacking yet."

"I'm ready for it," Finn said with his usual determination. "Tell me. Show me. I'll do whatever I have to do."

"He's telling the truth there, you know," Caoilte said with a laugh. "He can't be stopped. He has the vigor of a hundred men. It's very wearying sometimes."

"I believe he has the spirit," Crimall said. "I'm just afraid he hasn't the time. You see, he's yet to learn the bardic skills to be accepted by the Fianna."

"Bardic skills?" Finn repeated, not understanding.

"Aye, Finn. It's the high bards of Ireland who keep the knowledge of our past and spin out the songs that record our present. What we are lies with them, all our wisdom and our great deeds, and our mistakes too. You see, a man of the Fian is more than a fighter and a hunter. He's a man who also honors wisdom above all else. To be accepted, he must have the bard's skills for shaping songs, and he must know the twelve books of poetry."

"It sounds a great deal to be learned," Finn admitted.

"It is. Most lads who wish to join the Fianna study under a bardic teacher for many years to learn it all. You have less than a quarter of a single year to do the same."

"There must be some way it can be done," Finn said. "I mean to go to Tara at Samhain."

"If you're bound to try, then you must go to Finnegas. He was the greatest teacher of the bardic ways in all of Ireland when your father and I were boys. He was our own teacher. If you could have his help, and if you were swift enough of mind, you might succeed. But he must be old now, and I've no idea as to where he might be found."

"I would," piped up the Little Nut. "I've heard of this Finnegas myself. The other bards I've met here and there in my travelings speak of him. But they say he's given up the bardic calling, oh some seven years ago that was."

"Given it up?" said Crimall. "What for?"

"To fish, they say. He's set himself down on the bank of the river Boinne to fish, and nothing else. No one knows why. Some think that he's gone mad. He might not help you, Finn."

"I'll make him help me," declared the irrepressible young warrior. "Somehow I have to make him help me!"

Finn tied the shield upon his saddle and turned to the others of the clan gathered about him.

"Well, I'm ready. There's no delay for me now. I'll need every day."

"Finn, are you certain we shouldn't go with you?" asked Crimall. "The Brugh na Boinne is very near to Tara. It will be very dangerous for you there."

"That's why I'll not risk my clansmen in this," Finn replied firmly. "This is something that I must do alone. Besides, I'll attract less notice by myself than with a score of men. Believe me, Crimall, it is the safest way."

"You are the one who leads now," his uncle said. "We will stay here. But at Samhain time, we mean to go to Tara with you."

"That you will do," Finn promised. He looked around at the other men. "We will all go to prove that the Clan na Baiscne is not yet dead."

The Fian warriors greeted this with shouts of enthusiasm, but a high and strident voice cut across it.

"Wait now, Finn MacCumhal!"

They looked about to see the Little Nut and Caoilte approaching them, their own horses saddled and ready for traveling.

"Don't think that you'll be leaving me behind here!" the harper said as he reached the group. "You've no knowledge of that part of Ireland. You'll never find this bard alone."

"But my friend, I don't want you to be hurt!" Finn reasoned.

"You know well enough I can't be hurt by a mortal so long as I have my harp or my whistle. And it would be a real danger to me if the King-of-the-Hill knows I'm not with you." He folded his arms and fixed an unwavering stare on Finn. "So I'm going, and that's all there is to it!"

Finn laughed. "I can see there's no moving you in this. And I'll welcome the company, as always." He looked at Caoilte, who had stood quietly through this exchange, his expression wooden. "And what about you, Caoilte? What are you meaning to do?"

The warrior shrugged. "It looks as if my task is finally over. I've fulfilled my oath to you. I'm my own man again. It's time for me to be moving on."

"But you're still an outlaw," Finn reminded him. "You'll not be safe."

"You could stay here with us," Crimall suggested.

Caoilte shook his head. "I've never been much for staying. I might make my way back down to Corca Dhuibhne and take up service again. It's the proper place for the likes of me."

Finn felt a sorrow in him at that. It had not occurred to him before that the dark warrior might not be staying with him. Still, he knew he couldn't hold a spirit as free as Caoilte's. He tried to put on a cheerful front.

"Well, there's nothing left to hold you," he agreed. "You've done more than was needed. You've given me a warrior's skills and seen me here." He put a hand on the other's shoulder. "I owe much to you, Caoilte. Wherever you go and whatever you do, you'll be my friend."

"I had better be!" the dark warrior told him, smiling. He clasped Finn's arm, meeting his gaze for an instant in silent fellowship. Then he abruptly turned away, climbing onto his horse. He took up the reins and looked down at Finn.

"Good fortune to you," he said. "You'll make a fine chieftain, I think, if you don't manage to get yourself killed first." His eyes went to the harper. "Good-bye, Little Nut. See to our young friend. And to yourself."

He turned the horse and urged it away. Finn and the others watched him ride off. It seemed to the young warrior that there was much he still needed to say, but he had no words. When Caoilte had disappeared from sight, he shook off the regret and turned briskly to his clansmen.

"Well, we'll be starting now ourselves. Ready, Cnu Deireoil?"

The harper nodded, and they both mounted. Finn looked down at his uncle.

"Farewell for now," he said. "If all goes well, we'll meet at the Brugh na Boinne and go on to Tara."

Crimall lifted a hand in a final salute and the pair rode away. They angled to the north to skirt Lough Dearg before turning toward the east. They rode on in silence for a time, each lost in their own thoughts. But finally Finn spoke: "It seems as if my life's becoming nothing but departings lately."

Pulled from his reverie by these words, the Little Nut nodded. "True enough, lad. Believe me, I know the leaving's hard."

This sympathy raised a question in Finn's mind. "Tell me, what brought you to leave your own home?"

"Boredom," the harper said flatly. "The life of a Sidhe is beautiful enough, peaceful, comfortable, safe. Ah, it was like death to me. The mortals' world may be quite harsh and cold, but it's exciting too." He sighed and added, "Though, mind you, there's times I'd not mind visiting home for a bit."

A fluttering above drew Finn's attention then. He glanced up to see a black bird soaring above, sweeping across, then turning lazily to sweep back.

Finn continued to note the bird as they rode on. It was very curious, he thought, that the creature stayed above them, flying in wide circles, but never disappearing from sight.

"Do you see that raven?" he at last said to the harper.

"How could I not?" Cnu Deireoil replied. "It's a very large one. Like a hawk it looks."

"It's very curious about us," Finn said musingly. "It's been above us since we left the camp."

"That is a bit odd," the little man agreed, giving the gliding bird a harder look.

"More than that. I think I've seen that bird about before."

"Before? What do you mean?"

"In our traveling. I've noticed great blackbirds flying close above us many times. I saw one above us when we left the bruidhean. I saw one above us on our last hunt. A great raven, just like this one."

"And both times we ran afoul of the Others soon after," Cnu Deireoil added.

Finn met his eyes. "You're thinking what I am then."

"That those of the Sidhe could be in this? Of course I am. Your Tadg may have them tracing our every move."

"How can we be sure?" Finn asked.

"I've an idea," the harper told him. "Let's just look for a thicker place in the woods."

Soon they came upon an area where the foliage of the trees formed a canopy so dense that it concealed them completely from observation from above. They rode through it quickly to its far side, where the trees gave way to a small open glen. Here they dismounted, well within cover, and peered cautiously out. The raven swept by above them, flew ahead, then wheeled about to pass above the thick area again.

As soon as it had flashed by and was momentarily out of sight, the harper moved from the trees and threw himself down on the open ground, assuming a sprawled attitude that impressed Finn by its impression of lifelessness. He crouched back in the shelter of the trees, tense and waiting.

The bird swept into view again. It soared by, but then banked into a sharp turn, angling back and down toward the tiny figure. Cnu Deireoil's idea had worked. He had drawn the attention of the raven.

It pulled into a tight spiral above him, clearly giving the situation a careful scrutiny as it dropped down. Finn watched anxiously as it came ever lower. Would the ruse take it in?

At last it fluttered to a landing on the ground some way from the motionless body. It hopped cautiously forward, pausing often, its sleek, glowing blue-black head twisting sharply from side to side as it examined Cnu Deireoil with its glinting eyes. Drawn by its curiosity, it came closer, closer, closer. Only an arm's length away from him, it stopped to stare intently, seeking some sign of life.

This it got. For the harper suddenly jerked his head up and met the raven's black gaze with his own. In the instant their eyes locked together, Cnu Deireoil recognized the power within the bird.

"So, you are a child of the Morrigan," he said triumphantly.

With an angry caw, the raven flapped its wings and began to rise away.

"Quickly, Finn!" the little man called. "It is an agent of the Sidhe! Stop it!"

In two strides Finn was out of cover. The bird was off the ground already, stroking powerfully upward with its great wings, pulling itself higher. Finn lifted the hunting spear he had held ready. The raven reached the height of the treetops, turned to soar away into their cover. Finn launched his weapon at the tiny target as it began its graceful sweep.

The spear flew unerringly to its mark, the head thumping into the raven's body, impaling it, knocking it into a shapeless bundle that plummeted from the sky, smashing to earth.

Finn and Cnu Deireoil moved to stand over the dead raven. The sleek, elegant body looked now like a pile of ragged black wool.

"Now at least we can travel safely without all the Sidhe folk of Ireland knowing where we've gone," the harper said with satisfaction.

"For how long, I wonder?" Finn asked, his gaze lifting again to scan the sky.

Chapter Twenty-five

THE SALMON OF KNOWLEDGE

The scrawny figure moved down to the bank of the broad, sparkling river. It crept along the shore, its lean head crooked forward on a long neck, searching the ground before it carefully. Finally the proper place was spotted. The being stopped and, pulling its long robe about it in a fussy manner, settled down right at the water's edge. Long arms held out a square net. The head thrust far forward, like that of a turtle, eyes peering fixedly down at the moving surface. The lanky form stiffened. Now it might have been a peculiarly shaped tree stump rooted in the riverbank.

From a safe distance away, two pairs of curious eyes closely observed the strange behavior of this creature, sheltered from its view by a screen of brush.

"Do you see?" Cnu Deireoil told his companion softly. "It's just as I've heard. That's all he does the whole year around. It must be madness."

"It could be that you're right," Finn reluctantly agreed, staring at the motionless form.

"How do you expect to get help from a ragged creature like that?" his companion wondered.

Finn shrugged. "There's no other choice. I have to try."

"All right then," Cnu Deireoil said resignedly. "I'll keep a watch on you. But just you be careful how you approach him. Even a sane bard is a touchy sort of creature. I've met enough to know that. It's like a child speaking to a parent you should be. Cajole. Plead. Ask him to take pity on you and become your teacher." He paused, looking out at the bard again, then added, "Likely he'll still turn you away."

This rather doubt-filled advice did little to bolster Finn. Still, he was determined to have a try. He unstrapped his sword, giving it into the care of Cnu Deireoil. Then he moved out from their cover and up the river's bank toward the man.

He tried to establish clearly in his mind the kind of attitude he must take. Above all, he must show a great respect. The closer he came to the crouching man, however, the more he wondered if he wasn't making a mistake.

The figure had not moved since taking up position. It was still in that awkward, stiff attitude, as if some enchantment had frozen it. The only sign of its life was the eyes, shifting restlessly back and forth across the rippling water. The body was even more gaunt than it had seemed at a distance. Bony elbows and knees thrust out through holes worn in the tattered robe, which Finn realized had once been a splendid garment. The finely textured cloth was worn to filthy rags and the rich, golden fringing had been mostly torn away. The man himself was as unkept as the gown, his graying hair a matted tangle about his shoulders, an untrimmed beard masking all but a sharp nose and bright, thick-browed eyes.

Finn stepped up close beside him and stood quietly, waiting for the bard to acknowledge him. But the bard seemed not to notice, all his attention fixed on the water running close beneath his nose.

Finn cleared his throat and then, somewhat hesitantly, ventured a greeting: "Ah . . . hello," he said, as pleasantly as he could.

There was no response. Finn tried again.

"Have you had good fortune fishing here?"

Still no reply. He might have been a bird chirping in a tree for all the interest the crouching man was showing. Finn scanned the riverbank with the practiced eye of a fisherman, gauging the water's depth and the play of currents.

"You might find more fish if you'd try over there by that rock," he suggested helpfully.

This, finally, brought results, but only minor ones. The scrawny body tensed, almost vibrating. The eyes narrowed with irritation.

"I've come a long way to see you," Finn said with more insistence. "It's very important that I speak to you."

The lips moved behind the screen of beard. The voice came like the sound of a hinge grown rusty from long disuse.

"Go away!"

"Go away?" Finn echoed, his own voice growing sharper with rising anger. "Look here, I'll not go away until you talk to me. I need your help!"

"Well, I don't need you bothering me!" the bard rasped back. "Can't you see I'm fishing? Go away!"

Finn remembered the Little Nut's suggestions. Swallowing his anger, he dropped down beside the man, forcing a pleading note into his tones.

"Please, Great Ollamh, I must learn from you. I must have the wisdom that a chieftain of the Fianna of Ireland must have. Please teach me as you taught my father. I am the son of Cumhal MacTredhorn."

"I don't care who you are!" the man snapped, tearing his gaze from the water with an obvious effort to glare at the young warrior. "I am fishing. It is all that I care about. I've no time or interest in the likes of you!"

"Why?" demanded Finn. "You can at least tell me that."

The man sighed deeply. "All right, if it will make you go away the faster." The gaze swung back to the water, taking up its intense search again. "There is a salmon here. For seven years now I have been waiting to catch it. Nothing else is of any importance to me until that has been done."

"A salmon?" Finn said. He looked at the water and then back to Finnegas. The man was indeed mad, he reflected sadly. "But, Great Ollamh, no fish can be that valuable."

"This one can," the old bard said impatiently. "It's

221

not just a fish. It is a fish of great powers, and it is meant only for me!" He glanced at Finn, saw the openly skeptical look in the young man's eye, and his temper flared. "I know. You think I'm mad. Well, I am not! Seven years ago I was given the prophecy that I would catch and eat a salmon that would come to me here. From that salmon I would gain knowledge greater than that of any man. Think of it, boy! It's a prize worth waiting for all these years, isn't it? Now, will you go away and let . . . ME . . . BE!"

On these last words the bard's voice had risen to a shout, the sound echoing away across the wide river. Realizing what he had done, the old man quickly lowered his voice to a whisper, adding threateningly: "The gods help you if you've made me frighten it away!" Then he dropped back into his crouching position, becoming silent and motionless once more.

"Wait!" Finn whispered back in desperation. "You can't do this. I can't reclaim my father's place without you. Don't you understand?"

There was no answer. It was again as if the man had been turned to rock.

"I won't leave here!" Finn said stubbornly. "I'll stay until you help me!"

"Not . . . until . . . I catch . . . this fish!" came the response through clenched teeth.

Finn felt defeated. He wanted to pick up the wretched man and shake him. But he knew that force would not make the bard help. There was nothing he could do. He climbed slowly to his feet and started to turn away. But then he paused, staring down at the water.

Just beneath the surface, close to the bank where he stood, something was moving. That it was large he could tell by the high ripples it created as it shot toward the crouching Finnegas like an arrow from a bow.

The bard saw it, saw the huge, dark shape beneath the water. With an exultant hoot he leapt forward, spreading the net out between his hands. He splashed down atop the moving thing, disappearing beneath the

222

waves, rising again almost immediately, arms clasped about something that struggled within the net.

"I have it! I have it!" he cried out happily, battling the creature thrashing wildly to escape.

"Let me help you," Finn volunteered.

"No!" the bard shouted back. "I'll do this myself!"

And he did. With a great effort the scrawny man fought his way to the shore, carrying and dragging the writhing bundle. Putting all his strength into a great heave, he managed to get the netted fish out of the water. Then the drenched, dripping, exhausted man dragged himself out after it.

Panting for breath, he looked down at his prize. It was indeed a salmon that lay within the tangled net, its blue-green scales and white belly glittering as it flopped madly to free itself. Finnegas gazed at it with the pride of a man seeing his first son. Then his eyes lifted to the young warrior standing over him, and a curious light came into them.

"Seven years I've been sitting here, waiting for this salmon," he said thoughtfully. "Seven years, and not a sign of it. Then you come here, and within a moment's time, the fish is all but throwing himself from the water at my feet!"

"It was your good fortune," Finn said.

"Maybe. Maybe. Who was it you said you were again?"

"My name is Demna, son of Cumhal," Finn told him, reverting to his true given name for this formal purpose.

"Well, Demna, it seems you've brought me luck. Maybe I can be of help to you after all—if you're willing to serve me."

"I'll be most happy to do that, Great Ollamh," Finn said eagerly, his hopes renewed. "Anything you wish."

"Can you cook well?" the bard asked.

"I've been well taught," Finn answered.

"They're not necessarily the same thing. But it will have to do. My own cooking is something only barely eatable, and I want no chances taken with this." He climbed to his feet slowly, greatly wearied by his battle. He lifted the loaded net with a grunt and held out the still squirming catch to Finn. "I want you to take this salmon and cook it for me. Can you do that?"

Finn took the fish, looking at it and then at Finnegas uncertainly. "Are you sure you want me to do this?"

"I do," the bard said firmly. "Come with me."

He led his new pupil away from the riverbank to a nearby clearing. There sat a small and badly weathered hut of wattle and daub. With its bony frame poking out here and there through holes in the daub, and the wind-tattered condition of its gray thatched roof, it looked rather like the bard himself.

"There, lad," the still dripping man said, pointing to a tumbled pile of rocks near to the hut. "You can build a fire and cook the salmon there." He pulled himself erect and said with pride, "I mean to go and make myself ready for this occasion." He looked down at himself. "I've let myself get a bit shabby these last seven years."

"Yes, Great Ollamh," Finn said, holding back a smile as he looked at the bedraggled figure. "Just a bit."

The bard shot him a glare at that, and Finn sobered quickly, asking: "And how would you like the salmon cooked?"

"Broil it, lad," he ordered. "You'll find a spit there." He stepped forward, lifting an admonishing finger as he went on. "And listen to me, boy: prepare it carefully! Eat none of it yourself. If you want my help as badly as you say, you'll give me your word. The salmon is for me and me alone!"

"I'll eat none of it, Great Ollamh!" Finn promised. But he was wondering just how much he did still want the bard's help. His madness seemed to have abated little since making the catch.

Finnegas stared searchingly into the young man's eyes for a long moment, then he snorted. "Well, I suppose I can trust you," he said grudgingly. "Get on about it, boy. I've waited long enough for this!"

He turned and shuffled into his little hut. Finn

went to the stone fireplace and kindled a small fire, feeding it from a meager pile of sticks. He set up a rusting and badly bent iron rotisserie, then took the salmon from the net.

It truly was a magnificent fish, plump and as long as his arm. He cleaned it carefully, exposing the fresh pink flesh of its insides. He slipped it onto the skewer, fixed it into the supporting frame, and began slowly to rotate the fish over the flames.

While he was cooking, he heard a sharp whistle from the trees close by. He looked around to see the face of the Little Nut peering out cautiously from the cover.

"How is it going?" Cnu Deireoil called softly.

Finn looked around quickly to be certain Finnegas was still inside his hut. Then he called back. "Fine! Fine! At least, I think so. But get away. I don't want him to see you."

"All right. I'll make camp a short way upriver, in case you need me. How's the old man?"

Finn lifted a hand and tapped his temple in reply.

"Good luck, then," the harper said, and withdrew into the shelter of the trees again.

Only moments later, the bard reappeared. He had dried and neatly combed out his hair and beard. They now formed a single bush of gray about the small patch of exposed face. Even the thick eyebrows had been brushed, and now flared upward dramatically.

He had exchanged his threadbare robe for one of brilliant white edged with gold. An exquisitely wrought torc of twisted gold bands was about his throat. In his hands he carried a large platter, also of gold.

"You look very fine, Great Ollamh!" Finn complimented as the bard approached.

"Thank you, boy," he answered, clearly pleased. "I've had this robe of mine folded carefully away all these years, awaiting this." He lifted the platter. It had been newly polished and shone softly. Its edge was deeply embossed with curling designs and set with precious stones. "I've kept this, too, knowing I would have need of it one day. I've cared for it as I would my

225

child." He looked down upon it lovingly. "It was given to me by the high king himself, many years ago. It will be suited to such a momentous feast."

"As you say," Finn replied, trying to sound non-committal.

The bard fixed an irritated gaze on him. "You still think I'm mad, don't you? Well, never mind. Just see to the cooking and bring the salmon to me when it is done!" He thrust the platter into the young man's hands, wheeled about, and stalked back into his hut.

Finn returned his full attention to the fish, taking great care to keep it turning slowly to cook all sides evenly. It was doing very well, the skin of it browning and crisping beautifully. At least he would make the peculiar bard pleased with his cooking, he told himself.

But even as he thought this, he noted one spot that had begun to darken too fast. The moist, hot flesh was boiling, and a great bubble rose up beneath the skin, threatening to burst. Fearing that his perfect meal would be blemished, Finn acted instantly. He thrust out a thumb and pushed the blister down. But the oozing juices burned his fingertip, and in pain, he instinctively shoved the damaged thumb into his mouth to suck on it.

To his amazement, he found that this tiny taste of the salmon was like a mouthful. The warm, rich, meaty flavor of it flooded his senses. It was most peculiar, like a surge of energy, like lightning flashing within his mind. He felt suddenly very aware, of himself, of his thoughts, of the world around him. For an instant everything seemed to shine with a brilliant clarity that made him feel as if he had been only half awake before.

He jerked the thumb from his mouth. The sensation faded instantly. He stared at his thumb in wonder, then looked down at the cooking fish. Was there some power in this salmon, as Finnegas had said?

He reminded himself sharply that this was nothing to do with him, no matter how curious he was. He had made a bond to serve Finnegas, and this he would do faithfully. The salmon was thoroughly done now and

226

must be served. It and whatever power it had belonged to the bard and to no one else.

So, with these noble thoughts, Finn carefully eased the broiled fish from the skewer and slipped it, steaming and fragrant, onto the golden platter. He carried it with slow, certain steps to the hut door and, raising it before him in a triumphant gesture, stepped inside.

The bard was seated behind a worn and warped plank table, covered now at one end with a dazzling white cloth and set with a silver knife and a candlestick holding a burning taper. It seemed ready for some sacred ritual, and Finnegas sat behind it, proudly upright, face glowing with excitement, like a high druid ready for a great sacrifice.

Finn set the platter before him with a flourish and stepped back. The bard examined the salmon critically. He picked up the silver knife and prodded tentatively at the skin. It fell open, the succulent fish done to a flaky perfection. He looked up at Finn.

"It seems cooked well enough," he admitted. "But we will see."

He lifted a large morsel on the knife point, bringing it toward his mouth. Finn could see the trembling of his lips, the expectation in his eyes. The man could barely stand it.

Then another thought occurred to him. He glanced suspiciously up at the young man again. His voice was demanding.

"Boy, you didn't eat any of it at all now, is that right?"

"No, Great Ollamh!" Finn responded promptly. "You can see that yourself. I had none of it."

That might have been enough, but then Finn's ingrained need for honesty came into play again. Under that searching stare, he had to tell the complete truth. "Of course, I did lick some juice from my thumb after I burned it touching the fish."

"What!" Finnegas sat back as if he'd been struck. "You tasted it! You couldn't have!"

"It—it was an accident!" Finn said haltingly, shocked

by the violence of the man's reaction. "It was just a small touch. I've eaten none of—"

"I mean, how could it happen, boy?" the other shouted. He banged both fists on the table with his full might to punctuate his words. "It . . . is . . . not . . . possible!"

Finn stood stiffly, not knowing what to say. He believed the man had passed from simple madness into raving lunacy.

"It's not possible," the bard repeated, speaking with greater control this time. "No, the prophecy said that it was the one named Finn alone that would taste the salmon. And you said your name was . . . something else . . . what was it?"

"Demna, Great Ollamh," Finn supplied. "That's the name I was given at birth. But most of my life I have been known as Finn."

This news seemed to draw the bones from the old man. He sank back limply in his seat, his face draining of its color. "Finn!" he repeated hollowly. "You are Finn." He looked down at the fallen bite of pink, succulent fish that had a moment before been so close to his mouth. So close. His voice reflected his sense of desolation at its loss. "Then it must be you that the prophecy was speaking of, not me."

"I don't understand," Finn said.

"Wait! Wait!" the bard told him irritably, holding up a hand. "Give me a moment to get used to this. It's a hard thing to discover after seven years."

He looked around him at the decrepit hut, down at the table and the waiting salmon. Then he sighed and seemed to pull himself together, sitting upright again.

"All right," he said in brisker tones. "If it's to be that way, it will." He arose, stepped aside, and gestured to the seat. "Sit here," he ordered Finn. "It is now for you to consume the entire salmon!"

Chapter Twenty-six

BARDIC TRAINING

Finn looked blankly at the man. "I still don't see."

"Oh, you don't?" said Finnegas. He sighed and glanced upward as if appealing to some invisible powers. "And this is the one the gods have chosen for such a gift?" he asked. Then he looked back to the young man. "Now, listen to me, lad: it was prophesied that this salmon would be consumed by one named Finn, and that he would gain great knowledge as a result. I thought it was to be me. Clearly I was wrong. It was you. The fish all but killed itself to come to you when you arrived. You tasted of it before I did. So now you must sit down and eat it all."

Finn looked from the salmon to the bard. "But are you certain?" he asked uncertainly. "You've waited for so long. I don't mean to take away—"

"Look, the salmon is yours!" Finnegas snapped testily. "Don't expect me to be gracious about it as well. Just sit down here and eat the bloody salmon, will you?"

Finn obeyed with alacrity, springing into the seat, taking up the knife, and all but diving into the fish. The bard watched him closely as he cut into the warm flesh, raised a piece, and put it into his mouth. Finn found its taste rich and savory, but he chewed and swallowed without real enjoyment under those staring, disappointed eyes.

"Seven years," the man muttered darkly, watching piece after piece disappear into the young man. "Seven

years I sat here, letting my joints stiffen. And for this!"
He leaned forward. "Tell me, what is it like? What is
the power doing to you?"

Finn considered, then shrugged. "I don't feel anything," he said.

"Oh?" Finnegas said. "You must need more. Keep
eating."

"Excuse me, please," Finn managed to get out
around a hot mouthful of salmon, "but will you still be
willing to tutor me after this?"

"Tutor you?" the bard repeated. "You are a bold
lad, asking me that after stealing away my salmon!"

Finn fell back to eating, silently, eyeing the man.

"Still," Finnegas went on heavily after a time, "I
suppose you are the one who's been chosen. And you
say you are Cumhal's son?"

"Yes, Great Ollamh."

The bard sighed again. "Well, then it seems I'm
meant to help. The fish must be some sign of some
future greatness for you, and I'm clearly the one who
must see you properly trained." He paused, considering, then went on as if to himself: "I'm to be an instrument. I suppose that's always the lot of a teacher; to be
the instrument for someone else's winning of their goals.
Still . . . I had hoped . . ."

"Does that mean you will help me?" Finn asked
hopefully.

"Yes, I will," Finnegas answered, "if I must. But if
you are as leatherheaded as your father was, it'll not be
easy."

"Is there so much to learn, Great Ollamh?"

"Of course there's much to learn!" Finnegas replied indignantly. "The storyteller's calling is the most
exalted in Ireland! His authority is next to that of the
king himself. Why, even to become an ordinary bard
requires seven years of study. Becoming a *filé* or an
ollamh requires twelve."

"Seven years?" Finn said, taken somewhat aback.
"Why?"

"Because of the amount of material. A bard must
know the twelve books of poetry. Each concerns a

230

different class of tales: courtships, destructions, tragic deaths, cattle raids, encounters with the Others, and the like. There are three hundred and fifty in all. You'll begin with the simpler ones, and move slowly on to the more difficult. You'll be learning the art of composing the poetry yourself at the same time. Some go on beyond the seventh year to learn the higher forms of verse and the ancient Poet's Speech, but you'll not likely be doing that. As it is, you're very old for beginning the training."

"Yes, I am," Finn admitted. "That's why I'm afraid I haven't got quite the whole seven years to learn the bardic ways."

"What do you mean?" the bard demanded. "How much time have you?"

"I . . . ah . . . hoped to be finished before this Samhain," Finn said reluctantly.

This last revelation could bring no new astonishment to Finnegas. He nodded, as if he had expected something of the kind.

"Samhain," he said in a resigned way. "Of course. You want to gain the knowledge of seven years in sixty days. Certainly. Why not? It should be simple then."

"Good!" Finn said, much relieved. "I was fearing that you might be upset by that." And with his appetite freshened by this good news, Finn resumed his eating of the salmon with a real will.

Less than a day's walk eastward along the Boinne River from the hut of the ollamh, a chariot carrying Tadg, high druid of Tara, rolled to a stop.

"Wait for me here," he commanded its driver, climbing from the back of the wicker-sided car.

The man looked nervously toward the high, rounded hill that rose abruptly and ominously from the smooth lowland along the river's bank.

"You'll not be gone long, will you, High Druid?" he asked hopefully. "It's said that the Others live within that hill. People who venture here have been taken Away by them and never seen again."

231

"You will be safe so long as you stay here," Tadg assured him. "But I warn you: do not wander!"

"I'll be doing none of that, High Druid," the driver said most emphatically.

Tadg nodded and started away from the chariot toward the base of the hill. The driver watched him with apprehension, wondering what dark and terrible secrets a man of such powers was seeking in this haunted spot. He saw the druid come close to the base of the hill, then stared in shock as Tadg's form began to shimmer, like an object seen through a haze of heat. Its outlines grew quickly hazy, its colors faded, and it was abruptly gone.

Frightened by the magical disappearance of his passenger, the driver glanced quickly around him at the landscape, feeling suddenly very much alone. His impulse was to urge the horses away at their best speed and leave this cursed place. But somehow he knew that to disobey the high druid's order would be a great deal more unpleasant to him than anything that might happen to him here. He waited.

Tadg, meantime, was striding up the hillside, unconcerned by the fact that he was now invisible to the outside world. He had penetrated the barrier that both hid and protected all dwelling places of the Tuatha de Danaan from mortal men. As a member of this mystical race himself, the druid had no difficulty in passing through the shield of energy raised by the powers of Manannan MacLir many years before. But no one not of the Other could breach that defense without the permission of those who inhabited the enchanted realm contained within its circle. Should the driver have tried to follow Tadg, he would quickly have found himself led astray, sent off in some other direction, far from the hill, disoriented and lost.

Tadg reached the crest of the hill. It was slightly flattened, providing a platform for a large ring of standing stones. It was composed of a dozen large pieces, taller than a man and crudely shaped into pillars, spaced widely about the open space. In the center of this ring, three men awaited him.

He knew them well. In the center stood Bobd Dearg, a lean, intense, darkly brooding man who was the chosen leader of all the de Danaan clans of Ireland. To his left stood his brother, Angus Og, a fair, youthful, and spirited man whose cheerful disposition helped to balance Bobd Dearg's somberness. On the right loomed the gigantic form of their father, the great Dagda himself, most powerful champion of the de Danaans, his hard, thick body and broad, battered face making him seem like one of the stones himself.

Tadg moved through the circle and crossed the open area to stop before them. His expression was one of displeasure.

"Why have you summoned me here?" he demanded impatiently. "I have duties at Tara."

"You have a duty to us," the Dagda growled, taking a step forward. "When you're called, you come. Don't be forgetting yourself, Tadg. You live in the mortal world because we allow it. You're still subject to our rules."

"You allow it?" Tadg responded scornfully, unimpressed by the giant's blustering. "I am the son of Nuada. My father was your own high king. I do as I wish."

"Your freedom to live in the outside world was agreed upon by us all, you must admit," Bobd Dearg said in more reasonable tones. "It was intended that you become part of their life, watch them, help us to understand them, not interfere with them."

Tadg eyed Bobd Dearg coldly. "Why don't you say out what you mean."

"Very well," the de Danaan ruler agreed. "We believe it is time that you give up this drive to destroy the son of Cumhal."

"What?" Tadg cried in disbelief. "How can you say that? You know what insult has been done us. My daughter was brought to deny her own people, to accept the mortal world over her own."

"This boy called Finn had no part in that," Bobd Dearg said.

"He is a product of the obscene union," Tadg said

233

slowly, gratingly, through clenched teeth. "He is a symbol of the violation of my family, of our whole race. His existence is a continued insult to me that I will not tolerate!"

"You were wrong in asking our help," Angus Og now stated. "The Shadowy One has come to us. She told us what happened at Cnoc-na-Righ. We have met and we have talked with the leaders of other Sidhes. All of us are agreed. The Tuatha de Danaan have no right to interfere in the life of Finn MacCumhal or his comrades."

"I might have known you would argue so," Tadg answered with a sneer. "You always have displayed an unnatural liking for these beings who savagely tore Ireland from our hands."

"Be reasonable, man!" the Dagda bellowed irritably. "I hate what the mortals have done to us, and I'd be the first to match iron against them in a fair fight, but this lad carries our blood, too, and he's done us no harm."

"So," Tadg said, his chill glance moving from man to man, "you are telling me that you will no longer help me to exact the vengeance that is owed to me?"

"We're asking you to understand that there is no need for vengeance at all," Bobd Dearg replied. "Muirne's choice was her own. It was made for her love of Cumhal. The crime you see is in your own mind. Your need for revenge has already destroyed your daughter and Cumhal. It has interfered with many lives. It is enough. Let it be finished."

"I will not," Tadg angrily shot back. "The insult was to me, not you. You cannot understand. Until the blood of Cumhal is utterly wiped away, my honor is not clear. If you have chosen not to help me, then choose as well not to hinder me. Nothing will keep me from my end. Nothing!"

With that, he wheeled and stalked away from the three men, who stared after him in some dismay at his defiance.

"The man's obsessed," Angus Og pointed out. "He'd

bring all the mortals of Ireland to war if it served his purposes."

"Well, he's alone now," said the Dagda. "What can he do?"

"He has great magic," Bobd Dearg told him. "Even among our own druids he's known to be very powerful. Who knows what he could do?"

"That may be," the Dagda admitted, "but I know that if he tries to use our people in his schemes again, it will go hard for him." He clenched a massive fist. "I'll see to that."

Tadg, meantime, had reached the base of the sacred hill. He strode angrily back toward the Boinne River, fuming with indignation over this treatment by his own race. What fools they were, he thought. Had their defeat and their years of hiding away in their underground realms made them so weak, so passive that they could meekly allow this outrage? Well, he would not. He would find a way to act.

He was through the protecting barrier now. The chariot and driver were ahead. The man was looking toward him with a great smile of relief. A hard day's ride would see him back in Tara, able to begin devising some new plan.

But suddenly he stopped. He stiffened, all senses alert. He turned and looked westward along the shining band of the river. A sharp breeze had arisen from there, tangy with the first scent of fall decay, damp and keen with the foretaste of coming winter snows. But it also seemed to carry a hint of something else, something that called up a hazy vision of his daughter smiling in the arms of Cumhal, of their forms blending, uniting to form another image of a handsome, insolently grinning, fair-haired youth.

He had not seen Finn before, but he knew that this was the hated boy. Tadg could feel his presence, as if he were close by, as if the druid could almost touch him, smell him, hear his voice.

Then the breeze died and the impression faded with it. Tadg shook his head irritably. The experience had disturbed him. Could the boy dare to be so close to

Tara so soon? He wished he knew. He lifted his eyes and scanned a sky already half covered by a swiftly moving front of thick gray clouds. He had searched the skies often lately but, as now, had always found them empty. When would he receive news from his ravens again?

Another blast of cold wind whipped about him. He shuddered and pulled his cloak tighter, then started on toward the chariot again at a quick pace. The suddenly changing weather was a reminder that he would have to begin overseeing preparations for the Samhain fete soon. The mortals would have to have their rituals.

He knew that the complex arrangements that would begin at Tara would be making the days until the festival pass very swiftly now.

"Back to Tara," he ordered the driver as he climbed into the car. "At your best speed. My time is very short!"

Chapter Twenty-seven

THE TRAINING ENDS

The fall passed very quickly for Finn. Each day he noted that a bit more warmth had faded from the air. Frosts came, and the trees the two sat beneath to work flared brightly with the changing of their leaves. The surrounding woods Finn hiked in alone to meditate or memorize grew emptier of their summer life, more barren, more brown, more skeletal in their look. And it rained more often; cold, heavy, clinging rain that made the trees and the worn hut droop as if in mourning for the passing of the season of warmth. On many days now, he and Finnegas huddled by the fire in the tiny hut for lessons while the wind shrieked across the fire hole and icy drops splashed upon them through holes in the tattered thatching.

Yet neither the stark life nor the constant, rigorous teaching of the bard were hardships for Finn. Instead, they reminded him of Slieve Bladhma and stern Bodhmall, surrounding him with a comforting sense of being home. The intensive learning itself was also pleasant because of its engrossing nature. He discovered that the vast oral literature of Ireland was a rich storehouse of customs, philosophy, history, and dreams from thousands of years of living in this land. He began to feel that he understood the people he had met more clearly. He could see how the savage and beautiful country had given them both a fierce independence and a single spirit that made them all one.

He found the new discipline of learning the ways of poetry interesting too. It was as exacting in its way as learning the fine skills involved in hunting or using a sword.

He studied as one possessed. Finnegas gave him no rest and no quarter, whipping his mind to greater efforts as Bodhmall had once whipped a weary child's legs to force him up one more hill. The bard taught him tricks for committing the many poems to memory and skills for learning with ever increasing speed. As with the rabbits in the field so long before, the perseverence forced him to gain greater swiftness and agility, but of the mind this time.

Even without the help of Finnegas, however, the mental abilities of Finn were far above normal. He mastered the bard's skills and tricks with a speed that amazed even the great ollamh, though his other teachers—Bodhmall and Crimall and Caoilte—would have expected it. Like them, Finnegas soon learned that this young man would not be kept from finishing what he had set his mind to do.

And so it was that on a chill, wet, blustery evening five days before the beginning of the Samhain festival,

Finn was able to stand before the ollamh to take his final bardic test.

Already he had been through a rigorous examination. The titles of poems chosen randomly from the twelve books had been thrown at him, and he had supplied a recitation of each tale that was correct to every single word. With all the proper inflection, emphasis, and embellishment, he had spun out the drama of Lir's Children, the adventure of the Cattle Raid of Cuailnge, the tragedy of Deirdre of the Sorrows.

Now he stood, collecting his thoughts, feeling somewhat uncomfortable under the ollamh's scrutinizing gaze as he prepared for the last part of his trial. He must prove his mastery of the poet's skills by reciting a poem created by himself.

He took a few deep breaths to compose his mind. He set his voice for the low, smooth, impassioned tones of a bard and began:

Spring is the most pleasant time, beautiful its
    colors.
The blackbird sings out his full song, the liv-
    ing wood is his holding.
The cuckoo voices a constant strain, welcom-
    ing bright summer.

Summer dries the rivers down, swift horses
    seek the pools.
The heather spreads out its long hair, and soft
    white bog-down grows.
Wildness comes on the deer's heart, the sad
    sea is lulled to sleep.

The harp of the woods plays music, there is
    color on the hills.
A haze lies on the full lakes, every sail fills in
    peace.
The high, lonely waterfall sings welcome to
    the warm pool, and the rushes speak.

Black as the raven's feathers is the bog, the
    cuckoo's welcome loud.

The speckled salmon is leaping, strong as the
  leap of a fighting man.
The strength of man is surging, the maid proud
  in her growing beauty.

The hot desire for racing horses grows in you,
  twisted holly leashes the hound.
A bright spear has been shot into the ground,
  the flag-flower shining golden under it.
Faultless spring is the most pleasant time, its
  colors beautiful.

He finished, took a long, deep breath, and turned
to look down at the bard, wondering anxiously what the
judgment would be.

Finnegas stared thoughtfully for a moment that
seemed an eternity, not speaking, giving no sign of his
reaction. Finally he nodded.

"It is . . . adequate," he said in a guarded way. "Of
course, no bard who meant to make his livelihood at it
would do so with such work, but for a warrior it is more
than fair."

"Does it mean that I've passed?" Finn asked with
rising hope.

A smile showed through the screen of beard.
Warmth filled the voice. "Of course it does, Finn.
You've earned the rank of bard."

Feeling suddenly drained by the tension that had
gripped him, Finn dropped limply down upon a bench.

"Facing my first warrior in a fight was not so bad as
that," he said with relief.

"You've more of the bardic learning now than any
man of the Fianna has ever had," Finnegas said, "certainly more than your father. And as for your poetry,
well, there's no comparing. Cumhal's was awful!"

"I owe it to your teaching, Great Ollamh."

"You call me Finnegas now, lad. I'm your teacher
no more. And it wasn't my modest efforts alone. In fact,
it's quite beyond me how you could absorb so much so
quickly. Are you certain there's been no effect on you
from that salmon? It might have sharpened your mind."

Finn shook his head. "No, sorry to say. I've felt nothing different from it, at least so far as I can tell."

"Ah, well," the bard said regretfully. "Then it was a fool's quest I was on, surely. I suppose it happens to all of us when we grow old. We're willing to chase after any chance of glory, even those in our dreams."

"If I could give to you the glory that you deserve, I would," Finn told him.

"Don't you be concerning yourself with me!" Finnegas said firmly. "It's only your own glory that you're to worry about. You've very little time. You and your comrades must be starting for Tara as soon as possible or you'll not arrive for the beginning of Samhain!"

Finn knew that he was right. Only two days before, the warriors of the Clan na Baiscne had come to join him there. They were now camped nearby with Cnu Deireoil, anxiously awaiting the outcome of his trial.

Finn nodded. "You are right, Great Olla—" He stopped as he remembered. Instead he smiled and said, "I mean, Finnegas." He looked around at the tiny, dripping hut, his expression sobering with regret. "I'm leaving once more, it seems. One more home. One more friend."

"You can never leave friends," Finnegas told him. "Even if they're never seen again, something of them stays with you."

"I've learned that," Finn said. "I've much of them with me now"—he put a hand on the bard's shoulder— "and of you. Thank you. Thank you for teaching me how to catch the hares."

"The what?" asked Finnegas, not thinking he had heard rightly.

Finn smiled. "I meant, thank you for giving me your skills. "You know, a woman named Liath raised me to believe that I must understand the beauties of the world to be truly complete. Now I see how important that is to me."

Finnegas lifted a hand and clasped Finn's arm. His gaze met the young warrior's searchingly and his voice was intense.

"Son of Cumhal, I wish you all good fortune. You can be a greater chieftain than your father ever was if you use your honesty, your wisdom, and your strength. But be careful. It's powerful, powerful enemies you've got. As close as Tara is to us, it's a long and dangerous way you have left to go."

"You really expect me to help you again, you treacherous ferret?" Goll MacMorna raged as he paced the parapet walk.

"There is no need for insults, Captain," Tadg answered in his soothing way. "What I'm asking you to do is for the good of all of us."

Goll wheeled upon him. "All of us? And is it for my good when you threaten my honor?"

"This lad may threaten our survival," the high king reminded him.

The three men had this time repaired to the high walkway around the inside of Tara's stockade for their private conversation. Below them, in the yard, activity was already building as the servants readied the fortress for Samhain. Beyond the wall the wide countryside spread away like a quilt of bright patches in its fall colors. But neither the bustle within nor the beauties without held any interest for the arguing men.

"My king," said Goll, "I am your loyal servant still, but I can't without guilt continue hunting this one young man. The warriors of the Baiscne clan are dead or scattered. There's no reason to think he could restore their strength enough to make a claim for his father's chieftainship. And if he has hidden alone for all of these years, he cannot have the skills that he would need even to be accepted as a Fian man. He cannot be any threat."

"No, no," Conn said quickly, shaking his head. "I can't believe that." In the months since Finn's existence had been discovered, the young man had become an ever-increasing object of dread to the aging high king. As if he were some deadly spirit of the slain Cumhal come back to seek revenge, the ghastly vision

241

of Finn's return filled Conn's waking thoughts and haunted his dreams. He had carefully noted Finn's travels, his progress, his victories, certain that the lad's quest would one day bring him here. He was convinced now, with the help of constant, gentle prodding from Tadg, that Finn wanted nothing less than the destruction of his power.

"My king, why are you coming to me again?" Goll asked. "I had thought that your druid had taken the search into his own hands these past days, since I had failed."

Tadg was not going to admit that it was only the refusal of the Tuatha de Danaan to help him any longer that had forced him to turn back to the resources of the Morna clan. His response was reasonable, placating, and quite false.

"I've taken on no search. That duty was and still is yours. I've merely used my own modest powers in a task that no one could expect your warriors to do: trying to locate the boy."

"Your powers," Goll said darkly. He stalked closer to Tadg, his expression glowering. "I warned you about using your magic in this. I'll have no part of it."

"Not so hasty, Captain," said the high king. "What Tadg has done seems justified to me. He's doing nothing that might unfairly harm this lad."

"Of course not," Tadg lied smoothly. "And once he's found, it will only be necessary for you to finish what you began. Send your men to insure that the Clan na Baiscne can never become a threat to us again."

Conn and the druid eyed Goll expectantly. The Fian leader looked from one face to the other thoughtfully. He understood too well his obligation to the king. His sense of loyalty told him that he must obey. Yet another part of him said that he had gone too far, that he had been drawn into acts that violated a greater loyalty to himself. He shook his head.

"No. I'll compromise myself no further." He looked at Tadg. "I can't trust you or your methods. I've acted once too often at your command. I'll do it no more." He turned a determined gaze to Conn. "My king, I'll do for you what I am bound to do. But unless this son of Cumhal does appear and challenge me, I'll do nothing against him. For now, there's nothing more to speak of."

He turned and walked away before Conn could reply. Tadg stared after him with open hostility. One more weapon in his fight to destroy Finn had been taken away.

"Your Fian captain begins to sound like Cumhal himself," he said.

The high king's head turned sharply toward him. "What do you mean?"

"Only that none of the Fianna can be relied upon. The concern of all of them is first with themselves. Goll is a fool. Finn has proven how dangerous he is. Every day he grows stronger. If we wait until he chooses to challenge MacMorna, it may be too late to stop him."

"What can we do?" the high king asked.

"Keep your own household companies alert," the druid advised. "Sooner or later he must come to you to proclaim himself Cumhal's son and lay claim to his rightful place. That we must prevent. My own efforts will go into discovering where he is now. He's still thought to be only a common outlaw to everyone in Ireland, and I have my own . . . agents . . . seeking him as well. Once I've found him, I will find a way to deal with him, I promise you."

"I'm growing a bit weary of your promises, Tadg," Conn told him irritably. "I've heard a great many of them lately, but I've seen no results."

But the druid was not listening to this criticism. His attention had been drawn to a black object that had swept into view from the western horizon. He stared intently at it. It was a raven, a large one. And as he watched, it banked into a descending spiral that brought it swiftly down toward the sacred grove below the fortress's hill.

He kept his eyes locked upon the bird until it vanished into the upper branches of an oak, then turned to Conn, face lit by a new hope.

"I'm sorry, my king," he said quickly, "but I must

leave you." His small mouth lifted in a wily grin. "I may have some news sooner than I'd supposed."

He departed swiftly from the fortress, striding down toward the grove with as much speed as his dignity would allow. He was filled with anticipation. It had been three score days since he had lost contact with the raven he had sent to keep watch upon Finn. Another bird dispatched to spy upon the Baiscne warriors in the Connacht woods had finally found the roving band again, only to report the young man missing. Since then Finn's whereabouts had been of primary concern to the druid. He had taken the only course left to him, charging the raven to stay with the clan in hopes that Finn would join them once again.

However, as the fall days had passed without any news, he had begun to fear that he might never hear. The use of the ravens might have been withdrawn from him along with the rest of the de Danaan's help.

Now he dove into the tangled shadows of the oaks, pushing through them impatiently until he reached the clearing. There the black bird waited, sitting quietly atop the skull upon the central post. Tadg wasted no time in approaching it and trying to establish communication with it. He felt relief when he saw the familiar glow arising within the glinting eyes and the images beginning to form.

Soon he was watching from high above as the warriors of the Baiscne clan gathered their belongings and boldly left the sanctuary of the Connacht woods for the first time in over sixteen years. With growing fascination he followed their journey across a changing landscape, always toward the north and east. Finally the travelers reached a place that he identified with some amazement as the Brugh na Boinne. He saw them come at last to a small hut along its banks. He gazed intently, hopefully, as two figures emerged from the hut to greet them. The image swelled as the bird swept down with breathtaking speed to pass, once, close above. For that instant the faces of the men were very clear.

Elation surged in Tadg. He had found the son of Cumhal once again!

Following this was a quick series of views showing the entire party leaving the hut, crossing the Boinne, and starting south. But this ended abruptly, and he found himself seeing only the shiny blackness of the raven's eyes.

"What is the rest?" he demanded stridently. "Show me where they've gone!"

The bird's response was a harsh single caw. Then, with a laborious flapping of its great wings, it lifted from the skull, climbing up from the clearing, through the almost bare branches of the oaks, and away. Tadg was left alone.

He understood. This would be his last message from the children of the Morrigan. The cursed de Danaans were doing as they had promised. He would have the help of the ravens no longer.

It didn't matter now, he told himself. He had what he needed to know. But that news was more alarming than he had expected. Finn was very close, as he had sensed before. He had apparently gathered the remnants of the Baiscne clan—an impressive number, Tadg thought, for a band that had supposedly been destroyed—and had started south. He could be heading nowhere but toward Tara itself!

But why? He had learned that the young man was no fool. He had to know that he would be facing swift execution as an outlaw before he would have any chance to prove his true identity and make his claim for the chieftainship.

And then the realization came to him: Samhain!

Of course. Finn could come freely, openly, arrogantly through the gates of the fortress, protected by the laws of peace. He could declare himself to one and all without fear of interference. And once he was known to be Cumhal's son, there would be no way the high king or he could act openly against the young upstart again. Nothing would prevent him from then challenging Goll MacMorna for the leadership.

This challenge must never come, he told himself fiercely. For, though Tadg hated the idea of it, he knew what more-than-mortal abilities and spirit Finn had likely been endowed with by his de Danaan blood. More than that, his growing knowledge of the lad and his own powerful, mystical sense were telling him quite strongly that, should a clash come, the Morna clan would no longer be able to stop Finn MacCumhal alone.

Something must be done to head off this threat, and soon. Finn must not be allowed to reach Tara.

He would see it done himself this time. It might be that the Tuatha de Danaan had abandoned him, but they could not rob him totally of help. He still had friends among his people. Some must still be loyal. Some must still be willing to aid him in such a just cause.

One old ally seemed his best chance for stopping Finn now. Conaran, son of Imidd, was his name. His intense hatred of the usurping mortals was well known. And his three daughters—yes, they would be the ones to do as Tadg wished, and quite willingly.

His grin was one of wicked satisfaction. He was far from beaten yet. He met the hollow gaze of the white skull upon the post, and then in a swift, savage gesture swung his bronze-shod druid stick up and knocked it from its perch.

The skull flew across the clearing, tumbling into the thick, crackling blanket of fiery autumn leaves. Its smooth dome cracked by the blow, its unhinged jaw askew, it looked up forlornly at the smiling druid.

"That for Bodb Dearg," Tadg announced loudly, defiantly. "He'll see, all of them will see. Nothing will keep me from having my revenge!"

Chapter Twenty-eight

THE CAVE

It had been a day since Finn and his companions had crossed the wide Boinne and headed southward. With most of the clan's warriors afoot, it would be two more days of traveling before Tara was reached.

Their numbers had swelled considerably since Finn had left them in the forests of Connacht. Crimall had not been idle while Finn trained with the ollamh. He had sent messengers to seek out every remaining member of the band scattered throughout Ireland. A score of warriors had come to rejoin the Clan na Baiscne and risk all in helping Finn make his bid for the place of his father. At least as many more had vowed to join them at Tara.

"There's many a strong young warrior, like yourself, who was an infant or yet unborn when the clan was broken," Crimall explained as they plodded along a road muddied by fall rain. "They have grown to manhood as servants to others, hiding their true blood as you have done, without honor, without pride. Now they see in you their only chance to have something of their own again. If there are enough to support your claim to the chieftainship, the Clan na Baiscne may live once more."

Finn looked back at the eager faces of the painfully young men marching stolidly along behind him. He had not thought before of all the lives he would be risking in this drive to fulfill his own quest. He recalled the carnage he had witnessed in his first battle with uneasiness.

"And what happens if there aren't enough?" he asked.

Crimall smiled grimly. "Then, when Samhain is ended, we may find ourselves deer to the Morna wolf!"

They moved on steadily southward and eastward from the Boinne. Dawn of the second day brought them to a wide, hard-packed main road that Crimall said led to Tara of the Kings.

"We'll not be traveling it ourselves, of course," he pointed out. "This next part of our journey's going to be the most dangerous. If the high king or the Morna clan have any suspicion that we're heading for Tara, they'll have every way guarded."

"Helped by the powers of Tadg," Cnu Deireoil added, looking nervously about. "With de Danaan magic against us, any fox or any tree might be an enemy."

Remembering the raven, Finn glanced cautiously around as well. Once, at the Boinne, he thought he had glimpsed the form of a great blackbird sweeping close overhead. But he had seen nothing since.

"Well, we'll take no chances," Finn's uncle announced. "I know a way across country that should get us to Tara without being discovered. It will take longer, but we'll still arrive before the fete begins.

Across country was, Finn found, a mild way of describing the tortuous route Crimall now guided them along. It seemed to be mostly up and down, across fields of jagged rock and through treacherous bogs, up wind-scoured cliffs and over rain-swept hills of barren stone.

It was midafternoon of the second day when Crimall brought the party to a halt. Leaving them to rest, he and Finn moved on ahead, scouting the way to insure safety.

For some time they moved constantly upward into an area of rugged hills. The stone around them was bare of vegetation and the sky above was heavily overcast, making the world about them seem all a dismal gray. They saw no signs of game and heard no sounds. Even the keening wind had died away.

Following the only passable route, they climbed a narrow cleft up a steep hillside, coming finally upon a wide ledge just below the crest. As they clambered up onto this level area, they stopped in surprise. Before them was a cave, like a jagged hole punched in the gray armor of the cliff face. And before the mouth of it were seated three figures.

They appeared to be old women, gray-haired and scrawny and hunched. They were engaged in some task around three upright sticks that so absorbed them that they seemed unaware of the arrival of the two warriors.

"What are they doing out here alone?" Finn asked in wonder.

"I don't know," Crimall said, "but let's be away. No use in having anyone see us."

"Wait!" came a high, faint, wavering voice from one of the women. "Don't leave us alone. We've need of your help to rid us of our curse!"

The pain and the immense weariness in the voice went to the heart of the young warrior.

"We've got to see if we can help them, Uncle," he said.

"No, lad," Crimall protested. "It's no good our delaying here on such strange business. These women are nothing to us. The journey of your own is all that matters now."

"Seeing to those who are needing help is always what matters first, Uncle," Finn said firmly, "or winning the kingship of all Ireland itself would mean little to me. Now, I'll not be leaving here until I see if anything can be done for them."

He started forward. Crimall realized his brash and stubborn nephew was not to be dissuaded. As Caoilte had so often done before him, he gave a sigh of concession and moved after Finn.

As the two came closer, they saw that the women were indeed very old, and quite wretched in appearance. The skin of their faces was darkened and deeply seamed as if countless years of sun and rain and wind had burned them, eroded them, weathered them away until the flesh was gone and the cheekbones, jaws, and noses were thrown into sharp relief.

The hair of the three was gray-white and very coarse, standing out about their heads in wildly tangled manes. Their eyes, fixed intently, unblinkingly on their work, were large, bright red about the light pupils, and tearing constantly. Their skinny lips were drawn back tightly in concentration, revealing teeth badly broken and decayed. All three wore tattered gowns of filthy yellow wool with the sleeves pulled up to reveal arms that were long and almost skeletally thin.

Finn realized that what occupied them so completely was the spinning out of fleece. Three tall and crooked sticks of holly wood were set upright in the ground before the opening of the cave, forming a large triangle. A thick hank of drawn wool hung upon the branches of each stick, and a woman worked at each hank. With long, bony fingers whose thick nails were like the tips of a cow's horns, they spun the wooden spindles tirelessly.

"They're an unpleasant-looking lot," Crimall commented softly to Finn, grimacing in distaste.

"Their appearance is not their own doing," Finn murmured back in an admonishing tone. He raised his voice to address them. "My good women, what is it that's troubling you?"

"It's cursed we are," said the one who had first called to him. Neither she nor the others looked up while she spoke, but only labored feverishly on. "A sorcerer of the terrible Sidhe folk has put it upon us. We have been slaves of it since we were girls, oh so many long years ago. We've been made to work here without rest, and it's only the hands of the greatest hunter of all the territories of Ireland who can lift the curse from us."

"I make no claim to being the greatest in all Ireland," Finn said with modesty, "but I've been a hunter since my youngest days."

"Is that the truth!" she said with eagerness. "And are you always shouting through the whole country with your great packs of hounds and tearing through the wild places, driving the badgers from their holes, and the foxes in their wanderings, and the birds on the wing?"

"Aye, I suppose that's right enough," Finn admitted. "It is the hunting that's one of the greatest joys of my clan, and of myself as well."

"Then it just may be that you are the one we seek, young warrior. See if you can come to us and pull our hands from these spindles. If you can, our labors will be ended. We will be free."

"I will try it then," Finn promised, starting forward.

His uncle stopped him with a hand upon his arm. "Finn, are you certain you must do this?" he asked.

"I told you, Uncle, I must do what I can," Finn said with determination and went on.

Crimall moved close behind him, a hand on his sword hilt, watching the hags carefully in case they should make some threatening move. The two approached the woman who had spoken first, stepping past the sticks of holly, into the triangle of space they formed.

As they entered it, a strange trembling, as from a sudden chill, fell instantly upon their limbs. Finn noted the tingling first and turned to shout a warning to his uncle.

"Enchantment! Go back, Crimall!"

But it was already too late for both men. The strange ague had swept through their limbs, leaving them unable to control their movements. They stood frozen to their spots, shaking violently, trapped within the triangle of sticks.

Around them the three hags now rose, letting drop the spindles. They gazed at the two captive men, their thin mouths stretching wide in gap-toothed grins.

"It was a fool you were to walk within the triangle," the one woman told them. "It's enchanted wool that hangs upon the holly sticks, and its magic drains the will of fighting men. So now we have you, hunter. Now we will repay your bloody work, your ravaging of our fields and our fair creatures with your savage hounds and your cruel weapons. And we will do the same with any others of your company that come after you."

Finn struggled to move, to break free, to grip his sword, but the uncontrollable tremor was draining away his strength. He stood helplessly as the hags moved in upon him. They bound first him and then Crimall with thick ropes, winding them tightly about his body, securing his legs and pinning his arms to his sides with coil after coil until the two looked more like upright posts than men.

When they were both thoroughly wrapped, the three women approached Finn again, seized him, and lifted him from the ground. The ease with which they did this astonished Finn. Their strength greatly belied their hunched, scrawny bodies. They hoisted him to their shoulders and carried him into the cave.

It was very dim inside and, as they passed into the shadows, Finn could at first see nothing. The hags moved back a short way from the entrance, stopped, and unceremoniously dumped him onto the floor.

He fell heavily atop a lumpy mass of strange objects that snapped and rattled loudly beneath him. It was as if he had crashed upon a collection of brittle sticks and fragile pottery, shattering a great deal of it.

The three women turned and walked out of the cave. Finn quickly realized that being removed from the magic aura of the triangle had allowed his strength to return. With a determined effort he managed to pull himself upright. And, as his eyes adjusted to the cave's half-light, he was able to look about at his surroundings.

He found that he had been dropped into a great rubbish pile composed of human bones.

The remains stretched away to the rock walls on either side and back into the darkness behind him. There were an uncountable number of skeletons here, their disjointed bones jumbled together in a choppy sea of dull white. Close by him, an arm with hand still attached stuck up from the heap as if gesturing for aid. Beyond, a skull smiled at him from its perch atop a high pyramid of bones.

There were many tattered fragments of clothing

mingled with the ghastly remains. There were great numbers of weapons as well, the iron of spear points and swords bloodied by thick rust, the leather of shields and harnesses rotting away. He and Crimall were clearly far from the first hunters who had fallen prey to the grotesque trio.

The women reappeared at the cave mouth, carrying the wrapped figure of his uncle this time. They dropped him down into the bones beside Finn and then moved back to stand in a tight group at one side of the cave, staring down at their prisoners. Crimall looked around him and, uttering an exclamation of disgust, swiftly pulled himself up to a sitting position.

"By all the gods," he shouted at the hags, "what kind of monsters are you?"

"It's yourselves who are the monsters," said a man's voice.

Another figure had appeared at the cave's mouth. Finn peered searchingly at it, but he could see little of it against the bright background. The newcomer was slim and tall and moved with easy grace. He was clad in a robe so white that it seemed almost radiant about its edge.

"Who are you?" Crimall demanded.

There was no response to this. The man stopped on the shore of the sea of bones. He seemed to regard them silently for a time. Finally he spoke again, his voice a smooth, calm, oddly pleasing sound.

"So, you are the one called Finn. Yes, I see much of Muirne in you. But there is much of the vile MacTredhorn too. His coarseness has despoiled the fairness, the perfection of her blood as he despoiled her."

A sudden understanding came to Finn at these words.

"You are Tadg!" he said with certainty.

The druid arched an eyebrow in mild surprise. "So, you know about me. Very good! Too bad your acuteness of mind was not enough to save you from the trap. Yes, I am Tadg. And since you know that, tell me what became of my daughter."

"She . . . left me when I was a baby," Finn said quite truthfully, but using omission to protect his mother's hiding place. "I was told that she had died."

Tadg shrugged. "No matter. She was dead to me from the day she chose Cumhal. Now you will die, too, and it will all be finished."

"But why?" Finn asked. "I've done nothing to you."

"Your very existence is an insult to me," the druid scathingly replied.

"You're condemning me because of some hatred of your own. You are my own grandfather!"

"Reminding me of that does nothing to help you. It's your relationship to me that I must wipe away. And that I have finally arranged, through these fine women."

"Why should they be helping you in this?" Finn asked.

"There's no reason that you shouldn't know. They are the daughters of Conaran of the Tuatha de Danaan, once lord of this part of Ireland. He charged his daughters with the guardianship of it and of its wild creatures. That was their life and their pleasure, until the mortals came. Then they watched the birds and beasts they had so long protected ravaged by the new masters of the land." He smiled. "I'm afraid it drove them all quite mad."

A high-pitched, cackling laughter from the trio in response to this statement was enough to prove the truth of it to Finn.

"They vowed to take revenge upon any hunter they could," Tadg went on. He lifted a hand and gestured about the room. "As you can see, they have done very well at it. Of course, the well-known passion of the Fian warriors for the hunt has made them a particular enemy, so they were most eager to help me in my own revenge. Now I will leave you in their gentle hands. Good-bye, son of Cumhal."

He turned to walk away, but Finn called after him.

"Wait. Can you just leave me here?"

Tadg paused and looked back. "Of course I can. I've really no desire to witness what I'm certain will be a most unpleasant end. I only came to have a first and final look at you. It is enough to see you helpless here and know that you are doomed."

"The others of our clan will come."

"It will be too late for you. And, if they come, they will only meet the same end as yourself. I must go. I'm needed at Tara. The Samhain festival begins in just two days. I'm sorry, but it seems you'll not be attending it."

And before Finn could reply, he had walked out of the cave.

"A friendly sort, your grandfather," Crimall remarked dryly. "What now?"

The three women stepped back to the cave wall where the weapons of scores of victims formed a high mound. With care each one selected a good sword, checking the edges of the blades for keenness with the tip of a skinny finger.

"Now I think that we'll be dying," Finn answered his uncle.

The hags moved toward them, crunching heedlessly through the field of bones. Their appearance of frailty was all gone from them now. They looked tall, sinewy, and hard.

At the feet of their prisoners, they stopped. One of the trio leaned down over Finn. She stroked his cheek and smiled.

"This one is very pretty, sisters," she croaked out, looking up at them.

"Yes. Very pretty," another one agreed. "Such fine hair! It seems a shame to leave him suffering. Why don't we kill him first?"

"Yes! Kill him first!" cried the third, and the high, hideous screams of laughter from all three echoed in the cave. For the first time Finn found himself regretting the attraction that he had for women.

They closed in around him, swords lifting. He struggled madly but hopelessly against his bonds. The weapons swept down. He threw himself sideways, rolling from beneath the descending blades. They smashed harmlessly into the bones. He tried desperately to wiggle away, only burrowing into the heaped remains.

"Hold him!" a sister cried, and one of the hags

leaped astride him, pinning him down while the other two came up on either side, raising their swords above his neck.

"Now you will be torn apart as our poor creatures have been," one of them promised.

"No he will not!" said a voice.

Startled, they turned their gazes toward the cave mouth. Finn lifted his head to look as well. Again the figure of a man was silhouetted there. But not Tadg this time, Finn saw. This man was clad in a dark cloak, a shield and sword in his hands. A warrior.

He stepped forward. As he moved out of the light, his features became visible. Finn's heart lifted in joy. It was Caoilte MacRonan.

"Let them go," he told the three sisters in a reasoning tone. "Let them go and you'll not be harmed."

He was unaware that he was dealing with lunatics. One of them shrieked, "Kill him, sisters!" and the trio swept upon him with the swiftness and savageness of attacking hawks.

Their sudden assault surprised the warrior. He barely managed to fend off their first flurry of wildly flailing blows. They became a whirlwind wailing about him, forcing him to wheel constantly in defense. The watching Finn realized that his comrade was fighting to hold them off, not striking back, reluctant to harm women, even ones such as these.

Then a sister darted in beneath his shield as he lifted it to fend off another blow. She thrust out, her sword point aimed at Caoilte's undefended belly. He spun to the right. The blade slipped by his side, slicing through his tunic, skittering along his ribs, scoring his flesh. It was not a dangerous wound, but it was surely painful. With it, the warrior's temper flared and his patience with the women reached an end.

Giving an angry bellow, he struck out with all his power. One blow severed a scrawny neck, and the hag's head plopped into the company of a legion of fleshless ones. A second well-aimed cut clove the waist of another sister to the spine, toppling her into the piles of bones.

Still the third hag was not ready to give up. In the grip of her insane lust for blood, she leaped upon him, howling like a wounded wolf, wrapping him with her lanky arms and legs, knocking him from his feet. They crashed down together into the mass of bones and thrashed about. Caoilte battled to throw her off while she clawed at his face with her hornlike nails and tried to tear his throat out with her jagged teeth.

Finally he worked the round shield between their bodies and then rolled over atop her, forcing her beneath him. His full weight upon the shield pinned her there while he brought his sword up, pressing the point against her throat.

This seemed to return some sanity to the woman. She ceased her struggling and cried out to him imploringly: "Oh, Champion, I put my body and my life under the protection of your bravery. And it is better for you to have your comrades back than to take my blood. I swear by the gods my people swear by, if you release me I will free your friends and do you no more harm!"

With that, Caoilte relented. He rose, letting the hag climb to her feet. But he watched her carefully, sword ready, as she went to the captives and began to untie their bonds.

"I never thought I would see you again, Caoilte!" Finn said to his friend. "What are you doing here?"

"I've been watching you since you left the Boinne. I thought an extra bit of help hidden away would be of use, especially knowing your talent for walking boldly into danger. It's a guardian you still need, my lad."

"You are right," the abashed young warrior agreed. "Once more I owe you my life."

With the ropes finally unwound, they moved outside the loathsome cave, driving the hag ahead of them. Here Finn drew sword and hacked down the holly sticks, scattering the strands of fleece to the winds.

"You'll not use this trap against unknowing men again," he told the woman. "But you are free to leave here. I've no wish to harm you or any of your people. Remember that."

He and his comrades watched the defeated hag slink away into the rocks of the hillside and disappear. Then Finn turned to Caoilte again.

"Does your coming here mean you've decided to stay with us?"

The other nodded. "I realized after I'd left you that I'd spent all my life seeking something, and I had found it with you. So I came back."

"I'm glad," Finn told him, grinning. "And once I have my father's place, you'll be a man of the Fianna, if you wish."

"I think we'd best just get to Tara first, all right?" Caoilte answered in a prudent way.

Book Four

FINN'S TRIAL

Chapter Twenty-nine
INTO TARA

The chariot bounced sideways into the turn, crashing into the one racing beside it. Both cars overturned, their teams tearing away. Two more chariots coming up from close behind were moving too fast to avoid the wreck. They ran full upon it, their horses caught up in a tangle, the frail cars splintering apart, the drivers trying to jump clear.

A lone survivor of the disaster, escaping just ahead of it, sped away up the course to the accompaniment of a lusty cheer from its supporters in the large crowd.

"A lucky win that was," Caoilte commented as he and the rest of the Fian band moved past the racing track.

On either side of them, other sporting events were in progress across the wide meadows below the fortress hill of Tara. There were several heated contests of hurling going on, each with its own screaming crowds of ardent fans. On several other courses there were more races being run with a variety of participants: horsemen on slim, long-legged steeds; lean, sharp-nosed hunting dogs; even fleet and wiry-limbed young men. In other fields, warriors competed in wrestling matches, spear throwing, and other tests of the warrior's strengths and skills.

"I wouldn't mind doing some competing here today," Caoilte said as they passed a spear-throwing contest. He grinned. "With Finn, we'd be certain to win a prize or two."

"We want to be bringing no extra notice to ourselves," Crimall reminded him.

"So far, we've had no notice at all," said Finn. "No one seems to be looking for us, Uncle."

"Maybe. If we're fortunate, your Tadg convinced the king that you are dead. Still, we can't be taking any chances now. You just keep that cap firmly upon your head. It's like a beacon your hair would be to them."

The young warrior was now sporting a large cap of fox fur. It was tipped at a jaunty angle, as if he were proudly displaying a new bit of finery at this public gathering. But its only purpose was to hide the shining white-gold hair.

Ahead, the great hill of Tara itself had become visible, and Finn's attention now went from the spirited games to it. The slopes around the high king's fortress were bedecked with bright pavilions, colorful banners, and rows of market stalls. They were alive with a constantly milling crowd of thousands.

"I would never have believed there were so many people in all of Ireland," Finn said, almost overwhelmed by the sheer numbers.

"Ah, well, they come from all the provinces for this one," Crimall said. "All the great festivals have a fair with them, and there are few larger than this."

"I find them a wonderful place to go, myself," Cnu Deireoil remarked, smiling with pleasure at the scene. "It's another thing that makes your mortal life more enjoyable. There are no fairs in the Sidhes."

"It's true enough that everyone likes a chance for bartering and play and friendly contesting," Crimall agreed. "It may even help to keep the fighting down, bringing the clans together to talk, and giving the young men and women a chance to meet. Many a wife's been found at the fairs."

They moved up the slope and entered the busy avenues of the market stalls. All kinds of products were displayed. There were foods, cloth, household goods, artwork, weapons, and many other things from the corners of Ireland and beyond. They created a rich collection of varied textures and materials and hues to excite the senses.

Energetic bartering went on all about them. Finn noted that some of the most intense haggling, accompanied by emphatic gestures, involved cattle and horses. The argument over the value of one sleek, black-coated steed had drawn a crowd as avid and partisan as those at the matches below.

Through the milling crowds roved entertainers—jugglers and balladeers and musicians of all types. There was another and more unusual form of entertainment too. In various open spots, men in bardic dress stood upon raised platforms, addressing attentive groups in their resonant tones. As he passed by, Finn overheard snatches of discourse on history, on family genealogy, and on the laws of Ireland.

"They're a part of every fair," Crimall explained when Finn pointed them out. "It's a fine chance for them to bring their teaching to the common folk who have little other chance of hearing it."

Finn tended to stop often to observe these marvelous new things in fascination. His comrades were constantly urging him along.

"Don't be so slowing of us," Crimall finally said impatiently. "They'll be starting the first of the meetings at the dun soon." He pointed upward. "Look there. The warriors are already going in."

Finn's party was through most of the fair by now, and had reached the edge of the open area maintained below the walls of the fortress. Groups of cloaked men were visible moving up the roadway from the markets and the pavilions of the camps and passing through the gates.

Finn delayed no longer. He moved briskly upward with his clansmen, his attention now wholly on the timber stockade looming above. He noted that a pair of warriors stood at the gates, stopping and speaking to each group before allowing them inside.

"There are guards passing the warriors through," he pointed out. "How will we get by them?"

"Let me see to that," Cnu Deireoil said, pulling

the case from his harp and grinning widely. "It will be my own pleasure."

"And what clan is it that you're from?" one of the guards asked as Finn's band approached. He looked over the mixed and somewhat shabbily dressed lot of men. "I see no colors among you that I know."

"Well, you might say that they're with me," the little man spoke up.

The guard looked at him and laughed. "With you? And who are you to be needing such company?"

"Maybe the greatest harper in Ireland is all," he announced proudly. "I've music to charm any ear. Listen!"

He strummed a few notes on the instrument. The attention of the two men was seized at once. They cocked their heads, their faces taking on that foolish expression Finn had seen before.

"You find it most captivating, I can tell," Cnu Deireoil said. "Now, we'll just be passing in. You don't mind at all, do you?"

They shook their heads.

"I thought not." He gestured to the others. "Go ahead, lads. I'll just keep them occupied until you get past. Hurry."

The warriors moved quickly through the gates and into the yard. Cnu Deireoil kept up his playing until the last was safely inside. Then, with a cheery "Hope you enjoyed the tune," he trotted after them.

The guards stood captive of the last, lingering notes until the next party of clansmen accosted them. Then they shook their heads and gazed about them in bewilderment. By this time, Finn's party had merged with the scores of other warriors in the fortress yard.

"The magic always works best on those of duller wits," the harper commented. "Two like that'll likely not even remember we were here."

Now the Teach Mi Cuartha, the main hall of the high king, was ahead. Finn looked up at its massive outer wall and felt the first internal tinglings of anticipation, of excitement and nervousness combined. This was the final goal of his journey before him now, he

264

thought. At last he had come to the place where all he had learned would be brought to its testing. He recalled his feelings when he left Slieve Bladhma, and he realized that it had then been for Bodhmall and not himself that he had set out, ready to fulfill a duty that he had been taught to believe in but had not felt. But here, with the hall before him and the loyal warriors at his back, he knew that his reasons for acting had finally become his own.

As Finn and his comrades joined the men making their way through the main doors of the hall, they were unaware that they were doing so almost literally beneath the nose of Conn himself. For the high king was now looking down upon the warriors crossing the yard from an upper window of the royal quarters, a smaller structure set not far from the hall. Close beside him stood the high druid Tadg.

"This may be the largest gathering we've ever had," he commented. "I'm very pleased with that." He glanced around at Tadg. "Especially if there will be no unwanted guests."

The druid's gaze darted to the only other occupant of the room, a slim, blond-haired young man who sat at a nearby table, listening attentively. He was Art, the son of Conn.

"My king, should I speak . . ." Tadg began hesitantly.

"It's all right, Tadg," Conn assured him. "You can speak before my son. He knows the tale of Cumhal and this Finn. Someday, possibly soon, he'll be having to deal with these arrogant Fianna men himself to rule Ireland."

"Very well," Tadg said. "Then I assure you again, my king, that Finn is only a tattered pile of rotting limbs. Likely his clansmen are as well by now. There'll be no challenge, at this or any other Samhain."

"I am relieved to hear that, finally," Conn told him, emphasizing the last word. He looked down into the yard again. "Well, the warriors seem to have all gone into the hall. It's time for you and me to join the others for our entrance."

Meantime, Finn and his group had by now made their way inside with the rest. Here the awe Finn had experienced over the other sights of the festival was overshadowed by his first view of the famed hall of Tara na Righ.

None of the other halls he had seen in his travels had matched the splendors described in Liath's tales. But here her glowing descriptions paled beside the real thing. The room was vast, the space enclosed over a hundred feet across and rising at least four stories to the peak.

The outer area was divided into seven compartments for the seating of the ruling classes. The walls between them were not of wickerwork but of red yew wood elaborately carved with curving lines and stylized animals interweaving in complex designs. The outer edges of the partitions were banded in gleaming bronze, as were the thick roof poles and the beams that ran upward to the peak. On the walls above the compartments were hung the shields of the many clans attending. In the open central area about the large fire pit were tables enough to seat hundreds of their warriors. These tables were now crowded, with many other men standing, filling every available space. The compartments were all closely occupied, too, with the exception of a single empty one opposite the main doors.

A loud horn blast came from somewhere outside the hall. At the sound, the warriors standing tightly packed about the door pulled back, clearing the way for a column of men who started in.

"Careful now," Crimall warned quietly." It's the high king's procession coming."

Finn and Caoilte shifted in front of Cnu Deireoil, hiding him from sight. Finn turned his face away, watching from the corner of his eye.

A group of ollamhs in their brightly colored robes of office led the parade, striding by in solemn majesty. Behind them came the high druids in their gowns of brilliant white. Leading them was one that Finn knew at once. For even though his face had been shadowed before, the shape of the head and body were a vivid image in Finn's mind. He gazed for the first time upon the features of his grandfather, surprised that one so cruel could still have the delicate, gentle looks of his mother.

Tadg and his druids moved past the group of Finn's men, his gaze actually sliding over the young warrior. Then they were gone and a new party was entering the hall. Four men in colorful warrior dress first, each with a different, brightly patterned cloak, all richly adorned with gold and jewels, all strutting with the unmistakable arrogance of leadership.

"Who are they, then?" Finn murmured to Crimall.

"It's the kings of the four provinces," his uncle whispered back. "Munster and Leinster at the front, Ulster and Connacht behind. Ah, there'd be no such closeness of those four without the Samhain peace, I can tell you that!"

Behind them strode another whose own air of haughty aristocracy proclaimed his rank like a trumpet's blaring. Finn needed no one telling him that it was the high king of Ireland himself he was seeing now. He peered stealthily but with great curiosity at this ruler whose deeds were already legend, who was held up as a great and honorable man, yet who had conspired in the death of his father.

Slightly behind and close on either side of the high king, as if on guard, moved two other men. One of them Finn discovered with some astonishment that he knew. He had seen that hard, dark face somewhere. But where? He searched his memory, and then an image came clear: that same face, streaming with rain, staring in surprise, revealed for an instant by a lightning flash.

"Who is that man behind the king?" he asked.

"Him that was called Aed, leader of the Morna clan," Crimall replied. "The stout one with him is his brother, Conan."

When all had passed, Caoilte expelled a great sigh of relief. "I'm very glad that's over."

"At least you could see something besides a man's

backside," came the complaining voice of the Little Nut from behind him.

The procession moved on, along an avenue through the tables, around the central fire, toward the one empty compartment on its far side. There they mounted a raised platform set within the space and grandly took their seats about a long plank table. The high king sat at the center, the other kings ranged on either side. Druids filled the left end of the tables, bards the right. Behind Conn the two Fian warriors stood protectively.

"It's the most powerful men in Ireland gathered before you now," Crimall explained to Finn. "The highest ranks of judges, bards, and priests, with the five kings. They make up the examining board. It takes their agreement to verify any claim."

"What do we do?" Finn asked.

"For now, we wait. They'll open the ceremonies and begin to accept the candidates. First will come the craftsmen and artisans, presented by their clan chieftains. Then will be the new members of the bardic and druidic orders. Last come the new claimants for nobility. That's when your turn will come."

So they waited. At first, Finn observed the proceedings with a certain interest. Tadg and other of the druids went through an elaborate ritual, invoking the support of the gods in this enterprise. Then the high brehon stepped to the front of the dais.

"Those gathered here are now one in the acceptance of the Samhain peace," he announced. "The first session of the Fete of Tara may now begin. Chieftains, bring forward your candidates."

One by one the various spokesmen rose to present their people. For most, simple nods from the members of the board were all that was needed for approval. In some few cases, there was a brief discussion of qualifications, but always the acceptance came.

The ceremony plodded on from man to man, into the afternoon. Finn's interest gave way to growing restlessness. He watched the golden rectangles of light slanting in through the high windows of the hall crawl across the floor and lengthen with a slowness as agonizing as that of the ceremony. But, finally, the confirmation of the new chieftains began.

Here it was the province kings who put forward the men from their tuaths who would now serve as clan chieftains. There were only a half dozen of these, replacing leaders who had died—largely by violence—during the year. When the last one was confirmed, the high brehon moved forward on the dais again to announce the formal close of the ceremony.

"Now's the time, lad," Crimall said. "Quickly!"

"There being no more—" the high brehon began.

"Wait!" Finn shouted. "There is one more!"

Men around him turned to gaze in curiosity. Tadg pulled himself stiffly upright in his seat, wonder filling his face at the sound of this voice. Conn only looked puzzled at this violation of tradition. The high brehon stepped to the edge of the dais, peering out across the crowd.

"And just who are you to be making this claim?" he demanded.

Finn pushed farther into the central area and leaped up onto a table. He yanked the cap from his head and shook out the hair he had bunched under it. The flow of it shimmered in a shaft of sunlight.

"Surely you know me?" he said. "I am the one called Finn."

There was a roar of astonishment. Conn, stunned by his surprise, sat back, staring, speechless. But Tadg's wonder at the escape of the younger warrior was not enough to hinder his quick wit. He jumped to his feet, shouting urgently: "He is an outlaw! Kill him. He means the king harm!"

Around Finn a hundred hands leaped for their swords. His own blade flashed out in reply. Would he after all be killed before he had a chance? If so, he'd not go easily. Below him, Caoilte, Crimall, and the others of his company drew as well.

But the fight never came.

"No!" cried Goll MacMorna, striding forward. "He is protected by the Samhain peace. Any man attacking him answers to me!"

He drew himself up, his hand resting on his sword hilt. No man there dared challenge Goll or the Fian power. All moved back from Finn, sheathing their blades.

"Good," Goll declared. "Now, let us hear him out."

Surprised by this support from such a source, Finn put his own sword away, his comrades following his lead.

"I thank you," he said. "For I am no outlaw. The men I killed I killed fairly, and only to save myself. My true name is not Finn. I am Demna, son of Cumhal MacTredhorn."

This announcement created an even greater uproar within the hall.

"He lies!" shouted Tadg. "He cannot be. None of the family of MacTredhorn has survived."

"You know that it is true," Finn replied, "as does Goll MacMorna and the high king himself!"

Conn blanched at this accusation. Could the boy know the truth? Could this son of Cumhal who had appeared like some spirit from the dead expose him here, reveal his treachery to the assembled power of all Ireland? He cast a look of dismay at the high druid who had failed him.

"The high king knows nothing of you," Tadg was responding. "You have no proof of your identity."

"I am his proof," came the soft but clear, firm voice of a woman.

All eyes went to one of the compartments where sat an assemblage of noble families. A woman had arisen there. She now shrugged back the hood of her cloak, revealing her head to the company. Her hair was a shining flood of light about her slender shoulders.

"I know that this warrior is the son of Cumhal MacTredhorn, for I bore him, and I was MacTredhorn's wife!"

Chapter Thirty

THE SON OF CUMHAL

"Muirne!" said Tadg. The shock was like a blow to him this time. He dropped back heavily into his seat.

"There are many here who must remember me," she said, looking around the room. Then she directed a chill look at the high druid. "And I'm certain that my own father will not deny me."

"I thought that you were dead," he managed to get out in a choked voice.

"I remained hidden so that my son might be safe. This man, who is my husband now, protected me."

Mogh Nuadat rose beside her, slipping an arm about her shoulders.

"This is an outrage!" spluttered the king of Munster province. "The man is infamous! He constantly challenges my leadership and even defies your own authority, my high king. His coming here is unbelievable impudence!"

"I know that as well as you," the dismayed Conn growled back in frustration. "But the peace protects him too."

"I thank you for your graciousness, High King," the cocky little chieftain said, smiling mockingly. "I am most happy to be here."

While this exchange was going on, an astonished Finn bent down to speak to his companions.

"How is it my mother came to be here?"

"That's my doing," Caoilte admitted. "I did return to Corca Dhuibhne as I said I would. I told your

271

mother what you planned to do, and she was determined to come."

"Why didn't you tell me?" Finn demanded.

"I thought you might not approve," his friend answered simply.

Finn straightened and looked toward his mother across the crowd. She met his eyes, and he felt the warmth of their contact filling him. Then her attention turned back to the men upon the dais.

"There was no longer a reason for my hiding," she told them. "My son is here, and I have come to support him in his claim. After his birth, I had him hidden in the glens of Slieve Bladhma. And should any doubt the truth of that, I have brought others to testify. They are servants of my husband's house. The ones who raised my son."

She gestured to one side. Two other figures rose at the table, and Finn felt yet another thrill of surprise as he recognized Bodhmall and Liath.

Bodhmall drew herself up proudly, sending her hard, fearless gaze toward the high king. Liath eyed them timidly, then turned to Finn with a great smile of joy.

The presence of these three fired the young warrior's spirit with a new assurance. He faced the men on the dais boldly.

"Do you still question my identity?" he demanded.

The high king was much discomfited. This audacious lad had put him in a difficult spot, and he was acutely aware of the hundreds of expectant gazes upon him. They were watching for some fatal error, he was sure. They were waiting, like wolves around a cattle herd, for him to show some sign of frailty.

"We have no doubts of your being Cumhal's son," he answered carefully.

"Then I claim my father's place as chieftain of the Clan na Baiscne," Finn announced.

Now it was Goll MacMorna who moved forward to reply.

"Wait now, young warrior. We may accept that you are MacCumhal, but that does not mean you can claim a chieftain's place. You must have a clan to lead, and there can be none of your own left."

"As you would know better than any, son of Morna," Finn shot back. "But you are wrong." He turned to those in the crowd behind him. "Men of Baiscne, make yourselves known."

The warriors with Finn pressed forward, joining him, forming around his table as other warriors moved back to give them room. And, as they did, yet other fighting men moved from the crowd in all parts of the room. Other warriors of the clan, come from their scattered hiding places about Ireland, were now declaring themselves courageously. There were many more than Finn had expected. When all had assembled, he was surrounded by over a hundred men.

"Here is your clan, MacMorna," he said with pride. "Its men have chosen to join me, and I demand my right to lead them."

Goll felt some dismay at the size of a clan he had thought forever broken. But he showed no outward sign of it. The face he turned to Conn was stony.

"He has a fair claim, my high king," he admitted flatly. "He may ask to be confirmed as chieftain. But, if he wishes to take his father's place as a Fian leader, he must first prove himself worthy to be accepted as a Fian warrior." He looked searchingly at Finn. "Are you prepared to undergo the trial for membership?"

"I am," Finn answered without hesitation.

"Very well," Goll said. "Then tomorrow, at first light, they will begin."

"You took a great risk coming here, Mother," Finn told Muirne in a gently scolding tone.

He and his companions were now in the pavilion of Mogh Nuadat. Following the feast of the first Samhain night, the chieftain had asked them to join him in his own encampment below the fortress hill. He had provided Finn's clansmen with comfortable accommodations amongst his warriors.

Nuadat had certainly denied himself no comforts in

273

his traveling. The felt-covered structure of interlaced sticks was secure against the fall winds, warmed by a central fire, outfitted with comfortable pallets of luxurious furs on which the guests now lounged.

"When I heard from Caoilte what you were planning, I knew that I had to come," Finn's mother replied. "I knew that you would have to prove your identity. That's why I stopped at Slieve Bladhma and fetched Bodhmall and Liath as well."

"We were so happy to come," Liath told him. "When you left us, I feared I would never see you again."

"I was as certain that we would," the gaunt woman said with her customary assurance.

Finn turned to Mogh Nuadat. "And why didn't you keep her from coming here? I thought you were determined to keep her safe."

The chieftain grinned. "You know I can deny your mother nothing. And in this, she was right. But it wasn't unprotected she came here. There was little risk."

"I'd say that's true enough," Caoilte said. "He has nearly his whole company here."

"And they'll be at your service, if it's needed," Nuadat told Finn.

"I thank you, but it will not be. If the time comes when I must challenge MacMorna, it will be only my clansmen against his, as is proper."

"Ah, I'd give a shield arm for another chance at them," Crimall said wistfully, his hand gripping his sword hilt. "It seemed impossible to me that they defeated us before."

"Well, there'll be no challenging at all until I've passed these tests. Will they be difficult, Uncle?"

"That I'm certain of, though I don't know exactly what they'll be. It's for the Fianna captain to decide. All I can say is that they'll test your abilities as a warrior. But that'll be no trouble for you, lad. Your skills are greater than those of any Fian man I've known."

"So long as the tests are fair," Cnu Deireoil said.

"What do you mean?" asked Finn. "Do you think Goll MacMorna would try something to make me fail?"

"Goll's always been known as an honest man, even with his enemies," said Crimall. "I don't think he would be playing tricks with the other Fianna chieftains about."

"I think that it's my father the Little Nut is thinking of," said Muirne. "He's the greatest danger here. It was a great sorrow to me to learn that he was involved in this. It's made me realize that it might have been him behind the death of Cumhal as well. He was against my giving myself to a mortal."

"Every day you become a source of greater wonder to me, Wife," Mogh Nuadat said, smiling at her. "I knew it was a special woman I had married, but not one of the Others!"

"It's not as marvelous beings you should be thinking of us," she said. "We're only people as yourself, endowed with some magic by Queen Danu and Manannan MacLir long ago. And those powers were lost to me when I chose to be an inhabitant of your world. I'm a mortal now, and that is enough." She put a fair, fine-boned hand upon the chieftain's dark, broad one and he beamed with pleasure.

"Is that true for you as well, Cnu Deireoil?" Finn asked the harper.

He nodded. "It is. Unless we eat of the food MacLir provides and renew ourselves within the magical boundaries that guard the Sidhes, we're no different than you are. It's only my little skill with the music that I managed to bring away to protect me and find me some comfort as I roam."

"But my father still gains his sustenance from the de Danaans," Muirne said, "and he is a druid as well. That makes him very powerful."

"But would he dare to try anything with all of us watching, any more than Goll would?" asked Coailte.

"With the magical forces available to him," she answered grimly, "there may be many things that he could do unknown."

* * *

"I don't know if I want you doing anything more against this son of Cumhal," the high king told Tadg.

It was late in the night that they were meeting in Conn's private quarters, having waited for the rest of the fortress's population to retire so they might safely discuss their problem.

"What do you mean?" said the druid, not understanding the king's sudden reluctance to act.

"It may be that he knows of my involvement in his father's death. If he is angered, he may expose me."

So that was it, thought Tadg. Conn was more frightened of the Fianna turning upon him for his treachery than he was of Cumhal's son. Such thinking he knew he must alter at once.

"He cannot do anything to you if he is not alive," Tadg pointed out in his soft, reasoning way.

"That's hardly a comfort, Tadg," the high king stormed. "So far, none of your schemes to destroy him has succeeded. If you try and fail again, he may decide to use his knowledge against me."

"I cannot believe he has such knowledge," Tadg argued. "And if he does, it only makes it more vital to you that he be destroyed. Think of it, my king. Once he became captain of the Fianna, he would control you. He would be a greater threat than Cumhal. Nothing could stop him from using the Fianna to his own ends."

Conn knew that the high druid was right. He could envision himself living in fear, acquiescing to this upstart MacCumhal's every whim.

"All right, Tadg," he conceded. "But with all the highest authorities in Ireland looking on, how can we act now?"

Tadg smiled. "It is the Fianna leaders who are testing him. It is they who will destroy him. As before, the Morna clan will take the blame."

"What do you mean?"

"I mean, my king, that our young warrior will find his trials a bit more difficult than he could ever imagine."

*   *   *

276

As the dawn sun lifted above the top of the fortress's stockade, its light fell upon a scene of great activity. In the center of the yard, two men were digging a small pit under the watchful eyes of Goll MacMorna and his brother Conan. About them a crowd was gathering. The high-ranking ollamhs and druids were coming from their quarters within the dun. The province kings and their retinues were coming to the fortress from the smaller duns maintained as residences for them on the hill nearby. And from their encampments below, the Fian chieftains and their warriors were moving up toward the gates.

All were eager for the coming show. As they gathered within the yard, the air of excitement rose. Like water rising slowly to the boil, the sound increased, from murmuring to a louder burbling of talk. It surged suddenly higher when a new ingredient was added; Finn and his company. They moved in through the gateway and crossed the yard to Goll.

"I am ready," the young warrior announced.

"Good," the Fian captain replied. "So are we." He turned to the two diggers, who had now reached waist depth. "That's enough."

Conan moved closer to him to speak in confidence.

"They could go deeper," he suggested.

His brother gave him an exasperated glance. "You'd have it up to his chin, I suppose?" he asked scathingly.

"Just trying to help," Conan muttered, stepping back.

As the two diggers climbed from their pit, Goll turned back toward Finn.

"Son of Cumhal," he announced, "this will be a test of your speed and your dexterity. You will be buried to the waist in this hole. Nine of the best spearmen of the Fianna will cast their weapons at you from the distance of nine furrows. They can throw at you whenever they wish. Their aim is to strike you!"

He paused for a moment at this point, allowing it to register upon the young warrior. Perhaps Finn's realization that the test was a matter of life and death would change his mind.

But the peril made no impression upon Finn. He merely waited politely for the captain to go on.

"There is something else," Goll said. "All you may use to defend yourself is your shield and a staff of hazel wood. Do you understand?"

"Of course," Finn assured him calmly. "May we begin now?"

He removed his cloak and the sword harness, handing them to Caoilte. He slipped his shield onto his right arm, settling it firmly. Goll then took the hazel staff from one of his warriors and presented it to Finn. The young warrior examined it carefully. It was a smoothly polished rod two fingers thick and as long as his arm. The wood made it strong but supple. It flexed easily in his hands, showing no signs of weakness.

"It seems all right," Finn said, whipping it around him experimentally.

"You've no need to fear that," Goll said sharply, catching the implication. "There's no man in Ireland would say that Goll MacMorna is not an honorable man."

"I see," said Finn. "Is that why your clan destroyed mine? Is that why my father died?"

"Your father had taken too much power to himself!" Goll returned heatedly. "He had broken the bond of all Fian warriors to serve the will of the high king before all else. He had to be challenged for the leadership, and that challenge was a fair one!"

"It may be you thought you had cause," Finn conceded. "But I am not my father. Why were your warriors sent to hunt me down?"

Goll hesitated. "That . . . was not something that I did willingly," he said at last.

"It was at the high king's order, wasn't it?" Finn asked. "He wanted no chance of my father's clan rising again."

Goll didn't answer that directly. He stared for a long moment at the young warrior, and then replied in determined tones: "I give my word to you now that what has happened will not happen again. From this day on, only the law of Ireland and the honor of the

Fianna will determine what happens to you, and I will put my own sword to the seeing of it!"

Finn looked into the unflinching eye of the Fian captain and saw no falseness there. He nodded.

"I believe you, son of Morna. But when I have won my father's chieftainship, you know that there is something else I must regain as well."

"*If* you win the chieftainship, the next choice is your own," the other replied.

For a time they stood motionless, their iron gazes locked, their tall, hard figures set like those of two stags preparing to contend.

Then one of the Fian chieftains asked, "Are you ready?"

Finn gave a sharp nod of acknowledgment. He stepped down into the pit. Goll directed the diggers in and they began to fill the hole, pushing the dirt in about Finn's legs, packing it tightly, trapping the lower body quite effectively.

As this was being done, Finn looked around him at the watching crowd.

"I see that the high king isn't here," he remarked.

"The high king has nothing to do with this," Goll told him. "These tests are for men of the Fianna. Your success will be judged by our chieftains alone."

With Finn secured, the nine chosen Fian warriors moved forward. From a rack of spears crafted especially for this purpose, each chose a weapon. Then they formed a ring about the pit, facing away from Finn. At Goll's command, they began to pace outward. The crowd fell back before them, opening up a circular space like a wheel, with Finn as its hub and the spearmen its spokes.

"I notice that my father is also missing from the gathering," Muirne commented to Caoilte as they moved back.

"Likely he wants to avoid speaking to you," the dark warrior replied.

"I hope that is the reason," she said, her voice touched with worry.

"Don't be fearing for your son," Caoilte assured

279

her. "I know what he can do. This test will be a simple one for him."

"Of course it will," she agreed, putting on a brave smile, trying to ignore the chill of fear she felt.

From the upper window of the high king's quarters, Tadg and Conn watched the preparations closely. Conn's face was drawn with his concern, but the druid's expression was smug. For, early that morning, he had visited the armory where those special spears were kept, taking along certain items of his magic craft. Only he knew that the weapons now contained a power that would endow their throwers' arms with a brief surge of strength. The spears would speed to their marks with an incredible speed.

It would be impossible for Finn to escape them all.

Chapter Thirty-one

THE DEADLY TRIALS

In the yard, the spearmen continued to back away until Goll judged that they had reached the distance of nine furrows. He signaled them to halt.

Finn prepared himself for the defense. He knew his back would be most vulnerable. He would have to twist from side to side with speed, wrenching himself violently around to defend himself from the spearmen behind him. If they were good—as he was certain they were—they would only fire when they felt he was least able to turn and fend the missiles off. The throws would come very quickly once they began.

He looked across to his companions. His mother

and Liath stood with arms about one another, offering mutual comfort. He gave them a wide, confident smile.

"Are you ready?" Goll asked.

Again he nodded.

"All right then," said the captain. He stepped back from the warrior in the pit and raised his voice to call out: "Spearmen, you may throw at your own will!"

Finn began to swivel his head rapidly back and forth awaiting the first attack, shield and stick held high. There was a long moment's delay as the spearmen evaluated Finn's movements for possible openings and eyed one another to gauge who would throw first.

Finally, one man leaped forward, firing his spear at the young warrior's back as his head began to turn the other way.

The weapon shot toward Finn with a velocity that astonished its thrower. But its speed actually saved Finn. For, before he could turn completely away from it, he caught its movement in the corner of his eye. His trained reflexes gave him just time to swing around and throw up his shield.

The spear hit the upper edge with tremendous force, slamming the head through the thick layers of leather, tearing away the straps. The shield was wrenched from Finn's arm and carried away to fall out of his reach.

Finn's arm was tingling. He stared at the spear impaling his shield in disbelief. Never had he encountered a spear thrower with such power—even himself. If the others were as good, he was going to have a very hectic time saving his life.

The hectic time came almost instantly. Seeing Finn shieldless, the other warriors quickly began launching their own missles. He began to twist his upper body with greater speed. He had only the hazel stick for defense now, and he lifted it in both hands. He remembered Caoilte's training and the dark warrior's often repeated warning to always keep an eye on the opponent's weapon. He must focus all attention only on those incoming, glinting iron points.

The lightning reactions those baby hares had long

before forced him to acquire now stood him in good stead. His movements were a blur. The rod struck out at each spearhead as it came within reach, sweeping around, right and left, the thin wood whipping against the metal points, snapping them aside.

Liath gave a cry of fear and hid her face against Muirne as the spears seemed to converge upon Finn. But in instants it was over. All the remaining spears were grounded, heads deeply buried in the earth, shafts quivering, forming an outward-slanting fence about the unscathed young warrior.

The crowd gave a collective roar and surged forward, shouldering through the spearmen, who stood staring in amazement at their failure.

"A grand show that was!" Caoilte told Finn as the diggers moved in to free him. "I don't think I've ever seen you move that fast before."

"I've never had to before," Finn told him.

With the dirt removed, Finn climbed from the hole. The clan chieftains of the Fianna came in close around him, examining his upper body carefully.

"There's not a single mark upon him," one of them finally reported to Goll. "He has passed the test."

"You did well," Goll MacMorna grudgingly admitted.

"The spearmen were good," Finn told him, eyeing him closely. "They were better than I would have thought any man could be."

"What do you mean?" the captain demanded.

"Never mind," Finn said quickly, for the face of Goll had told him that the man was truly puzzled by his statement. "I only meant to praise their skill. Shall we be getting on to the next trial?"

Goll seemed to accept this. He nodded. "If you wish. For the next trial we must move down to the woods below the hill."

At his orders, the Fianna men quickly began to stream out through the gates and down the slope. The other watchers, not wishing to miss what was to come, joined in the exodus. As Finn and his own company moved after the rest, he had a chance to speak to his comrades.

"Mother was right, I think. Tadg is taking a hand in this. We'll have to be on guard."

"It would be nice to know what for," Cnu Deireoil commented unhappily.

In the high king's quarters, Conn was watching the departure of the victorious Finn with growing despair.

"Did you hear the cheer for him when he won the test?" he asked the druid. "They like him, Tadg, just as they liked his father. It's happening again, Tadg, and you can't stop it!"

His voice had risen to a strident note on these last words, but they brought no reply from his high druid. He turned to find the man gone.

"Oh, no!" said Conn. "What's he meaning to do now?" He considered, then he shook his head. "No. Better not to know."

Tadg, meantime, had arrived at his sacred spot within the grove of oaks. He had anticipated the possible failure of his first attempt and had made arrangements for another. The cauldron boiled already over the fire of ash and yew. The ingredients were prepared and waiting. He had only to slip them into the steaming brew and begin the incantation that would raise the spell.

In moments the cloud was writhing up from the bubbling liquid, growing, lifting over him. He looked up at his creation with satisfaction. His own magic was still strong. He had once again called up this force to aid him, and he would now send it out to work his will.

It was only fitting, he thought. It had helped to destroy the father. Now it would help defeat the son.

By the time the high druid was prepared to put his newest scheme into operation, the great crowd with Finn MacCumhal had gathered by a large wooded area on the far side of the fortress hill. Its numbers had been swelled considerably by hundreds of folk attracted from the fair by this event. For word of mouth had quickly spread the knowledge that the son of the legendary Cumhal would be the one tested. That made the contest more interesting than any race or hurling match.

Finn looked around at the enormous crowd with curiosity. They seemed most excited, and many seemed to be exchanging coins.

"What are they doing?" he asked.

"I'll go see," Cnu Deireoil volunteered. He moved off to talk with several of the folk, then returned, grinning widely.

"They're wagering," he announced. "Ah, they'll bet on almost anything, that they will."

"Wagering?" Finn said, feeling somewhat indignant at this liberty. "That's a bit unfeeling, isn't it?"

"Ah, no. It's just good sense, lad. Why waste such a fine opportunity? I've put a bit on you myself. The odds are very good. Two to one against you."

"Against?" Finn repeated in dismay.

"It's very few men who are good enough to come through this test, so they say," the Little Nut explained.

"Put a bit on Finn for me as well, harper," said the enterprising Caoilte. He smiled at Finn. "It'd be a fool who'd not want to bet on such a certain thing, wouldn't it?"

Finn smiled in return. "It would only be a help to my confidence."

Goll MacMorna now approached them with a retinue of his warriors. While two men carefully fastened Finn's long hair up upon his head with pins, the Fian captain explained the next challenge.

"You must run the length of these woods and return," he said. "A band of Fian men, led by myself, will pursue you. You'll have only the start of the length of a tree branch before we come after you. If any of us catch you or wound you in your flight, if your hair is undone by hanging branches or a stick cracks under your foot, you have lost."

Finn could see why few men were good enough to come through the test. But he thought of the rigorous forest training Bodhmall had given him and he told himself that it would help him to succeed now.

"I am ready," he told Goll.

He and the captain's band moved to the edge of the woods. They gathered by the trunk of a large tree while Finn moved into the woods until he reached the end of one of its lower branches.

"We will begin when you do," Goll told him.

Finn searched the underbrush ahead, picking his path. He took a few deep breaths, calming his mind. Then he was off.

He shot away like a startled deer. The suddenness of his move left the Fian warriors staring for a moment before they gathered themselves and set off in pursuit.

The young warrior had no difficulty in quickly outdistancing his pursuers. In little time he was far ahead, streaking through the woods as if there were no trees to slow him, leaving no mark of his passing, making no sound.

Behind, the Fian warriors pushed ahead at their best speed. But the rotund Conan—not quite in the ideal condition of the rest—accompanied their run with his complaining.

"I knew that this test would be useless," he puffed. "We already knew he had a deer's speed. This is . . . as the night . . . in Slieve Bladhma . . . once again!"

"Save your wind!" shouted his brother. "Keep on! No one can outrun the best men of the Fianna!"

But he was wrong. Finn was outrunning them, and easily. He reached the far end of the patch of forest long before them, turned, and started back. He skirted the pack of his would-be hunters still heading the other way without their knowing and without slowing his pace.

He felt the glow of triumph burning in him now. He had only to return to the waiting crowd and the chieftainship would be his!

He kept up his best pace, anxious to be through the remaining portion of the woods. So intent was he on the way ahead that he did not notice the first, faint wisps of fog begin to flit down, ghostlike, through the trees around him.

It was the change in atmosphere he became aware of first. A gust of air swirled suddenly about him, clinging and chill and heavy with a scent like that of a coming rain. Curious, he glanced around. The tendrils of fog, now grown to thick streams, were coiling down through the trees, twining about them, weaving through their branches in a serpentine way.

His eyes followed the tendrils up until they reached their source. Then he stopped, staring in astonishment. An enormous cloud was dropping rapidly down upon the woods. So dense was it that its gray swollen belly seemed to swallow the trees as it moved toward the ground. To Finn it was like some grotesque creature that had seized the woods with its tentacles and was now pulling itself down to feed upon its prey.

His long familiarity with nature's forces told him that this was nothing usual. This was something to be feared. He started ahead at his full run, but he had only gone a few steps when it dropped around him.

The gray-white blanket wrapped him in its clammy folds. It shrouded the trees around him and in an instant he was nearly blind. Objects in his way became vague shadows, visible only when they were very close. He slowed to a walk, knowing a quicker pace would bring certain collision.

He was sure now that this was some magic of the vengeful Tadg, meant to slow him, disorient him, make him easy prey for the hunters. Well, nothing was going to defeat him now, he told himself fiercely. He had only to keep on moving straight ahead, toward where he knew the edge of the woods must be.

And then he realized, with a stomach-wrenching dismay, that the cloaking aspect of this fog was not its only or its most dangerous power. Somehow it was sapping his energy as well!

The farther he went through the billowing stuff, the heavier grew the weight that dragged upon him, as if he were accumulating layer upon layer of the moisture-laden air, carrying it along. It wore upon him quickly. His legs grew leaden. Each step became a greater effort, a greater agony.

He struggled forward, but with a growing sense of hopelessness. He could barely move now, and the accursed fog showed no sign of thinning before him. The Fian band must be moving up behind him now. Soon they would reach him, and he had a strong feeling that this enchantment would have no effect on them.

Still, he would not quit. He put all his energy into another step, forcing one leg to lift up from the ground, concentrating on shifting it forward, grunting with the strain as he willed it down again. Nearly exhausted from the work, he took a deep breath and then doggedly began the whole routine with his other leg. The notion flitted through his mind that he would look quite absurd to any observer.

An odd flutter in the shadows ahead of him caused him to look up from his half-lifted knee. He saw that, in fact, he was being observed. A figure—indistinct but definitely human—was visible not far away. It moved forward, seeming to glide in the fog, and its outline grew clearer. He saw that the figure was not only human but distinctly female as well. His initial fear that somehow one of the pursuers had already come before him faded away. He watched her approach with a curiosity that soon turned to recognition.

It was the Shadowy One of Cnoc-na-Righ who stepped up before him. She smiled.

"I said that we would meet again, Finn MacCumhal," she told him. "You seem to have a talent for getting yourself into traps."

"I've been told that before," he said ruefully. "But, can you help me?"

"That is why I've come." She lifted a slender hand and took one of his. "I will lead you out."

Her touch sent a wave of vitality surging through him, washing away the fatigue. He was able to move freely again, and he let her lead him ahead. Together they climbed a slope that soon brought them out of the blanket of fog, onto the crest of a high ridge.

Finn looked back. The fog was a long band cutting across the woods below. A barrier he could not have avoided. He turned to the Shadowy One with a grateful smile.

"Thank you again for your help," he told her. "I owe so much to you—"

She pressed her fingers lightly to his lips.

"Please, no talk," she told him urgently. "We've little time before your hunters come, so listen to me. It was Tadg who sent this fog against you. The continued use of his powers against you has angered my people. For that reason I was allowed to come to help you. But it was only for this time. I'll not be able to give you help again. Instead, I can tell you this: if you're again faced with such a situation and you must learn what to do, use the power of the salmon."

"The salmon?" Finn said, not understanding.

"The salmon of knowledge," she said. "You must remember."

He shrugged. "But it gave me no power!"

There were shouts behind them. Finn looked around to see the band of Morna warriors moving through the woods just beyond the band of fog. They stopped, spotting him on the high ridge, gesturing emphatically toward him. Then they plunged into the thick cloud.

"They are coming," she said. "I can wait no longer."

He turned back and gripped her shoulders, holding her.

"Wait! You'll not escape me so easily this time. You must tell me about the salmon."

She gave him an exasperated look. "Finn, you must think! I can do no more for you. Think what you did when you first tasted the fish. Now I must go!"

She lifted up on her toes, leaned forward, and planted another long, warm, and most emphatic kiss upon his lips. Then, before the pleasantly surprised young man could react, she pulled away and fled gracefully into the trees. He was left with the lingering impressions of her smooth skin, her springlike fragrance, and her soft lips.

Her kiss had also left him with another tingling charge of extra energy. It erased the last effects of the fog's magic, giving him a feeling of vitality greater than when he'd begun the race.

He was going to need this extra vitality, for now the hunters of the Fianna burst from the fog just below him at an all-out run. Motivated by the nearness of their quarry, they were putting their all into a final effort to capture him.

Some of them whooped in triumph as they closed in. But their elation was short-lived. It might as well have been a fox that they were trying to catch as Finn darted away into the trees.

"Keep on! Keep on!" shouted Goll. "He's not out yet!"

And his men did keep on after the flying young warrior. But it was no use. As before, Finn quickly left them far behind as he ran the final distance to the edge and burst from the trees into the view of the waiting crowd.

A tremendous cheer burst from the watchers as he pulled to a stop before them, grinning broadly. Then he was surrounded by well-wishers so excited by his victory that little notice was paid to the Fianna pursuers when they stumbled, panting with exhaustion, from the woods.

Conan came out last, puffing, red-faced, barely able to keep his feet.

"I . . . told . . . you—" he gasped out to his brother.

"No more, Conan!" Goll snapped back, and pushed through the adulating crowd to Finn's side.

At his order, the Fian chieftains once more inspected the young warrior. They did it carefully, again and again, seeking any tiny scratch, any bit of twig embedded in the clothes, any single hair pulled out of its place. Finally all shook their heads and turned to their captain.

"He has passed," one announced. "He has won the right to become a man of the Fianna."

"Not until he passes the bardic test," Goll said sharply. He stepped close to Finn, meeting his eye. There was a certain smugness in his expression. "I doubt you've had much chance to acquire the poet's skills hidden away in your glens all these years."

Finn smiled modestly. "Some," he said. "I was taught by an ollamh named Finnegas."

There was a gasp of amazement in the surrounding crowd.

"Why, he's said to be one of the finest bards in Ireland," a Fian chieftain said in an awed tone.

Goll's smugness faded. The look he now fixed on Finn was stone.

"Of course," he said with a certain resignation in his voice. "Such a thing I should have guessed." Then he shook his head, trying to recover some confidence again. "Still, it must be tested. We will return to the dun. There the high king's own ollamhs can determine just what skills you really have."

Chapter Thirty-two

A CHIEFTAIN OF THE FIANNA

At the orders of Goll MacMorna, the crowd began to break up. The nobility started back toward the gates of the fortress. The common folk drifted back to their fairgrounds. As the people scattered, Finn was joined by his companions. He accepted the congratulations of the warriors, gave great hugs to Muirne and Liath and even a protesting Bodhmall.

But then the young warrior's joyous expression turned to a grim one as he glimpsed someone through the thinning crowd. For Tadg himself had arrived to witness the successful outcome of his newest effort and was now standing, frozen, staring in dismay at the victorious youth.

Finn stepped toward him, determined the wily druid would not avoid a confrontation this time.

"Well, my grandfather!" he said. "You seem unhappy at the outcome. Not as you expected again, is it?"

"What do you mean?" Tadg shot back, still off balance from this unexpected turn.

"I mean that you failed," Finn said. "That's twice in the same day, I think."

Muirne understood the meaning of this. Angrily she moved toward her father too.

"So, my loving parent," she said with heavy scorn. "You have used your powers against my son again!"

Tadg had by now recovered his self-control. His response was assured and cool.

"I've no idea what you are speaking about. These tests are a matter between MacCumhal and these Fianna men."

"Don't lie to me," she told him hotly. "I look at your face and I see the truth of it. I knew that you disliked Cumhal, but I never believed that you hated him, and me as well for marrying him."

The attention of many, including Goll MacMorna, turned to them at this. Tadg was aware of their notice and it clearly made him uncomfortable.

"I had nothing but admiration for the man," he said quickly, sounding a bit flustered, "and nothing but love for you."

"Love!" she said with a derisive laugh. "Oh, yes. So much love that you've avoided speaking to me since I returned."

"I have been . . . very busy with Samhain," he hedged. "But I've worried all these years about what became of you. And you are welcome to return to my family now. You and"—he forced himself to smile weakly at Finn—"my grandson."

"Of course," she said. "You could be rid of your shame easily then. You could destroy me and my son as you destroyed Cumhal!"

"I played no part in the death of MacTredhorn," Tadg argued vehemently, glancing around at the curious eyes. "This is some madness that has obsessed you, Daughter. It was a struggle between the Fian clans that killed him."

"Was it?" she asked, glancing meaningfully toward Goll. "Or were the sons of Morna merely tools for you?"

Tadg opened his mouth to protest, but she gave him no chance.

"Good-bye, Father," she told him with finality. "You told my son that I was dead to you a long time ago. I am happy to remain so."

With that she turned and walked away with great dignity.

"You've given me several causes to take your life, my grandfather," Finn added. "But I would never be able to harm one of my own blood. Good-bye."

He joined his mother and, accompanied by the rest of their party, they started back toward the fortress gates. The high druid, flushed with shame at this public humiliation, stared balefully after them.

"You lying hypocrite," came a voice from behind him.

He turned to see Goll MacMorna watching him. The rest of the crowd had departed now, leaving the Fian captain, his brother, and the druid alone at the edge of the woods.

"What is it *you're* speaking about then?" he asked irritably.

"I heard what you told her," said Goll, moving toward him. "But it was she who spoke the truth. You did everything you could to see Cumhal dead, and you've done the same for his son. You've even used those black powers of yours today, haven't you?"

"Of course I have," Tadg admitted, waving the fact away with a careless gesture.

"So you did play some trick with the spears. I was thinking you had after I talked to the warriors who threw them."

"Yes, I did. And what else was I to do? You must know by now that he can't be stopped any other way. Your tests don't work."

"I warned you against using your druid treachery," Goll told him darkly.

"You're a fool," Tadg answered harshly. "Our purpose is to stop him. If it takes my powers, then I will use them. Otherwise he will take the leadership."

"If he challenges me, I will fight him," Goll told him. "I've said I would do so."

"You will lose. You would have lost to the Baiscne clan in your last fight with them." He fixed Goll with a chill, commanding eye, all pretext at diplomacy now gone in his anger. "It's time you understood. Just how do you think you'd be where you are now, my grand captain, without my powers?"

"What are you telling me?"

"That it was an enchantment sent by me that sapped the strength of Cumhal and his men and gave you the victory."

Goll understood. "Of course. The fog. Like the one in the woods just now." He jerked his sword from its sheath, stalking toward Tadg, face twisted with his wrath. "I'll kill you for what you've done!"

Conan moved in, quite swiftly for all his bulk, and seized his brother, pulling him back.

"No, Goll! What are you doing?"

"He's dishonored us!" the captain shouted. "Don't you see? We won the leadership with treachery! His treachery!"

"He is still a high druid, Goll," his brother reasoned, fear in his voice. "To harm him would bring their powers against us."

"Listen to him, Goll," Tadg advised, backing away, his arms upheld before him. "No greater crime can be done in all Ireland than harming a man of the druidic class."

Goll shook off his brother's grip, but he made no further advance upon the druid. His first madness had passed. He slammed his sword back into its sheath.

"All right, Tadg. I won't kill you. But I'll see your treachery exposed. I'll see you stripped of your position."

Tadg smiled, once again confident. "Denounce me and you denounce yourself as well. If your honor is so important to you, think how little would be left to you if your part in this conspiracy were known. No man of the Fianna, no man of Ireland would trust you."

"He is right," Conan put in dismally. "No one would believe that we didn't use the druid's help to gain the leadership."

Goll shook his head in frustration. He had only tried to fulfill the obligation he felt to the high king, and it had brought him to this.

"So, keep your precious captaincy, MacMorna," Tadg went on. "And keep your loyalty to the king as well. Challenge the Clan na Baiscne if Finn succeeds in becoming their chieftain. Let me help you destroy them as we did once before."

"Your nerve is very great, Druid," growled the Fian leader. "Now you expect me to take part in more of your treachery?"

"I expect you to do as you promised long ago and see the clan of Cumhal wiped away! They are still dangerous to the king. It is for him this must be done. Refuse and you risk breaking your bonds of loyalty."

"I am loyal," Goll shot back, "but only to the high king. I will obey orders, but only his, not yours. I know now that it's only your hatred of Cumhal and his son that moves you. You've used me and the king to your own ends. Well, maybe I can't stop you, but I'll do nothing more to help you. Conn may call me disloyal if he wishes, and you may threaten me with dishonor, but nothing will bring me to disgrace myself or my clan again!"

"So, it is over," the high king said mournfully, slowly pacing the floor of his quarters. "MacCumhal has passed the last of the bardic tests. Goll must accept him as a man of the Fianna, and tonight I must recognize his lawful right to the clan chieftainship." He stopped and cast a desperate look toward Tadg. "And you're certain Goll will do nothing to help?"

The high druid shook his head. "He is useless to us now. Why, he'd likely give the leadership back to Finn's clan if he had the choice."

"Then we can try nothing more," said Conn. "Without the Morna clan to take the blame, it would be too risky. I fear Finn MacCumhal, but I fear exposure more. It could bring the Fianna to open rebellion!"

The lines that age had etched in Conn's lean face drew into deep furrows around his mouth and between his jutting brows, making him seem suddenly very old, very worn. He dropped wearily down onto a bench, letting his head fall forward into his hands.

"Perhaps we cannot act directly," the high druid agreed. Then, in a careful way, he added, "But there may still be a way that we can bring this brash young warrior to his death and seem blameless in it."

Conn lifted his head and looked toward Tadg, his expression one of mixed hope and puzzlement.

"A way? What is it?"

"It is nearly Samhain eve. We could send him against Aillen."

The high king drew back, aghast. "The son of Midhna? No! We wouldn't dare to do that!"

"Yes we could!" Tadg earnestly replied. He moved to Conn, sat beside him, leaned in close. All his powers to cajole, to reason, to convince were brought into play now, in this effort to manipulate the high king just once more. "Think of it. I know the mind of this Finn. I know that he could be brought to accept such a challenge. We have only to offer him a prize so great he cannot refuse it."

"But such a thing would mean the destruction of Tara as well!" said Conn, still appalled by the utter ruthlessness of the suggestion.

"A few buildings, my king," Tadg reasoned smoothly, "easily rebuilt. Perhaps a few lives." He met and held the eye of Conn with an intense gaze. "But what are they against the rule of Ireland? You must choose, High King. Who will rule after you? Will it be your own son or the son of Cumhal?"

In the bright, icy gaze of the high druid, Conn could see the image that had so long filled his nightmares—himself kneeling before a laughing white-haired youth. It seared his mind. He squeezed his eyes tightly closed to shut it out.

"All right!" he cried in a tortured voice. "All right! Whatever must be done!"

"Demna, son of Cumhal, you have passed the trials and shown yourself fit to become a man of the Fians of Ireland," pronounced Goll MacMorna. "Is this what you wish?"

"I do," said Finn.

On this second night of the Samhain festival, the young warrior stood before the dais of the high king. About him in the great hall were assembled the warriors and nobility of Ireland. Above him on the dais stood the Fian captain, his expression solemn as he continued the acceptance ritual.

"If you would be approved by these assembled chieftains of the Fian clans, there are four *geasa* which must be laid upon you as final condition for your admission. You must be gentle with all women. You must take no man's cattle by force of arms. You must not keep to yourself that which is needed by any other man. You must not fall back before nine fighting men or less. Do you accept these vows of chivalry?"

"I do," said Finn.

Goll looked about him at the Fian chieftains. "Is there any among you who disputes the right of this warrior to enter the ranks of the Fianna?"

There was no response. Goll nodded, looking back down to Finn.

"Son of Cumhal, you have been accepted in our company. It is a life of great sacrifice and hardship you have chosen, but a life of great adventure, too, and its joys will reward your labors a hundredfold."

"My captain," Finn responded with all the graciousness he could muster, "no grander honor could be given me. I pledge my life to the honor of the Fianna."

He bowed low, and a great cheer went up from the assemblage, led most enthusiastically by Finn's own comrades. When it had died away, Goll MacMorna retired to his place behind the high king, who now arose to address the young warrior.

"It is not only a place in the Fianna you have won, son of Cumhal," he said. "It is also your right to lead a Fianna clan, that of your father. So now I, too, welcome you. Come forward."

Finn mounted the dais and strode forward to the table of the high king. He drew his sword from its sheath, reversed it, and held the hilt out toward Conn.

"As the chieftain of the Clan na Baiscne, I come before you now, my king, to get your friendship and to give you my service and my loyalty."

He met Conn's eye boldly, his face expressionless. He knew that, like it or not, he was now bound by ancient oaths of loyalty to the high king. But he wondered if Conn could sense the loathing and mistrust he felt for one who had conspired in his father's death.

The high king could sense these feelings behind the stony young face, and his stomach churned in fear. Finn might just as easily denounce him here or drive the blade of the sword into his heart as offer him its hilt. Tadg was right. There could be no comfort again in life until this boy was dead!

Still, the winner of a hundred battles, the proud leader of all Ireland could show his feelings no more than the one he faced. With an air of total command, he gripped the weapon, taking it from Finn.

"You are son of a friend, young warrior," he said with towering sincerity, "and son of a man I trusted. Take your sword." He reversed the weapon again, passing the hilt back into Finn's hands. "And now, in honor of your acceptance here, come and sit with me tonight and give yourself to drinking and pleasure."

Finn moved around the table. Conn took his hand and led him to an open place at his right.

"Sit here," he said, "between myself and my son."

The warrior sat down, feeling a bit uncomfortable here, by the high king, surrounded by his glittering court. He looked toward the king's son, Art, and found the young man examining him in a critical and rather haughty way.

"So, you are the one I have heard so much about,"

Art remarked. "I understand you were raised in the trees, or something."

Finn did not like the superior air or the soft, pampered look of the son of Conn. And he most certainly did not like the insolent tone of voice. He was reminded of the first boy he had ever met, the chieftain's son whose arrogance had led him to attempt the drowning of the naïve Finn. Finn was naïve no longer.

"I was raised to hunt and to fight," he responded with pride. "It is such skills that make a Fian warrior the finest in Ireland."

"The Fianna are useful," Art conceded in a bored way, "so long as they know their proper place."

There was no doubt, Finn told himself, that he was not going to get along with the king's son.

The evening's ceremonies completed, the feasting had begun. Great platters of food and tankards of drink had been brought to fill the tabletop. Goll and his brother had left their official places to join the others at the high king's table, dining at one end, beyond the province chieftains. At the opposite end, among his peers, sat the high druid Tadg. Finn caught his eye once, but the man only looked quickly away. This made the new chieftain uneasy. Could his vengeful grandfather still be contemplating some move?

Finn's gaze traveled on about the room. For a moment it paused on the compartment occupied by his clansmen and friends. He was pleased to see them so joyously celebrating his—and their—success. But then his attention moved on to Goll MacMorna, and a new and grimmer process of thought began.

Now that he had achieved his chieftainship, what next? Clearly, if he must complete the restoration of his clan's honor, he must reclaim the captaincy of the Fianna. This meant that a challenge of the Morna clan must come.

His eyes went from Goll back to the rejoicing warriors of the Clan na Baiscne. There were so many young faces there, flushed now in an almost childlike exuberance. How many of them had not yet been initiated into the Fianna? How many had not even fought

298

before? And how many would die for his challenge, willingly sacrificing themselves for the honor of the clan?

He looked again toward Goll. He believed now that the captain had acted out of a sense of loyalty to his king. And he believed that the means had been within the accepted rules governing challenge. Goll had taken the leadership fairly. Could Finn commit his warriors to a certainly bloody attempt to regain it out of some need to fulfill his personal destiny? A destiny he had not chosen himself? Yet, the high king had acted in a treacherous way. He had condemned Finn's father to death. To let him win without some retribution . . .

Finn's mind was whirling. It was all so complex! Back in the quiet, isolated glens of Slieve Bladhma it had seemed so simple. There had been only Bodhmall's teachings then; her unquestionable, emotionless logic. The dark and evil Morna clan was clearly his enemy. His only goals were to avenge the clan, to restore its honor, to regain its rightful place.

But then had come his journey. A stream of impressions from it rippled through his mind: a hurling game, the Little Nut, Luachra, Firbolgs, Caoilte and Cian, the Dovarchu and the three hags, Mogh Nuadat, Tadg, Finnegas, and so much more. His experiences in the world had changed him. It was not a matter of ideals anymore; it was people who were neither good nor bad, and truths that seemed often contradictory, and loyalties that were often in conflict. Where was his honor amongst all of that?

Honor. Always there was that word again. It had been with him, dominating him, all his life. Caoilte had said it was a foolish thing, a thing that killed men. Maybe he was right. The tangled web of honor had entrapped his father, Tadg, Goll, the high king. How many had it destroyed already?

He realized that Goll had noted his musing stare and was returning it with a frown. It seemed to Finn that the captain, this man who fate had made his adversary, was trying to fathom his thoughts, trying to guess his intent. Finn wished that he knew it himself.

Beside him, the high king arose. The eating was largely over now, and it was clear Conn meant to make some announcement. He waited until the roar of conversation in the hall faded away, and then began to speak.

"I had no mind to be casting a deep shadow on the brightness of tonight's celebrations, so I waited until now. But now my time has come. Tomorrow night is the eve of Samhain day. Tomorrow night all the powers of the worlds beyond our own knowing will be free to roam the lands. And all of us here know what power it is that will come upon us as it has these nine years past."

The others there may have known, but Finn certainly did not. He listened attentively as the king went on.

"Since that first night, Tara has been in thralldom to this monster, forced to submit to this humiliation, because no champion could be found who would face his threat.

"And so, tonight, with this greatest assemblage of Ireland's warriors ever seen at Tara, I have determined to make a new offer. It is a final plea for someone to restore our dignity to us. If there is among you a fighting man of Ireland who can defeat this danger to Tara's existence . . ." he paused and gazed about him at the crowd before going on with greater emphasis, ". . . then I will give him whatever inheritance is right for him to have, whether it is small or great!"

There it was, thought Finn, a thrill running through him. There was his chance to regain his father's place without a fight. He could win it! He could wrest it back from the hands of the very man who had ordered it taken. He had no idea what this threat was, but it didn't matter. He would face it. He leaped to his feet.

"My king!" he said.

Across the room, in the compartment of the Baiscne clan, Caoilte groaned.

"No, no!" he said, grabbing the arm of Cnu Deireoil tightly. "Tell me he's not about to do what I think he is!"

On the dais, Conn had turned to the young warrior, his wooden expression masking the elation he was feeling.

"Yes?" he asked.

"My king," Finn announced, "I will be your champion!"

Chapter Thirty-three

A PROMISE OF HELP

"I knew it! I knew it! I knew it!" Caoilte repeated, each time with greater heat. "It's many foolish acts you've charged blindly into since I've known you, but none so bad as this!"

The feast was ended, and it was a gloomy lot of Finn's companions who had gathered in the pavilion of Mogh Nuadat to discuss his recent decision with him.

"Don't be too angry with me, Caoilte," Finn told his friend. "I've done this to save lives. Don't you see? I can earn the leadership without risking the clan!"

"Noble reasons, but you're still a fool," the dark warrior shot back. "You don't even know what it is you'll be going against."

"That's never slowed our lad down before," Cnu Deireoil pointed out.

"But those times were not like this," said Caoilte. "I've talked to many about this monster. It seems he is of the Sidhe folk."

"I've heard of him," said Muirne. "His home is a hill not far from here. He's said to possess strong magic. But he's not allowed to use it beyond his Sidhe."

"He can on Samhain night, when all the supernatural forces are unleashed," Caoilte added. "And it's then that the mortals become the targets of his nasty tricks.

"Nine years ago, he decided that Tara itself would make a grand object of his Samhain foray. He came here during the evening feast and demanded a staggering tribute. The high king refused and some of his warriors made the mistake of challenging the man. They died, and all of Tara was burned to the ground."

"Burned?" Finn said, surprised. "By one man? But how?"

"Aillen has more than a single talent, it seems," Caoilte darkly explained. "First, he has a skill with the harp much like that of our little friend. All who listen fall into a deep trance. But, most importantly, he can breathe a stream of fire as thick as a tree's trunk and as far as even you can hurl a spear."

"Breathe it?" Finn said, not believing that he had heard rightly.

"From his mouth," said Caoilte. "It sets ablaze everything in its path."

Finn turned to Muirne. "Mother, you say you know of him. Can all of this be true?"

She nodded. "I'm afraid so, my dear. Though his powers can be used only once a year, it is at Samhain when they are strongest."

"Strong enough that no one has dared challenge him again," said Caoilte. "Conn has paid tribute every year since."

"This has an evil stench to it," said Cnu Deireoil. "And it comes from our druid friend, I'd say. Finn, you've been drawn into another of Tadg's snares."

"Maybe," admitted Finn. "But I've made my bond to fight, and—"

"And you will fight," the harper finished with a faint smile. "I know."

"Besides," Finn added, "even if this is some plot by my grandfather and the high king, it is still a real threat that someone must deal with."

"The question is how," Caoilte said bluntly. "You

can't go against such a being without something to protect yourself."

"You may have some protection from the flames already," said Finn's mother. She lifted the gold hem of the handsome four-folded cloak that he wore. "Is this the cloak that you said was given you in the Sidhe at Cnoc-na-Righ?"

"It is."

"Then it may be made of a fabric that is nearly impossible to destroy. It was created by de Danaan magic to last as long as its wearers. Try it."

Finn unfastened the garment and hung one corner in the flames of the central fire. For long moments he held it there, but the material showed no signs of singeing or even discoloring from the heat. Finn pulled it back and looked at it with awe.

But Caoilte was unimpressed. "That might block the flames for a time, but it'll not protect any uncovered flesh."

"It might shield me long enough to let me strike at this Aillen," Finn said.

"You won't be doing anything if you're not awake," Caoilte pointed out. "The fire is your second problem. The first is this enchanting music. He'll be putting you to sleep with his tune long before you can come within a spear's throw."

Finn turned to the Little Nut. "Can you help me?"

The harper shook his head sadly. "My own magic is very weak compared to his. The effect of my tunes can be overcome by a strong will, but no one within hearing can escape Aillen's. Every listener will be overcome with sleep, and only the coming of the morn after Samhain will release them from the spell."

"And there's no protection?" asked Crimall.

"Not from me. Even I'm not safe from the magic. And my own music will have no effect on him."

Finn looked around the fire at the circle of faces. Some shifted uncomfortably. Some even looked away. All shared the same sense of despair, of frustration. They could think of nothing else that might help the young warrior.

303

Finn's gaze moved around, and then stopped abruptly on the face of Bodhmall. The gaunt woman was staring into the fire with an intensity that Finn had seen before.

"Bodhmall," he said softly but urgently, "what is it? What is it you're seeing?"

"A man," she answered at once. "A strange, worn, crippled man. He creeps about in the darkness of the camp alone, fearing every move, every sound. He peers from the shadows at our pavilion. He wishes to see . . . to see Finn MacCumhal! But he is afraid."

She broke off suddenly, shaking her head. Then her gaze jerked around to Finn.

"He has a way to help you!" she told him with an intensity unusual for her. "I could feel it in him. Finn, you must see him! You must see him now! Tonight!"

The others, save for Liath and Muirne, were staring at Bodhmall in puzzlement, not knowing of her seer's power. Finn ignored them. There was no time for explanations.

"How can I see him, Bodhmall?" he asked.

"Go out now, into the encampment. Go away from the tents of the people, away from the dun, down into the empty stalls of the fair. He will come to you. He is afraid. He'll only come to you if you are alone."

"I'll do it," he said.

"Wait!" said Caoilte. "I don't know where this woman's getting her notions, but if there is something lurking out there, it could be another snare. You'll go nowhere alone."

"I agree," said Crimall.

"I trust Bodhmall's judgment," Finn said stubbornly. "It's saved me before. I'll do as she asks."

Caoilte and Crimall exchanged a look. Both knew well enough that Finn would not be swayed. They nodded.

"I'll be back soon," he told the group reassuringly, then slipped from the pavilion into the night.

It was very still, the almost constant moaning of the fall wind about the hill having died away. Most of the hundreds in the many encampments below the

304

fortress had retired. There were a few faint sounds of talk, a distant laugh, some stray notes of drifting song, and little else.

He moved down through the camp toward the market, looking about him warily. A few people were still stirring, moving in the avenues, shifting about before the fires. None seemed to be watching or following him.

In the market area, even the few signs of human presence were gone. No lights burned in the avenues. No people remained. The only sounds were the snorts and restless stamping of penned livestock disturbed at his passing.

He moved more slowly, more cautiously now. Much as he trusted Bodhmall, he still needed the warning of Caoilte. He kept a hand upon his sword hilt.

He moved deeper into the large market area, feeling his way along the maze of avenues, through stalls and huts and pens. With the fall moon hiding behind a screen of light clouds, the shadows about him were very dense. There were uncountable places to hide.

The keen hunter's senses were fully alerted here. Eyes probed every suspicious spot of black, ears harkened for any sound of movement. It was the ears that warned him first. He heard the faint rattle of a stall's plankings, jarred by a passing body. Carefully, carefully, he turned to glance toward the sound. He saw it: a shadow indistinguishable from the others save in one fact. It was following him.

He kept on moving, watching, letting this strange figure trail after. The man was afraid, Bodhmall had said. He was shy of contact like a fawn in the woods. Finn sensed he must be treated as a fawn. Any aggressive move would make him bolt. Only patience and the assurance of safety would bring him in.

The tactic worked. By the time Finn had wandered, with apparently peaceful aimlessness, into the heart of the market area, he had become aware that the figure was closing in. He stopped, leaning against the post of a produce stall as if to rest. He watched out of the tail of his eye as the shadow crept closer, closer,

305

closer through the patches of darkness. Finally it was nearby.

Then came a voice, creaking and quavering as if long unused.

"You know that I'm here, don't you?"

Without making any other movement, Finn replied. "I do."

"I knew it. I knew it! Any good man of the Fianna would. And, is it the son of Cumhal that you are?"

"It is."

"I've been hoping for a chance to see you, that I have."

"Why?" Finn asked.

"First come closer," came the reply. "Over here, into this shelter. It's safer here. Come on. You've my word there's no danger. You've the word of another Fian warrior."

The man's speech was rather wild and broken, but Bodhmall had said he meant to help. Finn had no other choices. He moved into the deep shadows behind a stall where the man crouched.

The faint light revealed a figure as wild in looks as in his manner of talk. He was wretchedly thin, clothed in a ragged tunic and cloak. Unkempt hair hung about a lean, worn face and tangled with a straggled mustache and beard. He stood hunched forward, left shoulder down, left arm hanging in an odd, crooked way. The man's head was thrust out of his skinny neck like a crane, and he peered up at Finn with a bird's sharp, glittering gaze.

"You say you're of the Fian?" Finn asked, not able to keep the whole of his surprise out of his voice.

There was a harsh, crow-rasping of a laugh from the man. "Ah, I know it's a hard thing to believe, looking at me. But I was once, that I was. I was a warrior of the Baiscne clan same as yourself. And I was a comrade to your father. It's Fiacha I'm called."

"I've heard of you!" Finn exclaimed. "My uncle told me you were one of the clan's best fighting men. But he thought you were killed in the battle with the sons of Morna."

"They thought it as well," Fiacha answered with another cackle of laughter. "Cut right to the bone I was. Nearly took off my shoulder, as you can see." He lifted the maimed and nearly useless arm with an effort. "I was left in the woods for dead. But I wasn't dead. No, no! I wasn't dead. It was the last of the clan I thought I was, and me crippled. Still, I knew that there was a reason I'd been saved. It was meant that I be the one to repay the sons of Morna for what they'd done. So I came back here, and here I've stayed. I've been nothing but a poor, nameless cripple to them here. I've cleaned the yard and stables for my keep. I've polished weapons that I'd once have used myself. But all the time I was waiting, watching, knowing that one day my chance would come."

Finn listened in fascination to this tale. What this man had suffered, what he had endured through the years, sustained only by his sense of a purpose, was incredible.

"But why didn't you come to us when we first made ourselves known at Tara?" he asked. "Why didn't you rejoin the clan?"

The man looked away. "Well, I was ashamed, you see," he said in a subdued way. "I couldn't have my old comrades finding out what a wretched thing I'd become. I wanted none of their pity. And I knew that I was useless to you. It seemed that even my waiting here all these years had been for nothing."

Then his head came up again. The smile had returned, the eyes were bright with a renewed energy, and an excitement was back in the strange, rusty voice.

"But tonight I heard of the challenge, so I did. And I knew that I was meant for something after all. You need help and I can give it! They think Fiacha is a broken, harmless man, so they do. But he'll show them!"

"How?" Finn asked. "What can you do?"

Fiacha cast a suspicious look about them, as if to assure himself that no one was nearby. Then he sidled in close to Finn, his voice dropping to a conspiratorial whisper.

"It's magic I can give you, so I can! Magic that can

keep away all spells. It'll save you from the enchantment." His mouth stretched in a rather gap-toothed smile.

Finn leaned down to whisper back, "And just how does this magic work?"

The smile vanished. "Ah, no, no!" Fiacha said sharply. He cast another searching glance around, his head whipping, gooselike, on his scrawny neck. "No talk of it here! They're all around, you know! They'll hear! They'll know! And that'll be the finish for all of us! There can't be anyone else who knows, not even you, until it's time."

"But can't you tell me anything?" Finn asked. "How will I get it from you?"

Fiacha shook his head. "No more now," he said with finality. "I've been with you too long already. They'll find I'm gone. They'll see us together. I've got to be getting away!"

The man's eccentric behavior was doing little to inspire Finn's confidence in him. Still, the young chieftain couldn't overlook any possible avenue to salvation.

"If you can help me regain the leadership of the Baiscne clan, you will be an honored warrior among us forever, that I promise," he told Fiacha.

"It's enough to know I've not waited here for nothing," the man replied. Then he grinned and winked broadly. "We'll show them, eh? We'll show that Morna clan!"

He turned and started away into the darkness.

"Wait!" Finn called after him. "When will I see you again?"

"You'll see me when it's time," Fiacha called back over his shoulder. "It won't be safe before. Just when it's time! Don't fear, son of Cumhal. I will be there!"

Finn watched him until he had faded from view among the shadows of the stalls. Then he turned to call softly into the darkness.

"He's gone. You can come out now."

Two figures moved from the shelter of a stall and came toward him. The faint light revealed them as Caoilte and Crimall, both rather shamefaced.

"How did you know we'd followed?" Crimall asked.

"I didn't until now. I just guessed that you might."

"We weren't going to let you come here alone," Caoilte said defensively. "We only meant to keep you safe."

"I know," Finn said, smiling. "It's all right. But you saw there was nothing to fear from him."

Crimall shook his head. "No. Poor Fiacha," he said sadly. "I couldn't believe it was the same man I knew. The last time I saw him, he was a hardy young warrior, cheerful and bold and fearing no man. Now"—he hesitated, then forced himself to go on—"now I'm afraid whatever he's suffered has done for him. Finn, it must be he's gone mad."

"That may be, Uncle," Finn said, looking after the departed Fiacha. "But right now he's also the only chance I have."

Chapter Thirty-four

THE FINAL CHALLENGE

The eve of Samhain was darkened by an oppressive cover of gray-black clouds. They shrouded the late afternoon sun, creating an eerie, twilight atmosphere. The wind that had all day keened dismally about the fortress hill had died away. The air was heavy with the scent and feel of moisture. There was an ominous stillness, a sense of the world's holding its breath in expectation, as comes before the rising of a storm.

But it was not the forces of a natural storm that were to be unleashed upon the world this night. It was the powers of those realms beyond the mortal ones.

And all across Ireland, people shuttered tight their homes and huddled close about their comforting fires, praying to whatever protecting spirits that they knew for the safe passage of this terrible time.

At Tara, however, none of the inhabitants huddled within its buildings. Just below the main gates of the fortress, Finn MacCumhal stood with his uncle, Caoilte, and Cnu Deireoil, watching the last of the high king's people departing.

The entire population of Tara had wisely determined to remove themselves to a prudent distance for the contest that was about to come. Most had taken up positions on a distant edge of the ridge on which the fortress sat, well out of the reach of enchanted music or magical fire. With great disapproval, Caoilte watched the last fugitives hurry away, laden with their possessions.

"They could show a bit more confidence in you," he said irritably.

"I'd want none of them risking themselves by staying," Finn told him. "I've sent all the others to join them, and I expect you three to go there as well. You'll be no help to me. You'll have no defense against the music."

"Neither will you, it seems," Crimall remarked, looking around him. "There's no sign of my poor old comrade Fiacha, and not likely to be, I'm thinking."

"Maybe you could stop your ears against the sound somehow," Caoilte suggested.

"Even deafness itself can't keep out the magic of this spell," said the Little Nut.

"Maybe you could charge at him and come close enough to have a fair cast before the music has its effect," said Crimall.

"The effect takes only a moment, so I've heard," Cnu Deireoil replied. "And the sound of his playing travels far ahead of him. I'm afraid even the speed of our lad won't be enough."

"You're a great mine of cheering information, so you are," Caoilte told him.

Finn looked toward the lowering sun.

"It'll be time for his coming soon. I'd better go. You get away now, my friends."

"Finn," Caoilte began, "maybe I—"

Finn held up a hand. "I know what you're thinking, but you can't help me this time. It's my challenge, and it'll be only me against him."

Caoilte sighed. "Be a fool to the very end, then. But don't be expecting me to grieve over your ashes."

"You know, it's been the three of you more than any others who've helped to bring me here," Finn told them with great earnestness. "I wanted to tell you that, no matter what happens now, I'm grateful for what you've done."

"Get on with you!" Cnu Deireoil replied. "You sound as if you were making a poem for your own funeral. There's never been anything that could stop you, lad, and there isn't now!"

Finn gave the hand of each man a final clasp and started down the hill. He had taken only two good throwing spears and the cloak of Cnoc-na-Righ with him. No other weapons would be of use in this fight. He knew his only difficulty would be in getting close enough to make use of either.

He strode down along the avenues of the fair market. Around him a few straggling merchants were hastily packing up what goods they could and abandoning their stalls. As Finn looked around at them he reflected that all of this, and the high fortress above, would be a blackened ruin at the next sunrise if he failed.

In the distant crowd, Conn watched Finn's movements attentively. He, like the other high-ranking nobility, was mounted, prepared for a rapid move should a victorious Aillen decide to turn his wrath upon them.

Finn's company had refused to participate in such a defeatist show. So had Goll MacMorna and the other Fian men, much to the dismay of Conan.

As Finn moved into the market avenues, Conn leaned down toward Tadg, who stood beside him in his chariot.

"Finn's gone out of sight," the high king said

worriedly. "There's no chance he might be planning some trickery?"

"Our Fian chieftain?" Tadg said with a smile. "Never! His sense of fair play is as strong as Goll's."

"And what about your man of the Sidhe?" Conn asked. "Can we be certain he'll come?"

"My king, there is no doubt," the druid answered smugly. "By now Aillen has left his mound and discovered that no tribute has been given. He is likely already on his way here, burning—if you will excuse my little joke—for revenge."

Conn gave him an odd look. "There's little amusing in the destruction of Tara," he said.

"But think of the destruction of MacCumhal!" Tadg replied.

Below them, Finn had reached the end of the market area. He stopped by the last stalls and looked out over the wide gaming fields beyond. The sun, a faint glow buried in the clouds, was dropping toward the horizon. Evening was upon them, and Aillen's coming would be soon. And what would he do then?

"Hisst! Hisst!" came a hoarse whisper.

He turned toward it. A hand was beckoning from behind a wicker wall of a market stall. He moved closer.

The head of Fiacha poked out suddenly, craned about on his thin neck as he surveyed the scene.

"No one else left about, eh?" he asked.

"Just ourselves," Finn said. "The rest are far away by now."

"Ah, it's safe then!" the man proclaimed triumphantly. He gave a rasping crow-laugh. "I've done it. I've got it. And now the magic's yours."

From behind him he pulled an object, thrusting it into Finn's hand. The warrior grasped it, looking at it in surprise.

It was a spear, very old and very worn. Its wooden pole was badly battered, even splintering in spots. Its metal head, which seemed once to have been of a smooth and gleaming silver, was nicked, blunted, and blackened as if by intense heat.

"This is it?" he asked. "This is your magic?"

312

"Oh yes! Oh yes!" the crippled man assured him excitedly. "It's a spear that will keep away all magic. I've heard the tales of it. It's very old."

"Where did you get it?"

The man cackled again in trumphant glee. "From the high king's own armory, so I did. I went in and out and his own guards never saw a bit of me! I've got the Fian skills yet, so I have. But you see why no one could know of it until this time. Now it's too late to stop you from using it."

"This came from Conn's armory?" Finn said. He looked from the weapon to the grinning man in puzzlement. "But, if it's his spear, why hasn't he used it himself?"

A look of great bewilderment overspread the man's face. His eyes flicked to the spear and then back to Finn.

"Ah . . . I don't know that," he said with rising uncertainty. "I—I'd not thought of it before." He considered, then brightened with a new idea. "Maybe he doesn't know how to use it!"

Finn regarded him dismally. "And have you some notion that I do?" he inquired.

The man was stricken. He sagged, as if the enormity of his mistake had drained all his substance from him.

"By all the gods!" he exclaimed in a hoarse voice. "By all the gods! What I've done is useless to you!"

Finn tried to maintain what graciousness he could in the face of this final dashing of hopes.

"Never mind," he told Fiacha. "You only meant to help me, and you risked your life in it. It's my own foolishness that's brought me to this."

"I'm sorry. I'm sorry!" the man wailed. "But I know its magic's real! If we could discover how to use it."

It was then that the words of the Shadowy One came back to Finn. If he needed to know, he could use the salmon's power.

But how? Her last, cryptic hint was that he must do as he did when he first tasted it. He thought back over the events. It was Finnegas who had forced him to sit down and eat the fish, but only after he had already tasted it. How had that happened?

The image suddenly came clear to him. He had burned his thumb. He had thrust it, wet with the salmon's juices, into his mouth to cool it.

Without hesitation, he lifted his hand and plunged his thumb into his mouth. The action startled Fiacha who, ironically, looked at the young warrior as if he had gone mad.

"What is it you're doing, lad?" he asked.

Finn wasn't listening. His mind had been suddenly filled with a bewildering flurry of images, thick as the flakes of a blizzard or the bright fall leaves in a strong breeze. The salmon's gift of knowledge was his after all, as Finnegas had thought. Now it was flooding him with information so quickly he could grasp nothing but fleeting impressions, stray bits and pieces of ideas. He had to focus, fix on the single question of the spear.

And as he forced his mind to concentrate, the confusion faded. Almost instantly the knowledge he sought was there, like a puzzle piece dropped neatly into place. He jerked the thumb from his mouth and turned to Fiacha, beaming.

"I know!" he cried. "Fiacha, if I place the spear's head to my temple, it will protect me from the music's spell. It will work! Your spear will work!"

Relief filled the worn face of the crippled man.

"Ah, my lad! I don't know how it is you've discovered that, but you've given my life back to me, so you have."

A movement on the fields beyond caught Finn's attention. He looked toward it searchingly and his expression turned grim.

"It looks as if it's my own life I'm to try saving now," he said. "But you've given me a fair chance at it, Fiacha. Be away quickly. I must go out and meet our visitor before he comes near the hill."

As Fiacha scuttled away, Finn started out across the playing fields. Far away, a tiny figure was moving toward him. The being was afoot, but it was too distant for any other details to be observed. Still, the young warrior kept his hearing sharply attuned for the first notes of the enchanting music.

He was close enough to see that the approaching figure was carrying a large, crescent-shaped harp when the first high, sweet strains of its plucked strings drifted to him. Instantly he was aware of a grogginess, like a darkness filling up his skull. The sleeping spell did, indeed, work quickly.

Without delay he lifted the spear, touching its battered point to his temple. He was elated to find that its magic worked quite as well. The drowsiness withdrew from his mind like a night creature shying back from the sun.

As the being moved closer, the lack of his music's effect must have become clear. The music grew in intensity, the tune faster, louder, ever more urgent in its tone. Finn only strode on, finding the melody pleasant, impressed by the skill of the harper, but untouched by the spell.

He was close enough to see the features of his adversary now. Finn discovered that this monster who had threatened Tara's survival for nine years was anything but monstrous in appearance. He seemed a young man, very slim and rather frail in build. His face was long, its features elegant—almost effeminate in their careful sculpturing. His hair was a high, curling backsweep of deep reddish gold, beautifully arranged. A silver tunic was covered by a cloak of brilliant green. The vast collection of jewelry that adorned him scintillated as he glided forward with a graceful stride. He wore no weapons and he carried nothing but the large and exquisitely worked harp he played.

Just now, however, the smooth perfection of his features was marred by a worried frown. Clearly, he could not understand why this man stalking toward him had not tumbled to the ground in sleep. His fingers flew more rapidly across the strings. The music of the harp swirled around Finn like a storm wind seeking the chinks in a house's wall. But it found no weakness. Finn kept the spearhead clapped firmly to his temple and strode on.

The youth came to a halt. He stopped playing and lowered the harp, staring across the field at Finn in exasperation.

"And just what is it that you're doing?" he demanded in a high and strident voice. "No man has withstood my spell before."

Finn came to a stop as well. He judged he was now just within range for a long spear throw. But attack was his last recourse.

"I've my own magic to protect me," he told Aillen. "I'll not be put to sleep."

"Is that right?" the other said scornfully. "And just who is it that you are?"

"Finn MacCumhal is what I'm called," Finn told him with pride. "I am a warrior of the Fianna. I've come here in the service of the high king to keep you from Tara. There will be no more tribute paid to you, Aillen, son of Midhna!"

"No tribute paid to me," the youth repeated in a mocking voice. "Your high king told me that nine years ago. He woke to find his grand hall a smoking ruin."

"This time I will stop you," Finn told him coldly. "Be away from here. I've no quarrel of my own with you, and I've no wish to harm you."

"No, you only want to keep me from my bit of fun!" Aillen shot back. "My only chance to come into the world, to use my powers, and you're wishing to take it from me. Well, I will not have that!" He stamped his foot like a petulant child denied his favorite toy. "No mortal will tell me that I can't have what I wish on Samhain night. So *you* stand away from *me*, Finn MacCumhal!"

He started forward again, striding haughtily.

"Stop!" Finn called, lifting one of his throwing spears. "Don't come against me. You know that your power doesn't work!"

The youth smiled. "Ah, but I have another!"

His mouth dropped open and from it burst a stream of fire.

Like a geyser exploding from the ground, the flames shot toward the warrior. Finn had not wholly believed the tales of Aillen's fiery breath. His misjudgment almost killed him. The burning stream had a speed and a range greater than that of a hurled spear. He had barely time to throw himself from its path, rolling away as the flames crackled over the spot where he had stood.

He scrambled to his feet. Aillen was turning toward him, drawing breath for another blast of fire. Finn cocked and hurled his spear as the second blazing column exploded from the youth's mouth.

The distance was too great and Finn's throw too fast. His spear went wide, while the flames nearly caught him. They licked at him as he leaped away, searing the exposed flesh of his throwing arm.

He started off at a run, moving in a wide curve about his opponent, hoping to come behind him. But Aillen's reflexes were nearly as swift as his. The youth spun about, sweeping the stream of fire in a great arc meant to cut down the desperately racing Finn.

He couldn't keep ahead of it. Abruptly he stopped, turned, set himelf, and launched his second spear.

Aillen shifted the blazing column up into the path of the weapon. It plunged into the flames and was instantly consumed by the incredible heat of the magic energy. The spear pole burned away. The iron head dropped harmlessly onto the sod.

But this prolonged attempt to finish Finn ended there. With all of Aillen's breath momentarily expended, the stream of fire weakened and died away.

While the youth prepared to draw wind for another devastating blast, Finn had a brief respite to act. He had only the spear of Fiacha left to him. He had to be certain he did not miss again. He had to be close.

Lifting the old weapon, he charged directly toward his opponent, yanking the cloak from his shoulder as he ran. Aillen filled his lungs and expelled another searing jet. It stretched out from the young man's mouth toward Finn, licking out at him like a great, curling tongue to wrap him in coils that would char him to the bone.

Finn waited until it had nearly reached him, then flung the unfolded cloak up before it. The column of fire slammed into the center of the square of emerald cloth like a fist, rolling back upon itself. The cloak became a sack about it, drawing it in, enclosing it, then falling with it, pulling it to the ground.

There was a sharp explosion and a puff of blue-white smoke. Only a steaming pit remained.

Now Finn was close. He could see the dismay in Aillen's face as he saw his fire blocked. He could see the young man's narrow chest expanding as he began to draw breath for another spurt of flame. There was no more time. Ignoring the agonizing pain in his burned arm, Finn drew back his final spear and launched it with all the power left to him.

This time his aim was true. The blunt, battered point struck the chest of Aillen, piercing through the swelling lungs.

As the lungs were rent, the tremendous energy magically building there was released. It erupted from the chest and head in a great, terrible blossom of flame. The body stood upright for a moment longer, flaring like a torch. Then it toppled to the ground.

Finn moved toward it. He looked down upon the blasted smoldering corpse that had once been a beautiful young man, a master of the harp, a living being.

Another bond had been fulfilled, Finn thought. Another life had been taken in this long struggle. Maybe, this time, it was the final one.

His eyes lifted toward the hillside, toward the watching crowd.

"Now, my grandfather and my high king," he said with a grim satisfaction, "it is your turn to pay."

Chapter Thirty-five

A RECKONING

In the Sidhe within the mound of Aillen, there was much keening that night over a son of the Tuatha de Danaan who would not return.

On the hill of Tara, the great Fortress of the Kings was ablaze with light. Hundreds rejoiced within its main hall, freed of the curse that had been upon them for so many Samhain nights.

Below the hill, the sacred enclosure of the druids was dark, save for a single, tiny fire burning before its hut. There sat the brooding figure of the high druid Tadg. He stared intently into the fire, trying to shut his ears to the sounds of merriment a night breeze carried to him from the hall.

Suddenly the breeze sharpened to a gust. It howled through the trees about the enclosure. It swirled down within the stockade, teasing at the fire. Tadg looked up as the aroused flames lifted higher. Their wavering light threw long shadows from the skull-topped posts along the narrow yard. They seemed like bony fingers pointing frantically toward the black square of the enclosure's entrance. Then the wind was abruptly calmed. The fire died back to a soft glow. The shadows faded.

But now a dark figure loomed in the opening, nearly filling the space with its enormous bulk.

It started forward. Tadg watched with hard and glittering eyes as it moved slowly, relentlessly along the avenue of skulls. Before the fire it halted, towering over the seated figure of the druid. He looked up into the

319

features now revealed by the fire's ruddy light: the broad and weathered features of Dagda, most powerful and most feared champion of the de Danaan clans.

"I warned you, Tadg," the Dagda said, his voice an ominous rumble. "I promised that if you went on using the power of our race for your own ends, you would pay. Tonight you've brought death on another of our people. Tonight, it is finished. From this time, your own powers are gone from you. You will leave the mortals' world and find yourself a hidden place where you will stay alone. Do you understand?"

Tadg nodded, saying nothing in reply.

"It is only your own pride and your own hatred that have brought you to this, man!" the giant told him, angered by his impassive acceptance of this sentence. "Have you no remorse at all? No regret?"

The eyes of the other flared with a defiant light.

"From what he has done to me, my hatred of Cumhal's son has only grown the stronger," he said with icy deliberation. His gaze lifted to the glowing fortress above. "Someday yet, Finn MacCumhal will be brought down, if all of Ireland must be destroyed with him!"

But a burst of laughter drifting down from the great hall only seemed to mock his dreadful vow.

There, in the brightness and warmth, the merriment had reached its height. But now, with the Samhain rituals and the feasting done, a hush fell upon the gathering. All eyes turned expectantly toward Finn as he rose from the table of the high king.

"Samhain night is nearing its end, my king," he said so that all could hear. "My portion of the bond that we two made has been fulfilled. Now it is time for you to fulfill yours."

Conn had dreaded this moment through all the evening. He knew what would come, but there was no escape left to him. Slowly he climbed to his feet, facing this youth who beamed triumphantly at him. He could see the fierce independence in Finn's eyes, hear the defiant tone in his voice. And never before had the young warrior looked so much the picture of his father.

"I will fulfill what I have pledged," he said, forcing a taut smile. "And what request is it that you're making of me?"

"I think that it is already known to you, my king," Finn told him. "I wish the captaincy of all the Fian clans."

A murmur of surprise went through the listening crowd. But it was followed quickly by a loud cheer of acclamation. And though the supporters of Goll voiced their denial, it was clearly the opinion of a minority. Finn was the hero of the day. Like his father, he had won the hearts of the people.

The high king quickly raised a hand to silence the uproar. He tried to put enthusiasm in his voice when he spoke again.

"Your feelings have been made known," he told them. "Finn MacCumhal has saved Tara, and the reward we pledged to him has been rightly earned. His request will be granted."

He turned to Goll MacMorna, who now rose. The face of the Fian captain was without expression, and Conn felt new fears churning within his vitals. Would Goll—the always loyal Goll—defy him now? Would he challenge this royal command, or would he still obey and save his high king from humiliation?

"Son of Morna," he began in a tentative way, "it is my will that the leadership of the Fianna be given to the son of Cumhal. Is it your choice to quit Ireland, or to put your hand into the hand of Finn?"

There was a long silence. The eyes of the two chieftains locked together. Finn wondered, like Conn, whether Goll would accept this without an argument. He did not know that to the Morna leader there was no other choice.

Here, thought Goll, was his chance to restore his honor, to correct the injustice, to restore what treachery had taken. He walked forward, down the length of the table, followed by the gaze of everyone. He stopped before Finn. Conn looked from one to the other apprehensively. Then the son of Morna spoke.

"By my word," he said, "I will give my hand to Finn."

He lifted his hand and Finn took it in a firm clasp. The high king watched them, knowing his nightmare had been realized. From now until his death, he knew, it would be this fair-haired, smiling youth who truly ruled Ireland, not him.

It was the final night of the Samhain festival. Most of the fair's stalls had already been dismantled. The visitors were preparing to depart the following day. The hillside below the fortress was quiet and nearly deserted.

The evening was bright and clear. The stars were sharp points in the chill fall sky. Finn gazed at them appreciatively as he wandered alone, feeling rather glad to have this brief time to himself. It had been a long time since he had been alone, as he had been so often in Slieve Bladhma, with just nature as a companion. Things had changed a great deal since then, and he knew that from now on he'd have little time to himself ever again.

But then a hand lightly touched his arm. He turned to find that he was not alone. His mother had joined him. She fell in beside him and they continued on together across the hillside.

"So, my son, you've won what it was you sought," she said. "Is it happy you are now?"

"I feel that I'm where I was meant to be," he answered.

"There may be great troubles and great pain ahead for you," she told him, "and your father's fate may still await you."

"If I'm to lead the Fianna, such things are as they should be. I'm content to accept them."

She stopped abruptly, facing him. "But it needn't be so. You have done all you need to do. You have restored your father's clan. You have redeemed his honor. You could be free of all the rest. You could be free of all the mortal cares and pains that you'll be facing. You are of the de Danann world as well as the mortal one. My blood has made you so."

She lifted a hand to his arm. Her voice took on a tone of earnestness.

"You could go away. You could go to the lands where there is no suffering, no death, only beauties beyond your knowing, and love, and a life that never ends. Please, my son, go! Give up the warrior's destiny."

"It's a glowing vision that you offer me, Mother," he said, smiling. "But I've traveled much of Ireland in my journey here, and I've learned many things. It's taught me one great truth: I'd not give up this country if I were to get the whole world in its place, and the Country of the Young along with it."

For a long moment she held his gaze. Then, recognizing the truth of his words there, she nodded in resignation.

"Yes, I expected that answer," she said. She smiled too, but there was a sadness in it. "It's truly your father's son that you are, Finn MacCumhal."

Glossary

Here is the approximate pronunciation of some of the more difficult names:

Baiscne	Bask-na
Bodhmall	Bah-mall
Caoilte	Kweel-ta
Cnu Deireoil	Nu Der-ee-oil
Cumhal	Koo-al
Domhnall	Don-al
Muirne	Mur-na
Tadg	Teig

The following are terms about which the reader might appreciate having some further information:

Almhuin	(All-oon) The name of the home fortress of Finn MacCumhal. Located near present-day Kildare.
Bantry	A territory of Celtic Ireland located in what is now County Kerry.
Boinne	Now the Boyne River, located in County Meath. Along its banks are many sites linked to the Celtic and pre-Celtic eras, including Knowth and Newgrange.
Brehon Law	A vast and complex body of ancient Irish laws much admired by modern judicial scholars for their thoroughness in covering many types of social relationships with great justice.
bruighaid	(Brew-y) The official entrusted with the running of public houses of hospitality in Ireland. A very honored profession.
bruidhean	(Breen) A public house of hospitality, usually set up on the junction of several roads. It was intended to serve the needs of any traveler without charge and is an excellent example of the characteristic hospitality for which the Irish are known.
Carraighe	(Kerry) This territory of ancient Ireland is today known as Kerry. It is in extreme southwestern Ireland.

Cnoc-na-Righ	Now called Knocknarea, this hill is found not far from present-day Sligo. The legendary Queen Maeve is said to be buried in a large passage-grave on its top, and its base is surrounded by many mounds marking the site of neolithic burial tombs.
Connacht	(Kon-akt) One of the five provinces into which ancient Ireland was divided. It was comprised of the land that makes up the present-day countries of Galway, Mayo, Sligo, Roscommon, and Leitrim.
Corca Dhuibhne	(Corn-a-Gween-eh) Meaning "Seed of the Goddess." It is now called Dingle Peninsula, a most popular scenic attraction near Tralee, in southwest Ireland.
crannog	A small artificial island situated at the edge of a lake, defended by a wooden stockade.
curragh	A small boat of bent lath strips covered with hide. St. Brendan is said to have used one to visit the New World, and a larger version of such a craft crossed the Atlantic in our own time.
Dovarchu	(Da-var-koo) Though the word translates literally as "water dog," it is used to refer to a Master Otter, an Irish version of the Loch Ness monster. Over the centuries there have been many sightings of such

creatures in Irish lakes. Finn is credited in the legends with killing a number of these creatures. His slaughter of one in Lough Derg in Donegal is said to have supplied its name (Red Lake). The Lough Lein monster is included on the long list of others slain.

fidchell (Fid-kell) A board game having some similarity with chess, played with pieces of silver and gold. After war and hunting, this game and hurling were the most popular pastimes of the Irish fighting man.

Lough Lein (Lock Leen) This is the present-day Lake Leane. It is located near Killarney in the county of Kerry.

Mogh Nuadat (Ma Nu-a-dat) A legendary ruler of Munster and a notable opponent to Conn of the Hundred Battles. After freeing Munster from the cruel subjugation of the warlike Ernaan, he warred against and won concessions from the high king of Ireland. Conn was supported in these fights by the loyal Morna clan of the Fianna, but not by Finn and the Baiscne.

ollamh (Ol-laf) The highest rank of Irish bard. The position of such men was very high in Irish society (as the poet's still is today). He was ranked second only to the king in honor, and first in sacredness.

Samhain	(Sam-an) One of four great yearly celebration days marking the changing of the seasons. The date of Samhain, along with many of the Celtic customs and beliefs associated with it, has been retained by modern society under another name: Halloween.
Sidhe	(Shee) A name for the hidden dwelling places of the mystical Tuatha de Danaan race. Later the word came to be used as a name for the inhabitants of these underground places as well. The legendary beings exist, though much degenerated, in popular modern Irish folklore as leprechauns and banshees (Ban-Sidhe, meaning "woman of the Sidhe").
Slieve Bladhma	(Slee Bla-ma) A section of hills and glens associated with the family of Muirne's grandfather, Nuada of the Silver Hand, once high king of all the Tuatha de Danaan tribes.
Tir-na-nog	Legendary Land-of-the-Ever-Young. It is felt to be the home of the Tuatha de Danaan, and has been often visited by Irish heroes and stray travelers. Unfortunately not included in any modern guidebooks, it is known to lie somewhere in the mists of the Western Sea (the Atlantic).

Tuatha de Danaan (Too-aha dae Don-an) A race of beings with long lives and great magical powers. They once held sway in Ireland but withdrew to hidden, underground dwellings after their defeat by the invading Milesian tribes. They take little direct action in the affairs of mortal man, but they do watch over him with interest and sometimes help or hinder him. The belief in these beings (often called the "Other") still exists among some in Ireland today. The Banshee and the Leprechaun are the most popularly known modern remnants of the de Danaans.

ABOUT THE AUTHOR

KENNETH C. FLINT is a graduate of the University of Nebraska with a Masters Degree in English Literature. For several years he taught in the Department of Humanities at the University of Nebraska at Omaha. Presently he is Chairman of English for the Plattsmouth Community Schools (a system in a suburban community of Omaha).

In addition to teaching, he has worked as a freelance writer. He has produced articles and short stories for various markets and has written screenplays for some Omaha-based film companies.

Mr. Flint became interested in Celtic mythology in graduate school, where he saw a great source of material in this long neglected area of western literature. Since then he has spent much time researching in England and Ireland and developing works of fantasy that would interest modern readers.

He is the author of four previous novels, A STORM UPON ULSTER, RIDERS OF THE SIDHE, CHAMPIONS OF THE SIDHE, and MASTER OF THE SIDHE. He is currently at work on another novel about Finn MacCumhal.

"A book to treasure."
—Morgan Llyewelyn, author
of *Lion of Ireland*

the last rainbow

by **Parke Godwin**
author of *Firelord* and
Beloved Exile

He was a headstrong young priest who would some day be called Saint Patrick. She was the passionate young queen of the ancient Celtic race called Faerie. In a strife-torn twilight land where the pagan gods still ruled, she taught him the powers of the earth and the pleasures of love. Together, they discovered a miraculous destiny in the enchanted realm that lay beyond the Last Rainbow.

Buy THE LAST RAINBOW, on sale March 15, 1986 wherever Bantam Spectra Books are sold, or use the handy coupon below for ordering:

Bantam Books, Inc., Dept. PG2, 414 East Golf Road, Des Plaines, Ill. 60016

Please send me _____ copies of THE LAST RAINBOW (25686-6 • $3.95 • 4.50 in Canada). I am enclosing $_____ (Please add $1.50 to cover postage and handling). Send check or money order—no cash or C.O.D.'s please.

Mr/Ms _____

Address_____

City/State _____ Zip _____

PG2—3/86

Please allow four to six weeks for delivery. This offer expires 9/86. Price and availability subject to change without notice.